HATE HUNTERS

HATE HUNTERS

Mari Georgeson

Originally published as "I Hate Hate!" in November 2022.

Cover design: Kari Brownlie

For Lolly and Basil

CHAPTER ONE

THE ADDENDUM

Alma felt pretty in her inexpensive, yet stylish white sundress as she waited in line outside the office of Birth and Death Certificates. The flowers on her dress were perfectly spaced. There weren't so many as to overwhelm her own, natural beauty, nor were there too few. Alma and the dress were in a perfect symbiosis of beauty. She smiled at the woman in front of her, a Latina woman with a sleeping toddler in her arms. Three other children stood beside the woman, each one two inches shorter than the last, like steps: all quiet, obedient, calm. The mother had a long, thick, messy black ponytail. It was substantial—like the tail of an actual horse. Behind Alma stood a Middle Eastern couple, the woman in a headscarf, the man solemn and serious, as if posing for an old daguerreotype.

The line spilled out into the old art deco lobby of the Bureau of Health building. A stone statue of a nurse towered over the lobby and watched over them all. Her hat, her stethoscope, and her sensible shoes were rendered in exquisite, almost hyperrealistic detail.

Alma noticed she was the only phenotypically white person in the line. Strange, she thought. Didn't white people get born and die, and file records of their having done so? She smiled sadly. She supposed not. She supposed if you were to ask any of these people in line, all of them beautiful shades of brown, all of them most surely with long, complicated, unpleasant histories with Caucasians, both here and abroad, they would answer that no, in fact, white people did not get born or die. They were always just "there." Here. There. Everywhere. Invited, uninvited, it didn't matter. They were always there. And they weren't going anywhere anytime soon.

That was why Alma was so excited to finally be getting rid of her white stain. Or was it whyte, with a *y*? No, yes, she was right. It was white. White referred to the people, the race, and "whyte" with a *y* referred to the characteristics—privileged, insensitive, murderous, colonial, etc. They were, for all intents and purposes, synonymous, but still, the distinction was made by those most well versed in tolerance theory. But, yes, it was her actual whiteness she'd be shedding today, with any luck.

The Chromosomal Birth Certificate Addendum Program was brand new. She would be one of the first. And while that was exciting, it was also worrying, knowing how bureaucracies could be. She hoped they'd have it together. As she stood in line, she imagined the million ways it could go wrong, the conversations that might ensue:

"Your DNA report isn't notarized. You need to get your DNA report notarized."

"But it didn't mention that in the packet."

"I'm sorry, Eve Genetics isn't one of the officially recognized labs."

"But it was listed on your website."

"Our computer's not set up for it yet, come back in a month."

"But the website said you started doing it on the fifteenth."

"New York City doesn't participate, we're too overwrought with real work. Try Albany."

"But the website said Albany didn't do it, and you did."

"Twenty-three percent isn't high enough. Twenty-five percent is the cut off."

"But ..."

Once inside the office of Birth and Death Certificates, Alma took a number and sat down in a yellow plastic bucket chair. The office apparently hadn't been redecorated since the 1970s. The digital readout on the wall displayed the number 1658. She looked at the piece of paper in her hand—1777. She passed the time pleasantly, watching people, and trying to guess what languages they were speaking. Finally, the woman behind window two called her number.

Alma approached the window, and was greeted by an African American woman with short hair and a small, gold Star of David dangling from her neck. "How can I help you?" the woman said.

"I'd like to ... uh ... alter my birth certificate, please."

"Name change? Date change? Gender change?" the woman asked, mechanically.

"It's ... a ... chromosomal addendum, I think it's called?"

"Oh!" The woman looked her up and down. "A race change. Interesting. That's a new program—let's see, I think Sara's handling those for now. I haven't had the training yet. Sorry. You didn't actually have to wait in line. Sorry about that. I'll just call her."

"No. No. I didn't mind waiting in line at all."

The woman picked up the phone and made a call, then set her eyes on Alma again. She leaned forward and in an excited, hushed tone asked, "What race are you changing to, I mean, if it's not rude?"

"No, not at all," Alma said. She waited for the words to come out of her mouth, but they were stuck. She stood there awkwardly, shifting from foot to foot. Finally, she told herself she had nothing to be ashamed of. She was who she was, and she had the science to prove it. "African American," she said.

The woman stared at her for some time, contemplating her features.

"Twenty-three percent," Alma said. "Mostly from the area around Nigeria and Mauritania. Oh, and Niger I think."

The woman continued staring. Finally, she broke out into a warm smile. "Well shit, welcome!"

"Thank you!" Alma said.

"Honestly, I think DNA testing is great," the woman said, "because it just confirms what we already know—or should know—that we're all connected. One big happy family of man!"

"Exactly!" Alma said, and then, motioning toward the woman's Star of David, said, "Have you? Is that how you ...?"

The woman touched the pendant. "Oh this? No. No. I converted when I was eighteen. I just felt called to it. No.

Yeah. I haven't done the testing. Truth be told, I've always been a little scared to do the whole DNA thing."

"Yeah, I get it."

"I mean, I feel pretty sure about who I am."

The click clack of heels could be heard approaching, and a woman walked up to Alma and held out her hand, introducing herself as Sara. She had on a navy-blue blazer and a pretty, patterned silk blouse. "This is so exciting!" she said. "You're our first chromosomal addendum! A pioneer!"

Alma followed Sara back through the waiting room to an air-conditioned office appointed with lush green plants. She took a seat across from Sara at a large wooden desk. She retrieved an envelope from her purse, and handed it over to Sara.

Sara studied the report, her eyes moving quickly down the page. Her face was heavily made up, and Alma got the sense it wasn't so much for glamour's sake, as it was to cover up some minor yet lingering imperfection.

Sara looked up. "Impressive!" she said, smiling at Alma. "Twenty-three percent sub-Saharan African ancestry—within a 98.7 percent degree of certainty! Thirty-one percent British Isles. Fourteen percent Scandinavian. Twenty percent Benelux. Six percent Iberian. The rest is central European with trace amounts of eastern Mediterranean/Levant. Cool!" She paused and studied Alma for a moment. "Am I correct in assuming this came as a total shock?"

"I had every reason to assume I was Dutch and English all the way back."

"Wow!"

"Yet," Alma said, tilting her head, "on another level, I can't say it was a complete shock."

"I think I know what you mean."

"I mean, I never really clicked with whiteness, you know? I always just had the feeling that something was ... off. Ever since I was a little girl."

"I know exactly what you mean," Sara said, leaning forward.

"Have you ...?"

"Yes," Sara said, and then in an excited whisper, "18.5 percent Plains tribes!"

"Jesus! That's amazing!"

"And that's not all! I've got another 2 percent Cherokee/Algonquin!"

"Holy ..."

"I know. But ... I have to be very sensitive, you know. I can't go around wearing it on my sleeve, as it were. It's not as easy, with Native. I mean, I definitely have the blood percentage to make the claim. Not, of course, in a political way, like fishing or gambling rights, or anything like that, but ... What I mean is, with Native American it's a little more complicated. I had to apply to the tribe, show supporting documentation, things like that."

"Of course."

"They get the ultimate say—which is only fair. That's how it should be. Only horses and dogs should be measured by blood percentage, you know."

"Totally," Alma said. "Good luck! I hope you get it!"

"Thanks. I don't see any reason why I wouldn't. It's more just a formality at this point. My great-great-grandmother was born on a reservation, so ... I have the records."

"That's so cool."

"Anyway," Sara said, "even without it being official yet, my life has changed. Just knowing it changes you."

"Did you always know? I mean, did you feel, like, a connection to that culture?"

"Well. Yes. I mean I always knew about my great-great, so I was sort of on the lookout for things from that culture. But not ..." she straightened up, "you know, not anything offensive. No dream catchers or anything like that. I was always very respectful. But in answer to your question, yes, I did feel an affinity, which, when the test came back, was very much affirmed. And you haven't had yours for very long, I see from the date of the report, but just wait, you'll see, more and more things will start falling into place for you. Parts of yourself that you never understood will make sense to you: ways of looking at things, affinities, vague sensations. Not so much the culture. Like in my case, it's not an affinity with nature, or a tendency toward a matriarchal, or nonhierarchical society, or an attraction to shamanism, psychedelics, or anything like that. Because it hasn't been proven that any of those things get passed down through the genes. But as we know, trauma *does* get passed down. I'm sure you've heard of genetic whisperings. Those kinds of things started falling into place for me. Like, I finally understand why I'm so afraid of white people."

"Exactly. Me too," Alma said. "I've always felt like an outsider."

Sara cleared her throat. "So, I'll make copies of your documents, and if everything goes well, your official amended birth certificate should be ready in six to eight weeks. This is so exciting! Just so you know, we're not able to change the race of your mother or father, or your race, as stated on the original certificate, but you will be provided with an asterisk, stating your updated ancestry."

"Great! Thank you!" Alma said. She began to get up

from the chair, but then sat back down. "Actually, I was wondering. Is there any way to get a temporary certificate? You know, like how at the DMV you can get a temporary driver's license, until the real one comes?"

"Yes of course," Sara said. "Just bear with me." She turned to the computer and typed Alma's details onto an official form. She walked over to the printer and then handed the sheet of paper to Alma. It had the agency's logo and stated that—ALMA WILLINGSBY—had successfully applied for and had met the burden of proof of—BLACKNESS—as determined by the State of New York, a proud member of the Virtuous Federation of the United States of America.

Exiting the building, Alma was walking on air. Nothing had changed, yet, in another way, everything had changed. She was not the same person who had walked in. All the people on the various squares and plazas of the municipal area of downtown—going to court, coming from court, registering documents, taking civil service exams, selling hot dogs, eating hot dogs, drinking coffee, laughing and talking, taking photos, soaking in the sun—looked different to her than they had before. They looked smaller, more benign, less significant somehow. And she felt taller. Actually, physically taller. Like there was more space between each of her vertebrae. And her entire being was somehow more cushioned, more springy. She felt alive, and she also felt as if the ground was alive. And she felt like she was connected to the ground, and had sprung from it. There was something wild, instinctual, natural about the way she walked now. If she were to meet a predator, she would be prepared. If she were to sense an intruder, she would be prepared. It was as if she was surveying her territory. Yes! That was it! That was the feeling.

It was her territory. For the first time, she felt like she belonged to the land. To the earth. And she felt like it belonged to her. She felt a connection to it. It was so strange. So primal. It was such a natural thing, and yet she had never felt it before. It was a completely new sensation. Why? Why was she feeling this now? This new bodily sensation? What had changed? She had always been the same person, it was just that now she was officially ... she had the documentation ... That was it!

She stopped. And she stood there as things began to fall into place in her mind. People jostled by her. A few bumped into her and said, "Excuse me." She didn't care. She didn't turn around, she didn't say "Excuse me" back. Because that was it. Although she was the same person she had been before, she'd now taken her rightful place in the world. The world now recognized her for who she was. Not someone whose ancestors had stolen this land, betrayed and murdered its original inhabitants, then forced others to work it, but someone whose ancestors had been brought here against their will, then forced to work the land. Yes. That was it. Her ancestors had bought this land with the time-honored currency of blood. It was bought and paid for. Her place on this earth was bought and paid for. She could now hold her head up high.

She didn't want to go home. She had too much energy. She wanted to survey her new land with her new eyes, her new self. She wanted to be out. Be connected. Be wild. Be free. Celebrate. Mark the occasion. An idea came to her. She looked up an address on her phone. She walked south on Broadway until she came to Wall Street, then kept moving south, zigging and zagging down narrow streets, until she was well within the bounds of the old Dutch city, surrounded by tall grey buildings whose cool dampness she felt on her skin, even in the summer heat. She walked past the business men and women just beginning to spill out of their offices, the narrow streets now crowded with people rushing by. She took a few more turns and arrived at an out-of-the-way, seemingly forgotten street, quiet in the midst of all the hustle. And then she came to it, the Barry Street Bus Depot. It was little more than an empty lot with cracked pavement, and just a few city busses hissing on one end of it, waiting to begin their routes. It was an old and little-used hub—set to be cleared for good in the wake of the recent discovery of what was believed to be the oldest slave burial site discovered in the city to date. Historians had long predicted its existence, and had pored over ancient maps and letters, finally zeroing in on its location. The outlines of six coffins had been confirmed using ground-penetrating radar. While plans were being made for a memorial and possibly a museum, the actual burial site, about fifteen square feet on the south side of the lot, had been cordoned off with cement stanchions and yellow police tape. Wreaths, bouquets, cards, candles, and other objects of tribute lined the perimeter.

Alma approached the site. She had a strange and sudden urge to feel the ground beneath her feet, so she slipped off her beige flats, and wiggled her toes on the hot, cracked concrete. She let out a deep breath and sunk further into her body. She walked over to the cordoned-off area, and stood there, silently, trying to imagine the people buried beneath. They were her ancestors, in a way—metaphorically if not literally. She wondered who they were, who they'd been. She got the idea that maybe she shouldn't be standing atop them, so she got down on her knees. Once her knees were on the concrete, she regretted for the first time—but definitely not the last time—wearing her white cotton sundress instead of pants. Tiny pebbles and specks of what she hoped wasn't glass dug into the skin of her knees. She brushed them off with her hand, and tried her best to clear the area. She kept adjusting her position until she was about as comfortable as could be expected given the circumstances. She bowed her head low to the ground, and found herself wishing she knew how to pray. But she assured herself it would be okay. They would understand. She would just greet them. Like she would any other people she didn't know yet. And if it was awkward at first, so be it.

"Hello," she said, quietly, into the ground. And then waited. "Hello," she repeated, then sunk further into her position. "My name is Alma Willingsby. I know we've never met before, and I'm sorry, I don't know your names, but it's just ... we might be related. No. No. Probably not. Not literally, but, perhaps we share a journey ..."

Alma lifted her head and wiped off her knees again. She didn't feel like she was saying the right things.

She bowed down again. "So. I'm Alma Willingsby. Sorry. I already said that. What I wanted to say, is, you know, thank you. Thank you. I think in some way you made my life here possible. With your suffering ..." It was still wrong.

"No," she said. "I'm sorry. That's what I want to say. I'm sorry. And I love you. Yes. I love you." Alma lifted up her head again, suddenly not sure what she was doing there. There was silence all around, just a few horns honking in the distance, and the quiet hissing of the busses. She looked at all the items of tribute that had been left on the ground. The discovery of the site had only just been announced, and many of the flowers were still relatively fresh. She wondered how the people beneath felt about all the attention. Maybe they were overwhelmed. Maybe they were alarmed, frightened, disturbed. Maybe they had grown used to the silence: the soothing sounds of the busses, the mellow thoughts of the bus drivers. And now there were all these visitors, with their outpourings of grief and respect.

She put her ear to the ground again, and she waited. For what, she didn't know. A connection. A feeling. Yes. The communication would be silent. She wouldn't use words.

She closed her eyes and she imagined the earth beneath the concrete. The cool, wet earth. She imagined she was going down deeper into the dirt, reaching down. One foot down, two feet down, three feet down ...

Gradually, the city sounds faded from her mind, and she thought she began to perceive the silence of the earth. Her body was completely still. It was peaceful. Relaxed. She no longer felt the pebbles and the other worrying things that were sticking to her knees. She was expectant. Open, ready. Ear to the ground.

She waited.

Then she waited some more. She let her body relax further, so it almost folded in on itself, and she sunk her ear closer to the ground. She let go. Let go of everything. Let go of the day, the office of Birth and Death Certificates, her new identity, her old identity. She let go of it all, and she just listened.

She tried to listen to the dirt. She tuned into what she imagined to be the sound of the earthworms. They emitted a quiet, self-satisfied buzzing sound. She pictured a thread, a simple thread, emanating from her and reaching down into the ground, down, down, down, winding through the dirt, trying to locate her spiritual ancestors below. And then she thought, what if they have a thread too, and they're trying to reach me? She felt a jolt of energy. She was so tuned in to the minute intricacies of the situation, to her ideas about what might be happening beneath the ground, on a subtle plane, between her and some deceased beings, that for her, the vision solidified, and intensified, and things became less subtle and more real, very real, until she could have sworn she heard a very loud trumpet, three clear and foreboding notes, "BOOM BOOM BOOM!" So loud, in fact, that she could feel the reverberations throughout her body. Was it a warning? Was she disturbing the dead? Did they want her to GET THE FUCK OUT OF THERE? Was it Gabriel, announcing end times? Whatever it was, it gave her a feeling of terror and impending doom. Her heart began to skip and jump wildly, and she scrambled to her feet.

And then she was face-to-face with it. Not Gabriel. Not the angry ghosts of the old Dutch cemetery. But fifteen tons of glass and steel, hovering over her, bearing down on her, less than a foot away. It was the BxM44 express bus, hissing and raring to go. The driver, a round-faced black man, glared down at her through the window, and pressed the horn once again with a fearsome relish. The sound was so soul shattering she couldn't move. Then the driver honked again, and then, against all logic and civility, inched the bus forward, until it was just centimeters from her face. He honked again. There was no mercy, no sympathy, no compassion in his round face. He was not to be reasoned with. He would kill her if he had to.

Alma dove out of the way as the bus went careening off to begin its long route. She landed on her elbows. She caught her breath for a moment. She got up and inspected herself. Her right knee was skinned and she had a gash on her left forearm.

Slightly shaken, but undeterred, she walked back over to the cordoned-off burial site. As she knelt, her right knee sent pain signals to her brain. But she remembered how well she'd been able to concentrate before the interruption. How she'd been able to quiet her body's protestations. She wondered if she would be good at meditation now. She'd never been good at it before.

She put her head down to the ground, closed her eyes, and took a few breaths, trying to recapture the mood of before. Where was she? Yes. The cord. She'd been sending a cord down through the dirt to her spiritual ancestors. She began to picture it again, going down, down, down.

She turned her head to the side and was very surprised to see a young woman kneeling beside her, not three feet away. More shocking still—the woman was wearing the exact same dress as her! She stared in amazement, marveling at, among other things, what a great dress it really was. The other woman was taller, and significantly larger, yet the dress looked fabulous on her too—but in a completely different way. The dress seemed to have a magical ability to contribute to each woman's unique beauty.

The other woman, who took no notice of Alma, prostrated herself on the ground, her white arms outstretched toward the yellow police tape. Her long, shiny, black hair fell loose around her body. She was whispering quietly. Almost chanting. Alma could hear bits and pieces of what she was saying. "... am not worthy ... so much pain ... please accept my pain from having caused you pain ..." And then the woman expelled a soft, extended moan. She looked up for a moment, and caught sight of Alma.

"Nice dress!" Alma said. But the woman didn't acknowledge her. Her face was blotched and tear stained. She prostrated herself to the ground again, continuing her lament.

"Such suffering, such nobility, dear Mother and Father, I know I can't begin to comprehend. I bow down to you, I lower myself before you, Mother, Father, of suffering and grace, it's all I can do. I wish the ground would swallow me up and I could be down there instead of you. You don't deserve it, I do. I am sorry. I am sorry for everything. But my apology means nothing to you. I have trodden everywhere, all over you, on my happy feet of privilege! I have danced on your grave, and now I'm here to make amends. To throw dirt on my face. To atone. But I cannot. I cannot. No matter what I do I cannot."

The woman's voice grew louder, more emotional.

"I can't imagine your suffering! I can't even imagine it! Tell me how it was for you! Give me some of it!" she demanded. "Give me some of your suffering! Give it to me! Give it to me! Give it to me! I want to take it all! Forgive me! Forgive me! Forgive me please!" She was openly bawling now. "No, don't! Don't forgive me! Don't you dare! I don't deserve it!" She was pounding the concrete with her fists. "Don't forgive me! Don't forgive me! Don't forgive me! Punish me! Please! Punish me! I want to be lowly forever! Forever and ever! I will keep apologizing to you! Dear Mother and Father! But don't accept it! Ever! I am your lowly servant!"

Alma bent down again. She focused intensely, trying to block everything out. And then she heard only silence. She kept sending the string down and down and down into the earth. And then her mind went blank. And she visualized nothing. After a while, she felt as if something was holding her, cradling her in its large hands. A warmth spread out all over her body, and she smiled.

She got up, and she performed a very slight bow toward the burial site, more social than worshipful, as if to say, "Thank you, see you again." She walked away, enjoying the feeling of the hot concrete on the soles of her feet so much that she forgot for a moment that shoes existed, and that she'd come with a pair of them, and that she would need to leave with them.

She turned around and looked at the spot where she'd left her shoes. They weren't there. She looked around the lot. They didn't seem to be anywhere. There was lots of junk lying around. There was a newspaper wafting about in the breeze. There were some small metal objects—parts—they seemed to be parts of something. There was an old pair of cheap black discarded shoes.

The other woman had now risen, and her arms were outstretched to the heavens, and she was yelling, "Mother! Father! Goddess! God! Forgive me! Forgive us all!"

Alma walked over to the old black shoes. Maybe they would fit. She needed something. She couldn't very well go back into the city barefoot. She picked them up, and it was then that she noticed the insoles—and began to make out a familiar pattern—cute little terriers with bows. And then she realized the shoes weren't black at all, they were formerly beige, but covered with tire tracks. They were her shoes! She gingerly slipped her bare feet inside. The shoes were floppy and the life had gone out of them. She noticed a young man off to the side taking pictures of the wailing girl. She was surprised the woman hadn't attracted more attention. But it was a strangely remote little outpost, in one of the busiest parts of the city.

CHAPTER TWO
THE SPECIAL PROJECT

"So that's why we here at Baker, Carter, Ludlow and France felt it was important to call and let you know that *we know* ..." George paused for effect, his feet up on the antique, bespoke mahogany desk, crafted not long after the firm's founding in 1822, "that the incident in Russia, the so-called terrorist incident on Tuesday, had absolutely nothing to do with Muslims or Islam."

There was a momentary silence on the other end of the line. "No ..." Wali Hossein said, from his law office in Dhaka, considering carefully, trying to remember the facts. "I'm pretty sure those people were Muslims. From Central Asia, I think. Terrible! Sixteen people, George! Sixteen people dead. And what were they doing? Going to work? Coming home from work? Who were they bothering?"

"No, I mean they weren't *real* Muslims," George said, "and what they did has absolutely nothing to do with real Islam."

"Of course they were not real Muslims!" the Bangladeshi

said, a note of dignified umbrage in his voice. "They were not real humans! It is disgusting."

"Exactly, and we here at Baker, Carter, Ludlow and France know that Islam is a very peaceful and nonviolent religion. In fact, if I may quote from the Quran," George cleared his throat, "'Whoever kills a soul unless for a soul or for corruption in the land—it is as if he had slain mankind entirely. And whoever saves one—it is as if he had saved mankind entirely.' That's from surah 5, verse 32."

"Yes! That is very true!" Wali said. "Islam is like a light in the darkness! It is like a lantern that leads humanity to the sacred part of its own soul. Islam teaches peace. All the great religions do. And hopefully, we will all get there one day. All of us! Peace for everybody! Peace for blacks, whites, Christians, Jews ..."

"Yes!" George said, taking a little spin around on his comfortably cushioned ergonomic chair. "And what breaks my heart is when people have no trouble using the words 'Islamic terrorism,' but refuse to call the shit we have going on here, right here in the good old U-S-of-A, by its true name —terrorism—just because the perpetrators are ... you guessed it ... white! For example, just the other day, a white man shot up a packing facility in Modesto. He killed twenty-seven people! And nobody has once used the word terrorism!"

"Yes. I heard about this," Wali said. "I am so sad for you. My heart reaches out to you, George, and to all my American brothers and sisters."

"I mean this ... *this* is terrorism. What we have going on right here. This is the real shit. There's no question."

"There is no question in my mind," Wali said. "It is terrorism and it is terrible."

"And I'm talking about right here in the Virtuous Federation," George said. "I'm not even talking about all the shit going down in the Patriot States."

"Yes. It is terrible. And also such a shame about the Peaceful Bifurcation of America," Wali said. "I mean, it's not a shame that it was peaceful. But it's a shame about the bifurcation. I always looked up to America so much. It was so unique—all different kinds of people, all different kinds of ideas, and yet somehow everybody made it work. Too bad the different sides couldn't agree in the end. It was such a great democracy!"

George paused. It hadn't really been a bifurcation, although many people understood it that way. The United States was still united. It was just that different states had formed unions of sorts, based on their beliefs and a presumed common way of life. But George didn't see the point in correcting Wali.

"No, trust me buddy," he said. "This is the America you always loved. That other one, the Patriot Federation—that's nothing but a bunch of gun-toting bigots. This is the one you want. This is the America you love. Right here."

"Still. A shame. Did I ever tell you I did part of my undergrad at Alabama?"

"Yes, I think you've mentioned it."

"Roll tide!"

"Indeed."

The Bangladeshi continued, "But back to terrorism, George. This is not how man was meant to live—with terror in his heart. Man and woman were meant to live in peace. In brotherhood and sisterhood. But, unfortunately, this is the history of humanity. Terror and love. Both. Together. Always. They both exist in us all."

"See, that's what I'm talking about," said George. "Violence is a *human* problem. Not a Muslim problem. In fact, Islam is *less* violent than other religions."

"No. We are all guilty. We are all terrorists. The terror is in all our hearts, George."

"Yes, but what I mean is ..."

"We are all brothers!" Wali continued. "It's just bullshit when they try to tell us any different! They try to tell us that because we are from different countries, different races, different religions, we have to be enemies. But that's not the case! They are selling us a line of bullshit, George. Because we are the same. We are absolutely, 100 percent, the same. I guarantee you. And this is not just some crap I am saying because I don't know the meaning of the word pain, the meaning of the word suffering, the meaning of the word enemy! I do. I know those words very well. Have you heard about 1971, George? Well, 1971 happened right here. Right outside my office. Blood was flowing on these very streets! They killed my uncle—my grandfather's brother. He was an amazing man. A very cultured man. He was a lawyer, an intellectual, a diplomat. They made him ambassador to Korea, and he came home, to fight for freedom for my country. Because he cared about my country. The Pakistanis were slaughtering Hindus. Raping women. It was genocide. Genocide! Right here. Right here in Dhaka. Right where you were! Not far from the Chinese restaurant—remember? Madame Wong's? I took you to Madame Wong's. Remember? Blood was flowing right there, George. Right outside Madame Wong's! Right outside my office. Everywhere. He was murdered. My uncle. They say he was tortured first. We never even found his body."

"I'm so sorry," George said. He looked out his window. Manhattan was just waking up, it was still groggy and clutching a latte, whereas he'd already been to the gym and knocked out three calls as part of his cross-cultural understanding project—his personal mitzvah, his passion project—three very important calls. Three calls that might just change the world. He did this once a week. It was his way of giving back.

He caught sight of the Lucite cow statue on his windowsill. It had a basket of fruit on its head, and it was dancing and typing on a computer. He smiled. The statue commemorated a very important cattle-for-computers deal his firm had helped broker between the governments of Brazil and China.

Wali continued, "But even with all that has happened, do you think I hate the Pakistani? No. I don't. The Pakistani is my brother, George. Everyone is my brother. You are my brother. You are black, I am Bangladeshi, I don't care. We are brothers. We are all brothers. We are all sisters. Don't listen to any of this nonsense they are telling you!"

George glanced at the printout of last week's so-called Islamic terrorist incidents. His project consisted of preemptively phoning his Muslim business associates around the world and assuring them that he didn't hold them or Islam in any way accountable for these incidents. He liked to address each incident at least once in his calls. This time there was the Moscow subway bombing, which he'd just covered with Wali; a mosque bombed in Baghdad—he could cross that out, it was simple internecine fighting, irrelevant; a busload of Christian pilgrims killed in Egypt—okay; a knife attack on a Dutch train—maybe; a suicide bombing in a Cameroon market—okay; four farmers hacked to death in Nigeria—yes; a man in Berlin exiting a liquor store "stabbed about the neck"—a lone crazy most likely, definitely not terrorism ...

the list went on. The broad search words he used to compile his report netted a lot of incidents that couldn't be considered terrorism in the strictest sense, and he crossed those out.

Next on his list was Amir. Unlike Wali, he'd never met Amir in person, but they had a good relationship.

"Assalamu alaykum!" came the pleasant, youthful voice on the other end of the line. Amir Rizwan was a British-educated engineer/MBA, and was second in command at Pakistan's Municipal Bureau of Construction.

"Wa alaykum assalam! Amir! My friend! It's George Lake —Baker, Carter, Ludlow and France."

"George! How are you? How are things in the Big Apple?"

"Well, I can't complain. I guess it's the same here as everywhere, you've got your good people, your bad people, your in-between people. Did you hear about our mass shooting at the Northlake Mall?"

"Oh, yes. I'm so sorry. That was in Texas, right?"

"Tennessee."

"Oh. I'm so sorry. It's been on the news here. My heart really goes out to you guys."

"Thank you, but I assure you, it's nothing out of the ordinary here. Business as usual. And of course, as usual, it was committed by ... wait for it ... a white, Christian male. No surprise there!"

"Oh that's terrible. I hadn't heard religion played a part. That's awful."

"Of course you hadn't heard! That doesn't surprise me at all. When the perpetrator is white, nobody calls it terrorism. I guess he just doesn't 'look the part,' if you know what I mean."

"What do you mean?"

"According to the media, the only kind of person who commits terrorism looks ... a certain way, if you know what I mean. Which brings me to the purpose of my call. Amir, I just wanted to reach out, in this terrible time, and let you know that we here at Baker, Carter, Ludlow and France know that every group has its bad eggs. We've got our bad eggs, and plenty of them, and you've got yours. And just as the Northlake shooter doesn't represent all Americans, we know that the Tunisian-Dutch knife attacker over the weekend certainly doesn't represent all Muslims."

"No," Amir said. "He certainly doesn't."

"And we know that the vast majority of Muslims are peaceful, hardworking, God-fearing, productive members of society."

"Of course," Amir said. "But," he paused, "extremism is and always has been a problem. It's a big struggle for us here right now, actually. I don't know if you know, but Pakistan used to be quite a secular country, well, I mean relatively. It's always had both strains, but it seems the Islamists are really gaining ground, especially lately, it's alarming. There's always been fighting between sects—Shiites and Sunnis—but now, there's this new religious fervor. You've got the tele-mullahs preaching on TV all day, the stabbings, the shootings of religious minorities, the school bombing in Peshawar, the bombing in Lahore, the almost universal demand for the execution of ..."

"Yes, it's exactly the same as here," George said. "People are people. Terror is equal opportunity. It doesn't have a brand—it's generic. So, yeah, that's it, man. We here at Baker, Carter, Ludlow and France just felt it was important to say it out loud. Because silence can be damning, and you shouldn't have to read between the lines. We're stating it loud and proud. We do not confuse the heinous acts of the *mistaken Muslims* with the 1.8 billion peaceful and loving true Muslims living in the world. Basically, we don't feel you have anything to be ashamed of, nor should you have to answer for the acts of the mistaken Muslims."

"Well. No. Of course not. I don't."

"If anything, we should have to answer to you. Because we're the ones creating conditions all over the world that spawn such *noblerage* and spur the mistaken Muslims to take such desperate actions. We leave them no choice!"

"Well, it's complicated, but ..."

"Say no more! Let me be the one to do the talking, for once. Let us be the ones to do the explaining! It's about time! Let the West finally stand up and take responsibility. Yes! I'm not afraid to say it. *I'm sorry!* I take responsibility. *I'm sorry!* I, George Lake, take responsibility. I'm manning up! I'm sorry and ashamed about everything America has done in the world."

The calls to Abu Dhabi, Dubai, Jeddah, Tunis, Qatar, Dakar, Kenya, Tashkent, Brunei, Jakarta, and Kuala Lumpur went equally well.

By the time George hung up the phone there were beads of sweat forming on his forehead—but in a good way. As a young man, he'd initially been drawn to the law out of a passion for social justice. He'd pictured himself defending the downtrodden, overturning unjust convictions, and spearheading equitable legislation.

Of course he'd been greatly inspired by Arun Merriweather—tolerance theorist par excellence and founding father of the Virtuous Federation. George had had a poster of him in his bedroom growing up. It was that famous photo, where Arun was standing on the dais in front of the Royal

Palace in Amsterdam, draped in the pink flowers given to him by the Dutch schoolchildren, receiving the first ever eponymous Merriweather Award for Genius in Tolerance. Arun was dashingly handsome back then, with his Anglo-Indian bone structure, his shocking blue eyes, and his insouciant youthfulness.

But George had been exposed, by chance, in his second year of law school, to a certain Professor Cornelius Treadway, who'd set his world on fire with his passion for the global free market. According to Treadway, the marketplace wasn't the greedy, rarified concoction of a capitalistic system, as it was so often portrayed, but a sacred institution, an ancient tradition practically synonymous with being human, coded into our DNA, as old as time, and, as such—almost certainly African in origin. To Treadway, the marketplace was nothing short of the vital flow of energy itself, without which there could be no jobs, no goods, no food, no growth, no opportunity, no learning, no culture, no progress, no ideas—in short, no life. Treadway was so passionate, and his teaching style so electrifying, that George was able to harness this energy and subsequently coast through the drier courses, like Securities Regulation, Antitrust, International Investment Law, and even Derivatives—on a wave of unbridled enthusiasm of the type normally reserved for team sports or war. He was hired by Baker, Carter, Ludlow and France after doing his summer internship at the firm's Hong Kong office, and he hadn't lost an ounce of enthusiasm in the decade and a half that had ensued. He'd traveled the world, learned several industries, and spoke smatterings of eight different foreign languages. He'd made partner quickly.

And now, with his passion project, George had come full circle. He was, as he'd always dreamed of, providing justice to the oppressed. Only he wasn't providing it in the legal sense, he was doing something even better: he was providing justice in the emotional sense. Phone call by phone call, all by himself, early every Monday morning—before even the first-year associates arrived—he was restoring stolen dignity to victims around the globe. He was offering them a sense of being understood, of being seen as a part of the whole, of having their basic goodness and humanity affirmed—of being viewed charitably. *This* was the new capital. And George was at the forefront of facilitating its flow. He was shifting the global conversation. George stood up and looked out his window. He took in the Hudson River, the skyline of Hoboken. He focused out further, all the way to the horizon, which was getting brighter and brighter with each passing moment.

He looked around his office at all the celebratory statues commemorating the various deals he'd worked on—visual representations of his achievements. "Deal tombstones" or "deal toys" they were called. The firm had them made to celebrate important closings. There was the dancing cow on the windowsill. And on the bookshelves there were several others: a statue of a syringe in the colors of the Indian flag—orange, white, and green—celebrated a hard-won pharmaceuticals manufacturing deal; a tire with hot-pink flames bursting from it commemorated a Taiwanese chemical conglomerate's acquisition of an Italian race-car parts manufacturer; a boat with a beautiful couple dancing on it fêted a Mexico/Qatar off-shore oil partial privatization agreement. He loved looking at his statues. There was something comforting to him about making the intangible tangible. If he'd been religious, his apartment probably would have been littered with icons and candles.

He wondered what his passion project's hypothetical deal statue might look like—this project that brought peace, comfort, and emotional justice to the world. An image came to his mind. An image of a loving presence standing on a mountaintop, arms outstretched, welcoming the whole world, regardless of race, creed, or color. Christ the Redeemer! Yes. The Christ the Redeemer statue in Rio de Janeiro. No. Well, obviously the statue couldn't be Jesus himself. But perhaps it could reflect the essence of that gesture somehow. But how? And it couldn't be Mohammad either. For obvious reasons. No. The gesture had to be distilled down to its essence. It had to be something abstract. He tried to visualize it. A pair of arms? An abstract pair of arms? A hug? Maybe just a circle? And then it came to him. A heart! Yes. A heart. A simple, universally understood heart. He pictured it. A simple round glass pedestal, with a clear glass heart on top. Yes. Simple, yet powerful. Because when it came right down to it, that's exactly what his project was brokering in. The most precious commodity in the world, more valuable than oil, more stable than gold. Love—the universal currency.

There was one more name on the list. George brought his hands together in a loud clap and then picked up the phone. Nadim Farhan was partner at an in-country law firm in Cairo. He was a brilliant lawyer, educated at one of Islam's oldest and most prestigious universities. A robust man, with jolly cheeks that belied an inclination toward fierce debate and contrariness—sometimes downright orneriness, he'd played consummate host to George on several occasions, keeping him up till the early hours drinking thick, sweet coffee at his favorite *ahwa* in downtown Cairo. They'd sit in the elegant old coffee house debating law, politics, poetry, philosophy, chess—and things George had never even imagined could be up for debate.

On their days off, Nadim had taken him around to see the sites—the Pyramids, the Sphinx, the old Mediterranean city of Alexandria, Luxor, Aswan, and Abu Simbel near the Sudanese boarder. Sometimes Nadim's wife, Layla, and their two small boys had joined.

"Mistaken Muslims!" Nadim bellowed on the other end of the line. "That's the craziest thing I've ever heard! Why do you keep using that term? What is this term? It is so silly!"

"Because," George said, "I'm just letting you know that they're not real Muslims. That we know that. We all know that."

"How do you know?"

"Because, we know that no true Muslim would act like that. They're mistaken. They're taking the Quran out of context. They have a mistaken reading of Islam. Because Islam is a religion of peace."

"No true Muslim!" Nadim bellowed again. His tone was one of murderous delight. A large jovial cat toying with its dialectical prey. "Well, I think first of all you should get your logical fallacies straight! I believe the expression is 'no true Scotsman.' Anyway, listen, George, you really have no idea what you're talking about. I mean, thanks for the well-wishes and all, but if you'd read your history, you'd know that Mohammad and his companions were some of the biggest spillers of blood the world has ever known. Islam has nothing —I repeat—nothing, to do with peace. It prescribes war. War, war, and more war, and then when that's done, more war—until all else besides Islam has submitted or succumbed. And then, trust me, when only Muslims are left, there will still be more war, against the 'mistaken Muslims,' as you so delightfully call them. That is, against any Muslim who any other Muslim doesn't agree with. So thank you again for your well-wishes, but really—it really is quite funny what you are saying."

"Man. Come on. Listen to yourself," George said. "There is no way Islam has cornered the market on violence. And to think so is racism. Pure and simple. Textbook racism. There's no other name for it. I mean, look at all the terrorism we have here, and nobody even calls it terrorism. The Tennessee mall shooting, the Canton cardboard box company shooting, the Missoula motel shooting. I could go on. But who are people afraid of? Muslims. That's just messed up, man. And if you don't see that ... then I just don't know what to say. Whites are the ones to fear, and they always have been."

"Oh! Brilliant!" Nadim shouted, in disbelief and delight. "Did you just call me a racist? And then go on to talk about whites being murderers? You realize that 'white' is a race, right? And you do know that race is involuntary? Right? An accident of birth. And you do own that it's wrong to judge a race, any race, by the actions of a few, do you not? Now, an ideology—that's a different story. It is quite within the pale to judge an ideology for what it preaches, teaches, and inspires. I mean if you want to judge white supremacy, go right ahead. You'd be quite right. That's an ideology. And so is Islam—and it's a particularly murderous one at that. Trust me, my friend. Read. Just read."

"I don't know about that," George said. "All I know for sure is that it's racist to call every single crime committed by one group of people by the name terrorism, and then to never use that word at all with another group, it's the worst kind of stereotyping ..."

"It has nothing to do with *words*, George! If the crime is

committed to inspire terror in the name of an ideology, then it's terrorism. It's not because a Muslim happened to commit it. Do you think my people don't have regular criminals? Run of the mill scum that just so happen to be Muslim? Of course we do. Murderers, drug dealers, mafia, thieves, rapists —we've got them all. And they are not terrorists, and nobody calls them that. Because their crimes have nothing to do with Islam. Now when someone carries out an act because it was prescribed by this bloody religion ..."

"Oh my God! Open your eyes!" George shouted. "You don't think Christianity is bloody? Ever heard of slavery? Ever heard of the Spanish Inquisition?"

"Abolished, abolished. And it's quite revealing that you are citing examples that are hundreds of years old for Christianity, versus things that happened yesterday, last week, every day in Islam. Don't you see that you are arguing against yourself? You are comparing Islam with the Middle Ages. And you would be correct! You have hung yourself, my friend. Why has Christianity moved on and Islam never has? Ask yourself that. And while you're at it, ask yourself ..."

The discussion went on much longer than George had anticipated, and when he finally hung up, he was in some distress, his faith in his beloved project teetering. But after a few deep breaths, it became clear to him that Nadim was suffering from a particularly virulent form of internalized Islamophobia, which colored his whole worldview—to the point that it was almost impossible to argue with him. It was sad, really. He'd seen it before in his own community. People overidentified with the oppressor and maintained a naive belief in the goodness of white, Western life—despite all evidence to the contrary. But he wouldn't give up on his friend. No, quite the opposite. He would keep calling, and he would find a way to get through. It was important. It was critical. In truth, Nadim's attitude only underlined the importance and urgency of his project.

In fact, he decided, he would actually go ahead and make a deal tombstone, a statue, for his project. And maybe T-shirts too. Yes! And he'd take it public. He'd let people know about it. It was too good to keep hidden! People could learn so much from it! He'd get it on TV, maybe. Yes. He had to. Who was that woman? Marine something? What was her name? She had that show—*Hate Hunters*, where she outed racists. And that other show, *Bridge Builders*, where she featured people's tolerance projects. Yes! He'd get his project on TV!

He reached across his desk and tore off a sheet from his gold-leafed company notepad and wrote a reminder to himself:

"Muslim understanding project, find a way to publicize. Take it to the people! *Hate Hunters/Bridge Builders*?"

CHAPTER THREE

THE PLAY

Jackie Krucic was seated in the eleventh row of the third balcony of the Avondale Theater on Broadway's Great White Way. Each row was about three feet above the last, which made for a spectacular, unobstructed view of the stage, but also, a sensation of teetering perilously on the brink. To her right, an elderly couple sat with their opera glasses at the ready, and to her left, a group of four well-dressed ladies about her age, in their late fifties, conversed quietly, in the expectant, hushed tones of theatergoers everywhere. Jackie, a full-faced, rather curvy woman with pale blonde hair, was there by herself. She was always by herself. Tonight, however, she felt a sense of camaraderie she hadn't felt in some time. It had been years since she'd gone to the theater, and she wondered why. She liked being part of the audience. It was anonymous, yet at the same time, everyone was connected somehow, as if gearing up to go on an adventure together. True, she was probably the only one in the audience who'd been court-mandated to attend, but still, no one would be immune to the allegations of *Danger's Tweets*, the triple Tony

Award-winning musical about the devastating effects of casual racism. The elusive magic of theater lay in the fact that it not only offered escape, which function was reflected perfectly in the decor of the Avondale—the two gold columns on either side of the stage rose up several stories; the proscenium arch was carved with elaborate Poseidons, mermaids, and other fantastical creatures; and the balconies were adorned with dizzying arabesques—but it also confronted you with reality. It took the most exalted, as well as the most troubling, aspects of human nature, and paraded them across the stage for all to see. It was an inescapable mirror. Tonight, all would stand accused, all would be indicted, and all would stand trial. All would be pardoned or damned. Together.

A hush came over the audience as the house lights dimmed. The first soft, heavily stringed notes emanated from the orchestra pit, like a lazy summer breeze, carrying just the first few hints of autumn.

Jackie leaned forward.

A young woman enters the stage. She's carrying a newborn baby swaddled tightly in her arms. She swirls around to the music, her ample skirt lifting into a wider circle as she dances. She looks lovingly into her infant's eyes. The two dance around as if in a happy dream. As if no one else in the world exists. After some time in this magical reverie, the woman stops and faces the audience, announcing, with a big grin on her face, "I'm a mom!"

She then begins her first musical number. In a beautiful, richly textured, but natural alto voice, she declares that all her dreams have finally come true, all the dreams she's had since she was a little girl. She's in love, she's a wife, and now, the crowning glory—this tiny precious life in her arms. She can hardly believe it's happening! But why not? she wonders. Why can't she believe it? New life is a miracle, without a doubt, she sings. But at the same time, it's also the most ordinary thing in the world. It happens every day. Babies are born every day. That's how people begin. That's how life begins. That's how life works. Which makes her realize he won't be a little baby forever. Her little boy will become a man. Her little seed will become a tree. The actress is singing all this as if she is just speaking to the audience, in natural conversation, as if everything is occurring to her in the moment; there is such a freshness and spontaneity to her stage presence—it feels like she's speaking directly into your heart. Then she sings the chorus:

"Small seeds, become trees."
"Small seeds, become trees."
"Small seeds, become trees."

She repeats the words as she swirls around with the baby again.

"Small seeds, become trees."
"Small seeds, become trees."

Then she sings about all the special moments that are to come. She sings about how nervous she'll be on his first day of school. How anxious she'll be when he first learns to drive. She even comically jerks her body back and forth as she imagines herself in the car.

"Small seeds, become trees."
"Small seeds, become trees."

Then she imagines him graduating from high school, going off to college, meeting a girl, getting married, the whole nine yards. While she's singing, a chorus of about thirty people enters the stage behind her, all dressed in muted colors, and they join her in singing, softly at first, then louder. They hold out their hands, as if beckoning the audience. Their voices become thunderous:

"Small seeds, become trees."
"Small seeds, become trees."

Their voices build even more:

"Small seeds, become trees."
"Small seeds, become trees."

The chorus and the mother exit, but they can all still be heard chanting the chorus from backstage:

"Small seeds, become trees."
"Small seeds, become trees."

As the singing continues, the back wall of the stage fills with projected photographs of smiling little babies, all in a grid. The pictures keep changing, more babies, smiling babies, all different races and colors. And the music continues:

"Small seeds, become trees."
"Small seeds, become trees."

Then the faces on the wall change to adult faces—young

adults, old adults, all colors and creeds, just like the babies. Black people. White people. Asian people. Happy people. Sad people. City people. Country people. Rich people. Poor people. People. People. People. The images just keep flashing. There are so many people! Then the images dissolve, and the stage goes dark. The audience applauds wildly. Jackie applauds with them. But there's a heaviness in her heart. She feels very in touch with her love for humanity at this moment. But since it's a feeling she doesn't often have, it's overwhelming, and she wants to cry. But she can't cry. She hasn't cried since she was a small child. So she's left with a feeling she calls "full of tears," or F.O.T. And F.O.T. is a very heavy, morose, tragic, yearning, hopeless, lonely kind of feeling.

In the second scene, it is some years later, and the family is in the full swing of busy, modern-day life. The baby boy is now a teenager, and there's a younger sister too, and of course the dad, Ryan, the love of the protagonist's life. There are a couple of musical numbers about their hectic lives—teenage problems, marital problems, and work problems, but nothing too heavy. It's basically a happy family. Electronic and social media are portrayed prominently—almost like a separate character. The family has cell phones in their hands at all times, and every time they type something, or get a notification, it's projected onto the wall behind them—the same wall where the babies were. Text messages, tweets, snaps, emails—they all go up on the wall. The messages are usually unrelated to the plot.

For example, during the musical number "What Ever Happened to Dinner at Six?" which talks about how the family never has time to eat together anymore, you see these notifications scrolling along the back wall:

"Tristan, where you at?"
"You won't believe your eyes! All dress shoes 20%–50% off!"
"Ryan, when you get a chance, let's talk re: the Leighton account"
"Poppy, why aren't you answering?!"
"#momtoteenagers #mycrazylife"
"Need a getaway? Travelhub has amazing deals to Miami!"
"Check out our new Mazdas!"
"Poppy! We're waiting!"
"OMG, love your dress in that pic!"
"You're due for a dental cleaning!"
"Check out our Oktoberfest deals!"
"Save the date: Summer Job Fair"
"Ha, Trist! 1st world problems, lmao!"
"Re: Upcoming Changes to Payroll"
"Sorry I couldn't get back to you, terrible migraine!"
"Yum! Jealous!"
"The tumor is benign! #Blessed, #prayerworks"
"Pretty trippy, huh?"
"WTF with this calc homework!!"
"Sun through the trees, #myhappyplace"
"Knock 'em dead, champ!"
"Check out my upcoming TV special!"
"You won't want to miss this episode!"

Most of the messages are apropos of nothing, which is great, because it shows how our attention is stretched in a million different directions at all times these days. And the actors are great too, with their split-second glances at their phones.

But pretty soon we notice texts of a different nature

mixed in. They are red and bolded, so they stand out from all the other random messages.

"Is she still awake? Can you talk now?"
"Missing you. I can't bear this situation much longer."
"Did you tell her yet?"
"I'm wearing the red panties. Can you get away?"
"I need you Ryan, you've been with her every night this week. Please, it's my turn. I can't live like this. You have to decide."

Meanwhile nothing is changing on the stage, everyone's still hectically pleased with their crazy lives. Eventually, however, it all comes out. Ryan leaves, and then it's just the three of them. After things have settled down a bit, the protagonist sings a very moving number about suddenly finding herself a single mom, called "My New Reality."

She has some ups and downs, and as she's trying to find herself as an independent person, she ends up getting involved in some pretty conservative, reactionary websites and chat rooms, and we see the messages on the back wall, in red:

"#buildawall"
"Bring back the American dream!"
"Reverse racism is real!"
"Last time I checked, marriage is between a man, a woman, and God!"
"ALL lives matter!"

But it's not a huge part of her life. Most of her messages are just routine stuff:

"Being a mom of two teenagers is the most frustrating, joyful ride of my life. #Arewethereyet?"
"Not looking for love—working on myself as an individual. Learning and growing! #metime"
"My daughter scored two goals in field hockey today! #Proudmama! #Myathlete #Shedidnotgetthatfromme!"
"Eating Ben & Jerry's, watching Real Housewives. Life is good!"

Tristan, the baby from the first scene, has turned into a really cool kid. He's very kind. He volunteers in food pantries, and he has a friend named Jessie, who he's known since kindergarten, who he kind of takes under his wing. Jessie is a good-looking kid, but a little bit socially awkward. He's always at the house, to the point that he's practically a member of the family. And it's pretty apparent he also has a crush on the mom, especially now that she's really coming into her own, discovering her voice, and starting to work outside the home. We often see him looking at her in amazement and adoration.

He has a solo number, where he talks about growing up in and out of foster homes, and wishing he had had a family like the Rowans, called "But I'm Grateful to be Here."

During all of this, the mother's red tweets show up from time to time:

"Sorry, last time I checked wasn't English our official language?"
"Why no wall yet?"
"My Tristan has a 4.0 GPA and 1520 SAT, but Stanford said no. Too white? Race-blind admissions now! #handoutshurtnothelp"

In one of the last scenes, we open on Tristan's classroom. There are about fifteen teenagers sitting at old-fashioned wooden desks. They are texting, talking, laughing, goofing around. Their typical teenage texts are scrolling along the back wall.

Jessie enters from backstage, aiming an assault-type rifle at the class. Nobody sees him at first. They just keep laughing and talking, looking at their phones, holding up pictures to show to one another.

"Hey!" Jessie says to the class, but his voice is quiet, cracking a little, like it's the first time he's talked all day.

Nobody hears him. The buzz of teenage conversation continues.

Finally, a girl turns around, perhaps looking for a friend who hasn't come yet, or the teacher, and she sees Jessie. She lets out a loud, piercing scream.

"Shut up! Nobody move!" Jessie yells, and waves the gun around. Everybody is quiet and perfectly still.

"Stand up!" he yells. "Everyone stand up!"

Some students stand up quickly, and their desks fall to the floor in the commotion. Others sit at their desks, frozen.

"Everybody up!" Jessie yells, his voice gaining authority.

A few more students stand up hesitantly.

"Jessie," Tristan says, in a soft voice, his arms outstretched. "Jessie, buddy, just put down ..."

"Now!" Jessie shouts, waving the gun around the classroom "Everybody up now!"

All the students stand up, except one girl falls to the floor, and repeats softly, "Oh my God, oh my God, oh my God."

"Quiet!" Jessie yells, pointing the gun at the girl. She is silent.

Jessie points the gun at an African American boy who is standing. "You!" he yells. "Get over there!" He points toward the wall at stage left. The boy looks around the class. He gestures to himself and raises his eyebrows, as if to say, "Me? Why?"

"Now!" Jessie shouts.

The typical teenage texts continue along the back wall.

"My morning face, ha!"
"Ugh, sick in bed, miss yoooooouuuu!"
"Love this place!"
"#Betruetoyourself"
"History sub sucks!"
"Hi Mila, it's Mom, do you have dance practice today?"

Tristan speaks again, "Jess. Just ... just put down the gun, okay?"

"Shut up!" Jessie yells, continuing to point the gun at the black kid, who starts slowly moving over toward stage left, never taking his eyes off the gun.

Jessie points the gun at a Latino-looking kid. "You! Go over there with him!"

The kid puts his hands up in the air. "Jessie, please ..." he says. Jessie shoots him and he falls to the floor. Everyone screams.

"Quiet!" Jessie yells, and shoots the gun in the air. "Nobody else talk!"

Tristan is inching forward, toward Jessie. The Latino boy is on the floor, clutching his stomach.

"You!" Jessie says, pointing the gun at an Asian girl. "Over there!" The girl runs over to the wall, without hesitating, joining the black kid.

Jessie goes through the class, systematically picking out all the minorities. He even asks one girl where her parents are from. She cries, silently, shaking, she cannot talk. He sends her over to the wall with the other kids.

Tristan all the while has been slowly sneaking across the room, and he's now just a couple of feet away from Jessie, slightly behind him. He is perfectly still. Then he reaches out his arms to make a grab for Jessie, but Jessie knocks him over with the butt of his rifle, not even looking at him.

"Move away, Trist," Jessie says, calmly, without turning.

Jessie then aims the gun at the kids against the wall. Tristan jumps back up and gets in front of Jessie. He lunges for the gun. Everyone is screaming. Shots ring out, dozens of shots, one after the other. There is chaos, and kids falling to the ground. Then there is silence. The stage goes black.

In the next scene, the protagonist sits on the ground, cradling Tristan's lifeless body. All is silent, except for her heart-wrenching sobs. She rocks him back and forth, kissing his face. Then she stops crying. She looks up. She has a faraway, dreamlike expression on her face. She begins to sing, in a quiet, shaky voice:

"Small seeds, become trees."
"Small seeds, become trees."

She gets down on the ground and lies with Tristan, hugging his body.

"Small seeds, become trees."
"Small seeds, become trees."

Then the chorus joins her on the stage, in their drab clothes. One of them announces loudly:

"Word seeds become deeds."

The actress keeps singing quietly:

"Small seeds, become trees."

The man repeats, loudly:

"Word seeds become deeds."

The actress looks up at him.

On the back wall, all the protagonist's racist tweets scroll by, along with others, more violent and extreme, until the whole wall is full of them.

"Make America White Again!"
"You will not replace us!"
"Hitler should have finished the job!"
"The South will rise again!"
"Blood and Soil!"
"White lives matter!"
"White Pride World Wide!"
"One race, one nation, end immigration!"

The protagonist reads the words, and then she looks back down to Tristan's body, and screams, finally descending into madness.

And the chorus just keeps singing, louder and louder:

"Word seeds, become deeds!"
"Word seeds, become deeds!"

Then all the schoolchildren from the previous scene enter and join the chorus, until it is a deafening roar that the audience can almost feel in its bones:

"Word seeds, become deeds!"
"Word seeds, become deeds!"

The singing continues, and the writing on the back wall becomes a list of positive movements and resources:

"#endracismnow"
"Hate speech is not free speech!"
"www.stopbullying.gov"
"Hate Crime Hotline: 800-555-7800"

And the cast continues singing:

"Word seeds, become deeds!"
"Word seeds, become deeds!"

The stage goes dark. There is silence.

The protagonist wanders alone onto the stage. She has aged; her face is lined. She is dressed in drab clothes, and she is hunched over. A little boy of about seven enters the stage, riding a scooter. He rides around for a while. Then he bumps into her by mistake.

"Oh! Hi!" says the protagonist, looking down at him, as if noticing him for the first time. She laughs.

"Hi!" the little boy says.

"What's your name?" the woman asks.

"I'm Andy!" the little boy says.

"Oh, how wonderful! Nice to meet you, Andy. I used to have a little boy just like you."

"Is he grown up now?"

"No sweetie. He's an angel. He's an angel in heaven."

The boy pauses. "What's your name?"

"My name is Mrs. Rowan."

"Hi Mrs. Rowan!"

"You know what, Andy, you can just call me by my first name. You can call me Danger."

"Danger?" the little boy says, screwing up his face. "That's a funny name."

"I guess it is."

"Why do you have the name Danger?"

The protagonist shrugs. "My mom gave it to me. It was her name, and her mother's name before her."

"But ... you seem like such a nice person!" Andy says.

Danger looks at him with a distraught, bewildered expression. "But I am, Andy, I am a nice person."

And then the stage goes dark.

CHAPTER FOUR

THE BODEGA

Jackie stood outside the theater. She smiled, happy to be part of the general milling about. People smiled back. She pretended to herself and others that she was waiting for a taxi, or a husband perhaps, or a friend to return from the powder room. The sidewalk was sparkling, and the theater marquees lit up the night, so there was a strong sense that the drama and excitement continued. She lingered as long as she could. Until she was almost the last person. She finally forced herself to start walking, out into the truly anonymous city. Luckily, she always had Mohammad, her stalwart, the owner of the bodega on Ninth Avenue, and a habitual oasis of warmth in her life.

"I would join you, but as you know, I am both Muslim and diabetic," Mohammad said, reaching down behind the counter for his water bottle, and then raising it to join Jackie in a toast. That was their routine. She stopped by the bodega every night. Sometimes she picked up a few items. A box of crackers. A chocolate bar. An orange. Sometimes she didn't. But the end result was always the same. She lingered at the counter conversing with Mohammad and sipping gin. She always offered him a drink from her silver flask, purchased at a thrift shop and monogrammed with the initials GVM, and he always regretfully declined, citing his dual diagnosis: "I would join you, but as you know, I am both Muslim and diabetic."

"I just came from *Danger's Tweets.* Have you seen it?" Jackie asked.

"No! It is extremely sold out! How wonderful that you got tickets! I've been trying for months! How was it?"

"So emotional! An emotional roller-coaster ride! And I had forgotten how nice it is to go to live theater. I want to see everything now!"

"Oh, yes, I know how you feel!" Mohammad said. "I must go! As soon as I get tickets I will take my wife and daughter." He then touched his plastic bottle to her metal flask. "To the theater!" he said.

"To the theater!" Jackie said, and took her first sip of gin that day. As always, it was welcoming and disappointing.

She raised her flask again. "To friendship!"

"To friendship!" Mohammad said, raising his bottle. Then he raised it again. "To America!" he said.

"To America!" Jackie said.

A large, muscular man with a singsongy Guyanese accent, wearing a burnt-orange suit and a straw hat, walked up to the counter and purchased a box of Marlboros and a lottery ticket. He took his time picking his numbers, then informed Jackie and Mohammad he would tip them generously from his winnings.

"How much!" Jackie shouted.

"Yes, I hope you remember your friends!" Mohammad said.

"I guarantee you, I never forget my friends!" the man said, and nodded towards them. As he left, the heat from the night outside entered through the open door.

Mohammad continued, "See, that's what I mean. America is the greatest country on earth. We are all brothers and sisters. Black, white, Mexican, Jamaican, Muslim, Christian, it doesn't matter. We are all related. Like now, for example. We are here together, talking to each other. You, me, Freddie ..." He gestured toward the door. Mohammad got a feverish glow in his eyes every time he talked on this subject, which was often. "We are all from different places. We have different backgrounds, different ideas, and here we are treating each other with respect and friendliness. This is a wonderful thing. We are learning from each other. That is what America is. America is at the forefront of the world in that way. A beacon of the future. In the future there will be no divisions. We will not talk about different kinds of men the way we talk about different kinds of animals. Because in reality, there is only one category. Human. All those divisions —religion, race, nationality—they are not real. Tagore, the greatest poet of my people, put it well when he said, 'Patriotism cannot be our final spiritual shelter; my refuge is humanity.' And this is what is happening in America. Humanity is right here in America. Humanity in all its forms, trying to live together in peace. Not always succeeding —but mostly succeeding. And *trying*. That is the important part, Jackie. We are trying. It is very special."

Jackie nodded. She completely agreed with Mohammad on all those points. Why couldn't her tolerance counselor, Alma, and the rest of the world see that? Mohammad was stating her opinions exactly. She just couldn't express them as well as him. Then she remembered. Alma had given her another assignment—besides the play. She reached inside her purse and took out her cell phone. She held it awkwardly in her hand, not really sure of the etiquette. She wasn't exactly part of the selfie culture. Should she just say, "Wanna take a picture?" Apropos of nothing? She supposed now was as good a time as any, now that they were on Mohammad's famous "black, white, Christian, Muslim, Chinese" theme.

"Yes, exactly," she said, lifting the phone.

Two blonde girls with long tanned legs and short denim skirts walked up to the counter. They purchased a large bottle of water, a ready-made chef's salad, a tray of sushi, and a box of Petit Écolier cookies. They asked for extra napkins.

"You know, when I first came to this country," Mohammad said, handing the girls a generous pile of flower-patterned napkins, "when I arrived at JFK, with my wife, I got off the plane, got our luggage, went through customs, and the first thing I did when I got outside—I got down on my knees, and I kissed the ground. I looked up to my God, and I said, 'Thank you! Thank you for bringing me to this place I have heard great things about, this place I have dreamed about since I was a little boy. Where all men live beside one another. Men from all different countries, continents, religions. They form a society together. This is the land I have dreamed of, and now I am here. Thank you!'"

Jackie imagined Mohammad as a younger man. It wasn't that hard. He still had a full head of thick, mostly black hair. She imagined him kneeling on the ground next to the taxi line at JFK, his young wife standing slightly off to the side, smiling nervously.

She went to take another sip of gin, and instinctively made the gesture of offering the flask to Mohammad.

"You know, I not only have diabetes," Mohammad said,

holding up his hand to refuse the drink, "but it seems like God, in his infinite wisdom, has decided to give me every disease of old age. Not just one. But every single one! He didn't forget one! And I'm not even sixty! But for some reason he really wanted to remind me, 'Mohammad, you are old!' He wants to remind me all the time. 'Mohammad, you are not young anymore.' 'Mohammad, don't do this!' 'Mohammad, don't do that!' 'Mohammad, you are getting old.' He really doesn't want me forgetting that. Sometimes I look in the mirror, and I think, 'Mohammad, maybe you are not a young man anymore, but you are not old either. You are in the middle! Mohammad, you are in the middle. You are not too bad!' But as soon as I say that, God gives me another disease, to remind me I'm old. I have diabetes, high blood pressure, cholesterol. I have a bad heart too." He put his hand on his heart. "Arrhythmia! It's a mess! I'm at the doctor every other week! I'm like a specimen, a lab experiment! They have to keep examining me!"

"I'm sorry," Jackie said. "But you look very healthy." She made a motion of flexing her biceps like a muscle man. "Very strong. You must be doing well. I hope you are doing well." She put the cell phone back in her purse.

"I am healthy. God willing. For now! But only if I stick to my plan. I have to take my medication and I have to follow my diet. But this is life, you know, this is the way it is. I could question it. I could say, 'God, why me?' I could become very depressed. But I don't get depressed. I feel very happy," Mohammad said, ringing up a lemon, a carton of milk, and an avocado for a middle-aged woman with short hair and a wool skirt suit in the dead of summer. The woman nodded at Jackie.

"Do you know what we believe about illness?" Mohammad said.

"What?"

"We like to say that illness is a love letter from God."

A young Latina woman in a powder blue T-shirt walked up to the counter carrying a bottle of dish soap and three sponges.

"Think about it," Mohammad said, ringing up the girl's items. "How long has illness been around? Since the beginning of time, right? God created man and illness at the same time. They're brothers. Cousins. Sisters. Whatever. Man and illness. Illness and man. Why?" Mohammad turned to the girl. "That will be $6.49, please, Miss.

"Together. Always," Mohammad said, and intertwined his fingers to show how interconnected man and illness had always been. "Why? Why has illness been our constant companion?"

The girl reached into her worn leather purse and handed Mohammad a ten-dollar bill.

"Because," Mohammad continued, "when he is healthy, man doesn't think about God! When he is laughing, singing, dancing, having a good time with his family, God is nowhere. Man forgets him completely. When man is working, making good money, living in a nice house, he is not thinking about God. No! When things are good, man ignores God. He thinks only about the world, and not about God. And this makes God very sad. Because we are like his little children. He loves us. He longs for us. He wants us to be near to him. But we don't even give him the time of day when things are going well. We forget all about him. We think we don't need him anymore. So God created illness, and he sent it to man. As if by post! Because the minute man gets sick, he talks to God. When man gets sick, he always has God on his mind—night and day. He has God on his lips, in his prayers, in his heart. And this makes God so happy. It fills his heart with joy. Finally, he is not lonesome. He is reunited with his beloved creation. This is why we say God created illness as his love letter to man. Here's your change, Miss, have a blessed night!"

"Thank you," the girl said, placing the change in her purse.

"Jeesh!" Jackie said. "It seems to me he could have thought of a better way."

"A better way?" Mohammad said.

"Yes. To get his children to call. I mean what kind of God ... why would God ... why would people worship a god who ... Never mind," Jackie said, and took another sip of her gin.

Jackie noticed that the young woman's fingers were shaking as she fiddled with her purse. And then she looked at the girl's face and noticed that a steady stream of tears was falling from her eyes. She must have been crying the whole time, Jackie realized. Just going about her business while crying! Amazing! Jackie felt a pang of jealousy at the girl's ability to cry, which was quickly overshadowed by compassion. "What's wrong?" she said to the girl, leaning forward to get closer.

The girl shook her head, embarrassed and overcome with emotion.

"Drink?" Jackie said, shaking her flask back and forth, putting a deliberately silly expression on her face. The girl laughed, shook her head, and then her tears redoubled. She reached into her purse and brought out a used tissue, almost completely disintegrated.

"Oh no! What's wrong Miss?" Mohammad said. "Here."

He handed her some flowered napkins. She took them gratefully, covering her face. Mohammad took out a folding chair from behind the counter and placed it off to the side, behind the lottery register. "Sit! Please. Sit, Miss." He helped her to the chair. She folded her body onto it and buried her head in her hands. "I'll get you some water."

Jackie walked over to the girl. The spot where they were was nicely hidden from anyone who might come in. The girl allowed herself to sob openly, her breath catching, her chest heaving up and down.

"What's wrong?" Jackie said. "I mean, if you want to talk about it. I'm a good listener. I won't judge you."

"Thank you," the girl said.

"Is it a man?" Jackie asked. She had a feeling it was a man.

A tiny burst of laughter came from amidst the tears.

Mohammad returned with a cold bottle of water. The girl took a few long sips, then got back to weeping. "Let it out," Mohammad said. "Just let it out. Crying is very good. It cleanses the soul! You will feel better after, I promise."

Jackie placed her hand on the girl's right shoulder, and Mohammad stood to the girl's left. Jackie felt a connection between the three of them, a circuit of energy that was strong and protective. She was happy she hadn't taken a picture earlier. This was the picture she wanted to keep in her mind.

After some time, the girl looked up, her expression lighter, more clear. She looked back and forth between Mohammad and Jackie. "Are jerk boyfriends a love letter from God?" she said. "Because if they are, I think God must really adore me."

CHAPTER FIVE

FATHER AND DAUGHTER

"America is the greatest country on earth," Mohammad announced. He had just fixed himself a tea with two spoonfuls of nondairy creamer and two Splendas. He placed it on the glass coffee table and took a seat in his habitual reclining chair. It was one in the morning and he had just returned home from a fourteen-hour shift at his bodega. His wife was upstairs reading her mysteries and his daughter, Ruby, was reclining on the nearby sofa in her pink pajamas. Her study materials were strewn everywhere: an Organic Chemistry textbook, an Anatomy and Physiology textbook, flash cards, laptop, tablet, phone, notebooks—and a Quran. In addition to studying to become a physician's assistant, Ruby was also memorizing the Quran. Mohammad was very proud of her.

Ruby didn't acknowledge her father's patriotic statement. She was concentrating on her Anatomy flash cards. She read to herself:

"A group of two or more tissues that have been adapted to perform a specific function."

"Organ!" she exclaimed. She turned over the card. It was organ. She let out a giggle.

The Real Housewives were on TV. A very tall woman in an elegant red sequined gown had just pulled the wig off of a short blonde woman. Everyone around them shrieked.

"You know," Mohammad continued, "my store is like a microcosm of America. We have everybody: black people, white people, Mexican people, Jamaican people ..."

Ruby rolled her eyes. This was nothing new. Her father often pontificated on this theme. "Dad," she said, trying to change the subject, "do you know what my Anatomy professor said today about diabetes?"

"What?"

"He said it's like starvation in the midst of plenty."

"Hmm," Mohammad said. "Starvation in the midst of plenty."

"Yes. Starvation in the midst of plenty. In other words, there's all this sugar in the blood. But with diabetics, they have no way of getting it into the cells where it can be used. And sugar is the fuel of all human life. So he calls it starvation in the midst of plenty. Isn't that poetic?"

"Yes," Mohammad said. "It really is very good. A perfect way of describing the condition."

"I swear, he has such a unique way of putting things. I love his class. I could listen to him for hours."

"Starvation in the midst of plenty," Mohammad repeated, and took a sip of his tea.

On TV, the wife who had grabbed the wig was telling her side of the story. She wore a brilliant diamond bracelet that sparkled like sunlit water against her brown skin.

"But as I was saying," Mohammad continued, "from my experience in my store today, I can say with certainty that the great experiment of America is working. I had a very interesting experience today. A woman came into my store and she was very upset. She was crying."

Ruby read the next flash card, "A large, multinuclear cell that breaks down bone tissue. Important in remodeling."

"Osteoclast!" she said out loud.

"What?" Mohammad said. "Anyway, we were able to help this woman. Together. Me and this other white lady. My friend, actually. Jackie. We listened to the girl, we comforted her, and we gave her advice. And she felt better. And it just goes to show that all humans are the same. She left my store feeling much better. It was like magic. It was like a sign. A sign that we are all meant to be living together. That we all have something unique to offer: blacks, whites, Christians, Muslims ..."

"Dad, stop, please!" Ruby said. Then, catching herself, she softened her tone. "I know your position. I mean about the blacks and the whites and the Christians and the Muslims, and the Jamaicans and the Mexicans and the Chinese. You talk about it all the time. And you know exactly how I feel. America's not the Shangri-La you think it is. Now, can we please just agree not to discuss it?"

"But you see, that's exactly what I'm saying, my love. I now feel confident that America really is the Shangri-La we had hoped it was."

"Dad, I know you want to believe that. You had a dream. And you sacrificed everything to come here with Mom and have me here. You left behind everything you knew." Ruby put the flash cards down and leaned forward on the couch. "And I appreciate it, Dad, I really do. You meant well. But seriously, you can't tell me your head is buried so deep in the sand that you can't see what's really going on. Yes, there are a lot of races here, but that doesn't mean they all get along, and it doesn't mean they're all treated equally. Least of all you and me."

Ruby leaned back and picked up the flash cards again.

On TV, one of the wives was arguing with her husband about the price of a bathroom remodel. Mohammad and Ruby watched in silence for some time. The husband was trying to explain how he didn't want to spend all that money, especially since they'd just recently remodeled the kitchen.

"He should listen to her!" Mohammad said. He turned to Ruby. "Do you know what the two most important words in a marriage are?"

Ruby rolled her eyes. "Yes, Dad. They are 'Yes, dear.'"

"Exactly. 'Yes, dear'!" Mohammad said, and laughed to himself. "Because you know she will eventually get her way. Every time. So why not just avoid the war? You must always tell your wife, 'Yes, dear.'"

"Ha ha," Ruby said.

Mohammad continued, "Anyway, I don't know what you're talking about, love. I have so many friends. And they all treat me equally. People at my store, they have conversations with me every day, and we all get along in harmony. White people, black people ..."

"Dad!" Ruby said, placing the pile of flash cards down again. "They're not your friends, Okay. America is a racist country. And somehow everyone knows it except you. And besides, even if your delusion were true—even if you were right, and all the blacks, whites, Christians, Muslims, and Jews were getting along, even if it was one giant lovefest, and everyone was dancing the Hokey Pokey together—our Prophet, peace and blessings be upon him, says we are not supposed to take those people as friends. I mean it's fine that you do business with them. Don't get me wrong. We're allowed to do that. We're allowed to be friendly, but they're not really supposed to be our friends. We're supposed to prefer other Muslims."

"That's simply not true!" Mohammad said, incredulously. "I don't know where you get that!"

Mohammad's eyes were drawn to the green Quran on the couch among Ruby's textbooks. He had never had the time nor the inclination for such scholarship. The way he thought about it, he'd grown up in a different time. When you were growing up then, in a Muslim country, or at least in *his* Muslim country, Muslim was just something you were. You didn't *emphasize* it so much, study it so much, define yourself by it so much. Because everyone was Muslim. Almost everyone. It was all you knew. You didn't have to try to assert your identity *against* anything else. And you didn't have to try to be perfect and follow it to the letter. You relied on God's mercy. You tried to be a good person. You fasted during Ramadan if you could. Gave money to the poor. But Ruby had really taken it to heart. It wasn't that he wasn't proud of her—he was—but still, he had a feeling she was drawn to the most harsh interpretations of things, and he didn't know why.

"I don't know, love," he continued. "I'm not so sure that verse is meant to be taken literally. Anyway, you're the last person I would expect to believe such things! You have always had all kinds of friends. In school, you had black friends, Hindu friends, white friends. You were always such a sweet and open girl. And you still are, my love. And that's why you want to help people. That's why you want to be a physician's assistant. That's one of the things I love most about you, my angel. One of the many, many things. And as far as Islam ...

well ... yes ... studying it is a great thing, it's a beautiful thing, an important thing. But even if you didn't study it, there is only one thing you really need to understand, and that is that Islam is peace. If you want one word for Islam, it is that. Peace. Islam is about treating everyone as a friend. Islam is about living in harmony with everyone. Islam is about helping people. Islam is about loving people. That's the most important thing to know about Islam. Everything else ... well, I'm not saying it's not important. But loving people, that's the most important. If you do that, you are a good Muslim. Automatically! And oh! How could I forget! What about your little friend Sofia? Your best friend. You two were inseparable! Ever since you were a little girl, it was Sofia and Ruby, Ruby and Sofia. Always together." Mohammad intertwined his fingers to show how connected the two little girls had been. "If you are looking for one, just find the other! Like twins! Like shadows! Where is Sofia? Look for Ruby! Where is Ruby? Look for Sofia! Sofia and Ruby! Ruby and Sofia! Muslim and Jew. Jew and Muslim. Together. Like twins! That's what Islam is! That's what America is. This is what I am telling you. Islam and America." He entwined his fingers again. "The American dream and the dream of Islam. They are the same."

Ruby flinched. "They are not, Dad. They're the opposite. America is the opposite of Islam. America is the enemy of Islam ..."

"That's not true, dear," Mohammad said, shaking his head. And then eyeing Ruby's green Quran again, "America didn't exist when the Quran was written, so therefore, the Prophet never talked about America. Therefore, according to the Quran, it's impossible that America could be the enemy of Islam ..."

"With all due respect Dad, are you really in a position to say what's Islamic and what's not? I mean, have you ever even *read* the Quran?" Ruby regretted her words instantly. "Sorry, Dad."

Mohammad turned towards the TV.

"It's just that that dream you have," Ruby continued, "of all the Muslims and Christians and Jews, the Mexicans and Jamaicans and whites, that's not even really the American dream. They say it is but it's not. The real American dream is mostly about money. Money and sex. Fornication and idolatry. And oppressing all the Muslims and blacks and Mexicans and Jamaicans—all your friends you're always talking about."

The woman on TV who'd had her wig ripped off was confessing to the other wives. She'd cheated on her husband. She'd been at a club, she said. She'd met a man. She'd drunk too much champagne and had gone home in a limo with him. The locks of her blonde wig were falling loosely around her face. Her long black eyelashes were wet. She pleaded with the angry group not to tell her husband; she swore that she would tell him herself. She promised she'd tell him that night.

"Islam means peace, my daughter," Mohammad said quietly. "You can trust me on that. It does. America is the dream of living together in peace. In that way, America is true Islam. Because Islam exists any time people are living together in peace. The word Islam means peace."

"No, Dad, Islam does not mean peace. You're talking like the Americans, and certain Muslims—it drives me crazy. Islam does not mean peace. It never meant peace. It's not that Islam is *against* peace, but it doesn't mean peace. Salam means peace. Islam means submission. Just because they have the same Arabic root doesn't mean they mean the same thing. In the Arabic root system, words that share roots are often related, but not always. There is no variation of the word salam that is "Islam." Islam means submission, every time. It's meaning is very clear. And peace will only come when everyone has submitted to Islam."

Mohammad looked up incredulously.

"It's true," Ruby said. "And you should *know* that. I hate to say it, but I think all your so-called friends—your Jamaicans and Mexicans and Christians and whites—they've polluted your soul. I'm sorry, Dad. I'm sorry to say that. I am praying for you. I am praying for your soul. And I hope it's enough."

Mohammad leaned forward and spoke softly. "It is I who should be praying for you, my daughter. You are a very smart girl—brilliant, actually. But I don't think you have a complete understanding of what you're reading. Is there someone you can talk to? Someone who can help you interpret what you read in the correct way? At the mosque maybe? I fear you are starting to sound like one of those ... mistaken Muslims—taking everything out of context. You have to be careful, love. You have to get the meaning of things. Not just the words."

"No, Dad," Ruby said, her voice uncharacteristically cold. "You are the mistaken Muslim."

They both turned toward the TV, stiff, quiet.

Ruby turned back to her flash cards. "Membrane covering bone surfaces, except at joints of long bones," she read.

"Periosteum," she said, quietly, and put the card down.

Mohammad studied her silently, and then turned back to the TV. All the housewives were happy again. They were having a champagne brunch at a restaurant. They were all dressed in pretty pastel suits. One of them raised her glass and toasted to their friendship. Mohammad turned back to his daughter.

"Did you pick out your birthday present yet?" he asked.

Ruby looked down. "Dad. You don't have to."

"Of course I have to!" Mohammad said, a little too enthusiastically. "You're my favorite daughter!"

"I'm your only daughter, Dad," Ruby said. And then she laughed, eager to move past their disagreement.

She picked up her laptop, and with a few clicks, found the page she had bookmarked. She showed the image to Mohammad—a beautiful ruby ring, set in gold, surrounded by diamonds.

"So beautiful, my love. Just like you. My Ruby."

"Really Dad, you don't have to," Ruby said.

"I insist!" Mohammad said. "Put in my credit card!"

CHAPTER SIX
WEDNESDAY MORNING HUDDLE

The Department of Tolerance ran towards the late side of things—with people generally showing up to work anywhere between nine thirty and eleven in the morning. The elite governmental agency was true to its name in that regard—it was quite tolerant. The weekly huddle took place every Wednesday at eleven thirty. Most people were still sipping on coffee or munching on a midmorning snack.

Ordinarily, it was the best part of the week for Alma. She liked spending time with her colleagues. She liked being face-to-face, discussing issues, and drafting battle plans to combat intolerance. Also, she really just enjoyed spending time with intelligent, normal people. Because while she loved her job as a tolerance counselor—the truth was, she spent the better part of her day arguing with racists. And her work wasn't just intellectually isolating, it was also physically isolating. The Department of Tolerance was located in a beautiful old building—the site of the original Mandelbaum's Department Store, constructed in the 1920s. The conference room still retained some of the original details—tin ceilings, huge arched windows, and intricate wood moldings.

But the rest of the floor—and the other five floors belonging to the agency—had been completely redone. It was all low ceilings, grey carpets, and grey cubicles. The cubicles themselves were particularly stifling. They were almost completely encased—ostensibly for privacy. The openings were barely big enough for one person to fit through.

So even on a visual level, Alma looked forward to the huddle each week. More specifically, though, she looked forward to the first part of the huddle—the part known as "new business." She actually dreaded the second part—the part known as "the grievance forum." The grievance forum consisted of ten to twenty to thirty to forty minutes—or however long it took—of people expressing their hurt feelings and anger about any cultural or gendered slights that may have befallen them in the workplace that week. The discussions typically went on for a long time, and became quite heated and confrontational—often without any understanding or resolution being reached. They were tense, to say the least. But of course, Alma understood the need for them. It was important to let people be heard. And, obviously, if the Tolerance Department didn't constantly and valiantly strive to honor the diversity within its own walls—practice what it preached, so to speak—what hope could there be for the rest of the world?

And Alma had a great deal of respect for "Tolerance in Tolerance," the internal committee that hosted the grievance forum. They were brilliant, and had many great initiatives. In addition to the grievance forum, the committee also hosted field trips and cultural hours to celebrate the diversity of the staff and the city. Last Tuesday, for example, everyone had spent the whole day at the Mexican Museum, taking in an art exhibit focused around themes of death and rebirth. The week before, they had all cut out at three o'clock on Friday to go to a Lebanese bakery. But perhaps the most exciting initiative of Tolerance in Tolerance was the Unique Whiteboard Initiative—wherein the nameplate was removed from everyone's identical grey cubicle and replaced with a blank whiteboard, on which people were encouraged to proclaim their own unique cultural heritage—using colorful Magic Markers. So whereas before, a grey cubicle might have indicated "Mark Johnson, Senior Human Resources Executive," on a gold nameplate, it might now declare—in bright, colorful, handwritten letters—which, incidentally, really helped offset the drabness of the office—something along the lines of "I'm Swedish, Panamanian, and gay! Respect my culture and I'll respect yours!"—or whatever unique combination of identifiers described the person.

That format, "I'm this, this, and this! Respect my culture and I'll respect yours!" had been the one initially suggested by Tolerance in Tolerance. But of course, the applications of the unique whiteboards were boundless. Further uses had been brainstormed: perhaps people would want to include "cultural clippings"—a treasured quote from a favorite national poet, or a "word of the day" in a native language; or perhaps a pet peeve—maybe some hard to shake stereotype that really irked the person. In addition, the fact that the unique whiteboards were erasable acknowledged and celebrated the fluid nature of identity; someone might later choose to transition genders, for example, or they might find themselves attracted to a new gender, or genders, or no genders, and so forth. The unique whiteboard would accommodate all of that. It was literally a blank slate. It was exhilarating. But for now, everyone seemed happy with the succinct, powerful, punchy feel of the original mantra, "I'm this, this, and this! Respect my culture, and I'll respect yours!"

It was a fascinating initiative, and through it, Alma had learned a great deal about her colleagues.

So Alma had come to today's huddle with her tall cappuccino, the foam stiff and thick, as only Xavier downstairs at The Dream Bean could make it, fully expecting to enjoy herself—at least for the "new business" portion.

But there was a glitch.

A very offensive photo was displayed prominently on the big screen at the front of the conference room. Melanie Diaz, an intern, was clicking back and forth between it and some of the news coverage, opinion pieces, and tweets that had sprung up like dandelions in the past week, all decrying the image.

Marine Schorr—the public face of the agency, and host of the popular TV show *Hate Hunters* and the slightly less popular show *Bridge Builders*—addressed the group from her seat at the head of the conference table. She looked intimidatingly flawless, as usual, with her perfect makeup, her perfect hair, and her natural-born, gym-developed prowess that made it look as if she was ready to unfurl and pounce at any moment.

"My thing is, it's just been done so much in the media already, and so many people know about it—I'm wondering if it wouldn't be overload?" Marine said. "I mean, don't get me wrong, I'm dying to run it on *Hate Hunters*. It's just begging to be used, and I know there's so much more to unpack for our viewers. But we need a new angle. And, also, I mean, it's just so bizarre! In a way, I'm wondering, what's the real teachable here? You guys have to help me out. Chime in, my tolerance theorists! I know it's wrong on so many levels, but what's the gist of it, exactly? What does it even mean?"

"It means so very much," said Wendy Watkins. Wendy was tall, and had strawberry-blonde hair that was always a little lank and scruffy, which only added to her somewhat superior, intellectual vibe. Wendy was an "Irish, Ukrainian, bisexual incest survivor!" and head of the Tolerance in Textbooks Committee. "It's a layer cake of offensiveness! Pardon my French, but it's a fucking gay fondant wedding cake of offensiveness! It's about white privilege, of course. And, I mean, the girls are aware of their white privilege, which is good ... I guess. But how clueless, how idiotic ... how tone-deaf ... do they have to be to think they can shed their white privilege by bowing down at a slave burial site of all places! No, it's not even that—it's the fact that they think white privilege is something that can be renounced. That just shows that they don't understand white privilege at all. I think that could be your angle."

"It's not just that," Braxton Hammond said. He was "Cuban, Samoan, Norwegian, and fabulous!" and worked in IT. "I mean *most* whites don't understand white privilege. That's par for the course. But this is worse! These two are literally on top of a sacred slave burial site, making a spectacle of themselves. I think we need to go for that angle. It's just so disrespectful."

"My thing is the dresses," said Derrald St. Phair, who was "African American, Caribbean American, trans, and demiromantic!" and a staff special projects consultant. "I mean, what was the point of the dresses? Like, 'Oh, let's go apologize to the people we brutalized,' Okay, maybe, but, 'Let's wear cute matching dresses while we do it'? I mean, what were they thinking? Like, 'Hey, Megan, let's look super cute!

We want to look cute for the cameras!' I just don't get that part. I swear, I just don't get white people sometimes." He sighed. "But, yeah, with those dresses, they found a way to make it about them."

"Maybe it was supposed to be like ... a flash mob?" Ray Diaz, no relation to Melanie, suggested. "And they were the only two that showed up?"

The group let out a collective "Uggh!" at the thought of a troop of them, instead of just two.

The photo everyone was talking about, now so prominently displayed at the front of the room, had been dubbed "flower butts" by the media. It showed two white girls on their knees bowing down at a recently discovered slave burial site, both of them wearing matching H&M flowered dresses. Their posteriors took up most of the frame, and parts of their bare, white, outstretched arms were also visible. The photo had come to light when the girl on the left, Bella Doheny, had proudly and unironically posted it all over her social media, with the caption, "Bowing Down to Renounce My White Privilege."

It was a meme in no time and had been mocked, decried, and dissected all over the Internet. It had also been the subject of several opinion pieces in the traditional press.

For example:

"Dear White People, Bowing Down to My Ancestors Does Not Help Present-Day Me!"

And:

"To the Two White Girls Wearing Dresses Made by Starving Children in Third World Sweatshops: What Are You Trying to Say, Exactly?"

And:

"The New Grave Robbers: Ancestral Appropriation is Real. And It's Dangerous."

No one knew the identity of the other girl. Alma stared intently at the stiff, thick, gleaming white foam on her cappuccino. Every once in a while, her eyes wandered to the right, where, on the table next to her, on a sheet of paper, Octavia Bravo was doodling cartoon puppies. The little dogs had big ears and big eyes, and they all looked the same—with a few variations—as if Octavia had learned how to draw them from a single YouTube tutorial. They were cute, the dogs, but in her present situation, Alma couldn't help but feel they were pitying her. Or mocking her. Octavia was well respected. She'd earned her PhD in Otherness Studies from New World University and currently served as senior theorist at the department. She also headed the Diversity in Gaming Committee.

Alma had worn the dress to work just once—about a week before the ill-fated flower butts photo was taken, which was very unfortunate, because, aside from the dress, Alma was almost certain that nothing in the photo could be tied to her. After all, the unidentified girl was, for all intents and purposes, just a butt, bare feet, and an arm—and as such, all but indistinguishable from any number of other youngish, medium-built, female Caucasian persons that roamed the city.

The strange thing was that she'd worn the dress to work at all. It was way too light and summery. But she'd paired it with a light green leather jacket that day. She'd been inspired, incidentally, by Octavia Bravo. Octavia was known for pairing unexpected items—exotic with pedestrian; cheap, mass produced with expensive; conservative with punky and edgy. Most days, Octavia looked like she worked at Vogue, rather than the Tolerance Department. In fact, even today, when Alma was studiously avoiding everyone's eyes, she was aware of Octavia's look—the large, red, lightning bolt earrings she wore complimented her small face and her short, floppy, asymmetrical haircut perfectly.

There could be no doubt that Octavia had noticed the outfit that day. She'd even complimented Alma on it. "Love! Love! Love!" she'd exclaimed, in her usual dramatic style, gesturing up and down with her pointer finger.

But if Octavia remembered the dress, she wasn't saying anything. She just kept drawing puppies.

"There's a lot to unpack here," said Marine, thoughtfully. "Actually, really, this seems to be *the* single hardest lesson for white people to learn. They just always want to center themselves in the narratives of black and brown oppression." Marine shook her head. "I think this photo—I think it's bigger than a single *Hate Hunters* episode. I mean, I think this photo can be *used*. You know what I mean? I'm talking TV spots, billboards, mailers. A good old-fashioned public service campaign! Where are my Public Messaging people?" Marine looked around the table.

Addie McCarrom glanced up from her computer, where she was taking notes. "On it, Marine," she said. Addie was "Irish, Black Irish, Irish Traveller, and a soupçon of Cajun!" and head of the Public Messaging Committee.

"Great call, Marine," Jean Lawrence said, "And now, we need to move on to the grievance forum. There's a sensitive item today." Jean was a "Romanian, Venezuelan, English-Irish cat lady!" and director of the Virtue Reinstallation Program—otherwise known as "Schooled!" She was also co-head chair of Tolerance in Tolerance. Alma was excited the meeting was finally moving on. Never in her life had she been so eager to hear about the emotional trials and tribulations of her colleagues as they attempted to navigate the uncertain world of the postcolonial, multicultural workplace.

"First, I want to thank Melanie for bringing the coffee situation to our attention last week," Jean said.

Everyone smiled at Melanie Diaz. Melanie smiled and blushed.

Jean continued, "Diane has informed me that we've switched vendors as of this week. The new company we're using follows ethical work practices—they have a B+ rating on Hadley's. And, they're 70 percent organic, with a goal of 90 percent in the next three years. According to them, it's just a matter of dealing with some of the in-country regulations in a few of the partner communities. So, while it's a little more expensive, obviously, that money goes towards paying the workers fairly. And, I think it should go without saying ..." Jean cleared her throat and put on a funny, announcer-type voice, "... Not having an offensive caricature of an indigenous coffee grower on the package —priceless!"

Everyone cheered. Alma joined in. She was happy about the new topic. The only problem was, "flower butts" was still up on the screen. She focused intently on the puppies.

"Next item," Jean said. "So, this is a tough one. A lot of people have expressed their outrage. But no one has been quite sure how to bring it up, or who would be the correct person to broach the subject. Well ... we still haven't figured it out, so I'm going to just come right out and say it." Jean paused and turned to Alma. "Alma ..." she said. She paused again. "Alma. What the fuck were you thinking? I mean Christ! In what universe did you think putting that sentence up on your whiteboard wouldn't offend people? Seriously!

'I'm African American! Respect my culture and I'll respect yours!' Just what the fuck were you thinking?"

Alma froze for a moment, then collected herself. "Oh. Yes. I can explain ..." she said.

"It was a rhetorical question!" Jean shouted. "We all know about your DNA test! We don't care. It doesn't make you black. Okay! It. Doesn't. Make. You. Black."

Everyone shook their heads. "No, it doesn't!" they said.

"DNA is not culture!" someone shouted. Everyone moaned in agreement.

"What you're doing is scientifically sanctioned cultural appropriation!" yelled someone else.

"And it's racist!" someone shouted.

"And the implications of your black ancestry are not cute!" someone else said.

There were shouts and murmurs of agreement.

Allison Corval stood up. Allison had feather-fine, flowing, golden-blonde hair, and was "Canadian-Prussian-Russian-German-Mennonite and Scottish!" "This is white privilege gone rogue!" she said. "It's unbelievable. It's next-level! Whites think they have a right to everything now! Even blackness! It's absurd!"

Everyone scoffed and nodded.

Allison continued. There were tears in her eyes. Allison was incredibly sensitive and compassionate. And although she was thin, happily married to the head of one of the most exclusive girls' schools in Manhattan, and incredibly beautiful—in the most culturally endorsed kind of way—she had an uncanny ability to feel everyone's pain exquisitely, particularly the pain of minorities and repressed groups. "It's unbelievable!" she continued. "It's even worse than the 1699'ers!" Everybody gasped. Allison began sobbing. Crystal Rodrigues stood up and hugged her, all the while shooting accusatory glances at Alma.

But Alma knew she wasn't anything like the 1699'ers—the umbrella term given to the miserable, ragtag groups of white people claiming to be oppressed because of their ancestors' tough times in Europe. They were always picketing for noble status outside the Tolerance Department. In fact, there were probably a few of them out there right now, with their giant, pathetic, blow-up, medieval torture devices, and their stupid placards with graphics of their European ancestors being whipped, stretched, pierced, burned, boiled, beheaded, impaled, and catapulted. They formed sinister brotherhoods with absurd names, like the Latter-Day Huguenots, the Waldensians, the Sons of Defenestration, the 1535'ers, the Tears of the Covenanters, the Barbary Slaves, and yes, the 1699'ers—apparently after some particularly sadistic quashing of a rebellion of Russian peasants in that year.

Allison was 100 percent right about people like them, of course. They represented the worst in white privilege—loath to cede superiority in anything—even, ridiculously, in suffering. Even worse than them, however, were the motley, unorganized, disheveled individuals that picketed about their sufferings in *this* lifetime, attempting to earn pity and claim nobility by flaunting their rotten luck. These descendants of privilege, sons of the eternally entitled, marched around with their pathetic placards showing their shocking X-rays and frightening pathology reports, their eviction notices and their debt collection letters, their dead babies and their deformed children, shouting their pithy slogans, "If you prick us, do we not bleed?" and "Our suffering counts!" and "You call this privilege?" Which was very disingenuous of them, of course—no, disingenuous was too mild a word. To ignore the research on the impact of genetic whisperings was not only disingenuous, it was racist. To claim that pain in one lifetime equaled pain compounded by centuries of systemic injustice encoded in genetic memory was not only ignorant, unproductive, and willfully anti-science, it was pure evil.

Of course, Arun Merriweather, the granddaddy of all tolerance theorists, had been the one to originate the theory of genetic whisperings—the mechanism whereby pain gets passed down through the generations.

Considered by many to be the intellectual founder of the Virtuous Federation, Arun's seminal work—*Orthosentia*—a collection of essays from the blog he'd written while on summer break after his third year at Oxford, had taken the world by storm with its refreshingly irreverent tone and revolutionary thinking. *Orthosentia* was one of the five foundational "books of influence" officially recognized by the Virtuous Federation, and without a doubt, the most important. Some even referred to it as the second constitution. In other words, everyone knew about genetic whisperings. So these so-called citizens of the Virtuous Federation who walked around claiming that their sufferings in a single lifetime were somehow equivalent to centuries of oppression were just ... there were no words. At least the 1699'ers, in their own twisted, deliberately misguided way, nominally acknowledged one of the most important theories on which the federation was founded, that pain was linear—passed down through generations.

In *Orthosentia*, Arun had poignantly illustrated the concept with a story—as he was wont to do. Referred to simply as "The Coffee Shop Story," every schoolchild knew it. It shall be included here—along with its introduction—in Merriweather's own words:

"History is destiny. And science backs this up. Innumerable studies have pointed to the subtle and spooky sensitivity of DNA, and it is now generally accepted that trauma can be passed down from generation to generation through our genes. At first it was observed, for example, that a mother who experienced physical or emotional trauma during pregnancy could alter the genetic makeup of her offspring, through a complex process involving certain genes being turned 'on' or 'off.' Then, it was observed that these traumas could actually be encoded in the genes, making their effects long lasting and not confined to just one generation. Now, it is theorized that there is an even more subtle process whereby all kinds of experiences get 'written' into our genes, in very complex and not yet understood ways, and not just during pregnancy, but throughout our lifetimes. These genetic 'stories' get passed down from generation to generation for all eternity. Obviously, it's not the events themselves that get passed down, so much as the feelings surrounding those events. The feelings translate into chemicals, and the chemicals act on our genes. To the point, it's mainly things like learned helplessness, low self-esteem, and collective depression resulting from systemic oppression over generations that are passed down through genes, as well as, interestingly, the opposite qualities, such as a sense of privilege, a feeling of entitlement, and a sense of safety and belonging. Thus our ancestors whisper to us, all the time, through our genes.

"Let me demonstrate. Say there are two couples, one white, and one historically oppressed, or noble. And let's say each couple tragically lost their only child, a toddler, to illness. You would think that they both shared an equal amount of suffering, and therefore are equally noble, or human. But, picture this, it's a few weeks after the funeral, or, let's just say that the period of acute grief and shock has passed. The white couple goes into a coffee shop, and because of their genetic whisperings, they take it for granted that someone will serve them a hot beverage with a smile. In fact, they do not even notice the person serving them. The world begins to open up for them in much the same way it always has; the world is 'at their service,' so to speak—quite in line with their genetic whisperings, that is, with their innate sense of privilege, their sense that the world is ultimately a safe and friendly place, and their inborn sense that despite their recent misfortune, things will be right once again—if not today, then tomorrow.

"Now the noble couple might walk into the same coffee shop, but in addition to the grief from the loss of their baby, they have all their other ancient whisperings. And it all gets compounded. What they hear whispered to them, subconsciously, is 'Do we belong in this shop? Is our kind allowed here?' 'If I give these people my money, can I trust that they'll keep their part of the bargain by giving me coffee?' 'Will they use up my country's resources for their own advancement, leaving me to starve?' 'Did I myself pick this coffee, sweating in a field somewhere?' 'Does the waitress feel comfortable serving us?' 'Does she feel it is *we* who should be serving *her*?' (In fact, if the waitress is white, her subconscious does in fact feel that they should be serving her, no matter what her personal beliefs.) All these messages are confusing, painful, and terrifying. They are all on a subconscious level—but no less powerful for being so.

"And it's all cumulative. As if it's all happening at the same time. Genes know no past, present, or future. So the whisperings and the recent loss get combined. The noble couple begins to hear subconscious messages that perhaps their baby died because it was never seen by society at large as having the right to exist in the first place, that it wasn't the right color, or religion, or that they, the couple, didn't have the right sexual orientation, etcetera. All these whisperings deepen their grieving and their sense of helplessness, and it becomes a vicious cycle, compounding as the years go by, and carrying down to their other children, should they have any —snowballing down through the generations.

"So let this serve as an answer to all the white people who have been pestering me with letters about their suffering, claiming they are not privileged, claiming they are noble! My answer is no. No. No. And no! I'll say it again—no. No, white gadflies, no, Caucasian contrarians, your suffering is not the same as the suffering of the people you've historically oppressed! Or, as my Indian blood says to my English blood, 'Your pain is not my pain!'"

Part of Merriweather's brilliance lay in his exquisite sensitivity to the implications of his dual bloodlines. Son of an English property mogul and an Indian chewing gum heiress, he was uniquely qualified to understand the viewpoints of, as he put it, "both conqueror and conquered, colonial and 'savage,' oppressor and oppressed." In fact, the title of his original blog was, *Colonizer, Colonized, I.*

But Alma knew she wasn't anything like the 1699'ers, or the entitled white cancer patients, kidney patients, and house-fire victims trying to pass themselves off as noble. She wasn't being a "white gadfly" or a "Caucasian contrarian." Because she wasn't white. She was black. And she realized in that moment that it didn't matter if anyone else knew it. Because she knew it. So she let the vitriol spill over her.

"She's worse!" Viridiana was yelling. "At least the 1699'ers stick to their own ancestry! Alma is stealing! She's stealing the old bones of Africans!" Viridiana was "Venezuelan. 100 percent. No, I am not white. Yes. I am blonde. But I repeat, I am Latinx, 100 percent!" and Alma had always liked her. Viridiana had once brought her an elaborate, hand-painted carnival mask from her trip to Venice, and Alma still had it hanging in her kitchen. Viridiana began to cry. "I'm not black," she said. "And I can't even begin to understand even a millimeter of their suffering. I can't even imagine it! They have it so much worse than me." She paused. "And I did *not* have it easy! I don't know if any of you have ever been told your whole life, by *everyone*, that you would amount to nothing!" She sobbed, glaring accusingly at Alma.

"She's stealing our graves!" someone said.

"She's making a mockery!" someone else said.

"I can't believe her! The nerve! The entitlement! The privilege!"

Alma let the staccato sentences hammer her as she concentrated on the puppies filling Octavia's page. "It's okay," they seemed to be telling her with their big eyes. "Everyone feels bad sometimes."

For some reason, an image came to her mind of herself as a little girl, with her big, ice-cube thick glasses, reciting the plot of one of the books she was reading to her parents. She had always loved reading, and by the time she was seven years old she was reading popular adult fiction. This image of herself seemed to be trying to tell her something. Not about books, or about reading, but something else. She looked at the little girl in her mind, in her yellow Snoopy shirt, proudly talking about the factory strike taking place in the novel she was reading—and the word that came to her mind was *unflappable*.

The room was in an uproar. Somebody said, "How can

she be a tolerance counselor? Should she even be trying to rehabilitate people? She doesn't have a clue! She's worse than her clients! She's more racist than they are!"

Suddenly, Octavia's pen dropped to the table—mid puppy. Octavia stood up. "Enough!" she shouted. And just like that, the entire room went silent. Octavia was "100 percent Filipina, and a hopeless *Dance Dance Revolution* enthusiast!" She continued, "I get that you all want to express your opinions. And I respect that. And I get that some of you may feel offended by what Alma wrote. Those are your feelings. And you have a right to them.

"But shit!" Octavia continued. "Insulting her work as a tolerance counselor? That's just unacceptable. We all know her work is impeccable. So at this point, it feels to me like you're all just basically berating her for the color of her skin. And there's nothing she can do about that, people! And while it's true that the white stain never fully goes away, Alma scrubs and scrubs at it, which is exactly what white people are supposed to do. She's an exemplar! She addresses her white privilege tirelessly. She does all the things white people are supposed to do. She respects/protects/elevates the noble races. She's one of the good ones!

"And she teaches other white people how to do exactly the same as her. And she's really good at it, people. You know that! Everyone knows that. Okay? So, leave her work alone. She actually educates and rehabilitates people. I've seen it. You've seen it. She's one of our best. No. Fuck it! She *is* our best! She's the best tolerance counselor we have!

"And you know what?" Octavia continued. "She made a mistake. Okay. She made a mistake—with the whole African American whiteboard thing. But cut her some slack! What do you expect? All we do is tell white people they're bad, they're evil, they're stained. We just keep repeating it, 'You're bad! You're bad! You're bad!' So she tried to change it. Was it misguided? Yes. But at least she's trying to change. Maybe she did it the wrong way. But it shows she's listening to us. Okay. She's trying to change. Fuck! Leave her alone!"

Alma looked up. Octavia was standing tall, chest up. Everyone else's heads were bowed. There was complete silence.

"And you know what," Octavia continued, "I wouldn't be surprised if one day you all find yourselves on the wrong side of history. I mean, who's to say Alma doesn't suffer from some kind of race dysphoria—that hasn't yet been discovered? You have no idea what it's like inside her head. None of us do. Maybe her genetic whisperings are shouting at her every day, 'You're black! You're black! You're black!' You don't know. I don't know. Maybe it should be up to Alma to choose her race, her identity. Maybe in a few years you'll all be ashamed of yourselves. You'll look back on this and think, 'Why was I trying to tell that woman who to be?' Like the way we feel about gender now. Look. I'm going to say that Alma can put whatever she wants to on her unique whiteboard. Because if we here at the Tolerance Department don't recognize the role of personal choice in identity—well, then we're all officially screwed."

Nobody said anything.

"I'm sorry," Octavia said, turning to Alma. "The only person we haven't heard from in all of this is Alma. Alma, is there anything you'd like to say? Please. Talk to us. This is supposed to be a two-way conversation."

"Well," Alma said, looking around from face to face, "I've heard everything you've said. And I want you to know that I acknowledge your feelings. I understand that my newly discovered identity has shaken and unsettled you. Now, I'm not going to sit here and insult your intelligence by talking to you about DNA science. I feel like that would be dismissive of everything you've just said. I'm going to choose to honor your feelings, because I respect you all as colleagues and as people. I will remove the offending sentence from my board."

Everyone nodded.

"Thank you," Octavia said. "And Alma, I would add that you don't have to put back Dutch and English if you don't feel that expresses your current identity. If I recall correctly, Tolerance in Tolerance told us that the boards are erasable for a reason, and that they are meant to celebrate the ever-changing, fluid nature of identity. So think about it, Alma. Play with it. That's what the initiative is for. Tell us who you are! Write down something that you currently celebrate about yourself. You are so many things!"

CHAPTER SEVEN

THE AMERICAN

Alma decided to wait for everyone to leave for the day in order to be able to rethink her unique whiteboard in privacy. She agreed with Octavia, there was no reason to go back to "I'm Dutch and English! Respect my culture and I'll respect yours!" No one in her family had been Dutch or English for quite some time. It wasn't like she'd grown up eating bread pudding, or clomping around in wooden clogs. And even if she had, Octavia was right again in that she should be more intentional, playful, and creative about her identity. Perhaps one should revisit one's identity every so often, as an exercise —an exercise in being human. The last person in the office, as far as Alma could tell, was Braxton Hammond, from IT. His cubicle was on the other end of the floor, and every time she wandered to the kitchen, ostensibly to fill her water bottle, she could hear him talking on his phone. From what she gathered, he was just killing time before meeting some friends for dinner in the Village. When she walked to the kitchen at 6:10, he seemed to have gone.

She stood in front of her grey cubicle, purple Magic Marker and eraser in hand, contemplating her whiteboard, and the sentence that had offended everyone so. "I'm African American! Respect my culture and I'll respect yours!" She stood back and repeated it in her head a few times. On the one hand, she couldn't see what all the fuss was about—why should it matter to anyone else how she described herself? But on the other hand, looking at it now, she had to admit it didn't fully describe her. Who was she, then?

It was pretty obvious that what everyone was trying to tell her was that she was white—and that's what they wanted to make sure she never forgot. But she couldn't very well put that on her whiteboard! Imagine, "I'm white! Respect my culture and I'll respect yours!" She laughed, imagining the grievance forum that would ensue if she wrote that.

What about "human being"? Couldn't she just say she was a human being? That was what she truly felt. More and more every day. The truth was, she was on "culture and identity" overload—in spite of the fact, or perhaps because of the fact, that her entire professional raison d'être was to foster awareness, respect, and inclusion for vulnerable cultures and identities. She decided to try it out. She wrote:

"I'm human! Respect my culture and I'll respect yours!"

She stood back and studied it.

"I'm human! Respect my culture and I'll respect yours!"

It was funny. It seemed to imply the existence of nonhumans who needed to be reminded to be respectful. Who was she warning exactly? Giraffes? Lemurs? Koala bears? They'd better respect her ... or else?

She tried something. She erased the second sentence. She stood back.

"I'm human!"

It was nice ... but, on second thought, it would probably be seen as a snub at the whole Unique Whiteboard Initiative —a repudiation of the very concept of identity. Or worse! It would be seen as an artifact of her white privilege and the naiveté it afforded her: "I don't see color!" "We're all the same!" "I'm colorblind!" etc.

What did the other white people put? Alma took a brief walk down her row of cubicles.

"I'm third-generation Polish, and I'm married to a woman! Respect my culture, and I'll respect yours!" was one.

"I am a proud Armenian American! Respect my culture, and I will respect yours!"

Alma wondered if Dave was really Armenian. And exactly how far back he was reaching.

"Mexican, Native American, Scottish, and Irish. Respect my culture, and I'll respect yours!"

Really, Sandra? Mexican? Native American? Maybe a great-grandmother. Or a great-great-grandfather. Why hadn't they given *her* hell?

As Alma looked around at all the unique whiteboards, it occurred to her that there was an elephant in the room. There was one unique identity that no one was talking about, that absolutely nobody wrote. Nobody. But it was 100 percent the identity that defined everyone the most. It impacted everyone the most, shaped them the most, and described them the most. It was the air they breathed and the water they drank, no matter what part of the world their ancestors came from, or no matter what country they had lived in until they were nine years old, thirteen years old, or eighteen years old. But for some reason, nobody wanted to say it. Nobody wanted to write it. Everybody almost seemed to be ashamed of it, to the point that they were coming up with some pretty far-fetched things to avoid it. They were a quarter Ukrainian, three-eighths Lithuanian, they were half Sicilian, three-quarters Irish, they were Latina, Latino, Latinx.

But nobody was ... American. Nobody was American. There were no Americans.

She thought.

Yes. That was it. She would do it. She would become the first American.

She erased the board, and with her Magic Marker she wrote:

"I'm American! Respect my culture and I'll respect yours!"

She took a few steps back to contemplate what she'd written. Why did it sound hostile?

"I'm American! Respect my culture and I'll respect yours!"

Ugh. It sounded like it was saying, "You're in America, learn English!" Was "American" just another forbidden identity, like white? Could it only ever sound arrogant, boastful, xenophobic, and brutish? But why? Why did it have to sound like that? All Americans weren't like that. They really weren't. Why wasn't anybody working on restoring dignity to the much-maligned American identity just like they were working on uplifting other identities? Couldn't the Tolerance Department, just within the confines of its own walls, begin to work on dismantling the negative stereotype of "American"? Wasn't it about time? She could spearhead the movement! With this one sentence she could take a step toward revisiting and redefining the American identity. She could highlight the diversity and subtlety, the unexpected and uncelebrated virtues of that identity.

And wouldn't that be a great thing? Wouldn't everyone benefit from that? Wouldn't everyone benefit from a *unifying* identity? Rather than all the fractioning ones? All the quarter third half Lithuanian Dutch Venezuelans with American birth certificates, American passports, American apartments, American friends, American lovers, American jobs, American children and American deaths? But still, nobody would admit they were American.

"What? Me? Oh no. I'm not really here. I'm just passing through!"

Well, she would. She would admit it. She would be the first American. A revolutionary. She would let go of the past and step into the future. And anyone who wanted to join her could. She took her eraser, and then she took the Magic Marker, and she fixed the sentence. She stood back. She read it:

"I'm American. I respect your culture."

Yes. That was it. It was beautiful. It was brief. It was not boastful, not threatening, not divisive. It was inclusive, gracious, dignified, benevolent, and welcoming. It was simple and elegant.

And it was perfect. Because, she now realized, "African American" had been wrong. Not because she wasn't African American—she was. But the thing was, she wasn't *just* African American. It was too limiting. When you were American, you were all those things. Everything and everyone affected you and contributed to you. You participated in it all, whether you realized it or not. You were white, you were black, you were Filipino, you were Lithuanian, and you were

Chinese. All those cultures contributed to who you were. But you were also American. That was important. American was its own thing. It was more than just a sum of its parts. It was not just a repository for other cultures, a top hat for another, more important identity. It was who we all were.

CHAPTER EIGHT
THE PITCH

"So let me see if I got this straight," Marine said, leaning forward, her arms forming a triangle on her desk. "You telephone Muslims after terrorist events, and apologize to them?"

George sat across from her. He was still taking in her physical presence. She was formidable on TV, yes, but in person, it was a whole other story. She was magnetic, imposing, brimming with life—so much life, in fact, that it was as if she had been issued twice the life force of a normal person. He was in awe, and completely overwhelmed. George considered himself to have somewhat of a charismatic presence, but he couldn't help but wonder if he would come off as invisible next to her on TV, should she decide to have him on her show.

Also, he couldn't stop thinking about the sign on her door, which had demanded, bizarrely, "I'm French and Italian! Respect my culture, and I'll respect yours!" As he sat there, he scrambled to find good things to say about those two rather impressive cultures—by no means unsung.

"Yes! Exactly!" he said. "I'm apologizing to Muslims. And thank you, by the way, for putting it so succinctly. The French have such a way with words, don't you think? 'Le mot juste,' as they say!"

Marine stared at him for a moment. "I love it!" she said. "What a great passion project! What a great tolerance project! It sounds like it might be perfect for *Bridge Builders*! I don't know if you know, but I'm trying to do more *Bridge Builders* shows—they don't seem to get the ratings, so my producers are against it. But still, I think it's important to focus on all the good people are doing. I think it's just as important to celebrate what's right as it is to denounce what's wrong, wouldn't you agree? I think we sometimes lose sight of that. And you, my friend, are a perfect example of the kind of bridge builder I want on my show. You are reaching out to a maligned group of people and letting them know that you respect them—that you're not buying into the negative stereotypes."

"Exactly!" George said. He struggled to find a way to work the ancient and illustrious Italian culture into the conversation. "Um," he said. His mind was blank. And then he had an idea. He cleared his throat, "And as the great Roman emperor and philosopher Marcus Aurelius once said, 'Men exist for the sake of one another.' What I mean is, we're all brothers, and we must help each other along."

"Exactly," Marine said.

"Exactly," George repeated. "We're all brothers. And sisters. All human beings rely on one another. We all affect one another. And I fear we've really dropped the ball as far as our Muslim brothers and sisters are concerned. I mean, first, in our inimitable colonial way, we interfere with their part of the world and make things so intolerable for them that they have no choice but to lash out in order to have their voices heard, and then, we turn around and blame them for the very so-called 'terrorist events' that our own violent actions have necessitated! I mean, Muslims are not violent. We make them violent. Islam is the most pacifistic religion in the world. If I may quote from the Quran, 'Whoever kills a soul unless for a soul or for corruption in the land—it is as if he had slain mankind entirely. And whoever saves one—it is as if he had saved mankind entirely.'"

"Oh, that's lovely," Marine said. The walls of her rather spacious office were lined with framed photos of herself posing with her cadre of "citizen hate hunters"—members of the general public who captured people being racist on film and sent her the footage. Many in the photos wore red baseball caps with the show's famous logo: a stylized outline of a young girl aiming a camera like a gun, and the tagline, "I hate hate!" On her desk was a photo of herself with a man in a grey sweater and glasses, both of them swinging a little blonde girl of about six between them. "I love it," Marine said. "I love this project. Do you have a name for it?"

"No. I don't. I've thought about it. But I haven't come up with one yet. You're right, though. It probably does need a name."

"Hmm," Marine said, thoughtfully.

"Hmm," George said, furrowing his brows.

"What about 'Peace Calls'?" Marine suggested.

"That's pretty good," George nodded.

"Or 'Dialing for Tolerance'?"

"I like that."

"Or no! How about 'Salam Brother'!"

"Very good," George said.

"No! I have a great one," Marine said, "'Salam Sorry'!"

She couldn't help but let out a little chuckle.

"That's very droll!" George said. "Très drôle!"

"No. Probably not," Marine said. "Anyway, my point is, I really like it. But there's just one thing that concerns me. Which is, I'm wondering if by featuring your project, we might not be inadvertently highlighting those rare, freak occurrences of so-called 'Islamic terrorism,' thereby reinforcing negative stereotypes for our viewers rather than dismantling them?"

"No. Yes. You're right," George said. "I see what you mean, absolutely."

Marine continued, "I mean, did you know that in the US people are more likely to be killed in a lawn mower accident than in an Islamic terrorist attack?"

"Of course," George said. "No. Of course. You're right. But I think that unfortunately, whether we highlight these rare occurrences or not, people will still stereotype. And I think that's what's unique about this project. It dares to speak. Because as we all know, silence doesn't help. Silence is where monsters grow, where suspicion festers. And I think our Muslim brothers deserve to know, with certainty, that they have our support. They need to hear it out loud. If not, they'll read between the lines of our silence—and read it as condemnation.

"And another thing. Keep in mind my firm and our clients are global, and they do business globally. So it's not like in America. They don't have the option of tuning this stuff out. They're confronted with these events on a weekly, sometimes daily basis—whether it be al-Qaeda, ISIS, Taliban, al-Shabaab, Boko Haram, Hamas, Abu Sayyaf, Hezbollah, Jaish-e-Mohammad ... You catch my drift. So I feel that if we don't outright say to the peaceful, true Muslims, 'Hey, we don't blame you for what these mistaken Muslims are doing,' well, it's like I said, they'll read between the lines of our silence and think we are accusing them. And we owe them more than that."

"Well, you certainly have a point," Marine said. "I think this would be very edifying for my viewers. A great way to show them how man ought to treat his fellow man—to show them that man must not be afraid to speak love, and to drive home the lesson that the vast majority of Muslims should not be held accountable for the actions of a few unstable, mentally ill individuals. But again, I'm concerned that by dredging up these incidents, which for all intents and purposes have sort of been shoved to the back burner—in order not to stir up hate, specifically Islamophobia—we might be doing the opposite of what we intend. What I'm trying to say is, it's probably best to let sleeping dogs lie, as it were. Of course, that's not to say that our meeting today hasn't been fruitful. Actually, I love the idea of raising awareness about Islamophobia." Marine rummaged through her top drawer until she found a pad of pale blue sticky notes. She wrote the word "Islamophobia" in large, tilting letters on the top note. She looked up. "Yeah. Thank you for reminding me about that. I'd like to do more on Islamophobia, actually."

"Yes, I definitely see your point," George said. "But before we let this go, I just want to bring up another aspect of my project that I think you might find novel, and, edifying, as you say, for your viewers, which is that typically, as an African American, I find myself on the other side of most of these tolerance projects. That is, I find myself as the maligned party, the aggrieved race, the oppressed group—the one that people are encouraged to learn about, to confront their prejudices about—to 'respect/protect/elevate' as they say. But in this case—in my project, that is—the situation is reversed. I get the rare and valuable opportunity to be on the other side. I get to be in the camp that does the 'respecting/protecting/elevating.' And it's unusual that people such as myself, black people, get this opportunity, being that we are so high up on the nobility tree. In fact, the only group higher than us is Muslims."

Marine leaned forward, her interest piqued. "Muslims are higher than blacks?"

George nodded.

"Are you sure?"

"Definitely."

"Hmm," Marine said. And then she added three exclamation points to the word "Islamophobia" on the blue sticky note.

"Yes," George said. "And they need all the friends and advocates they can get. So in that way, it's really a teachable moment. We have to let people know that just because you're in a noble group, or a sainted group, as some say, it doesn't mean there aren't groups more noble, more sainted—more victimized—than you, who need your help and your advocacy. And I think that I, as a black man, can model that behavior."

"Are you sure Muslims are higher than blacks?" Marine asked, looking skeptical. "I would think it would be the other way around."

"No," George said. "It's right there on the nobility tree schematic. Muslims are on the top branch. Their suffering is unparalleled. They are immutable."

"Immutable?" Marine asked.

George looked at her. He was a little surprised she didn't

know all of this.

"Yes," George said. "Immutable. You know, they never devolve to whyte."

"Devolve to white?"

"Yes," George said. It was basic tolerance theory. But he reminded himself that you didn't have to be a great theorist to be a great general, which Marine was. "Actually," George continued, "it's pretty technical stuff. I don't want to bore you. But, yes, most groups are mutable—fluid, that is. That just means that they are noble in certain situations, and whyte in others. Sainted in some situations, stained in others. It all depends on the context. Take for example the Jews. In the context of Nazis, they are respected sufferers—noble, sainted. But in any other context, they are considered whyte —or privileged, or stained, however you want to say it. In other words, they are the ones that need to apologize, to make amends. Almost all groups are like that. They are fluid. It depends on the situation they're in whether the noble designation applies to them or not."

"Strange!" Marine said.

"No, it's really not strange," George said. "It just sounds strange to say it out loud. Don't worry. Listen, you know this stuff, you just don't know that you know it."

"Hmm," Marine said. "So what you're saying is that black people can be white?"

"Well no." George stiffened, and cleared his throat. "Not exactly. I mean, yes, they can devolve to whyte, in certain situations. I mean whyte, with a *y*—not, of course, white with an *i*. But only with Muslims. You see, in that instance, between the Muslim and the African American, the African American represents the privilege of the West, so the Muslim is the more noble sufferer."

"So they can," Marine said. "Black people can be white."

"No, no. No. Not at all," George said. "I mean, yes. But whyte with a *y*, you see. Only whyte with a *y*."

"Whyte with a *y*?" Marine asked.

George shifted in his seat. It probably wasn't a good idea to be schooling Marine on tolerance theory when he wanted to be on her show. But he continued. "Yes. You know. I mean it's no big deal. Whyte with a *y* just means all the characteristics habitually associated with whites. That is—with unreformed whites. You know: privilege, colonialism, racism, insensitivity, cruelty, narcissism—things like that."

"So what you're saying is that certain characteristics can determine race, as opposed to just DNA?" Marine asked. She was jotting things down like crazy all over her blue sticky notes.

"Well, yes and no," George said. "Look, it's not important. I was just trying to point out that Muslims are above me. And they're immutable. They are the only ones that are immutable. They are always the aggrieved party, in every situation. Except of course for white, straight, cisgender men. They are also immutable. But on the opposite end. They are on the lowest branch of the tree. Always. They are always ... whyte. With a *y*. And they're always white with an *i*, obviously."

"So," Marine said, "what you're saying, is that other than Muslims and whites, with an *i*, race is fluid?"

"Well ... no, not exactly. Look. Forget it. You know what, it's all pretty academic. It's not important. Actually, it's not important at all. It's all from *Orthosentia*, which, as you know, Arun Merriweather could get pretty 'out there' with his theories."

Marine's face it up. "Arun Merriweather! I love him!" she

exclaimed. "Do you know Radhika? We've been on each other's shows!" Marine then tilted her head from side to side in the subcontinental fashion—imitating Radhika's famous gesture, and then, imitating her Indian accent, repeated the show's famous tagline, "Quite nice!"

"Quite nice!" George echoed. He let out a relieved laugh. "Quite nice!" He repeated. And then, "Très bon!" And then, "Molto bene!"

Marine laughed.

George laughed again, louder this time. There was certainly no one like Radhika Jagtap to lighten the mood! Now a lovable celebrity chef, she had been Arun Merriweather's servant once upon a time. In fact, she had been Arun's mother's childhood servant, accompanying her to England upon her marriage. A fixture in the Merriweather family for generations, she also happened to be the inspiration for *Orthosentia*. The story went that Arun had spied her from his parlor as she was hunched over pulling up weeds in the family's Knightsbridge garden—and that that simple image was what had set him on his life's mission. It's best to let Arun tell the story in his own words:

"There she was, her ragged, work-worn body stooped and humbled next to the towering, centuries-old oak tree in our garden. And that image, iconic and powerful, simple yet eloquent, burned itself into my brain instantly and permanently. I was never the same again. I set aside Churchill's *A History of the English-Speaking Peoples, Volume Two*, which I had been reading, and began contemplating the significance of what I was seeing. The first thing I noted was the contrast in heights. Radhika was so lowly, so close to the ground, even on her best of days, and the old oak was so lofty, shimmering in the breeze, its vantage point high above the rooftops. The second thing that struck me was not so much an image as a feeling, a sense that Radhika's old body was just as hard and knotty as the old oak—if not literally, then figuratively. And I felt my heart pour out to her. Just gush and bleed for her. I felt all the love and appreciation I hadn't felt in my twenty years of living, during which time I am ashamed to admit I had perceived old Radhika, when registering her presence at all, as something akin to a decorative table, or a steamer trunk —I felt all that love and appreciation come surging out of me, like a flash flood carrying decades of sticks and debris.

"And in that moment I dropped to my knees, clasped my hands, and exclaimed out loud, 'If I could, my dear Radhika, my noble, meek, earthbound creature, I would raise you up to the highest branches of that tree!' But even as I was saying it, my proclamation seemed so gauche, so unnecessary, so melodramatic to my own ears, and my words withered and died in the air before they even reached the ground. Because I realized that on some important, but unseen level, Radhika and her kind already were on the highest branches of the tree. And I and my ilk were on the lowest. And stupid me had just been too blind to see it. For just as Radhika was low and the tree was high, so it must be that the people who had their roots the deepest in human suffering had their branches highest in humanity. As the bard said, 'If you prick us, do we not bleed?' And I say, there are some who have been pricked and pricked and pricked and have bled and bled and bled. So if to suffer is human, then surely to suffer more is to be *more* human, and so the noble sufferers of the world, like Radhika, were *more* human. Higher up in the tree of humanity. I pledged right there and then to make it my life's mission to insist that everyone see things exactly the way I saw them at that moment, with the suffering people of this world in their rightful place as our teachers, our leaders, our saints. I pledged right then to come up with a detailed schematic to elevate those who have bled the most and humble those who have bled the least. That schematic would be a tree, just like the tree I saw that day. And I vowed to teach this schematic to the world!"

He kept his promise, of course, in both senses—he taught the tree schematic to the world, and he elevated Radhika. She was now a fêted celebrity and a household name. Even George, who got performance anxiety every time he had to so much as microwave a meal, enjoyed watching her cooking show, *A Clash of Cuisines*, where aspiring chefs were challenged to come up with unique culinary cultural combinations on the spot: "Polish and Peruvian! Go!" "Inuit and Mexican! Go!" "Japanese and Sudanese! Go!" And they would be off! Mixing and combining, sautéing and sous-viding, torching and plating ingredients that one would never have dreamed would go together!

The fact that Radhika was just a figurehead on the show took nothing away from her fame. At the judges' table, she positively beamed, her gold tooth glimmering. It was as if she was perennially surprised and thrilled to be eating, in the way of people who have known real hunger. She ate so quickly and so voraciously that the other judges occasionally had to wrest the plate from her gnarled, twisted hands in order to be able to taste the dish themselves. And her vote was always positive, no matter what the outcome. Her analysis was invariably "Quite nice!" much to the audience's delight. The show always opened with her sitting at a simple table in a humble-looking house, with a photogenic plate of food laid out before her—supposedly an old family recipe. Before taking a bite, she would recite the recipe in her native language, Marathi, while English subtitles flew by on the screen. George had once read that in reality, she only knew how to cook one dish. Lentils and rice. All the same, she was a cute grandmotherly figure beloved by all, a pop culture icon. There were mugs, T-shirts, pajamas, throw pillows, and a whole line of culinary implements with her likeness and the tagline "Quite nice!" She regularly killed it on the talk show circuit.

Marine laughed and nodded. "Seriously, I like your idea," she said. "I'm going to bring it to my production team. I think it's an excellent opportunity. In the meantime, keep thinking of a name. We need a name. Usually the tolerance projects I feature have interesting names. Like last week, I had that girl from Mississippi, I don't know if you saw it. She got everyone in her school to keep a journal about all the prejudices they noticed in themselves. Every time they saw someone from a different group, whether it was a classmate, the clerk at the 7-Eleven, or someone waiting to cross the street, they had to write down their honest initial reactions. That project was called, 'Who Is the Other Me in the Mirror?' I think that was a good name. Think of something like that."

"I will!" George said.

Marine then set about rifling through her desk drawers, and proceeded to present George with piece after piece of *Hate Hunters* merchandise. By the time he left her office, he had two T-shirts, a windbreaker, a duffel bag, a baseball cap, a beach towel, six lapel buttons, four pens, two hand sanitizers, three refrigerator magnets, two cell phone handles, and a sweatshirt—all with the *Hate Hunters* logo: the serious girl with her camera trained on racism.

CHAPTER NINE
SOLDIERS

Marine walked briskly along, ushering George back out through the offices. But they had to stop every few seconds so George could readjust the various items he was attempting to balance. "Sorry," he said, as he retrieved a *Hate Hunters* beach towel that had slid down his arm for the second time.

"Here, why don't I do this?" he said. He opened up the duffel bag and placed the towel inside, along with some of the other loose merchandise.

"There you go," Marine said. "I don't know why we didn't think of that in the first place."

"Yes, this is much easier," said George.

Marine studied him. He was all decked out in red *Hate Hunters* gear: the baseball hat, the duffel bag, the windbreaker—all with the logo. She laughed. "No one can accuse you of not hating hate!"

"No! You'd better believe I hate hate!" George said. Then, suddenly, from out of nowhere, there was a woman standing next to Marine. She had a very ethereal look—her hair was backlit by the late afternoon sun coming in through a window, calling to mind Botticelli's *Birth of Venus*. And it was almost as if she had a halo, a soft, glowing halo—as in Reni's *Assumption of the Virgin*. And her eyes—they were so soft, so incredibly kind—they reminded him of ... they reminded him of ... well he'd never seen anything like them. George's mother had taught art history at a small women's liberal arts college in upstate New York, and he'd inherited from her a deep and abiding passion for Italian Renaissance and Baroque painting.

Marine introduced them. "George, this is Alma Willingsby, one of our best tolerance counselors. Alma, this is George Lake. He's doing some really interesting work around Islamophobia."

Alma offered her hand. "Nice to meet you."

"Nice to meet you, too," George said.

"You look like you're leading the troops!" Alma said.

"Sorry?"

She gestured to his outfit and all the paraphernalia. "The *Hate Hunters* army!"

"Oh!" George laughed. "No, I'm just a humble foot soldier, I assure you."

"No! You look like a general! A brigadier, a commander, a colonel!"

George bowed slightly. "No, I'm just an infantry man, a humble ..." He stopped. He couldn't think of any more military ranks. He looked at Alma, and she looked at him. Neither of them spoke. Their eyes lingered for a moment.

Alma turned to Marine. "Listen Marine, I'm glad I caught you. I have Jackie in my office right now, and I'm happy to say, I think we've finally got her where we want her. I know—I've said that before, but this time, I'm convinced she really is changing. Did I tell you I sent her to see *Danger's*

Tweets? Well, it made quite an impression. She was very moved. She's telling me her thoughts about it right now—and I think it's going to be a big aha moment for her. I can just feel it! I think this might be what we've been working for all these years. So, listen, if you could just hold off on that footage a little bit longer ..."

"No way," Marine said. "The footage is ready to go. And that girl, the hate hunter who captured it, Brittney, she's been calling me every day, wanting to know when it will air. I've got to give my hate hunters what they want—you know how it is. Anyway, we have that whole segment on the Tamil culture that my team put together. It's good stuff. Really good. It'll probably air this weekend. Sorry, Alma."

"Please ..." Alma said. There was a note of such pathos in her voice, that George felt his heart jump.

"It's just that ... I don't know how she'll take it," Alma continued. "I'm really worried about her. It's not just the drinking ... it's everything—she's not good. Really, I don't know how she'll handle another public shaming."

Marine studied Alma. "Okay," she said, "we'll talk later."

Alma breathed an audible sigh of relief. "Thank you," she said. She turned to George, and was about to say something, but Marine wasted no time in whisking him out through the offices and into the reception area.

Near the elevators, Marine put her hand on George's arm. "It was a pleasure meeting you," she said. "And remember, think of a catchy name for your project!"

"Say, could I use the restroom before I go?" George asked.

Marine led him back into the offices and pointed him in the general direction.

A few minutes later, George stood in front of the bathroom mirror, scrutinizing himself. With his red windbreaker, red hat, and red duffel bag, he looked like a strange person loitering at a bus station. He removed all the red gear. He smoothed down the lapel of his suit. He waited until he guessed Marine was likely to be back in her office, and he drew in a deep breath. He couldn't believe what he was about to do. Basically, he was about to go wandering around a governmental agency, unauthorized, looking for a woman he'd met just once—for thirty seconds.

And if he found her, he had no idea what he would say to her.

"Did you feel the earth stop too?"

"Did your whole being stumble, like mine did, when we met?"

"Did you feel as though we recognized each other, even though we've never met before?"

More likely, he'd ask her for dinner. But that just seemed so ... mundane, so trivial—compared to the magnitude of what had happened.

Then he had an idea. She was a tolerance counselor—maybe she did private sessions. Yes. He could ask her about that. He could say he was interested in becoming more tolerant—which was true. Everyone should always be interested in becoming more tolerant.

Or better yet, he could tell her he'd like to consult with her about his Islamophobia project—that he'd like the perspective of someone well versed in tolerance theory. Yes! Perfect!

George stood in front of the mirror for some time longer. In the end, he chucked all his ideas and decided to wing it. That usually seemed to work for him. And he put the red *Hate Hunters* gear back on. He was a soldier, after all.

When he exited the bathroom, Marine was nowhere around. In fact, there was no sign of human life anywhere. Just grey carpet and grey cubicles for what seemed like miles.

He set off to find Alma Willingsby, the tolerance counselor. But as he began walking down the first row of cubicles, he realized it might be more difficult than he'd anticipated. The cubicles were deep, and enclosed, and there were no names on any of them—just large whiteboards, similar to the one on Marine's office door. And, like Marine's, each displayed a curious statement demanding respect.

One read, "I am a second-generation Andorran, third-generation Nuyorican! Respect my culture and I'll respect yours!"

George stood there, trying to work out if the statement could be referring to Alma.

Another said: "I am a proud Armenian American! Respect my culture, and I will respect yours!"

George wondered if that could be her. He couldn't remember what Armenians looked like. He made a mental note to come back to that one.

He continued walking.

"I am a gay man. Respect my sexuality, my right to love who I love, and I will respect yours."

George liked that one—it seemed to be wishing him good luck on his endeavor.

Another one: "I am one-quarter Mexican, one-quarter English, one-quarter Polish, and one-quarter Irish! I am 100 percent human. Respect my culture, and I'll respect yours!"

That could be anyone, George thought.

"Lesbian. Thespian. Humanitarian! Respect my culture and I will respect yours!"

He rounded a corner to the next row of cubicles.

"Bosnian, Welsh, Taiwanese Indigenous, proud corgi owner. I respect everyone!"

That was nice.

"Proud strong Muslima! Respect my culture and I'll respect yours!"

"Here. Queer. A quarter Japanese. Respect my culture, and I'll respect yours!"

It went on.

"Just your average, run of the mill desi queen! Respect my culture, and I'll respect yours!"

"Black. Loud. Proud! Respect my culture, and I'll respect yours!"

"Hungarian, Mexican, non-neurotypical human! Respect my culture, and I'll respect yours!"

He rounded another row of cubicles.

"100 percent Boricua! Respect my culture, and I'll respect yours."

It went on. And on.

George arrived at the end of the cubicles, confused about what his next step should be. There was just one more cubicle, all the way in the corner by a dark narrow hallway. George stood in front of it, and he read:

"I'm American. I respect your culture."

Something lit up inside him. He repeated it again in his head:

"I'm American. I respect your culture."

It was simple. It was friendly. It was neither proud nor humble. It was dignified. It was uncluttered: a refreshing relief from all the dizzying demands for respect. It was ... her.

CHAPTER TEN

THE ADMONISHMENT

"So in summation, while I was more than a little bit skeptical about the play's opening scene, which I found to veer precariously close to saccharine sentimentality," Jackie Krucic read from some scraps of paper in her hand, "when the house lights came on at the end of the play and there was nary a dry eye in sight, I certainly was no exception—in spirit, that is, because as I've mentioned, actual tears continue to elude me." She folded up the pieces of paper, put them back in her pink knockoff designer handbag, and looked up with an air of expectant self-satisfaction.

"Wonderful!" Alma said. "What a thoughtful review! And I agree. I had the same reaction at the end of the opening scene—with the baby photos and all that. I wasn't sure those emotions were quite ... earned, so early in the play, if you know what I mean—but then, wow! The play certainly delivered on its promise."

"It really did," Jackie said. "Oh, by the way, I brought you something." She reached in her purse and produced a dark blue box with a white ribbon on it. "Just a little something, to thank you for the play."

"You shouldn't have," Alma said.

"Open it."

Alma opened the box to find four perfect rows of macarons, organized by color: pale green, pale yellow, robin's-egg blue, and bright berry. Something about the quality of the colors struck Alma; they were thoughtful colors, "evolved" colors—about as far away from primary colors as you could get.

"Thank you, Jackie," she said.

"Go ahead, try them," Jackie said.

Alma took a bite of a green macaron, and a tiny explosion of cream and pistachio flavors went off in her mouth.

"It's the least I could do," Jackie said. "You know, seeing *Danger's Tweets* has been very important for me."

Alma nodded enthusiastically.

Jackie continued, "I mean, I loved the play, but also, since I lost my job, you know, my world has just gotten so small, and I'd forgotten how nice it was to be out among people. The thing is, in the theater, you're really sharing an experience. It bonds everyone, even though they're strangers."

Alma felt a pang of guilt. Like most of her clients, Jackie had lost her job and many of her significant relationships after her unseemly—but not necessarily criminal—behavior had been caught on film and featured on *Hate Hunters*. She did receive a meager pension after twenty-four years of working as a paralegal at the public defender's office, but Alma knew it wasn't easy for her. The more she saw of her clients' lives, the more she felt that if it were up to her, public humiliation probably wouldn't be the cornerstone of citizen rehabilitation.

Tolerance offenders would still go to counseling, get "Schooled!" and the like, but in her opinion, public shaming just wasn't effective. Either it unfairly harmed someone who had made a genuine mistake, an unfortunate misstep in an otherwise positive and productive life—in which case the punishment certainly did not fit the crime—or, as was the case with Jackie and many of her other repeat tolerance offenders, her "lifers," they felt the devastating and destructive effects of public shaming, without digesting any of its lessons—almost by definition of character. The experience just seemed to further entrench them in their retrograde points of view.

Alma contemplated the box of macarons on her desk, trying to decide which one to try next. It occurred to her that buying them must have been quite a financial feat for Jackie. Then, she had a strange thought. What if Jackie was secretly rich? What if, after all those years of complaining about how the Tolerance Department had ruined her life and made her poor, the whole thing turned out to be an elaborate ruse? She laughed to herself—she knew she was just projecting. Because much to her constant dismay, she herself was secretly rich.

Her father was an important airline executive, and she'd grown up on a sixty-acre estate—well, technically, it was more accurately referred to as a compound—on Long Island. Of the home's many amenities, including a lake, horse stables, and three separate English gardens, certainly the most noteworthy was the private ice-cream parlor her parents had had built for her as a child—her birthday parties had been legendary, of course, and her childhood in general quite happy. It was only as she grew older that she tried to distance herself as much as possible from her family's wealth. As a teenager, she was appalled at the thought of how many more times her father made than his employees—the baggage handlers, flight attendants, mechanics, ground crew, agents, the ones who did all the work, in other words—and she'd told him as much. They'd gotten into some heated discussions, and on more than one occasion she'd accused him of being a latter-day robber baron capitalist. He'd always laughed and called her a naive little communist and pointed to the fact that the airline created hundreds of thousands of jobs at all skill levels all around the world, not just directly, but also indirectly—in food, tourism, ground crews, and the like. He argued that the airline made it possible for families living apart to see each other, for immigrants to come to new lands, for people to see new places, learn new perspectives, try new foods, go to Disney World—God damn it—fall in love, go to hospitals in different countries for lifesaving surgery, and even send corpses home—all for a fraction of the price and time of a car, bus, boat, or train trip.

As an adult, Alma prided herself on living *mostly* within her means—with the one glaring exception of her Upper East Side classic six apartment. A classic six was an apartment built before the war having six rooms: living room, dining room, kitchen, two bedrooms, and a maid's room. Her father had originally bought it as a pied-à-terre to be used after meetings in the city, and Alma had held on to it for a few quite justifiable reasons. First, its location was undeniably convenient. Second—and there was really no getting around this one—she liked it very much. Third, it was already paid for. In other words, the damage was done. If her family sold it, all it would mean was that some other rich person—and undoubtedly one much less socially responsible than herself—would move in. That is to say, nobody who needed helping would be helped. Fourth, she considered it a piece of

New York City history, with its hard oak floors, working wood fireplace, and pretty moldings. It had several other curious features and quirks that she had grown attached to as well, her favorite of which was the 1920s-style intercom that connected down to the lobby—a black tube phone, like in the silent movies. If someone else were to buy the apartment, she could only imagine what kinds of trendy, expensive renovations they would make. They might convert it into an open-floor plan, create a kitchen island, or remove the claw-foot tub and install a rain shower.

Luckily, so far, no one from work had ever been to her apartment. When other friends did come by, their attention was usually successfully drawn away from its splendor by the deliberately humble furnishings—which were mostly shabby-chic curbside finds. When occasionally someone wondered out loud how she could afford it, she kept them at bay with vague references to the city's extreme rent control laws—implying that the apartment had been in her family practically since the neighborhood was farmland on the city's outposts. When people noticed her flying all over the world at the drop of a hat, she explained that her mother had been a stewardess—which, in fact, she had been, in the two years between earning her comparative lit degree from Barnard and marrying her dad.

"That is so true about the theater," Alma said, helping herself to a bright berry macaron. "I need to go more too."

"Maybe ..." Jackie said, "maybe ... we could go together." And then she added, "My treat." She paused, and then added more definitively, "Yes. My treat."

Alma wiped a fuchsia crumb off her lip. She took another bite of the macaron and studied Jackie. Her satiny white blouse was stained and a little too low cut, and her rather stubby, home-pedicured toes peeked out from scuffed, open-toed sandals. Alma wasn't supposed to socialize with her clients. But some of them were just so ... lonely ... so broken, you could see it in their eyes. So from time to time Alma deliberately ceased being a counselor and became ... a person. She'd take them out to lunch, buy them a coffee, take a friendly, human interest in them for an hour or so. They'd pass the time like fellow human beings—sharing observations, laughs, woes. It seemed to have a positive impact. And even though it broke the ethical and professional codes of counseling, she figured the moment the laws of being human stopped trumping the laws of being a counselor—would be the moment she'd cease being an effective counselor.

"I'd love to go, and it will be my treat," Alma said. "But Jackie, the exercise wasn't just to 'go to the theater,' as you know. I'm wondering if you noticed anything else about the play. For example, when I go to the theater, I often identify strongly with one particular character. So I'm wondering, did you see yourself up there on the stage at all? Were there any characters or incidents that you found yourself relating to—given all our discussions?"

Jackie lit up. "Well, it's funny you should ask, because to me, that's part of the magic of theater, definitely. I see it as a kind of collective dream, one that everyone in the audience gets to experience at the same time—and just like with a dream, I believe that parts of ourselves are represented in all the characters ..."

"Jackie," Alma interrupted, "how, specifically, did this play relate to you, Jackie Krucic? Which character in *Danger's Tweets* did you identify with?"

"Look. I know what you're trying to get at," Jackie said, the tone in her voice rising slightly. "I enjoyed the play. But as

I've told you before, while I know racism exists, and I know it's a problem, I do not consider myself a racist. Period. I am not a racist."

Alma dropped her head in frustration, and then continued, "Look, I think I know what's tripping us up. Let's just forget the word 'racist' for a moment. It seems like you have a lot of resistance to that word. The thing is, you're taking it too personally, as if we're applying it just to you. Like we're singling you out, trying to foist a label on you. Like we're saying, 'Jackie is a racist,' when, in fact, nothing could be further from the truth! The fact is, we are all racists—all of us white people—and there's no shame in it. Really, there's not. Trust me. The only shame is in not addressing it. Do you think I'm any different from you? I'm not. It's just our natural state. We were all born with the original sin of racism—also known as the white stain. It's in our blood. And unfortunately, the more we insist we don't have it, the more racist we sound. Because denying our racism—that's textbook white fragility. It shows that we're so fragile we can't handle being criticized, and we expect to be treated with kid gloves. Which means we think we are *special*, or better than others—in other words, racist! Get it? And if you think about it, there's no reason on earth we should be treated with kid gloves, because we've never treated anyone else that way. So you see, that's just the way it is. Think about it like this: denying it will get you nowhere. Denying it only leads you to the witch's dictum."

"The what?"

"The witch's dictum. I've told you about that before, Jackie. It means if you say you're not a racist, that proves you're a racist.

"What the ... but wait, what does it have to do with witches?"

"Oh, it's just a reference to witch trials and the way they tested if you were a witch. If you floated, it meant you were a witch, and if you sank, well, obviously, you were dead."

"Jeesh!"

"That's why you don't want to bring it to trial, so to speak—to deny it. You'll lose! But that's actually good news. It means you don't have to spend all your energy denying it and defending yourself. Because it's already been decided. The color of your skin has decided it for you. The color of your skin makes you a racist. It's done. Move on. Now you get to work on reforming it."

"The color of my skin makes me a racist," Jackie repeated to herself, mulling it over.

"Exactly!" Alma said. "So, it's not personal. That's what I'm trying to tell you. Everyone with the same color skin as you is a racist!"

"Everyone with the same color skin as me is a racist," Jackie repeated.

"Yes! So stop being offended! All you have to do is admit it! That's the first step. A huge step. And then the second step is to *demonstrate* to everyone you are not a racist. Well, no, I take that back, because you can never completely lose the stain, but you have to show you are at least trying to lose it, trying to reform, trying to change and become enlightened. If you don't do that, understandably, you'll make a lot of people quite uncomfortable."

"Well, then, it seems that as far as being a racist, I'm in a black hole of rhetoric from which there is no escape. So, fine, have it your way. Nevertheless, I must keep insisting that my main beef—and the reason I keep getting into trouble—is not with the other races, or the noble races, or whatever you call them, but with the complete breakdown, not only of society—but of the very idea of society! We seem to be living in a solipsistic nightmare where the concept of public space doesn't exist at all; in fact, the concept of other people barely exists. In public, people act as if they are in their own houses at all times; they have loud conversations on cell phones, they listen to music without headphones, they completely fail to acknowledge ..."

"Jackie, let's stay on topic," Alma said. "You keep saying that cell phones annoy you. But that's not the real issue, is it? Because the only people you get into altercations with over these supposed transgressions are noble people—minorities. Either you're hiding your biases from yourself, or you're being deliberately ..."

"No!" Jackie said. And then she whispered, "That's just it! The ... *hate hunters* ..." she looked around nervously, as if she believed that by referring to them, she might accidentally conjure them, "... only seem to materialize when I'm having these problems with ... nobilities ... or whatever you call them."

"Noble races," Alma said.

"I have an idea!" Jackie said. "Of how I can prove I'm not a racist! Just get a film crew to follow me around and film me all the time! You'll see that white people annoy me too. In fact, they're some of the worst offenders! The way they go on and on about their feelings and opinions loudly on their cell phones, as if anyone cares, as if their lives are a movie, or a reality TV show, or as if ..."

"No, I don't think that's the direction we want to go in," Alma said. "We want less public freak-outs, not more. Now, listen, I've told you all the various ways you can demonstrate you're making progress, and they're all really very simple. Much more simple than assigning a film crew to you 24/7. But you refuse to do any of them. And I don't know why. For example, I've been tracking your social media metrics since our last meeting, and you have yet to decry a single act of racism on the Internet—not on our tolerance feed or anywhere else ..."

"What's 'decry' again?"

Alma looked at Jackie. Her eyes were like deep wells, and Alma still didn't know what was at the bottom of them. They were at times accusing, at times accused, at times needy, desperate, sad—and then at other times, Alma could swear she detected something of the trickster in them, as if Jackie was playing her, playing all of them—as if she wasn't behaving badly out of ignorance or entrenched racism so much as going around the city doing performance art.

"Like I said, Jackie, it's easy," Alma said. "All you have to do is watch the *Hate Hunters* videos on our feed and then react with an outrage emoji, to show that you're angry, and that you condemn racism."

"Which ones are the outrage emojis again?"

"I told you, the little faces with the pounding fists ..."

"Oh yes. I have to decry. I need to remind myself." Jackie tapped her finger to her forehead and said, "Decry, Jackie! Decry, Jackie!" And then, "Wait, let me make a note of it on my phone."

"Good idea," Alma said. "Or, like I told you, you could just post a picture on your social media of yourself and your good friend Mohammad who you keep telling me about. If you posted just one picture ... just one ... that's all I'm asking ... that would be something. It would be huge, actually—something to celebrate. I could show it to everyone, and they would finally believe me that you are really making progress. Because according to the contact hypothesis, people who are friends with or have regular contact with someone from a group other than their own have their prejudices diminish greatly. If you can show me that that's indeed what you are doing, I'll be very proud of you, Jackie. It's not like I *want* to punish you. I don't want to expose you more. That's not why I'm in this—to humiliate people. No. I want you to grow. I want to work with you. All I'm asking is that you work with me too, just a little. Give me something, anything! Give me a picture of yourself with Mohammad, or decry. I'm begging you!"

"Mohammad or decry!" Jackie typed out on her phone. When she was done, she looked up expectantly at Alma.

"Now Jackie, I wish I didn't have to do this," Alma said, "but I'm going to have to show you the latest footage we have of you. I want you to see that it's ready to go and I want you to understand that we'll have no choice but to air it—possibly as soon as this weekend—unless you can show me immediate, concrete progress."

"No!" Jackie shrieked, in such a pitiful tone that Alma felt something grab in her chest. She wished there was more she could do to stop the footage from being shown, and, technically, there should have been. Her role as counselor was really two-pronged. She was supposed to rehabilitate people, yes—but she was also responsible for monitoring their mental health in the aftermath of intense public shaming. In fact, the department received a considerable amount of Jenny Meachom funds for her to do so. Jenny Meachom, or "Dream-Catcher Girl," as she was better known, had had an unfortunate photo taken of her at a music festival some years ago. She was stoned out of her mind, had a dopey expression on her face, and two giant, multicolored, feathered, dream-catcher earrings hanging from her ears. The photo had gone viral, and had become a meme, with scathing captions:

"Catch Dreams, Not Smallpox!"

"The Genocide Weaver!"

"Better Stoned Than Sorry!"

"Dude, Mind If I Appropriate Your Joint?"

But the fun had come to a screeching halt when Jenny was found dead in her car from exhaust fumes—a suicide at twenty-six. It turned out she'd suffered from untreated bipolar disorder, and according to friends and family, had been inconsolable about the memes. In Alma's opinion, the whole situation was doubly tragic—because she was murky at best about the supposed sin of cultural appropriation. She tended more towards theorists who believed that *all* culture was "cultural appropriation"—by definition. That is, without cultural appropriation, there would be no culture. To them, a living culture was like a river, and without tributaries, it would dry up, wither, and die. To them, the idea of "stealing" from a culture was absurd—and the idea that a "pure culture" could exist was inaccurate, dangerous, and racist.

But in reality, the Tolerance Department did little more than pay lip service to prioritizing mental health.

"Don't air it! I beg you!" Jackie said. "I'll show you, I promise! I'll show you I'm not the r-word! Listen. Just give me another chance. Remember the book I told you about? The book I'm writing? *The Expanded Self*? I'm still working on it. And I think I might have something for you by our next meeting. An outline maybe, the intro maybe too. Nothing much, unfortunately. But I think it will make you understand. I think it'll show you exactly what I find so frustrating about today's society, and it has nothing to do with race at all, nothing to do with the sainted, the stained, or whatever you call them ..."

Alma sighed. "Oh yes. Your book. *The Expanded Self*. Look, Jackie, forget the book—I mean, it's good that you're writing it and all. But this is more urgent. And, really, it doesn't have to be that complicated. You don't need to write a whole book to show me that you're working on your racism. I've given you the ways ..."

"Yes! Yes!" Jackie said. "Mohammad and decry! Mohammad and decry! I'll remember. I'll do it! I swear!"

Alma let out another deep sigh. "Okay, Jackie. I'm going to show you the footage now. I don't know if you remember this one. You were on a bus—again. And you were ... well, it looks like you were making fun of an immigrant—again. An elderly immigrant, no less. You were mimicking his accent. No, not even his accent, really—you were actually mimicking his language. You were making fun of his language. It's not pretty." Alma clicked a few times and brought up the video on her computer. "Oh, and Jackie, I have to warn you, it's not just the footage. They have a whole segment on the Tamil language and culture, which, apparently, is the one you lampooned—although I'm sure you didn't know it at the time. It seems it's a very ancient and revered language—a classical language—one of the oldest. Supposedly they were already speaking it—probably even composing epic poems in it—when our ancestors were still grunting around in caves." Alma pressed play.

The video shows Jackie sitting on a bus, wearing a tight red sweater and a floral scarf. Seated next to her is an elderly man talking loudly in a foreign language on his cell phone. Jackie is glaring at the man with a furious expression on her face, and whenever he says something into his phone, she speaks loudly back at him, trying to imitate—to disastrous effect—the consonants, vowels, and distinct phonemes of his ancient language.

"Lum de bum de bum de bumm!" Jackie says.

The man glances at her, then says something else into his phone.

"Pana dana dana dana!" Jackie imitates. "Rum da bum da bum bum bum!"

The man looks at her again, and returns to his call, trying to turn further away from her, toward the window.

"Dum de dum de dum aaaaargh!" Jackie screams, her face red. "Rumbumrumbumrumbum!"

And it all goes downhill from there.

Even Alma can't watch. She pauses the video. "I'm sorry, Jackie, but it just gets worse from there. And after the footage of you on the bus, there's a segment with Marine and Brittney, the girl who caught you on camera, just ripping on you. It's ruthless. And then there's the whole segment on the Tamil language—which … well, let's just say I wouldn't be surprised if it won some kind of journalism award. And unfortunately, there are other incidents as well—incidents we've been holding on to—not just the Tamil incident. The truth is, people love to get you on film. You're considered big game prey for hate hunters everywhere. A veritable white whale. There's one of you going off on a Sikh guy for watching a movie on his phone. And there's another one of you yelling at an African American kid for listening to rap. I mean, I'm pretty sure that's not someplace we want to go, is it Jackie? Do we want to go there?"

"No," Jackie said, her head down. "We don't want to go there." Then she looked up. "But it's just, I just wish everyone had a little more consideration for their fellow passengers. I mean, why can't they use earphones? They're acting like nobody else exists."

Alma sighed in exasperation.

Jackie continued, "The thing is, you say I don't like minorities, or saints, or whatever you call them. But what if the opposite is true? What if I actually like them ... a lot? What if I *miss* them? What if I miss them very much? I mean they're there—but they're not really there. Like the Tamil man, for example, he's sitting next to me, but he's not actually there, he's someplace else, and he's pretending I'm not there. What if that's what drives me crazy? The fact that he's there but he's not really there? What if I want to talk to him? What if I want to learn about Tamil? What if I want him to learn about my life? But he's not talking to me. He's talking to someone else, who's not even there, and he's pretending I don't exist! Not only that, he's not even letting me listen to my own thoughts. He's forcing me to listen to him. But he's not talking to me! He's not communicating with me! He's forcing me to watch his performance. That's what's wrong with the world, if you ask me. Nobody's talking to one another! Everyone's in these silos ... just trapped in their own little worlds ... ignoring everyone else ..."

"Jackie. Hold up," Alma said. "I think I'm having a breakthrough about your situation."

Jackie looked at her expectantly.

"Yes. I think I'm beginning to see what the problem is," Alma said, nodding her head. "Yes, yes. I think I've got it. Now please don't take this the wrong way, Jackie, but, here's the thing—he doesn't *have* to talk to you."

Jackie was silent.

"Yes. That's it," Alma said. "He doesn't *have* to talk to

you. That's the misunderstanding. I think you're still expecting America to be a melting pot. One big happy society where we all learn from one another and become a little bit more like one another each day. But it's not. See, that way of thinking is outmoded, and ... well ... racist. See, they don't have to try to adapt to our way. They don't have to ..."

"No. That's not what I ..."

"Wait. Listen. They don't have to try to fit in, make us happy, do our bidding, or act in a way that is pleasing to us. And the fact that you think that they do ... is nothing more than an artifact of your colonial psyche. I think we've hit pay dirt here! This is your core problem. See, you need to understand, I mean really understand, that the brown people of the world are no longer at your disposal, to do your bidding and perform in a way that is pleasing to you. It's now officially recognized that they have lives of their own, thoughts of their own, conversations of their own, languages of their own, and music of their own—and none of it has anything to do with you, Jackie Krucic."

"No, I didn't say ..."

"Because your time is done! Your reign on this earth is over! The Europeans had a great run. But it's over. And you have to face it. It's not *about* you anymore. It's just not. You need to step aside. Move over. Make way. Your time is done! Over! Finished! The sun has finally set on your empire!"

"Jeesh!" Jackie said. "You make it sound as if I was at the helm of the Niña, the Pinta, and the Santa María! I don't think you're understanding me at all ..."

"Alma?" A man's voice said.

Both women looked up. A black man dressed all in red

was standing at the door of the cubicle. It was the man Alma had been talking to earlier, in the hall, with Marine.

"Hi," Alma said, her face reddening slightly.

"Hi," said the man.

Everyone was silent for a while.

"Are those macarons?" the man asked, indicating the box on the desk.

"Yes," Alma said. "Would you like one?" She handed him the box, and he chose a blue macaron.

"Take another one," Alma said.

He took a green one. "Listen, I was wondering if maybe you'd like to have dinner with me ..." he said.

After the man had left, both women broke out into a slow grin.

Alma leaned back in her chair. "Sorry Jackie, I was lecturing you again. I shouldn't have been. We should be exploring ideas together here. And, frankly, you bring up some interesting points about alienation and isolation here in America. In fact, I myself have recently been rethinking the whole American identity thing. I think there might still be some hope for it. It might not be dead in the water just yet. Listen, I'll shut up. Why don't you go ahead and tell me about your book. I'm very curious to hear your thoughts."

"Oh! Okay! Well, so my thesis is basically that all human culture began as tribes. We were tribal. And the tribe was the basic unit of consciousness."

"Interesting," Alma said. She bit into a lemon macaron. It was not too tart, not too sweet, silky on her tongue.

Jackie continued, "So, it doesn't mean there was no individual consciousness during tribal times, but I believe—and mind you, I still have a lot of research to do on this—I believe that relatively little 'weight' was given to this level of consciousness."

"Hmm," Alma said.

"So at this point in our development," Jackie continued, "for all intents and purposes, groupthink prevailed. Survival of the tribe was paramount. Disabled children were sacrificed, the elderly abandoned on ice floes, the feebleminded stabbed in the chest. It was not wrong, per se, it was just a different unit of consciousness or identity. Acts such as those were the equivalent of cutting off a gangrenous limb. Society was like one body."

"Go on," Alma said, intrigued by Jackie's use of the word "per se." Intrigued by all her vocabulary, in fact. Had she come into counseling with this kind of vocabulary? With this ... intellectual curiosity? Alma didn't think so. Or had she? Lately, she'd been breaking it out a lot. In spurts. But the rest of the time, well—Alma sometimes wondered if Jackie didn't purposely play dumb. She had a thought. She wondered if Jackie was old enough to have been somehow given the message that women weren't supposed to be smart. She did the math. She didn't think so.

Jackie continued, "Then, as time progressed—and this was not linear, it happened at different times in different cultures—but generally speaking, as time progressed, consciousness moved away from the group, and toward the individual. So my theory is, there was some hypothetical point in time, that may or may not have actually occurred, when humanity was in a perfect equilibrium between its concern for the tribe and its concern for the individual; a perfect moment on the journey from group consciousness to individual consciousness—the apex, the crest of the hill, as it were. We don't know when this was or if it even happened. It could have been during the Renaissance, or the Industrial Revolution, or the 1960s; or it could have been in none of those times or places, but at any rate, what's abundantly clear is that we have long since hurtled past it. We've collectively charged past that ideal balance and into the realm of unbridled and unhealthy individualism—an inescapable vortex of unlimited individual self-expression, and I don't mean self-expression in the artistic, soul-searching sense, as was perhaps the case during the proposed fictional apex, the moment of perfect balance, but rather in the medical sense—like a cancer: the complete abdication of communal duty by a single cell in favor of unlimited self-replication—self-replication without meaning. Because that is what we are doing, Alma. Through social media, we are engaging in rampant narcissism—the usual checks and balances failed, bypassed. What we have is unlimited self-observation through the eyes of the other. And this is the 'expanded self' I'm talking about. We all parade our expanded selves about, like prized pets. On our cell phones, in public, walking down the street, conducting business, holding court, 'performing' for the passerby, meaningless performances of self, with no message except 'me.' We duplicate ourselves endlessly on Instagram, for no purpose other than duplication. No idea, no message, no communication. Except 'me.' Me! Me! Me! Me at the beach! Me at a restaurant! Me skiing! Relentless self-proliferation! A cell gone rogue! That's what I'm talking about. And the endless posting and reposting of articles and quotes and recycled opinions are also an extension of this meaningless 'self' and unfortunately what has come to pass for thinking."

Jackie's eyes looked feverish. They were once again bottomless chasms. It was as if she was talking about a nuclear event, a mass extinction of the human psyche.

"But this is where it gets weird," Jackie continued. "As this 'self-expression' increases, the actual self decreases, in any meaningful sense. Because it is no longer informed, communicating, reflecting, or open to new ideas or perspectives. In its endless proliferation, the self is actually starving. It is dying. And in its death throes, it becomes enthralled to the idea of the group. It needs the group to support it. To prop it up. So ironically, we have come full circle, to a new sort of tribalism. But it's a dangerous, less organic tribalism. It even plays out on the physical level; people are no longer where they physically are—on the street, in the classroom, or in the workplace. Their bodies are there, but they are not really there. They are instead connected at all times to their own tribe through social and digital media. They are no longer present in the marketplace of ideas. They just 'communicate' with their tribes. But this communication is empty. It's a vicious cycle. Without a meaningful self, there can be no meaningful group. And without true communication and reflection in a group, the self cannot be enriched, sustained, informed, have meaning. And so, with the self run amok, the group becomes a kind of shadow tribe, and there is a kind of totalitarianism, with a subconscious desire for murder, apoptosis, suicide, destruction. And I think this is where this revived race consciousness comes in. All the sainted and the stained, and the noble and the white that you guys keep talking about. The us and the them. It's a knee-jerk regression to mass tribalism, a stand-in for both the meaningful self and the meaningful group."

An important realization began to dawn on Alma. She put down her macaron.

Jackie's journey of awakening in the counseling program wouldn't just be in one direction—from racist to non-racist, although it would be nice if it included that someday. Because that's not how people worked. That's not how growth happened. Growth happened in fits and starts, and it happened in places you might not expect.

Jackie was growing as an intellectual before Alma's eyes. She was growing as a person and as a woman. She was taking Alma's teachings seriously. She was letting them sink into her mind, and she was giving them the respect of struggling with them, challenging them, arguing with them, and contemplating them.

She wasn't the same person Alma had met eight years ago. She was now thinking about ideas. She was writing about ideas. She was writing a book, for godsakes! And it sounded interesting.

After Jackie had gone, Marine popped her head into the cubicle.

"Well?" she said. "Did your Jackie have her aha moment? Does she finally get it?"

Alma tilted her head. "She doesn't get it. Not yet. But one thing I can say is she's really progressed. She's really thinking about this stuff. Struggling with it. She's actually ... she's writing a book ... about the dangers of tribalism, and the dangers of individualism. And I have to tell you, it's really thought-provoking. I'm proud of her. I'm actually proud of her. It looks like she's really finding her voice."

"Interesting," Marine said.

"Let's hold off on the footage," Alma said. "I'd like to be able to reward this, and not punish it. If you'll just trust me on this one, I think it will pay off."

Something about the calm in Alma's voice made Marine nod her head. "If you say so."

"Actually," Alma said, "why don't you just go ahead and destroy the footage?"

"Nice try." Marine laughed. "It doesn't work that way. But I'll hold off on it, if you say so. And I do love that you care so much about your clients. Listen, she's not Islamophobic by any chance, is she?"

Alma thought for a moment. "No, I don't think so."

"Because I'm on the lookout for incidents of Islamophobia. So let me know if you find any."

"I will," Alma said.

"I mean, with any of your clients. Let me know if you find any Islamophobia."

Alma nodded. "I will."

CHAPTER ELEVEN

AN EVENING IN

(ABOUT A YEAR LATER)

Alma took in the impressive selection of craft beers lining the wall of her local supermarket and spotted George's latest favorite, Breaker Six IPA, which he'd described as "moderately smokey, with hints of jasmine and clove," and grabbed a six-pack. For herself, on a whim, she chose Shoals, a medium-bodied pilsner which promised to be "slightly woodsy with a churlish rosemary finish."

It was Thursday night, and George was bringing over dinner. It promised to be a resplendent evening in. There were three new episodes of *Butterfly*, the police procedural drama about the beautiful forensic entomologist with a dark sense of humor and a penchant for risky sexual encounters, on streaming, and they planned to watch them all.

At the checkout counter, the man ringing up Alma's items drifted in and out of focus. She took an involuntary deep breath. Even after almost a year of dating, the anticipation of seeing George still made her nervous and excited.

She stepped outside into the frenzied energy of an unseasonably warm evening in late spring, the giddy awareness of longer days. She'd come straight from work and her Cuban heels clicked melodically along the sidewalk. She wore a grey and white striped wrap dress and felt pretty in it, even as she clutched a six-pack in each hand. She passed two girls around her age, also in dresses. Their faces and their décolletages glowed in the heat and fading sun. They spoke in quiet tones. The sky ushered in pinks and purples, and in the distance, children let out their last shouts before being called in for dinner.

Crossing Seventy-Fourth Street, a bus whizzed past Alma from out of nowhere, forcing her quickly back up onto the curb. She froze, tightening her hands around the cardboard six-packs, and the color drained from her face. On the side of the bus, larger than life, were the backsides of two girls wearing flowered dresses, bowing down at the Barry Street Bus Depot.

The Flower Butt Campaign was one of the most successful in recent history, and also one of the most ubiquitous. It was everywhere. On every bus, every bus shelter, and every subway car. And it had been going for the better part of a year and showed no signs of stopping.

Alma looked both ways and crossed the street. But she arrived at the other side a different person. Her dress now felt like an affectation, the heat felt sticky and foreshadowing of mosquitoes, and the thought of George sitting next to her on the couch all evening felt terrifying—like he would find her out.

She began the all-too-familiar routine of calming herself down. She stopped on the sidewalk and took in a deep breath. She reminded herself that no one knew it was her. No one. And if they were going to find her out, she reasoned, they would have done so by now. The girls weren't even the point anymore, she told herself. No one was interested. They had been so effective as a cautionary tale, that no one could any longer imagine that they were living people, with whole bodies and names and jobs and hopes and fears. They had taken on a sort of mythical, fairy-tale aspect. They were part of another realm. They were fictional. They had nothing to do with her.

She began walking again. Furthermore, she thought, if she were to step away from her own self-interest for a moment, she had to admit it was a rather ingenious campaign. Addie McCarrom and Messaging had done a fantastic job of explaining an admittedly nuanced and somewhat counterintuitive tolerance principle to the masses, using just a simple, memorable photo and a rather catchy tagline.

"Don't Be a Flower Butt!" the ad admonished, then went on to explain, "Centering yourself in black and other oppression narratives is just another way of making it all about you. Remember, when in doubt ... don't be a flower butt!"

It had become part of the vernacular. On the Internet, on TV, and in living rooms across America, people warned each other, sometimes earnestly, sometimes teasingly, "Don't be such a flower butt!"

It was good, Alma continued to reason. A woman with three babies in a triple stroller walked past her. It was a good thing. Not only was it a spectacular campaign, but, if she thought about it, it was kind of appropriate that she was the one providing the lesson. It was, in a way, a natural extension of her work as a tolerance counselor. It was the same work—just in a different form. By being in the photo, she was not only still teaching people—she was actually teaching more people than she'd ever imagined possible. And if she was really serious about being a tolerance counselor, which she was, and not just doing it for prestige and white redemption points, which she wasn't, then she shouldn't mind being the butt of the joke, as it were, as long as people were learning.

The progress of society as a whole was so much more important than her silly, privileged, individual life. She'd been given so many opportunities—why should she mind sacrificing a little comfort and peace of mind for the greater good?

Actually, if she thought about it, it was very fitting that one of the flower butts just so happened to be a tolerance counselor working for the Tolerance Department. Because what better way to show people that *all* white people, even so-called "expert" white people, made mistakes, and that that was okay. Although obviously, Alma hoped that neither the Tolerance Department nor the general public would become privy to that particular facet of the lesson.

She walked past what appeared to be a homeless man seated against a building. He was rolling cigarettes, and an orange tabby cat sat quietly among his things. The beer was getting heavy in her arms and the cardboard was beginning to dig into her fingers. She thought one of the boxes might tear. She placed it down on the ground and examined it. It was fine. She picked it up and started walking again. She was almost home. She felt better. She wasn't thinking about the ad. She wondered what restaurant George would be stopping at. She'd told him to surprise her. Maybe he'd bring steak frites from ...

"Aaaaaagghhh!" She let out a nervous shriek. Another bus with the ad was parked immediately to her left on Park Avenue, waiting for the light to change. God! she thought. She could swear the size of her butt had been enlarged in relation to her person in the photo.

She clacked quickly home, greeted her doorman, and let

herself into her apartment. She put the six-packs in the fridge and hurried back through her elaborately wainscoted living room into her bedroom. She opened the bottom drawer of her oversized dresser. She reached underneath the sweaters, and took out the offending dress. She folded it under her arm, and hurried to the apartment door. She looked both ways down the hallway. No one was coming, but just to be safe, she went into the kitchen, got a brown paper bag, and stuffed the dress inside.

In the garbage closet at the end of the hallway, she grabbed the silver handle of the trash chute, opened it, and held the brown paper bag over the black nothingness that led down to a dumpster in the basement. Why had she not done this before, she wondered. What had she been thinking? What if George had found the dress? She shuddered. He spent most weekends at her apartment, and the dress had been there the whole time, as they made love, made dinner, lounged around her apartment, got dressed, got undressed. What would he think if he found it? She knew, or thought she knew, that he felt the same way about her as she did about him. But how naive of her to think that nothing could change that.

She made a quick flick of her wrist to hurl the bag down into the abyss. But it wouldn't release. She flicked her wrist again. But she couldn't do it. She couldn't let go. Something was stopping her. She pulled the bag back out of the chute, removed the dress, and unfolded it out in front of her.

It really was a beautiful dress. She remembered how nice it had looked on her. And how she had felt in it. There was something about the dress. Yes. She didn't know what it was. But there was something about the dress. Or, maybe, it wasn't the dress at all. Maybe it was something else. But she couldn't throw it away. It was hers, somehow. It belonged to her.

Clutching it to her chest, she ran back into the apartment and replaced it in the bottom drawer. As she was doing so, the doorbell rang. She froze for a moment, then went and let George in.

George set Alma's plate down on the coffee table with a bow and a flourish, reminiscent of a French waiter in a children's show.

"Thank you," Alma said, somewhat shyly.

He joined her on the couch, and they both dug into their steaks as the darkly rhythmic theme music of *Butterfly* began.

The heroine, Sylvia, was dealing with family issues that week. She was at a bar in her hometown, drinking a little bit too much.

George pressed pause on the remote. "Babe," he said. "What's wrong?"

"Nothing," Alma said.

"I feel like it's too quiet," he said. "I mean, I know we're watching TV, but ... are you sure you're okay?"

"Yeah, I'm fine."

The screen remained paused on a shot of Sylvia leaning forward toward the bartender, an intense look on her face, while George and Alma ate in silence.

That night, she had a strange, vivid dream. In it, she was a woman from a long, long time ago—around 32,000 years ago. She knew this in the dream. She wasn't aware she was dreaming, per se, but she did seem to possess some sort of special understanding of what was happening in a larger context. She lived in the most perfect of interglacial climes—not too hot, not too cold. In other words, "sweater weather." Actually, it was even better than sweater weather. It was "sweater optional" weather. She wore a simple, sleeveless, animal-skin dress, and a refreshing chill nipped at her arms.

She was part of a peaceful clan, who milled about a pleasant and nondescript landscape in a jovial manner, exchanging ideas and customs with other tribes. She knew the particular era of human development she was in was extremely important—an epoch of unparalleled advancement. Many of the very things that made us human were on the rise—language, art, music, tools—and there was rapid transmission of this knowledge between groups. Each person was like an eager sponge, soaking up as much culture as they could from everyone they met: tools, words, gods, art styles, fashion, dance, drum patterns, new melodies ... It was a very heady atmosphere.

Alma's clan was known for an interesting game they'd invented. People came from far and wide to learn it. It went something like this: one team would form the outlines of various animals on the ground, using rocks. Perhaps they'd form a deer, a fish, a mammoth, a snake, an owl, and a rabbit—usually five or six animals, depending on the number of players. The animal outlines were not detailed—they didn't look like the actual animals—they were more of a schematic shorthand that everyone understood. Then the other team took turns throwing a rock and trying to land it in one of the animals. Whichever animal it landed in, they had to run to. But the trick was, they had to run "as" that animal. So if they landed in the rabbit shape, they had to sort of hop there, as a bunny would.

The tribe loved watching, for example, Aunt Erinnku lumbering as a bear, and Grandpa Grrruuu hopping as a rabbit, and Cousin Flichnu running as a deer. And no one enjoyed it more than Alma. Throughout the dream, her entire body was infused with a sense of laughter.

But it was much more than entertainment—and this goes back to all the crazy learning and advancing that was going on. Because with this game, Alma understood, her tribe had inadvertently invented adverbs. Primitive adverbs—but adverbs nonetheless. Because every time someone landed a rock in the rabbit zone, for example, people would say he had to run "rabbitly." And when someone landed in a fish, he had to run "fishily." And when someone landed in a snake zone, he had to run "snakily." It was a huge leap forward—a completely new category of language—and thus, in a way, a completely new category of reality. On some level, everyone knew it. They were alive and ablaze with the import and possibility of it. They couldn't stop saying "rabbitly" and "rhinoly" and "snakily." And it wasn't too long before the adverbs got ever so slightly more abstract. They'd talk about someone performing "hoppily" or "babyly."

One day a tribe from the western coast arrived. They'd heard about the game and wanted to learn. There were about fifty of them. Alma watched as they approached, and one man began to stand out from the rest. He must have been a chief, or a prince. He was large of stature, and dressed in incredible finery. The colors of his skirts were vivid—violet, indigo, crimson, viridian—the likes of which no one had ever seen. And the cuts of his fabrics and skins were outrageously innovative—so daring, so asymmetrical, so sleek. And his use of layers was ingenious. Alma could even make out the beginnings of "draping" consciousness in his designs. It was apparent that his tribe, and him in particular, were making incredible advancements in fashion.

As the man moved closer, Alma could feel her heart

opening and opening, and getting wider and wider. It was as if a light had entered her, and was breaking her open, jettisoning all the unnecessary parts of her.

The beeping of the alarm woke her up. She looked around at her white room, felt her fluffy, white comforter, and heard the hum of her air conditioning, and for a moment, she didn't know where she was. Then she slowly came back into her body and her surroundings. She looked at the other side of the bed. George was gone. His work started hours and hours before hers did.

She got out of bed, opened her bottom drawer, and took out the dress. Then she rolled it up tightly, and placed it in her purse.

At work, she waited until everyone was settled in their cubicles. She took out the rolled-up dress, placed it all the way in the back of her top desk drawer, then placed her purse in the drawer, as usual. With a small silver key dangling from the end of a red telephone-cord bracelet, she locked the drawer. Then she placed the key in the *Hate Hunters* pencil holder on her desk.

No one would find it there. And if they did, she'd just tell them she'd found it at a thrift store, and was using it with her clients as a prop—as a tie-in to the bus campaign.

CHAPTER TWELVE

THE EXPANDED SELF

Things were going well for Jackie. All footage was being held, and she hadn't been featured on *Hate Hunters* for quite some time. Countless other racists had gone viral since her (she kept forgetting to decry them!)—and she was finally becoming old news. People weren't recognizing her on the streets.

In order to lock down her anonymous streak, and distance herself as much as possible from the reviled character she'd been, she'd decided to make a few adjustments to her appearance. Her very thin, very straight, very pale blonde hair had helped to make her instantly recognizable, so she gave herself a perm. Objectively speaking, it was a disaster. Her hair was so thin, and so limp, that she had to re-perm it every two weeks, which made it extremely dry and frizzy. So she ended up with chin-length, luminously pale, straw-textured tiny corkscrew curls—causing her to resemble nothing so much as an aging version of a young Shirley Temple, which really drew in the eye, quite the opposite of what she'd intended.

She'd also been forced to admit that her decades-long penchant for low cut tops and high heeled shoes had become a trademark of sorts, so she jettisoned a good portion of her wardrobe. She scoured the thrift shops and eventually settled upon what she considered to be a French gamine look—mostly navy-blue trousers and red nautical striped tops. But whereas she was trying for chic and continental and devil may care, she didn't quite achieve it. Her new look only planted her more firmly in Shirley Temple territory.

But while her new aesthetic could be jarring at times, and tended to make her stand out in a crowd much more than she had before, at least with her new curly hair, her jaunty blue suits with gold buttons, her red striped T-shirts, and her brightly colored athletic shoes, she looked rather jovial, and, therefore, less recognizable as an angry racist. In short, her plan had worked, and she was able to relax a little on the streets without the constant fear of being hate hunted.

Not only did she *look* less angry, she actually *was* less angry. It would be impossible to overstate the impact that *Danger's Tweets* had had on her life in that regard. It had reintroduced her to the magic of theater—and she'd been going to some kind of show almost every night since. Each time she saw a show, a little more light entered her world. She loved being part of the crowd, feeling connected, and being entertained, but most of all—she loved watching, instead of being watched.

Theater turned out to be an expensive habit, though, so she'd gotten the idea to volunteer as an usher. She'd set about calling theaters, but they were mostly full, and had waiting lists. So she zeroed in on an off-off-Broadway theater near her apartment that had a sign in the window asking for volunteers. She called the number, but the phone just kept ringing and ringing and ringing. She inquired at the box office, and they confirmed she had the correct number, and it belonged to someone named Josh, who was the volunteer coordinator. They encouraged her to keep trying, as Josh was an extremely busy person. So she kept trying, but the phone always rang about twenty times, then disconnected. She started hanging around the theater every night, hoping to run into Josh. She kept asking for him, but he was never there. The sign remained in the window. Finally, she started going to the theater at nine in the morning. She'd stand outside all day, drinking coffee, leaving only for bathroom breaks. Then one day at around noon, a disdainful-looking young man of about twenty-two, with a rumpled tweed jacket and a navy-blue scarf wrapped around his neck in an excess of flair, let himself into the theater with a key.

"Josh?" Jackie said.

He glared at her, looking her up and down mercilessly. She introduced herself, and explained she wanted to volunteer. His face lit up.

He hired her on the spot. He went on to complain that the sign had been up in the window for over five months, and nobody had responded. Jackie tried to tell him she'd been calling diligently and that his voice mail didn't seem to be working.

"I hate phones!" Josh said, explosively, then explained that he was into "slow living." He only had a landline. Also, no TV, no computer, and no social media, which explained why he didn't recognize her. They were kindred spirits of sorts.

With her ushering job, she was able to watch *A Summer in Ketchikan* up to four nights a week, and on her nights off, she went to other shows. Not only was she having a great deal of fun, but she found that the addition of regular, enjoyable experiences to her routine gave her the emotional reserves she needed to be able to control her anger in a pinch.

One Tuesday morning, she was walking along Seventh Avenue, not far from Washington Square Park. It was a lovely spring day. Tulips were popping up everywhere. Women were wearing light coats, unbuttoned, with colorful dresses beneath. A group of men was working construction on a multilevel parking facility across the street, and in between the sounds of their machinery, their jovial voices carried on the breeze. It was a good morning to be alive. Everyone seemed to be communing in the excitement of spring—a delicious, unspoken, shared mood. Jackie was basking in it. Or she was trying to. Because a businessman had been following her since Fourteenth Street, shouting loudly into his cell phone, and Jackie couldn't shake him, no matter how hard she tried. It seemed every time she slowed down, he slowed down too, in order to emphasize some particularly important point to whoever he was talking to. And when she sped up, he sped up too. He was about forty, with a thick head of black hair.

Jackie tried her best to tune him out. She had several little tricks up her sleeve for times like these—when she could feel her blood beginning to boil. The old Tamil man was never far from her mind—a cautionary image of what would befall her should she misbehave in public again. She used him as a mantra of sorts. "Tamil. Tamil. Tamil. Tamil. Tamil," she repeated to herself.

The businessman was bellowing very loudly and theatrically, as if not only talking to someone hearing impaired, but also performing the conversation for the entire street:

"Yeah, no, that's what they were saying in Dubuque," he

was shouting. "So, hopefully we'll get the green light on that. I think that'd be really exciting. With their market size, I think it's a good fit. I'll tell you what, would you mind just cc'ing Lemmers on that?"

Jackie mumbled to herself, "Yeah! Let's just cc Lemmers on that! Okay? I think that would be a really great thing to do! I think Lemmers would really like to know! Let's tell Lemmers! Lemmers! Lemmers! Lemmers!"

Then she caught herself. "Tamil. Tamil. Tamil. Tamil. Tamil. Tamil. Tamil. Tamil," she mumbled to herself.

"Oh? Margaret told you that?" the man was shouting. "Oh. Okay. Interesting. Well, why don't I just touch base with my guys, okay? Yeah. Mm-hmm. Sure. No problem. Yeah, just go to the dashboard and bring up analytics. Yup. Exactly. Okay. Yeah. Great, let's hold off on the report then. I'll bounce it off Greggers."

"Greggers!" Jackie said, rather loudly. "Greggers! Let's bounce if off Greggers! Would you like me to bounce it off Greggers for you! Huh? Is that what you want! I'll just bounce it off Greggers! Or should I bounce it off Lemmers? Huh? Greggers or Lemmers? Lemmers or Greggers?"

She caught herself again. "Tamil. Tamil. Tamil. Tamil. Tamil. Tamil. Tamil. Tamil," she incanted to herself, for all she was worth, and then, "Seventy million people speak Tamil. Tamil is spoken in Sri Lanka and the Indian state of Tamil Nadu. Significant Tamil-speaking populations are also found in several other Indian states, as well as Singapore. The earliest written work in Tamil is an inscription found in ..."

"Yup! Yup!" the man was shouting. "That's fine. Chris told me you guys were going to be announcing it, and that actually works out for us. So thanks so much, by the way, because that really takes some of the pressure off my guys. So, yeah, it'll be good to get together and hammer out what the real issues are."

"Yes!" Jackie screamed. "Yes! Let's do that! That sounds very important! I'm so glad you let me know! I can't wait to hammer out the issues! Let's just hammer it out! Okay! Let's hammer! Where's your hammer! Get your hammer!"

The man stopped and turned around to see what all the commotion was. He studied Jackie, and spoke into his phone. "Great," he said. "Yeah, uh-huh. I'll just have Tamara check my schedule ..."

"Oh, Tamara! Great! Have Tamara check your schedule!" Jackie screamed. The two were standing face-to-face now, in the middle of the sidewalk. Jackie forgot about everything, she forgot about Tamil, she forgot about the witch's dictum, she forgot about *Summer in Ketchikan* and her newfound sense of peace—everything, she forgot it all. Her face was as red as her nautical striped tee and high-top shoes, and she was screaming at full throttle. "Yup!" she shouted. "Let's just run that by Tamara! Could you do that for me! Or maybe Lemmers! We could run it by Lemmers! Or what about Greggers! Yes! Let's get Lemmers, and let's get Greggers, and let's hammer it out!"

The man had a puzzled look on his face. He put away his phone.

"Maybe Greggers has a hammer?" Jackie continued. "Or Tamara? I don't know! Just tell me what to do! I'm at your command, Mr. Businessman! I'm at your service! I aim to please! Should I call Greggers?! Would you like that! Or should I call Lemmers?" Then she just began repeating, with increasing volume and contempt, "Greggers or Lemmers?! Lemmers or Greggers?! Greggers or Lemmers?! Lemmers or Greggers?! Greggers or Lemmers?!"

Then, in the middle of her rage, it somehow dawned on her that the man she was shouting at was white, and the significance of that. "Wait!" she shouted. Now was her chance to prove to Alma and to the world, for once and for all, that it had never been about race.

She reached into her purse and fumbled around for her phone. She felt a hairbrush, a box of Kleenex, a tiny umbrella, a couple of *Stagebills*, her keys ... The man was starting to walk away, so she yelled, "And Tamara! Don't forget about Tamara! I bet Tamara has a hammer! And Greggers and Lemmers!"

The guy stopped and turned around, and Jackie moved in closer to him. She held out her phone at arm's length, adjusting her position until both of their faces were on the screen. The guy had a round, somewhat pleasant face, and he looked genuinely confused. "What is this?" he asked.

For some reason, the image of both of their faces together on the screen had an uplifting effect on Jackie. But she felt it was important to keep raging for the camera. "Oh! I was just hammering things out with Tamara!" she screamed. "Isn't that what you wanted me to do? And Greggers! And Lemmers! I'm supposed to run things by Greggers! And Lemmers! Right? Isn't that what you said? I mean, I can only assume you were talking to me, because otherwise, why would you be speaking so loudly, with your voice booming up and down Seventh Avenue?! I mean, you certainly didn't want me to be able to think, or enjoy my day, or enjoy my own thoughts, so I figured it must be very important! So just tell me what you want me to do with Greggers! And Lemmers! Okay! I'm waiting! What do you want me to do with Greggers and Lemmers? Should I call Greggers and Lemmers?"

The man thought for a moment. "Sure, call Greggers and Lemmers," he said.

The unexpectedness of the response caught Jackie off guard. She suppressed a smile. She spotted a woman with green ankle pants and a denim jacket walking down the street. "Hey!" she shouted. "I'm Jackie, the racist! From *Hate Hunters*!"

The woman looked up and down the street, then took out her camera.

Jackie put her phone away and started yelling again. "You're sooo important, aren't you?" she screamed. "Soooo important, Mr. Businessman! Walking around with your expanded self!"

"My what?" the man laughed.

The woman in the denim jacket started filming.

"I mean *excuse* us!" Jackie continued. "Excuse us all for living in your world. I suppose we're just like pieces of furniture to you! Right? Because this is your living room, right?! You own this whole place, right?" She gestured around the street, and to the city at large. "It's not a public space, is it? It all belongs to you. And there are no other people here except you, isn't that right? No other people that matter anyway!"

"Excuse me, Señor," said the woman filming.

The man turned to her, as if noticing her for the first time. "What?" he said.

The woman took this as confirmation that he didn't speak English.

"Is she bothering you?" the woman asked, and then, loudly, "Ella molesta tu?"

"What?"

"Don't worry!" the woman said, enunciating every word

very clearly. "I am not La Migra! No soy la immigracion! La Migra no soy! No worry! Okay! Yo no soy La Migra!"

The man looked confused and turned back to Jackie.

"That's right," Jackie said. "You think you're so important, I hate people like you. Always having to prove to everyone how important you are. You're just so ..."

But the man's expression was so funny, Jackie couldn't keep a straight face. They both started laughing.

And laughing.

And laughing.

The woman filming became annoyed. "Is this some kind of performance art?!" she said, and walked away.

Jackie and the man laughed for quite some time. As if they'd both been waiting for this exact excuse to laugh with a stranger.

After a while, the man said, "You take care of yourself, okay?" and walked away.

"Hmm," Jackie said to herself, standing where the man had been. She watched several people walk by. "Hmm," she said again. A thought was forming in her mind. A young woman was coming toward her, wearing earbuds and talking quietly to someone on the phone. As she walked past Jackie, Jackie smiled at her. The woman gave her a little smile and kept walking. "Hmm," Jackie said. Then another woman walked by, speaking Chinese on her phone. Jackie waved at her and smiled. The woman held the phone away from her ear, apparently surprised and delighted to be greeted. "Hi!" she said.

"Hmm," Jackie said.

Then she started walking. And she smiled and nodded at everyone she saw—as a social experiment. The results were—most people smiled or nodded back—about 65 percent—

including some of the people who were talking on their phones. “Hmm,” she said.

She walked into a bar on Greenwich Avenue. She took a seat and ordered a gin and tonic. And there, in the cool darkness, among the noontime drinkers, she thought things over. Two drinks later, she came to the bittersweet conclusion that it had been *she* who’d had a grudge against the world—this whole time—and not the other way around. She dismounted the barstool, a little unsteady, but determined to make up for lost time.

Emerging into the early afternoon sun, she let her eyes adjust, then picked a direction and walked in it.

“Hello!” she said, to a retro hipster girl in thrift-shop Pucci.

“Hi!” the girl said, loudly, then lifted her big round sunglasses to get a better look at Jackie. She looked her up and down, taking in her jaunty apparel. She smiled in approval.

An old man with a walker was looking into the window of a cheese shop. “How are you?” Jackie inquired. The man looked up and smiled and nodded.

Then a young man in a tracksuit walked past her, talking loudly on his phone. “Hello!” Jackie shouted. He didn’t hear her, he kept walking.

She stayed out all day, flirting shamelessly with the world.

As it grew dark, she found herself in Times Square, an area she typically avoided—there were so many tourists, and you couldn’t get past them for all the selfie taking. Now, she saw it in a completely different light. It was a collection of wonderful human beings, all in one place. A perfect opportunity to get a jump-start on making reparations to the human race, to all the people she’d wronged—by being so curmudgeonly, so resentful, so slighted, so angry, and so purposely left out—by declining to join the great parade that was life. She would greet them all! Everybody! Everyone in Times Square! She would make amends! She stood there, in the middle of it all, taking it all in—the lights, the flashing screens, the people. She smiled at everyone—she smiled at a young family from Bolivia, she greeted a high school marching band from Des Moines, she waved at a soccer team from Maine, she said hello to a family from Sweden—and a hundred other people. Everyone was looking up at the lights, looking at each other, watching each other through their camera lenses. Jackie greeted them all.

And then there were the people dressed as characters, charging people to pose with them. Jackie greeted them too —the Disney princesses, Winnie the Pooh, Humphrey Bogart, a gold-painted mime, Abraham Lincoln, a naked cowboy, naked painted ladies. Jackie stood among them, in her sailor suit, with her magnanimous grin, greeting everyone.

"Hello?" a German man with sandy-colored hair was saying, trying to get her attention.

Jackie smiled. "Hello!" she said.

"Hello!" the German man said again, smiling.

He had two children, a girl of about ten and a boy of about seven, and he pushed them toward Jackie. They sidled up to her and hugged her. "Oh my goodness!" Jackie exclaimed, looking down at them. "Hello! My name is Jackie. What are your names?"

When she looked up, the father was taking pictures of them. And before she could fully take in what was happening, he handed her a five-dollar bill, took the children, and left.

Then a crowd gathered around her, and more children started running up to her and posing with her, while their parents took pictures.

And before she knew it, she was hugging countless beautiful children, from all over the world, on a magical spring night, under the brightness of seventy-foot screens. And not just children, adults too—men, women, teenagers, the whole world—she hugged and posed for pictures with them all. She began refusing money, insisting instead that people take pictures with her camera too, so she could remember them.

When the square cleared out, she hurried over to the bodega. She was relieved to see Mohammad was still there. She took a selfie with him, outside the shop, both of them smiling deliriously among the cut flowers for sale—roses, carnations, tulips, hydrangeas, pink peonies, white lilies, purple irises, daisies, azaleas, chrysanthemums, snapdragons ...

By the time she got home, it was two in the morning. And whereas she usually felt a force field yanking her into the apartment, beckoning her to safety, she now felt a force field pushing her out. She wasn't done with the world yet. She stood in the dark hallway, taking in the ever-present smell of nondescript food—seemingly a blend of everything everyone had cooked over the past six months—and nothing particularly interesting. She smelled weak soups, insipid teas, dry pork chops, wilting carrots. She steeled herself, and opened the door.

She kicked off her red high-tops, and flung herself onto her bed. She felt a wave of restlessness. She stared at her little studio apartment. It was so quiet. So small. So confining. Even the trellis pattern on the wallpaper seemed to conjure up the bars of a prison.

She sighed, and picked up her cell phone. She began scrolling through all the pictures from the night: her and Mohammad; her and the naked cowboy; her and the gold-painted mime; her and the mother and daughter from Mexico—Ana? Estela? Her with the brothers from Naples—she didn't remember their names. Her and the naked girl. Jackie studied the elaborate swirls of paint on the naked girl's body. "Jeesh!" she said. Her and Harry from Yorkshire. Her and the girl with green and white striped socks—Jackie didn't know if the girl was supposed to be a character—a cheerleader? Or if she was just an eccentric, outgoing New Yorker. "I love you!" the girl kept saying to Jackie, whenever they'd cross paths in the square.

Jackie put down the phone. She was still wide awake. New York was open twenty-four hours a day, she reminded herself. She didn't have to stay inside her little cell. But where would she go? Oh! There was a diner a few blocks down on Tenth Avenue. Perfect! She would go there. She would get a Denver omelet. She got up from the bed, grabbed her purse, and headed toward the door.

But somewhere in the ten feet between the bed and the door, she changed her mind. It was only a few hours until daylight—it would be better to go out then, she reasoned. It would be more fun. She'd wake up with the world, befriend it anew with a fresh face! She kicked off her high-tops again and lay back on the bed. She stared up at the ceiling. She decided to try to close her eyes for a couple of hours. But after a few minutes, she picked up her phone again. She began flipping through the pictures once more. But this time, she lingered on each one for a long time—her and Mohammad, her and the girl with green and white striped socks, her and the naked cowboy, her and the gold-painted mime ... And she began to relive each moment. Vividly. She felt as if she could actually smell the flowers outside Mohammad's shop—the pollen on the lilies, the sweetness of the roses, the freshness of the leaves. And she could feel the cool night air on her face. She could see the lights in Times Square—the towering, constantly flickering screens. She could hear the sounds—the excited fragments of conversations floating in the air, the clipped tones of the Nordic languages, the mellifluousness of Spanish ... the enthusiastic "I love you!" of the girl in the green and white striped socks.

And as she lay there on her bed, there was a smile on her face—as if it was all happening in real time. As if she wasn't trapped in her little apartment at all. As if she was still outside, in all those places—in all those places at once. As if she was still at the bodega, still in Times Square. As if she was—everywhere. As if she was huge. As if she took up the whole city. As if she was ... expanded?

An expanded self? Was she an expanded self? No. No, she wasn't. She wasn't at all. She was just hanging out, by herself, looking at some photos, and remembering a nice night in her life. In fact, she was the opposite of an expanded self. She was a contracted self. She was quiet, out of sight. She wasn't posting her photos on social media—stamping meaningless duplicates of herself all over the world, surreptitiously encroaching into everyone's consciousness, all the while pretending to be friendly, with innocent-seeming little captions, like, "Hey, just hanging out with my BFF Mohammad!" Or, "Hey! Check out this naked chick I met!" Or, "Here I am with sweet little Estela! Love you baby girl!" No, she wasn't doing any of that. She was just enjoying remembering the night, and all the lovely people she'd met.

But ... what if that's what other people were doing, when

they posted their pictures on social media? No. They weren't. They weren't doing that at all. They were doing something completely different. They were bragging, they were showing off, they were competing with other people. They were performing—trying to make their lives seem charmed, enviable, fabulous. It had nothing to do with what she was doing.

She started going through all the photos again, but since she'd been thinking about the pretentious ways people captioned their photos, she found herself coming up with little captions in her mind, just as a joke. She got out of bed, poured herself a gin, and sat down on the couch with her phone. Before long, she was laughing out loud at her imaginary captions. And through the blinds, the first morning light began to peep in.

She decided to write down some of her captions, just to amuse herself, and to remember people's names, where they were from—things like that. She looked for a piece of paper, but she couldn't find one. She went over to the nightstand and grabbed her red spiral notebook—the one she was writing notes for *The Expanded Self* in. She began thumbing through it, looking for a blank page. But she soon got caught up in reading her notes for the book. Eventually, she got the other three red notebooks from her bookshelf and started reading all of her notes for *The Expanded Self*, from the beginning.

At eight in the morning, she closed the last notebook. She walked to the bathroom, leaned over the toilet, and threw up.

When she got back, she sat down on the couch, and looked at the four red notebooks on the table, each with the word "notes" scratched onto the cover in heavy black ink.

Had she really compared people posting their photos on social media to ... cancer?

Because in her present frame of mind, it actually seemed like quite a sweet thing to want to do. To post your photos, to publish your photos, to share your photos with the world.

In fact, it occurred to her that it might be something she really wanted to do, right now. Possibly even something she needed to do. That it might be of the utmost importance that she expand herself a little—for no reason at all. *Especially* for no reason. Just for the sake of—her self.

She opened up her laptop and tried logging onto her old Facebook account. It had been years, so it took a little maneuvering. But eventually she got in. The first post on her feed was a picture of a little girl of about five, in pajamas, with damp, freshly shampooed hair. She was hugging a teddy bear and smiling from ear to ear. It was posted by Grace Dublin, Dan Dublin's wife. Dan had been the only person at the public defender's office who'd fought for her when she was fired. According to the post, the little girl was named Tara, and she was their grandchild. Jackie "liked" the photo.

Then she started uploading all her photos from the night. All her selves—all her duplicated, replicated, fabulous selves—with all her new friends. And with each picture she uploaded, her chest expanded a little, and a little more air came in. She wrote captions for each photo. And she thrilled in imagining her three remaining Facebook friends reading them. She allowed herself to indulge in the simple pleasure of seeing herself through the eyes of others, and imagining herself as *good*.

On the picture of her and Mohammad in front of the bodega, she wrote, "His bodega is like my church. I'm not kidding. He's my sanctuary in an often cold city. He always makes me feel welcome."

On the picture of her and the girl with the green and white striped socks, she wrote, "This girl had the prettiest smile."

On the picture of her and the brothers from Naples she wrote, "To my Neapolitan friends, I'll always remember the laughs we shared."

On many others, she wrote some version of "Only in New York!" She got through about forty pictures, then passed out, facedown, on the couch.

CHAPTER THIRTEEN
UNSETTLING NEWS

George walked through the glass doors of the firm, excited to greet the work week. His project hadn't been on TV yet. Marine complained bitterly to him every time they were at social functions together that her producers wouldn't let her do any more *Bridge Builders*. It just didn't have the viewership. But ultimately, it didn't matter to George. Mondays were still his favorite day. His project was making incredible headway. Witnessed or unwitnessed—it was powerfully shifting the nature of the conversation in the world.

He was particularly excited about the progress he'd been making with Nadim. On last week's call, for instance, Nadim had actually been at a loss for words, for the first time in over a year, and possibly for the first time in his life. He'd been so incensed at George's constant use of the term "mistaken Muslims," that he'd become emotional. He'd cursed, he'd stuttered, he'd sputtered, and then he'd just finally gone mute. He'd folded, basically. It was a huge breakthrough, as far as George was concerned. Because while he may not have been as knowledgeable, or as adept at arguing as Nadim, he was *persistent.* And that persistence was beginning to pay off. He would win him over.

It was not yet 1:00 p.m. in much of the Middle East and Africa, and George had a marathon session planned. He'd hit them all. He placed his briefcase on the desk and turned on his computer. The report detailing last week's "terrorist" incidents was compiled and ready to go. He pressed print. He grabbed the page from the printer and began perusing the doings of the mistaken Muslims around the world. Thirty-two killed in Burkina Faso, and fifteen mowed down in a restaurant in Mogadishu—both courtesy of al-Shabaab. Four killed in Nigeria, twenty-three in Chad, and ten killed by two female suicide bombers in Niger—all Boko Haram's work. Six killed in the Democratic Republic of the Congo by ADF. Twelve dead in Mozambique by Ansar al-Sunna. Six cops killed in Pakistan, and twenty-two civilians in Afghanistan—both by the Taliban. Six killed in Syria by three female ISIS suicide bombers. One killed in the Philippines—courtesy of Abu Sayyaf. And then in Cairo there was ...

The piece of paper floated to the floor, and George stood there for a moment, frozen. He picked up the paper, folded it, and put it in his pocket. He spent the rest of the day writing and answering emails about the Beijing/Tanzania/Macedonia hotel-chain deal. He did it without thinking, almost as if in a trance.

At 7:00 p.m. sharp, he walked through the doors of Amiro Das, the new Austrian Moldovan inspired bistro that he and Alma had been dying to try. He spotted her at a table in the corner of the rather grand dining room, with its shining brass fixtures, formal white tablecloths, and soft, muted, yellow glow.

They looked over the drinks menu. George ordered a

Dark Knight IPA, which was described as "brightly hoppy—yet with undertones of impending and titillating doom."

Alma settled on Hedgecrook Sour, touted as "cinnamony, crepuscular, and paradigm shifting."

Alma was clearly upset, and once the beer orders had been placed, she began explaining to George what had happened. It seemed to him she was explaining it in a very disorganized manner, perhaps due to the depth of her emotion. But it was also true that he himself was very distracted. It was hard for him to get the gist of what she was saying.

"The thing is," Alma complained, "just because the State of New York doesn't understand genetics, doesn't mean *nobody* understands genetics. *Somebody* understands genetics. *Geneticists* understand genetics."

When the beers came, she calmed down a little bit. George began to piece together what had happened.

"That's awful!" he said.

"I know!" she said, and slid the offending letter across the table for him to read. He picked it up. It was embossed with the official seal of the State of New York and it read:

"This communication shall serve as immediate and binding notice that the 'chromosomally-addended' birth certificate which was issued to you, at your request, by the office of Birth and Death Certificates of the State of New York—a proud member of the Virtuous Federation of the United States of America—is hereby rendered invalid. Any and all use of said document from this day forth shall be deemed fraudulent. Any attempts to present said defunct document to any public or private entity as a form of identification, or for any other purposes, shall be punishable by up to one year in jail, pursuant to New York State Penal Law, section 170.20."

George looked up.

"Isn't it crazy!" Alma cried. She explained that she was still reeling, not just from the news, but also from the unnecessarily harsh and accusatory tone of the letter, which seemed to imply that she herself had dreamt up the chromosomal addendum scheme—in dereliction of the law—when in fact she had merely been an enthusiastic early adopter—at the state's invitation!

"Unbelievable!" George said, and continued reading:

"The robust body of scientific research notwithstanding, it is the State's opinion that the science of genetics is insufficiently developed in the areas of racial and national ancestry designation—with the exception of the paragraphs relating to forensic criminal proceedings, as laid forth by the relevant sections of the New York State Criminal Procedural Law."

The letter then went on to use a number of disparaging terms to paint consumer ancestry genetics in an extremely unflattering light, equating the whole enterprise at one point to astrology, and asserting that individual results were best used, "for entertainment purposes only."

But of course the real story was that the state had caved to intense political pressure. Apparently, Alma's coworkers weren't the only ones incensed by the innovative and pioneering chromosomal addendum program. The "vanity birth certificate scheme," as it had come to be known in the press, had been characterized as selling "designer oppression" to wealthy New Yorkers—shamelessly hawking noble designations that otherwise would have had to be earned through generations of sweat and suffering.

"I'm sorry, babe," George said, reaching for Alma's hand on the table.

But she pulled it back in order to gesticulate. "I mean, I know it's just political. I know that. I *know* I'm still black. I mean DNA doesn't lie. So it's not that. But it's just ... I mean it's the tone, do you know what I mean?"

"They're idiots," George said. "Don't pay them any mind."

Alma continued. "I mean, isn't that kind of ... I mean, how can they ... just *rob* me of it like that. Don't you think that's a little crazy-making? Don't you think it sort of denies ... my existence? My experience? How can they just announce, against science, that I'm not ... *black?*" She whispered the last word.

George took a sip of his Dark Knight. His thoughts kept returning to the piece of paper folded in his pocket. The contents of it weren't available to his mind at the moment. It was as if he had encapsulated them in a kind of protective bubble. But the feelings associated with the piece of paper shot through his body. He tried to focus on helping Alma.

"Look," he said.

But Alma began speaking at the same time. "I mean, of course, I know I don't experience oppression in this lifetime, far from it, but I still have the genetic whisperings, right? So, yeah, it's kind of crazy-making." She paused. "Look, I'm not trying to compare my experience in any way to ... yours." She lowered her voice. "I know I can't begin to understand what it's really like to live as a black person in America today. Having to deal with not just your genetic whisperings, but also current-day racism and oppression at every turn. Obviously, I have no idea what that's like ..."

For some reason an image came to George of him and his

mother standing on the Ponte Sant'Angelo in Rome. She had taken him to Europe as a high school graduation gift. She had on a light blue shawl with sequins that dazzled in the moonlight. A lone ferry ambled along the black water of the Tiber below.

"I hope I haven't offended you," Alma was saying. "I'm really, really sorry. Really. Maybe I've been making too big of a deal out of this. Maybe New York is right. Maybe I have no right to this ... *word* ... I have no right to call myself *black*. I haven't earned it. Even if, you know, science says ..."

"Alma," George said, leaning in. "None of this matters. Look, whether you're black, white, purple, green—it doesn't matter. And furthermore, you've done more to battle racism and oppression than anyone I know. I mean, even if you're white ..."

Alma winced.

"What I mean is," George continued, "even if you *were to be* white, well, who cares! Because you're definitely not whyte with a *y*. You're the least whyte with a *y* person I've ever known—of any color."

Alma was quiet, sipping on her Hedgecrook.

"Look," George said. "This DNA thing means nothing. Absolutely nothing. Believe me. It doesn't matter."

Alma continued to brood into her beer.

"I never told you this," George said, leaning forward. "But I did my genetics too." He hesitated for a moment. He'd never told a soul. But looking at Alma's face, he continued, "I've got white in me too."

Alma looked up. But the confession seemed to have the opposite effect of what George had intended.

"Oh no," Alma said. "Babe. I'm ... I'm so sorry. Here I am, going on and on about my mixed blood, never thinking what that might mean for you. Never thinking about the *implications*. I'm … I'm so sorry. I didn't mean to be so insensitive. I know what that …" she lowered her voice to a whisper, "I know what that means. Having white on your DNA report. I'm so sorry. I'm so, so sorry."

She reached out to touch George's arm on the table, but he removed it with an involuntary flinch.

"No," he said. "It's not that. What I mean is, I think this race thing—maybe it's not as important as everyone's making it out to be. I mean, do we all really need to have these assigned *roles* all the time? It's … uncomfortable. I mean, yes, I'm oppressed, but is that the only thing I am? I think maybe that's one of the reasons I like working with …" He was about to say "Muslims," but he stopped cold.

Alma hadn't been listening. "God! I'm such an idiot," she said. "Can you ever forgive me? Wait. No. It's not about me. Forget about me. Forget about my feelings. How … how are you feeling? How did you feel when you found out?"

"I don't want to talk about it."

"No. No. Yes, of course."

They sat in silence for a while.

"Look," George said. "I'm really sorry. I'm just not fully here. I'm worried about something at work, actually."

"What?" Alma asked, eagerly.

But he didn't know what to tell her. What could he say? That he had possibly sent someone to … *prison*? By … *debating*?

"Nothing. It's nothing," he said.

The subject was dropped and they both worked hard to enjoy a meal that ultimately turned out to truly live up to the buzz.

CHAPTER FOURTEEN
THE TWEET

At home in his study, George reached inside his pocket and touched the folded piece of paper. A sensation like metal crashing against metal reverberated inside him. He unfolded the paper on his desk and forced himself to look at it. About three-quarters of the way down the page, in the midst of all the terror attacks, was the story:

"Cairo. Well-known Egyptian blogger in police custody. Nadim Farhan, 38, prominent lawyer and author of a controversial blog, is accused of insulting Islam in a tweet published last Tuesday. Farhan is awaiting trial and faces possible charges of blasphemy and inciting sedition.

"The tweet, which has since been removed, reads, 'Woke West keeps insisting Islamic terror groups are 'mistaken Muslims,' when we all know they're just following the example and commands of our bloodthirsty prophet.'"

George folded up the paper.

No. It must be a misunderstanding, he thought. Then, with stiff fingers, he picked up his phone and called Nadim's home phone number. It rang—a long, low beeping sound.

He pictured Layla's face. It was round, like Nadim's. He remembered the sound of her laughter. The phone kept ringing. He hung up.

He stared straight ahead. The door of the study was blurry around the edges. It seemed to shift, moving in and out of its frame. George put his hands on the desk to steady himself.

He took a deep breath. Even if it was true, he reasoned, in all likelihood, everything would be fine. Nadim was ... he was ... well, he was a natural-born contrarian. And he got carried away sometimes, that was all. He didn't mean anything by it. And everyone knew that. They probably just wanted to rein him in a little, teach him a lesson. Scare him. It was all just politics. He was a well-respected lawyer. He'd be fine. He'd be going home soon.

Then a cold sweat broke out on his forehead as he began to remember other stories. Stories that had appeared on his printouts every week for over a year. Stories about people in exactly Nadim's situation. People who had spoken out against Islam, or who had been accused of doing so, and what had happened to them.

He opened his laptop and searched through the archived weekly reports.

Raif Badawi, a Saudi writer, had been sentenced to ten years in prison and one thousand lashes.

Asia Bibi, a Christian farm worker in Pakistan, had been sentenced to death for insulting Islam. Her sentence had been overturned on appeal, but—horrifyingly—the governor of Punjab province and another politician had been assassinated for advocating for her.

Also in Pakistan, two men, Taimoor Raza and Junaid

Hafeez, had been sentenced to death over their Facebook posts. There were others.

Seemingly, no one was exempt. In Indonesia, a Christian governor had been jailed for blasphemy against Islam. Also in Indonesia, an ethnic Chinese woman had been sentenced to eighteen months in prison for complaining about a mosque's loudspeakers. Her case had incited riots, and the burning and ransacking of Buddhist temples.

In Bangladesh, it was open season on writers apparently. There was story after story of the killings of writers, bloggers, and publishers—all unpunished.

In Iran, a female human-rights lawyer had been allegedly sentenced to up to thirty-eight years and 148 lashes for defending, among other things, a woman's right to choose not to wear the hijab.

The stories went on and on. George forced himself to stop.

He typed "blasphemy laws in Egypt" into his search bar. From what he could tell, it carried a penalty of up to five years in prison.

In bed, George lay stiff and sleepless, his thoughts jumbled, his limbs cold and unconnected.

His mind jumped around, landing on different images: Nadim playing chess in a coffee shop in Cairo; Layla's round face; Raif Badawi being whipped; the cold, black Tiber River; Alma's pained face across from him that night at dinner; the folded-up piece of paper on the desk; Marine talking to him at a party, a glass of white wine in her hand; Bernini's angels on the Ponte Sant'Angelo, wielding Christ's instruments of passion: the cross, the nails, the whips, the crown of thorns, the lance ...

George tossed and turned, and the images kept coming.

After a while, one word came into focus. *Insisting*.

Insisting.

He rolled it around in his mind.

Insisting.

"Woke West keeps insisting ..."

What was the woke West insisting?

What had he been insisting?

He thought.

Then it came to him. That Islam was good. That's what he'd been insisting.

But why? Why had he been insisting that? What had been the impetus? He searched his mind. He tried to remember the words he'd used in debating Nadim. The logic. The exact nature of the case he'd been building every week for over a year. But nothing came to him.

It occurred to him that he really didn't know all that much about Islam. So what had been his point? He didn't know. And then, he realized, with a sinking feeling, Nadim probably hadn't known either.

Nadim had most likely felt ganged up upon. And that's what he'd been trying to say. That's why he'd been stuttering and sputtering and cursing, and that's why he'd finally gone mute. He'd been trying to say that he was getting it from all sides—not just from Islam, but also from the "woke West." From everyone. Everyone was singing the praises of Islam. Not just singing—insisting. Both Islam and the West were insisting. Nadim had felt outnumbered, and he'd lashed out, with a tweet.

And what did "woke" even mean? What exactly had George been so convinced he'd been awake to? The true, uncensored history of whiteness? The tyranny of the white man?

Because it dawned on him, now, with a shudder, that it was entirely possible that for Nadim, Islam *was* the white man. And if Islam was the white man for Nadim, then it was also the white man for Asia Bibi, for Raif Badawi, for the Bangladeshi writers—and for hundreds, or thousands, or even millions of others like them. Some living. Some dead. For countless others in the Muslim world—Islam was the white man.

And if that was true, then George had been championing the white man, relentlessly. Or, at the very least, the whyte with a *y* man. He'd been championing oppression, subjugation, and persecution—relentlessly.

He lay there, slack-jawed, uncomprehending.

And the thing was, he'd *known*. He'd known exactly how oppressively powerful the voice that protected Islam in the world was. He'd been reading about it for over a year. And longer. For as long as he could remember. And yet, he'd chosen to add to that voice.

He got out of bed and went back to the study. He unfolded the paper on the desk and reread the tweet:

"Woke West keeps insisting Islamic terror groups are 'mistaken Muslims,' when we all know they're just following the example and commands of our bloodthirsty prophet."

What a brave tweet, George thought. What a courageous shout into the darkness—what a brave, desperate, lonely shout.

CHAPTER FIFTEEN

WHIMBY

If Islam was the white man, then why had Arun Merriweather placed Muslims so high up on the tree, above everyone, above even black people? George took his old dog-eared copy of *Orthosentia* down from the bookshelf. It had pride of place between *Black Skin, White Masks* by Frantz Fanon, and *Pedagogy of the Oppressed* by Paulo Freire. He began thumbing through it, looking for clues.

He came to a chapter titled "Shifting Nobilities and the White Man by Proxy Test." It sounded familiar. He read:

"Oftentimes readers, having studied my various posts detailing the nobility/suffering tree schematic, and having found themselves happily encamped on the higher branches, have written to me in a state of mild annoyance at finding themselves treated with moral scorn in certain situations, as if they in fact resided on the lower branches, among the whites—as if they were the colonizer rather than the colonized, the oppressor rather than the oppressed, the stained rather than the sainted. These readers mistakenly think that if they're in the noble camp once, then they're in the noble camp always, when nothing could be further from the truth. I've always urged these readers to visit my previous entry titled, "The Sainted and the Stained," but apparently to no avail. They keep writing. So I shall review here.

"Imagine for a moment if you will an actual tree, with multitudinous branches, and now imagine that a breeze comes along, causing some of the branches to shift their position relative to the others. Where one was above, it's now below. Where one was below, it's now above. That, my friend, describes perfectly the situation of shifting nobilities. And we're all subject to it, with very few exceptions. This is important to remember. And it's a good thing. Because it keeps us humble. All of us, at any moment, no matter how oppressed we may feel, might find ourselves temporarily stripped of our nobility, and plopped down onto the lower branches, as it were, among the whites. We might find that it is no longer our turn to testify to our own pain and mistreatment, but it has fallen to us instead to respect/protect/elevate those on the upper branches, and also, of course, whenever possible, to admonish our fellow whytes for their collective despicable behavior. And here, again, I think, because of my own diverse bloodlines, I'm uniquely qualified to say that without a doubt, we are all sainted, and we are all stained. Well, most of us. Certain identities are fixed. But that's for another dispatch. For the rest of us—everything depends on the situation at hand. Here are some illustrative examples of fluidity:

"A Latina poet may be rightfully enraged at the idea of having her grammar corrected by 'old white men.' And she might publish a poem about such an indignity, and it would be beautiful, and it would also serve as an education—particularly to those lower down on the nobility tree. Another example, again, Latinos—and of course their white sympathizers—might vehemently protest a taco festival put on by white men, and they would quite righteously be considered aggrieved. A noble culture has been appropriated. However, if a Latino man, even one with a black grandfather, shoots an unarmed black teenager, he quite understandably devolves to white in that situation, and is correctly referred to as white. Because it's obvious that it's his white, entitled, racist blood —and not his noble Latino blood—that has whispered to him to kill someone who is from another race. We are sure of this because we know the kinds of things the various genetic whisperings say. Because we know history. So, you see, because Latino people are mixed, if not genetically, then culturally, it's a fluid noble identity. Sometimes it's there, sometimes it's not—it all depends on the context, or, as is often said, the narrative.

"It really shouldn't be too hard to understand. But I'll provide another example. Are we in Nazi Germany? Yes? Then to be Jewish is to be exalted, sainted, noble, aggrieved. Are we in New York City, and are we boycotting white male businesses in honor of women and people of color? Yes? Then the Jew has devolved to white.

"Or take the example of white women, who can rightfully be said to have suffered in the extreme, having endured, up close and personal, century after century of oppression, abuse, and dehumanization—not to mention general clumsiness and cluelessness—at the hands of white men. Make no mistake, they are the injured party. However, in most other situations—say, when compared to truly noble people—they would rightfully be considered the stained party—the colonizers.

"And so on. I'm sure you can imagine a thousand other

examples of fluid identities. And I suggest to you that if this describes you, as it does me, you shouldn't fight it, but embrace it. For the role of the stained is just as important as the role of the sainted, although perhaps not as glamorous. As the stained party, or the white, in a given situation, you have one of the most sacred duties there is, which is to respect/protect/elevate the sainted party, and—to provide harsh and humiliating remedial education to your fellow stained."

George found himself nodding enthusiastically, having momentarily forgotten the reason for his quest. He continued reading.

"Now, reality is obviously more complicated than my schematic tree suggests. So what do you do if you find yourself in a situation where there are many factors at play, and you are uncertain as to which party is the sainted and which is the stained, relatively speaking? How do you know who to view charitably, and who to view suspiciously? How do you know who to listen to, who has the moral high ground, who to champion? Well, luckily, there's a cheat—a simple trick which should allow you to instantly and intuitively discern who the noble party is, and thereby prevent you from having to decide an issue based on its merits alone, which would be a grave miscarriage of justice. Because while it's important to listen to what's being said, it's equally, if not more important, to listen to who's saying it. We must always look at the bigger picture when deciding what's fair. In fact, it's not as important that a single individual receives justice or is treated fairly, as it is that the historically oppressed group be given the benefit of the doubt in all instances. This is called narrative justice. And it's bigger and more important than 'individual justice,' or 'common-law justice.' After all, we're talking about balancing out centuries of wrongs. And it's okay to trample on a few rights to right a few wrongs.

"So how do we decide who occupies the noble position in a given situation, when it's not immediately clear? As I said, luckily there's a quick test, and it's called the White Man by Proxy Test—or, quite simply, the WHIMBY Test. To perform the WHIMBY Test, just ask yourself, 'Who would best be substituted for the white man in this situation?' Or, 'On which side are the white man's values most at play?' Or, you can broaden it to include the values of the West. So, a really common example of this is the case of women's rights in noble, non-Western, oppressed cultures. At first glance, you might logically think, 'If the noble man is oppressed, then the noble woman is even more so, we should listen to her, we should take her side.' But that would be totally inaccurate, and that's where the WHIMBY Test comes in. Think about it—to champion women's rights in a traditionally male-dominated, noble, oppressed culture would be to attempt to impose Western values on that culture, that is to say—it would be neocolonialism at its worst. Therefore, the women's rights agitators in such cultures can correctly be seen to represent the values of the white man. And therefore they are wrong. To side with them might be naively seen as justice on the individual level, but it would certainly be a miscarriage of narrative justice.

"The same goes for religious minorities agitating for rights in cultures that are more noble than themselves. Freedom of religion is a distinctly Western ideal. Therefore, religious minorities in those more noble cultures, however 'oppressed' they may be—and this holds true especially if the minorities in question are Christian—are correctly understood to represent the values of the white man; that is, they in no way have the moral high ground. Same goes for gays, atheists, herbalists, and journalists in those cultures. They are white, or whyte with a *y* for the literal minded among you. One should always give the benefit of the doubt to the noble, oppressed, dominant culture."

George raised his eyebrows. He realized that until today, he had indeed been subconsciously applying the WHIMBY Test to all the Muslim freethinkers he'd been reading about. He'd seen them as trying to impose Western values on an already beleaguered culture. He continued thumbing through the book. He came to a section in the appendix, titled "A Special Note About Muslims." He read:

"I have decided here to discuss a topic that might be considered somewhat of a special interest subject. A reader of my blog once wrote me asking why, in my tree schematic, Muslims were placed above blacks, given their rather extensive history of owning and trading in black slaves. Initially, I was somewhat taken aback by the question. First of all, I was quite shocked that one of my readers had decided to call into question the history of a noble culture. I found it to be in rather poor taste. Why would my reader feel compelled to try to malign a culture that was already injured, hobbled, and barely keeping its head up?

"Secondly, I felt at a distinct disadvantage in that I had no way to ascertain the identity of the questioner, and therefore I had no idea how to contextually evaluate his query. In short, I didn't know his race. He had a common, typical, Anglo name, and had taken the unusual and somewhat antiquated step of writing his letter out by hand and sending it by post. So I couldn't find out who he was by, say, looking up his social media. This left me in a quandary. I simply had no idea how much nobility to assign his argument. Was he a black man, who quite understandably wanted to exalt the position of his own historically oppressed people? Or was he a racist white pedant, stirring up mischief?

"It really was very annoying. I ended up having to do quite a lot of research. Much more than I would have liked. If I could have tailored my response to his positionality, it would have been much more expedient. For example, had I known for certain that he was white, which I'm strongly beginning to suspect he was, I could have shut him down on those grounds alone.

"In any case, I did my best to answer him. I didn't include my response on my original blog, *Colonizer, Colonized, I*, as I didn't think the topic was of general interest—only the one person had ever queried me about it. I felt that for most of my readers, the answer was intuitively understood. However, I shall address the issue here, for the edification of the future curious.

"So, yes, it does seem that, between the trans-Saharan, Nilotic, Red Sea, and East African trade routes, among others, Muslims did in fact import quite a large number of black slaves from sub-Saharan Africa into the Muslim world, as well as to other destinations, including India and China. And the numbers do seem to rival those of the transatlantic slave trade—of which trade to the US and territories that would become the US comprised less than 4 percent.

"Of course, the slave trade in the Muslim world is not as well studied as the transatlantic slave trade, for obvious reasons, chief of which being—it's rude. But I'll do my best.

"From Islam's inception in the middle of the seventh century until about the year 1600—so for about 950 years—there was a steady influx of about 8,000 black African slaves per year into the Muslim world. To the untrained eye, yes, that does seem like a lot. US numbers reached or exceeded 8,000 in only about 17 of the 250 years that slavery existed there—according to liberal estimates. But numbers can deceive, as we shall see.

"Then from 1600 to 1800, the average number of black slaves transported into the Muslim world increased to an estimated 10,000 per year.

"Then, in the nineteenth century, approximately 12,000 slaves were transported annually into the Muslim world, bringing the total number for that century to 1.2 million—nearly triple the amount of black slaves ever transported to the US. But again, comparison is misleading, which we shall get to later.

"And I'll end by conceding that, yes, by all accounts black slavery did seem to linger longer in the Muslim world. There are reports of a slave market operating in Mecca as late as 1941. And Saudi Arabia, Oman, and Mauritania were among the last countries to officially abolish slavery, in 1962, 1970, and 1981, respectively, although the actual practice lingered some years longer.

"Look, it's almost impossible to try to summarize a millennium and a half of black slavery in the Muslim world, and I deeply resent being forced to attempt to do so.

"But lest we get mired in false equivalencies, let me point out the obvious—all slavery is not equal. Slavery in the Muslim world was of a different nature entirely than slavery in the Americas. Now, just to be clear, slavery is a most barbaric, cruel, and inhuman institution, and it should never be wished upon anyone.

"But that being said, let's imagine for a moment you were a black slave captured in Africa, destined for the Muslim world—North Africa, for example. And let's suppose that you were one of the lucky few that happened to survive the actual slave raid. And let's further suppose you were one of the approximately 80 percent that survived the notoriously brutal Sahara crossing, for instance, and did not, like so many others, succumb to infections resulting from crude, unanesthetized castrations; illness; thirst; starvation; or exhaustion. Imagine your relief, then, at the end of your journey, to find yourself enslaved by a kindly, oppressed people, who practiced a peaceful religion—as opposed to a sadistic white plantation owner!

"A slave's lot in the Muslim world was about as far away as one could get from hard, enforced labor. On the contrary, it was domestic and delightful! One was taken into hearth and home, nestled to the bosom of the family—virtually adopted. And the numbers bear out this characterization! For the vast majority of the history of the Muslim slave trade, the ratio of females to males taken was at least two to one—the reverse of the transatlantic slave trade. It's well documented that slavery for women in the Muslim world was largely domestic and sexual—in other words, not so bad!

"And for the men, the possibilities were endless—well, not quite as endless as for white and Turkish male slaves. But in Muslim India, for example, several black slaves became rulers! Even in North Africa and the Middle East, some attained high positions in the household and administration, and others were conscripted into the military. And in the tenth century, one black slave even became a ruler of Egypt.

"Although it must be said, for some, the price was admittedly high. Unfortunately, for black eunuchs, removal of the entire scrotum and penis was the practice, whereas white children were often left with the penis intact—that is, until white eunuchs became scarcer and more expensive, and then all but disappeared as their countries of origin began enforcing antislavery laws.

"But still, if you were one of the one in ten black eunuchs that survived the operation, things looked pretty sunny indeed.

"Now it must be said that this rosy characterization of slavery in the Muslim world is currently under review. It now seems that, yes, during several periods of history, the lot of black slaves in the Muslim world was also in fact harsh labor, similar to the plantations of America. The salt flats of Basra come to mind, as well as the salt and copper mines of the Sahara, and the gold mines and sugar plantations of Upper Egypt. And then of course the clove plantations of Zanzibar —which at their peak boasted individual plantations with as many as 6,000 slaves.

"And when President Lincoln blockaded the Southern ports during the American Civil War in the 1860s, Egypt was quick to pick up the slack in the international cotton trade, importing some 25,000 to 30,000 slaves per year into that country alone.

"And admittedly, during these long and frequent but nevertheless completely uncharacteristic periods, it does appear that the life of a black slave in the Muslim world did rival in bleakness and brutality the life of an unlucky slave on an American plantation.

"But really, for the majority of slaves in the Muslim world, for the majority of history, the conditions really were ... Well it was a decent life. Of course, there's no denying that there were probably isolated incidents of heartlessness and cruelty on the part of Muslim slave owners toward their black slaves. However, such cruelty must be evaluated in its proper context. If you're unfamiliar with the concept of noblerage, I urge you to consult the chapter by that name. But to review briefly, a noble, oppressed group can only be pushed so far, over the span of so many generations, before their genetic whisperings begin to scream and howl for action. These screams are normally fuel for change, and they are quite beautiful to witness. However occasionally a noble group's noblerage is so great that they may have no choice but to lash out at an innocent victim—in this case, black slaves. But the Muslim slave owner is not to blame, as the rage is due to his own miserable, repressed state. As the saying goes—hurt people hurt people. Oh—and white people hurt people. Yes, hurt people hurt people, and white people hurt people—but for very different reasons. The cruelty of white people is based in their privilege, racism, and greed.

"Which brings me to another point about Muslims—but before leaving the topic of slavery, let me just add that the position of Muslims on the nobility tree cannot be evaluated solely on the basis of slave ownership. Practically every society throughout human history has engaged in this brutal practice at one time or another. Therefore it would be a particularly odious form of racism to suggest that Muslims be singled out and judged for this very human custom. But to return to the concept of noblerage, I have found that there is no greater indicator of the extent of suffering of a group than the degree of noblerage they possess. And as anyone can observe, hardly a week goes by without the resplendent noblerage of Muslims erupting somewhere on the planet, sometimes multiple times per week. Such explosions of noblerage, if mindfully observed, are majestic to behold. And here I will insert a special note to my fellow whytes: do your best to mindfully observe and sympathize with this rage whenever you can, and join in on it when at all possible. For if you can employ your hard-edged, inborn, sadistic *whiterage* in service of noblerage—any noblerage, not just Muslim noblerage—you can actually convert it, temporarily, into *diamondrage*—all of which I go into at length in the previously mentioned chapter titled 'Noblerage.'

"Anyway, I don't have time to get into all the ways in which Muslims are oppressed throughout the globe, and I'm quite annoyed that I should be expected to do so—just because my inquisitor decided to be a coward and hide behind the US Postal Service. My research on Muslim oppression in the world is very much ongoing, and perhaps my findings shall be published later in a book—or perhaps several books. But for now, I will say that I have witnessed firsthand that here, in Europe, many Muslims are very angry about their treatment. And while I have only been to India once, for my second cousin Ravi's wedding, I know that they are angry there too—as I said, I shall get back to you on the details. But I do know that throughout the world, Muslims are quite justifiably enraged about the mind-boggling gall of the usurper state of Israel, which has planted its white, impudent, colonial flag on a piece of land so tiny that it can only have been done as a taunt against Muslims. Imagine the sense of outrage and despair you might feel if your historical, visceral enemy carved out a nation for itself smack-dab in the middle of your rightfully conquered territory comprising some 50 nations! What would you do? How would you deal with such an insult?

"Again, I am bristling to know the identity and therefore the intentions of my inquisitor. Are you a fellow noble? If you are, I feel confident that by now, having read my explanation, you should be beginning to feel some sympathy for your fellow oppressed group—in spite of the bad history between you. Actually, I think if you really were black, or noble, you probably would have felt sympathy in the first place—and you never would have lashed out against a noble culture with your galling question. You would have known instinctively that all oppressed cultures need to protect one another from criticism, and you would have known that any criticism of an oppressed culture is likely be taken as a license to murder on the part of whites, who are genetically deranged and programmed to kill. And if you are indeed a white person, then shame on you. It shows incredible bad faith to shine an examining light on another culture when we've hardly run out of bad acts to examine in our own history. In fact, I can confidently say that we could scrutinize Western civilization for the next 300 years and never run out of shameful acts to decry. We all know that this is where the focus is supposed to be. There's no need for anyone to look elsewhere. If we can get our own shit sorted out, the rest will fall into place—trust me on that.

"You know, the more I think about you, the more infuriated I become. Why don't you just say who you are? Go ahead! Unmask yourself, if you dare! I have said who I am. I have nothing to hide. I'm half Indian, half English. Half conquered, half conquistador. Half colonized, half colonizer. Half sainted, half stained. Who are *you*? WHO ARE YOU!!!!"

CHAPTER SIXTEEN

THE 12 TRAIN

Beautiful woman on the 12 train,
Why are you hiding from me?
You've covered yourself from head to toe,
But your beauty's still plain to see.

Your hair, your cheek, your smile is a mystery,
But no matter what you do,
Your loveliness peeks through your pretty brown eyes,
And your soul's goodness shines through.

You're reading your Quran, so I won't disturb you—
Your mind's on the everlasting.
And it's not like I could really ask you to dinner,
I don't even know if you're fasting.

So goodbye pretty lady on the 12 train,
We'll soon go our separate ways—
But actually this train is moving so slow
It might be a couple of days.

Billy Skullet read over the poem he'd just written. It wasn't bad. The train he was on was traveling extremely slow—stopping, then starting, raising hopes, then stopping again. But mostly stopping. They'd been somewhere in the miles of underground tunnels in Queens for at least the last forty minutes. He'd gotten on the train in Manhattan, right after work, and was headed home—to the last stop in Queens. He'd grown tired of his word search puzzles a while back and was now engaged in in-depth character studies of his fellow passengers, one of whom had inspired the poem—a Muslim girl with her face entirely covered, except for her eyes.

He folded up the piece of paper with the poem on it and looked inside his "17th Annual South Jamaica Job Fair" tote bag for a safe place to store it among his thermos, orange juice, raisins, pen case, word search puzzle books, and large-print sudoku books. He found a paper pharmacy bag folded up at the bottom, and he placed the poem inside.

It really was a good poem, he thought again, and he wondered if it was *Skullet Family Times* worthy. At this thought, a wave of nostalgia passed over him.

His mother, who'd been an assistant language arts teacher at his elementary school, had wanted to foster an early love of language in him, and to that end, she'd come up with the *Skullet Family Times*. Every month or so, or whenever enough submissions had come in—his dad wrote about sports and news, his mom had an advice column and also covered family news and school happenings, and Billy submitted comics, riddles, poems, and short stories—she would put together an issue and make three copies of it using the school's mimeograph machine. There was always a great fanfare when it was "published." The three of them would sit around the kitchen table, reading the paper with great interest, announcing noteworthy findings and discussing them.

Every once in a while Billy still put out an "issue." And he'd imagine the paper's other two subscribers reading it up in heaven. He thought they'd really like this poem. He rested the tote bag back down on the floor between his legs, and turned his attention back to his word search book. He spotted the word "escargot," which had been hidden for quite some time. He circled it, and grinned.

"And the companions of the Fire will call to the companions of Paradise, 'Pour upon us some water or from whatever Allah has provided you.' They will say, 'Indeed, Allah has forbidden them both to the disbelievers.'"

Ruby's eyes were open wide as she read from her green, dual-language Quran. Surah 7, verse 50 had always grabbed her. Of all the descriptions of the afterlife in the Holy Quran —the sheltering date palms and eternally virginal maidservants known as houris on the one side, and the burning of flesh and reissuing of skin and re-burning of flesh for all eternity on the other—this one stood out the most in her mind, not only because it painted a clear picture, particularly in terms of spatial geography, with the fiery pit below, and all the inhabitants of paradise above, looking down, in an arrangement much like stadium seating, or at least that's how she pictured it in her mind—but also because it had a plot. A plot and characters. Characters with desires, wants, and needs. And a dialogue. Not much of a dialogue. But enough. With a little imagination, the whole scene was very dramatic. And for that reason, perhaps, the verse seemed to come to Ruby's mind a lot.

Like when she looked at her ruby ring, the one her father had given her for her birthday, which now sat poised on her fourth finger. To her, the ruby in the middle represented hell with its brilliant flames, and the many diamonds surrounding it were the sainted Muslims, bathed in God's light, looking down. But how were they looking down? That was the question. With what attitude? With what emotions? With scorn? With pity? Satisfaction? Schadenfreude? A sense of justice served? That was what made it interesting, and what made it literature, in Ruby's mind.

She looked up. The train was stalled again—"somewhere in Queens." In a tunnel. It was an old train, with hard orange seats, dirty grey floors, and no digital readout to tell people where they were or what was going on. It was a crowded train, and a lot of people were standing.

The relationship between the diamonds and the ruby, the Muslims and the infidels, was not simple. Not to Ruby, anyway. She believed that the Muslims felt genuine sadness as they looked down upon their fellow human beings suffering in the pit of fire, and that they wanted nothing more than to send them down a glass of water, maybe some fruit juice, or some dates. Maybe she was just projecting her own feelings onto them, but why wouldn't they? God had created man with compassion. He had put empathy and mercy into the heart of each and every one of them. Or most of them, anyway. After all, wasn't that why Ruby wanted to go into medicine? To give water to the thirsty? To heal and comfort the sick? There was no doubt that in man, God had created a true masterpiece. Man was complex—a whole universe existed inside him. He was full of feelings, passions, and ideas. But that was just it. If God's creation had ended with man and mountain and nature, then it would have been correct to assume that man was meant to live according to his feelings and his ideas—his own internal moral compass. But creation hadn't ended there. God had also given man prophets, and a book, a very clear book, with straightforward guidance. Why would he have done that if man was meant to rely on himself? Man was clearly meant to follow those prophets and that book, and not his feelings or his thoughts. Feelings and thoughts could be informative, and useful, but one had to admit that they had some pretty strange properties. They were not fixed, for one. They seemed to change from moment to moment, with every small breeze. They flipped and flopped all the time, and were often founded on misinformation to begin with. They were really nothing to base a life on. That's why God, in his mercy, had not left man afloat on his feelings and thoughts. He had sent to him clear, unwavering guidance, an instruction manual—two instruction manuals, actually: the Quran, and the life and sayings of the Prophet, peace and blessings be upon him.

In the verse she was reading, the Muslims obey God and do not send water down to the inhabitants of the fire. But if that decision were based on their feelings alone, Ruby felt, the Quran would have simply had them say, "No," when asked, instead of, "Indeed, Allah has forbidden them both to the disbelievers." In fact, she liked to imagine an extra line of dialogue in the scene, where the inhabitants of paradise turn to God and ask his permission to send down water, and God says no, so then they turn back to the inhabitants of the pit and tell them God has forbidden it.

And although he doesn't have to, God, in his mercy, explains his reasoning. In the surrounding verses, God reminds everyone of all the opportunities the infidels had to acknowledge the truth of Islam while they were on earth. And he points out that in their arrogance, they chose not to.

The train was still stalled, and the passengers seemed

antsy. They looked around, this way and that, trying to figure out, in the darkness of the tunnel, what was going on.

Ruby looked at the Arabic version of the verse on the opposite page. Although her speaking and understanding of the Arabic language had come a long way, the alphabet had yet to yield its secrets to her; it remained coy. The problem was that although there were twenty-eight letters, representing twenty-eight distinct consonant sounds, about half of those letters had doppelgängers or near doppelgängers elsewhere in the alphabet. Three letters looked like big identical *u*'s; three others were identical *t* shapes; two were identical *w*-looking letters; two resembled *e*'s; and two were like *b*'s. The rest were not identical, just "similar." Ruby couldn't for the life of her figure out why this had come about. It wasn't like there was a shortage of shapes in the universe to choose from. English *k*'s, *w*'s, *o*'s, and *f*'s, for example, were all very distinct looking, and no one would mistake one for the other. The Arabic look-alike letters were distinguished by the presence, absence, number, and placement of some tiny dots. But in cursive, where all the letters ran together like tiny waves along the shore, it hardly made a difference. The dots were just little splashes of foam around the general text. As a result, the page Ruby was trying to read looked to her like an indistinguishable mass of deliriously beautiful, infinitely repeated *w*'s, *u*'s and *i*'s.

The train jolted forward a few inches. Then it stopped. Then it shook. Then it jolted again. Then it kept moving. After it had been moving for a little while, the nervousness in the air began to abate—but not completely. Ruby couldn't help but notice that many of the passengers seemed to have their attention focused on her. An older white lady across the aisle from her, for example, with preposterously large blue eyes, made even larger by her thick glasses, was staring at her, her fists clenched at her sides.

This was nothing new. "Hey lady!" Ruby wanted to say. "Are you afraid I'm hiding a bomb in my burqa? Are you? You might be right." Ruby had been wearing the niqab—the cloth that covered her entire face except for her eyes—for the better part of a year, and she had been covering her hair for three years. She had many reasons for adhering strictly to the Muslim dress code, as she interpreted it. And she had reaped many benefits: subtle benefits, interior benefits—benefits of the soul. For one, her self-respect had increased. Islam was the most important thing in her life, and by dressing in the most pious way she could, she felt she was being true to herself. Strangely, she also felt that respect from others had increased—and she didn't know how that worked exactly, in an atmosphere of rampant Islamophobia, but it was true, she felt that other people respected her more. It was hard to understand or explain. And she felt closer to God, and closer to her Prophet, peace and blessings be upon him, at every moment, like she was touching the sacred in the midst of the profane. She felt less affected by all the haram—or forbidden—things going on around her. She felt pure, unpolluted, apart: as if she was moving around in her own private dar al-Islam—house of Islam—in the midst of dar al-harb—house of war. An unanticipated benefit of the face covering—a delicious, unexpected perk—was that she got to scare the crap out of Americans on a daily basis—just by going about her business.

It wasn't just the white lady across from her. The Hindu kid sitting three seats down from the lady kept looking up from his Game Boy, or whatever it was, and staring straight at her, as if monitoring her for sudden movements. A Latino man in his forties was hovering over her, supporting himself on the handrail. He had on a Mets baseball cap, and he seemed to be contemplating her shamelessly. Tiny beads of sweat were forming on his skin, and his lips were moving silently, angrily, as if he really had something he wanted to say to her. Like he might try to give her a piece of his mind at any moment. She wished he would.

A white businessman with grey hair sat in the forward-facing seat diagonally across from her. He looked rich. He was probably a lawyer or something. He was watching her out of the corner of his eye. What would he do if he was actually confronted with a bomb on a train? Would he take charge? Would he be a "hero"? Had anything in his soft, privileged life prepared him for that?

The problem with Americans was that they could dish it out but they couldn't take it. They waged war with seeming impunity on the Muslim world using their money, their power, their B-1s, their tanks, their Apaches, their M4s: and most disturbing of all, their immoral and illegal support of the apartheid state of Israel. And yet, their own skins remained relatively soft and untested. Their arrogant actions in the Muslim world would come home to roost. They would reap the wrath they had sown. They would realize they were not untouchable. They would realize that they, too, were human, vulnerable, mortal.

"Those poor, poor Muslim women. My heart really goes out to them," Kathleen Meyers thought to herself. She could see the fear in the eyes of the young girl sitting across from her. In fact, all she could see were her eyes. The rest of her was completely covered in black. She really felt for those women. Kathleen didn't know where exactly in the world the girl had come from, but she knew that wherever it was, she had probably been afraid there too. Afraid her whole life! And then she'd moved heaven and earth, gone through hell probably to get here—to America—hoping for a better life for herself and her family, only to find out that this supposedly free nation scorned her for her religion—for simply being who she was! Kathleen opened her hands wide, stretching them out. Then she made a gentle fist again. It was her own—probably irrational and superstitious—way of staving off the debilitating arthritis she felt was chasing her down through the generations—just waiting to get its grips on her.

Poor girl, Kathleen thought again. Americans suck! Why couldn't we just welcome her? Then, she remembered she had to write a note to Debbie about the Tablets in the Schools Fundraiser. She made a mental note to do so as soon as she got home—before she started dinner. No, actually, she would take out the chicken and preheat the oven first, then write the note.

One thing Ruby thought about from time to time was whether Sofia and her fiancé Anatoly would end up in the pit. It was still so shocking to her that Sofia had found love—seemingly the real thing—so early in life. Anatoly seemed to have appeared from out of nowhere, but once he was there, the two were inseparable. They even looked alike, like brother and sister—as if they had both spent time in the same womb—with their delicate features, their small, bird-like bones, their mousy-colored hair, and their same easy-going, passive temperament.

She imagined them in the pit. She imagined their faces, red and tearful, looking up, begging her for a glass of water. Of course, she would want to give it to them. She wondered if they would be holding hands in the pit—if they would be together in the afterlife, or if they would be tossed around and separated by the flames. There really wasn't an answer for that. The thing was, a lot of it didn't make sense if you thought about it too literally. Like how could the inhabitants of the fire enunciate enough to ask for water if their skins were being burned? Perhaps there would be breaks in the torture—after a new skin had been issued and before the next round of flames began. Ruby reminded herself that on a certain level it was all just metaphor. God described things man could comprehend, to explain things man couldn't comprehend.

Maybe Sofia and Anatoly would be in paradise alongside Ruby, sipping cool drinks under date palms, wearing silk clothing. They were good Jews, after all. And Jews were fellow people of the book, which counted for something. But if Ruby was being totally honest with herself, she knew they wouldn't be beside her. The Quran was clear, you couldn't recognize some of God's prophets, and refuse to acknowledge others. You had to acknowledge all of God's messengers, including Mohammad, peace be upon him, the final one. After all, Muslims acknowledged Moses, Jesus, and all the rest, so why couldn't Jews and Christians acknowledge Mohammad? It was sheer arrogance. They each thought they were special and that the messages had ended with them. And even when it had been their turn to receive the messages—the word of God—they had stubbornly refused to heed them. And they had corrupted them. The Jews had hidden and obfuscated the passages in their book referring to Mohammad, and the Christians had elevated Jesus, a mere man, to the level of God, and worshipped him alongside God. In doing so, they had committed idolatry—which was the most unforgivable sin of all. So yes, the Jews and Christians would be in the fire, writhing alongside the atheists and the polytheists.

Vikram sat on the train, staring straight ahead. He couldn't focus on *Song of Titan*, the game he was playing. The music just looped, and his character, Gulkkamar, shuffled back and forth, looking lost and goofy, like an awkward teenager on the sidelines at prom. Gulkkamar, despite his impressive size, his fierce half-man, half-beast visage, his long beard, his horns, his fire-throwing tomahawk, and his enemy-detecting shield—couldn't make a move unless Vikram told him to. He was utterly helpless. And Vikram hadn't told him to do anything for the past ten minutes. Because Vikram couldn't stop thinking about his mother.

It had been a Saturday, about a month earlier. Vikram was playing *Song of Titan* in his room, and his mother, Lalita, who had just finished putting away his laundry, was sitting on his bed, talking. Vikram wasn't listening—he was focused on the game. But there was nothing unusual about that. His mother could handle it. She was strong. She was like an independent avatar. Unlike Gulkkamar, she didn't need any input. She didn't need a nod, or a "really?" or a "go on ..." or an "oh, how interesting, that happened to me once ..." in order to keep talking. She was impressively self-sustaining.

And her stories were always the same. She was an environmentally conscientious raconteur in that way. She recycled faithfully. There were stories about her childhood in India, stories about the funny thing the woman in the shop said to her two years ago, stories about her sister's problems with her horrible, disobedient children, stories about Vikram's father's refusal to listen to her ... a whole repertoire. And when telling the stories, she always used the same tone of voice: amused and aggrieved at the same time. No matter what the story was, there was always an implied indictment —sometimes very subtle—not only against at least one of the characters, but also against you, the listener, for not listening enough—or for some other unspecified sin.

A few times a year, seemingly at random, she'd become briefly enraged, and shout that she wasn't being heard—but only for a moment, then she'd go back to normal, as if nothing had happened.

That particular Saturday, Vikram, as Gulkkamar, was navigating the treacherous landscapes and complex tribal systems of the Sabin Territories, when suddenly, out of nowhere, and for no discernible reason, he became more interested in the story his mother was telling than the story on the screen.

It wasn't as if he hadn't heard it a thousand times before. He had. He knew it by heart. It never changed. Not one word. And she was telling it in exactly the same way she always told it, laughing to herself at the exact same climactic moments. It was the one about the time she and her cousin Dev had snuck out to go to the movies as teenagers. First, they were scared about being caught the whole time and couldn't focus on the movie. Then, on the way home, one of the soldiers on the street had asked them if their father was C.G. Shetty—at which point they became so afraid that they ran off without answering. Later, they realized the soldier was a friend of Lalita's father, C.G. Shetty, and had been over to the house several times. But in the heat of the moment, they'd thought that Lalita's dad, a low-level bureaucrat at the Department of Public Works, had called the army on them.

Then, shaken, they'd lost their way home on their usual shortcut through the edge of a not-so-dense forest, all the while scaring each other half to death with stories of the tiger that had recently escaped from a nearby preserve. They ended up running deeper into the forest by mistake, where they huddled together against the trunk of a giant rosewood tree, terrorized by the sounds of owls and frogs until daybreak. When they got home, C.G. Shetty was a furious, nervous wreck.

Sitting there at his computer that day, after hearing the story for the thousandth time, Vikram suddenly couldn't understand why he'd never bothered to unpack it before, why he'd always just let the words skim over the surface of his consciousness. There were tigers in it, for God's sake. And soldiers. He got up from his chair, and he sat down on the bed next to his mother. Then he did the unthinkable. He asked her a question.

"What were the soldiers doing in your town?"

Lalita looked at him as if she didn't know who he was or how he had gotten there.

"What?" she said.

"Why were there soldiers in your town? Was there a war?"

"No. Nothing like that."

"Were they police? Military police?"

"No. They were soldiers."

"But what were they doing there?"

Lalita thought about it. "I don't know. Training?"

"Were there lots of tigers where you grew up?" Vikram asked.

"Yes!" she said. "More tigers than anywhere else in India!" Then they both stared at each other for a while.

"What other animals were there?" Vikram asked, and proceeded to grill his mother about the flora and fauna of South Karnataka.

"I have to go put your father's laundry away," she said, backing away from him on the bed. But Vikram insisted on asking her about tigers, leopards, elephants, jackals, monkeys, bison, deer, bears, boars, giraffes, alligators, capybaras, lions —many of which he knew didn't exist in India, but at that point he was having too much fun to stop. She responded with one-word answers where she could.

"Was Grandpa very strict?" Vikram asked.

"Yes!" she cried, grateful to find herself in a familiar rant. "You are spoiled! I let you do everything!" She got up and walked out of the room, her voice rising as she went, "Me and your father, we let you do everything. You have no idea!" She continued talking as she disappeared down the hall. "You have no idea how good you have it!"

Vikram stayed on the bed, aware of the space his mother had vacated. He sat there for some time. On the computer, Gulkkamar shuffled back and forth, unsure of how to proceed. That day, Vikram started keeping a journal, jotting down his realizations, hypotheses, and theories about life.

His first entries centered around his dawning realization that life was a game—all of life. Real life. Actual life. It was no more of a game and no less of a game than *Song of Titan*.

And, just as he was a player in his life's game, his mother was also a player in her life's game. Furthermore, his mother wasn't really the ancient, colorful, chatty songbird he'd always thought of her as. Not at all. She was young. Surprisingly young. She was only a few years older than him—in the grand scheme of things. True, she was forty-six. But how old was forty-six? How much wisdom could she have possibly picked up in a mere forty-six years? Surely not enough to make them essentially different creatures. They were very close in age if you really thought about it. He was seventeen, and she was forty-six. When you took into account the entirety of human history, they were uncannily close.

And—and this one was particularly shocking to Vikram —it was entirely possible that his mother's "India" game had had better graphics and features than his "American teenager" game. After all, her game had had soldiers, tigers, natural forests, a super-strict, old-fashioned father, a god with an elephant trunk, a goddess with eight arms ...

But it wasn't just that. He realized that, his whole life, it was as if he'd only ever seen his mother's avatar, her character, her game piece. But sitting there on the bed with her that day, he felt as if he'd come face-to-face with an actual person—with the quiet "I" inside of her, the one controlling her body, her character. And it was identical to—or possibly just another outpost of the exact same entity as—the "I" inside of him, the one controlling his body and his personality. And all her experiences—all her stories—they weren't just words. She experienced them exactly the same way he would have, if *he* were the one living her life. Just as deeply. Just as freshly. With just as much wonder, awe, confusion, pain, and pleasure as him.

Since that day, Vikram had been trying to get to know his mother. He'd been trying to talk to her and find out what her life had been like, what her life was like now, and what she thought about things. But the strange thing was, she wanted no part of it. She'd gone completely mute. She ran away whenever he tried to ask her questions. "Go away!" she'd yell. "Play your Poky Man!" She'd even accused him of trying to "exoticize" her.

Vikram looked at the other passengers on the train: the Muslim girl, the Latino man, the black man doing word puzzles, the old white lady with glasses, the goth girl. They were all playing different games, with different goals, different scoring systems, different obstacles, different enemies, different deities—but inside each one of them was a little "I," a universal player, fumbling at the controls. He wondered if all of them were as desperate to be known, and as unwilling to be known, as his mother.

He smiled. It was so funny how the tables had turned. He wanted more from his mother now than she wanted from him. It was a strange feeling, to be pushing on her like that, and to feel her pushing back. The train started to move. He leaned back and closed his eyes, and he thought about nothing.

"Why are you here! What do you want! Why don't you show your face!" Erica Cloughman screamed in her mind. Her thoughts were loud, pure, full of hate. She was glaring at a tiny Muslim woman at the other end of the train, a woman who, for all intents and purposes, was just a pair of eyes, surrounded by black cloth. "Seriously! If we are so godless, why do you people come here? If you think you're so much better than us, why come? Why!"

Erica leaned forward in order to glare more effectively. Her dyed black hair hung in her face, protecting the world from her rage and her rage from the world. The hate felt good. Strong. Clean. Purposeful. It was the opposite of that other feeling—"the feeling," as she referred to it in her mind —the nameless feeling that haunted her throughout her day at school. It didn't have a name, the feeling, but words like "dork," "idiot," and "ugly" weren't far off. The feeling made her want to hide, it made her want to be swallowed up whole by the earth. If the feeling were a prayer, the words would be, "Please don't look at me or ask me anything." And it would be repeated for all eternity. "Please don't look at me or ask me anything," "Please don't look at me or ask me anything," "Please don't look at me or ask me anything." The feeling wasn't always there when she was in class, but during free periods, it was deafening. It assaulted her during any unstructured time she had to spend around the other girls—all of them so confident seeming, so effortlessly close with one another—at Our Lady of Lourdes High School.

The feeling caused her to spend almost every lunch period by herself in a stall in a little-used restroom on the fourth floor, praying no one would come in.

Yet, Erica saw no irony in her sudden, rageful burst of Islamophobia—her irrational hatred of a woman, a stranger, who had basically given herself permission not to be seen, who had allowed herself to exist in the world as nothing more than a pair of eyes.

It wasn't like it would be the biggest tragedy in the world if Sofia wasn't with her in paradise, Ruby reasoned. The two girls were growing apart anyway. Sofia was spending all her time with Anatoly. And the last time Ruby had seen her, Sofia had actually been kind of rude. It had started out fine. They'd met at their usual coffee shop—with the beat-up couches, the shelves where you could take and leave books, and the red velvet cupcakes. It was the first time they'd seen each other since Ruby had started covering her face—wearing the niqab.

Sofia had been a little surprised at first. But the girls soon found their old rhythm. Before long, they were joking around. Sofia laughed hysterically at Ruby's attempts to drink tea under her niqab. Of course, that got Ruby laughing. She laughed so hard she spit out her tea and got the niqab wet. Then they pretended Ruby was sneaking alcohol under her niqab, and Ruby played it up, looking around dramatically as she took clandestine sips.

After the joking died down, Ruby shared with Sofia the reasons why she'd started wearing the niqab, and how it made her feel—how she felt closer to God, more in touch with her religion, and more self-respect as a woman. Sofia listened and seemed to be supportive, saying that Ruby should do whatever felt right to her—that that was the important thing. Then Ruby added that she also liked that it set her apart from the Americans. She felt sure Sofia would relate, not being American herself.

But Sofia seemed puzzled. "Ruby, what are you talking about?" she said. "What do you mean 'sets you apart from the Americans'? You're American, aren't you?"

"No, I'm not," Ruby laughed. "I'm not American."

"Yes you are," Sofia said, laughing—as if the idea was ridiculous. "You're even more American than me, you were born here." Sofia had been born in Russia.

"Being born here does not make you American," Ruby said.

"Well, it doesn't make you not American," Sofia said.

"Well, I'm not American," Ruby said, firmly.

"How? How are you not American?" Sofia asked. She seemed to be challenging Ruby—implying that she was putting on airs, or that she wasn't free to choose her own identity.

"How?" Ruby said. "How? I'll tell you how. First of all, I've never committed genocide on a people and then stolen their land. So—I'm not American. Also, I don't support Israel, who also stole the land of its native people, and then built an apartheid state on it. Again—not American. And I don't support the apartheid state that exists here in America today, where people are treated differently based on the color of their skin, where African Americans are incarcerated at five times the rate of whites, and where police brutality is disproportionately perpetrated upon African Americans. None of those things represent me, Sofia, so I'm not American. Get it? It's simple. I in no way support a system that keeps down all non-whites with systemic, institutionalized racism. So I'm not American."

"Yes, you are!" Sofia said, laughing—totally dismissing everything Ruby had just said. And then, she'd had the nerve to bring up the Armenian, Assyrian, and Greek genocides, out of nowhere! Saying that Muslims had committed at least those genocides that she was aware of, and probably more. And that people who lived in glass houses shouldn't throw stones.

It was crazy! Because neither of them was Armenian, Assyrian, or Greek, and therefore it had nothing to do with anything! There was no reason to bring it up—other than sheer nastiness. And besides, Turks—or whoever allegedly did those things—weren't really Muslims, not real Muslims anyway, so all Muslims couldn't be held responsible for their alleged actions. And to say otherwise was pure Islamophobia. She really hadn't expected that from Sofia. Also, Ruby hadn't even been trying to get into a political discussion in the first place. She'd simply been sharing her feelings, her very personal feelings, about wearing the niqab. So Sofia's reaction was totally inappropriate. It was the last time they'd spoken.

"Why isn't happy hour literally happy hour?" Gary Nuce thought, sitting on the depressing, stalled train. He was a middle-aged man in a cheap suit. The older you got, the more you felt those things, Gary realized, like the cheapness of suits. He'd been selling ad space at a durable medical equipment trade publication for the last twenty-five years. His skin bristled against his itchy pants. His socks were falling down. He could feel them slipping down his calves.

"I mean, there should be a real happy hour," he thought, "a happy hour that's literally about happiness. A happy hour that has nothing to do with drinking. Because what does drinking have to do with happiness? Nothing!"

That was certainly true. Drinking had not led to anything like happiness in Gary's life. It had cost him countless promotions, kept him in cheap suits, and almost cost him his marriage. It had taken the lion's share of his pride and dignity as well. And his youth.

"In the old days, people used to go out," Gary thought. "They used to socialize after work. What happened? Why do I have to go home right after work? What kind of life is that? Work, home, work, home, work, home—until when? Sixty-five? Seventy? And then what?

"I'm not a bad person. I think I deserve more. Sure, I used to be a drunk. But now I'm not. I've atoned. I've repented. So why am I still being punished? Why do I have to live like a machine? Home. Work. Home. Work. Home. Work. And why don't people go out anymore?

"Why aren't there happy hours where you can just be happy? There should be. At bars. They should have one hour, say between 6:00 and 7:00 p.m., where everyone *has* to be happy. It would be a rule. No matter what was going on in their lives the other twenty-three hours, they'd have to be happy for that one hour. And they'd have to smile. They wouldn't have to socialize, if they didn't feel like it, but they would have to smile. And they could wear name tags. There could be icebreakers, and games. And nobody would have to drink if they didn't want to. Because drinking has nothing to do with happiness. Not at all. And everybody deserves to be happy for at least one hour a day, damn it!"

She would not feel sorry for the people looking up at her, begging her for water as their skins were being burned, and then replaced, and then burned again, for all of eternity. She wouldn't feel sorry for Sofia. And she wouldn't feel sorry for the people on this train. It wasn't like they didn't have the opportunity to become believers—they did. Everyone on earth had the opportunity. If people didn't read, if they didn't research, then they only had themselves to blame. There was a book. With clear guidance. But they didn't read it. They were too proud. They were too proud to read God's book. Too busy parading around, with their genocides and their genitals on display. Completely shameless.

"Burn!" she said in her mind to the people on the train. "Burn!" she said to the white businessman, imagining the smug expression gone from his face, his business suit melting into his skin.

"Burn!" she said to the Latino man hovering menacingly over her, scowling at her, his lips moving in a private Islamophobic rant. She imagined him on the floor, consumed in flames, screaming, crying.

She looked from person to person: the snooty doctor in scrubs standing on the other side of her; the Indian kid, his eyes were closed now, but she knew he'd been staring at her; the older white lady across from her shaking in fear and making an involuntary fist. She imagined them all burning, screaming, crying for help. She saw the flames devouring their skins, their limbs, their bones. She heard their cries of agony. She closed her eyes, and her body shivered involuntarily with delight.

She wasn't sure what paradise would be like, whether she

would have an adoring husband, or wear gold bracelets, or recline in satin furniture, but she could imagine the feeling of it, or begin to imagine it. That was all God was trying to do in the Quran, in the hadith, he was trying to give men a little feeling of it, to bring them to the edge of what they knew pleasure to be, and then tell them it was even more. Because man's idea of pleasure was only a ghost of the pleasure of paradise. An anemic echo. God used words men could understand, to talk to them about things they couldn't understand.

"Man, their hair must be really fabulous," Dave Iborte thought to himself, in the detached, amused voice he used for his comedy routines. He was contemplating the Muslim woman seated beneath where he was standing. She was reading the Quran, and she was covered from head to toe in black cloth. The Jamaica-bound 12 train he was on had been stalled in the tunnel for what seemed like an hour. It had been stopping and starting, then stopping and starting again, then stopping. He'd boarded the train in SoHo, near the building where he worked as a doorman, and he was headed for the last stop in Queens—an epic journey on the best of days, let alone on days like these.

But at least he was using the time in a productive manner: making fun of another culture. Actually—he was doing an impromptu comedy routine in his head, inspired by the Muslim woman seated beneath him. Obviously, the routine would never see the light of day. As a Latino man, of course, all other Latinos were fair game. He had carte blanche. He could be merciless with Mexicans, destructive with Dominicans, pugilistic with Puerto Ricans, and vicious with Venezuelans; he could hate Hondurans, bash Bolivians, pillory Peruvians, and guillotine Guatemalans. He could do blacks, too, within reason. Latinos and blacks had limited comedy reciprocity. And, of course, whites were fair game for everyone. But Muslims—no way. Still, it was always good to develop material—it was good practice—even if he never used it. It helped with timing, delivery, and the creative process in general. And there might always be a scrap or two he could use. Plus, he was bored out of his mind.

"Man, their hair must really be fabulous," he continued, to himself. "I'm telling you, that must be some really gorgeous hair they have under there. I mean, how gorgeous must it be, that they have to keep it covered up to prevent men from going mad? Because me personally, I've seen a lot of beautiful hair—thick hair, shiny hair, wavy hair; blonde hair, black hair, red hair; curly hair, short hair, long hair—all kinds of beautiful hair—but I've never lost control over it. It's never driven me to the edge of sanity. Now—a nice pair of legs ... that's another story ..."

Dave paused for effect. He imagined the sound of ice clinking in glasses at Swizzlesticks, the comedy club where he performed at open mic every Tuesday night.

"But maybe that's just because I've never seen Muslim hair—not the good stuff, anyway," he continued. "Maybe I'm blissfully ignorant of its power, its capacity to inflict damage. And maybe those women are very wise to cover it up. Maybe they've been protecting me this whole time. Maybe they've been saving civilization itself! Maybe if they all uncovered their hair at the same moment, mayhem would ensue—society as we know it would cease to exist, because all the men would be writhing around on the floor having fits.

"But what must it look like, in order to do that?" Dave looked around the subway car, inquiring of his imaginary audience.

"Seriously? It has to be more than just thick and shiny and wavy. Maybe it's like sirens. No, I mean like actual sirens. Like each individual strand of hair is a cute little fairy, in a suggestive pose, beckoning you. Thousands and thousands of gyrating little sylphs, beckoning you. Imagine that! Then it would definitely make sense to keep it covered up."

He paused, looking around the subway car.

"And there's probably a special kind of shampoo for that hair too, if you think about it. Because have you guys wandered down the shampoo aisle lately?"

He paused again.

"Seriously, they have so many different kinds of shampoo these days, for all different kinds of hair. It's getting really specific. The other day, my wife came home with a bottle of shampoo for me. I was like, 'Thanks, babe.' But then I looked at the bottle. Do you know what it said?"

Dave lifted up his Mets cap about an inch off his head and looked around the car. "'For thinning hair.'" He put the cap back on, and shook his head. "That hurt. And now, I feel like my wife is giving me messages ... through the shampoo. I think if she leaves me one day, I'll probably find out about it on a shampoo bottle. It'll say, 'for hair that isn't there anymore, like our love ...'

"But back to the Muslim ladies. Think about *them* trying to find the right shampoo—that's a whole other set of problems. Because you know those little beckoning sylphs get unruly. Imagine those ladies walking down the shampoo aisle: Coarse hair? No. Flat hair? No. Poofy hair? Nope. Frizzy hair? Nope. Dry hair? Colored hair? Damaged hair? Nope! Nope! Nope! Where's my shampoo? I don't see my shampoo! Sulfate free? Dandruff controlling? Clarifying? Voluminizing? Lifting? Moisturizing? No! No! No! No! No!

No! I don't see mine! Oh, wait! There it is! Gyrating sylphs shampoo! Oh, and look, it's on sale!

"And *this* girl," Dave said to himself, looking down at the seated Muslim woman. He was gaining confidence now, imagining the sound of the audience at Swizzlesticks: the steady stream of individual chortles, punctuated by occasional torrents of uncontrollable group laughter. "Imagine how beautiful this girl must be, that she has to cover not just her hair—but her entire face. She must have ... like ... a criminal level of beauty. And you know, they must be getting more and more good-looking every day, these Muslim women, because I see more and more of them covering their faces. Their beauty must be exploding off the charts!

"But not all of them—that's the thing. Not all of them cover their face. So I'm wondering, how do they know which girl they are? Are they a face-covering girl, or just a hair-covering girl? Do they have an instinctual feel for the capacity of their own beauty to inflict harm? Or does someone have to tell them?

"Because, you know, that could be a potentially awkward moment. Like, maybe, they reach a certain age, and then, in a nightmarish hybrid of American beauty standards and Muslim modesty, someone tells them exactly how much of themselves they need to cover.

"Imagine the girl's family, on that day. They all gather round, and the dad is like, 'Sweetheart, congratulations, you're a woman now. This is a really important moment. And, well, I guess you've heard about the men writhing on the floor and everything—you know, the madness and mayhem your hair and face could now cause—and, well, baby girl, we know you love civilization just as much as we do, and we know you want to act responsibly. I mean, for real, you could cause a death; imagine if the person you distracted with your beauty was like ... an EMT, or an air traffic controller. There are cases like that, darling. So from now on, you're going to have to cover both your hair and your face when you go out. I'm sorry, baby girl, but think of it as doing your part for civilization. And society thanks you.'

"And then the young lady bows her head, aware of the momentousness of the occasion. 'Okay, Dad,' she says. And then, maybe there's a party. A very solemn party. Where nobody can see the guest of honor. Like a reverse quinceañera. Instead of 'coming out' as a woman, she 'goes in' as a woman. She disappears. Vamoose! Gone!

"And then, the next year, it's the little sister's turn. She looks up expectantly at her parents, ready to do her part for civilization. They look her up and down, studying her, and then finally, they say, 'Nah, sweetheart, you're good. Dress however you want.'

"Ouch! But no, you know what? I'd rather date the little sister. Anytime. Who needs all that weaponized beauty?"

A few seats away, Aracely Portelo was sleeping with her mouth wide open. A tiny trail of saliva made its way down her chin. Her head was listing to the left; one more inch and she'd be resting on the Indian kid's shoulder. She was tired all the time now, except tired wasn't the right word for it. It was more like, at any moment, her eyes might close and she'd simply cease to exist. Her body did this to her because it was using all her energy to create new life. Specifically, it was taking undifferentiated cells—the building blocks of life—and transforming them into bone, blood, brain, nerve, and muscle. In other words, she was very early in the first trimester, and she couldn't afford to make a mistake.

She was dreaming she was a bear. A large and powerful

bear. She was in what she assumed to be the Alaskan wilderness. The cold moisture of early spring hung in the air and licked her with its every breeze. Her fur was a little dirty, a little matted in places, but she didn't mind. The wind rustled it, leaving parts of her skin bare when it lifted. It was amazingly refreshing.

The mountains were in the process of coming to life, the snow on their peaks melting. Wild grass exploded through the dirt everywhere, and there was a loud rushing stream not far off.

Her limbs fit together exactly as a bear's would, and she moved like a bear, not a human. It was a strange sensation. Lately, she'd been dreaming a lot about being different things. She didn't know why, or how she got the information —maybe it was because she was literally in the process of becoming a different thing. Maybe everyone's DNA had the knowledge of how to become all things, how to create all things. And this knowledge came out at different times.

In the dream, she was alone. She owned the whole territory. She lumbered over to the stream, her movements big, imprecise, and powerful—like a large, happy drunk. Much to her delight, there were hundreds—no, thousands—of shiny silver salmon swimming up the river. Jumping and swimming. She stepped out onto a rock, bent over, held her mouth open, and waited for one to jump in. But they kept flying by her. She moved her head around, trying to aim at the salmon. But they kept jumping past her. Finally, one landed in her mouth, and she clamped down, like a trap.

The sound of Aracely's own teeth slamming together woke her up. Embarrassed, she kept her eyes closed. Very slowly, she opened her left eye just enough to see through a tiny slit. She tried to get a sense of the damage—of exactly how many people had witnessed her ravenous chomp on the 12 train.

She saw a quick blurry image: the grey floor, the black reflective nothingness of the windows, and the other passengers, all studiously ignoring one another. She slammed her eye closed. It was worse than she'd thought. Not only was it a standing-room only train--but much to her dismay, the engine wasn't running at all. There was absolute silence, which no doubt her loud chomp had pierced like a gunshot at dawn. Within seconds, she was unconscious again.

Billy Skullet's eyes were aglow. He couldn't believe it. He was really on a roll. He was finding word after word after word in his puzzle. It seemed like all the mysteries of acrostics had been revealed and laid bare before him. Mustache! Hair dryer! Clippers! Beard! Buzz cut! It was a barbershop-themed puzzle. He kept circling words. He felt unstoppable.

Then there was a loud, deafening noise. And then total blackness.

CHAPTER SEVENTEEN

THE IMPASSIONED PLEA

Alma and George sat on the couch, dazed, watching the ongoing coverage of the 12 train bombing. It had been over a month, and the images were still shocking: the rubble and the chaos, the smoke, the devastated expressions on the faces of the first responders, the wounded being lifted onto ambulances ...

Each day, more and more information came out about the victims. The dead: four high school students, three college students—two on exchange programs from Taiwan—a writer, an amateur comedian, a medical resident, a pregnant secretary ... the list went on.

And the injured: the department-store filing clerk with grave injuries to his face, the hotel night manager in a coma, the substitute teacher with a severe leg injury ...

And of course the mysterious, by now iconic, Ruby—no last name given. In the security camera footage, she is a tiny figure, shrouded in black, with only her eyes and her small, tapered hands visible. She's seen hurrying up the subway steps, running down the street, and then being tackled by an NYPD officer.

Her arrest had been followed by a flurry of emergency court hearings. What Officer Jose Ordoñez had called "reasonable suspicion"—he'd detained Ruby because she was fleeing the scene of a crime and her identity was obscured—the courts, after much intense deliberation, deemed "Islamophobia." The confession was thrown out, along with any evidence gathered; it was all fruit of the poisonous tree. If Ordoñez hadn't tackled her, she never would have been subjected to a search, or to questioning. The case was dismissed.

While many bemoaned the whole affair as an outrageous failure of justice, others saw it as a bright spot in an otherwise tragic time. Of course, the latter group was sorry for the victims and their families, and felt that, in theory, the perpetrator should have been punished. But at what cost, they asked? At the cost of having it be okay to arrest people just because they were wearing a burqa? They felt society had to draw the line somewhere. For them, the ruling was seen as a coup against institutionalized racism, and a triumph for narrative justice: for a new, more humane, more equitable standard of law.

And while Ruby's actual whereabouts were unknown—it was assumed she was in hiding or had fled the country—her image and spirit were popping up everywhere. Graffiti artists had painted her image on brick walls and sidewalks, deftly depicting her cloaked black figure and her elegant, feminine fingers with spray paint. A bronze statue in her likeness had even been erected by an anonymous artist. Four feet tall, and situated on a lawn in Battery Park, the tiny cloaked figure stared out over the harbor at the Statue of Liberty, imploringly or accusingly, no one was really sure which, as her face was covered.

The TV was now showing live coverage of a vigil for the victims in a park in Queens. Hundreds of people stood silently, tiny candles lighting their solemn faces. It was a familiar scene; there had been vigils practically every night in various plazas and places of worship around the world.

"So sad," Alma said, vaguely, as if in a trance.

George studied her. She'd seemed lost, on some level, ever since receiving the letter from the State of New York, in spite of her valiant and ongoing attempts at single-handedly resurrecting an exciting, positive, inclusive, American identity. He felt an ever so slightly perceptible distance growing between them, and it worried him. "I know," he said.

"Let's take a break from it," Alma said, and began flipping through the channels. She put the remote down suddenly. "Marine!" she exclaimed.

Marine Schorr was on TV. But it wasn't *Hate Hunters*, or *Bridge Builders*, or anything like that. She was alone on a dark set, sitting in a raised director's chair, bathed in a halo of light. She wore a simple black blazer, and her hair was perfect—as wavy as a very calm sea. She spoke directly into the camera, in an urgent, impassioned tone:

"So, folks, this is a personal piece—direct from my heart. This doesn't represent the views of my network, or the Tolerance Department, or *Hate Hunter*s, or any of that, okay. This is just me, Marine Schorr—an American—talking to you. Now, I know most of you have seen or heard about the little bronze statue, the little girl, that's standing in Battery Park, looking out over the bay at the Statue of Liberty. And that's what I want to talk to you about tonight. Because I went to see it, and I want to tell you, I was absolutely blown away by it. It was a life-changing experience for me—and that's no exaggeration.

"I don't even know where to begin. I think never has a piece of artwork affected me so deeply in my entire life. I mean there she is, you know, all humble, in her religious clothes, and she's looking out at the Statue of Liberty, which towers over her, and which, by the way, supposedly we all care so much about—give us your poor, give us your tired, yada yada yada—we all pay plenty of lip service to that! But here's this little wisp of a girl, this slip of a girl, this little Muslim girl, and she, and she alone, out of everyone, has the courage, the gumption, the moxie, to stare this lady straight in the eye, and ask, 'Where were you for me?'

"You know. At least that's how I see it. Where were you for me? Where were you for me when I was being hunted down by a white police officer, just for exercising my right to dress the way I want, to pray the way I want, to worship the way I want? *Where were you for me?*

"And where were you for me, when this very same white officer, Officer Ordoñez, was chasing down Muslims in Afghanistan? In one of my own countries? And where were you for me, Miss 'Give Me Your Tired Give Me Your Poor,' when I was tired and poor? And I was given to you, as you requested? Where were you for me then? You hunted me down in the street for the way I dressed!

"I mean, it's just incredible, the power that a work of art can have. And by the way, I think the artist did a fantastic job with her eyes, I mean they're just so expressive! And those fingers! Those dainty little fingers! I think the artist did a brilliant rendition of her fingers.

"And of course, I'm not condoning violence. Of course not. And I mean, supposedly she confessed. But one has to wonder just how exactly they got that confession. Think about it. I mean, they've got Ordoñez out there on the street, who did two tours in Afghanistan, where soldiers have the word 'infidel' tattooed on their chests, and call the enemy 'haji.' Should we really be surprised he's out there on the streets of New York hunting down Muslims?

"And if they've got *him* out there on the streets, I'd hate to think who they've got in the confession room! You know? That's all I'm saying. Now, I'm not saying for sure it was a false confession. No. What I'm saying is, we don't know. And I'm also saying that even if she did do it—well, I don't condone it—but really, shouldn't we be asking ourselves what got her to the point where she had to do something like that?

"And of course, the NYPD is saying it wasn't Islamophobia. Well, what the heck was it then? I'd really like to know. And somebody's quoting Ordoñez as saying he had a 'gut feeling.' Really? Seriously, NYPD? Intuition? Spidey sense? ESP? Is ESP now one of the officially recognized tactics of the NYPD? Give me a break!"

Marine looked at the camera and said nothing for a few moments.

"I mean, don't get me wrong, I know the NYPD's job is to catch criminals. But it's not like they don't have other tools at their disposal—tools other than Islamophobia, I mean. It would have been one thing if she'd been caught honestly—using DNA, or any of their other fancy technology. I mean who's to say they couldn't have found DNA on the bomb? I wouldn't be surprised, with all the technology we have at our disposal in the privileged West. So in a way, maybe there's some divine justice in the fact that it was her faith itself that protected Ruby. Just a slip of a girl and a simple piece of cloth were able to foil all our expensive white-man technology. Think about it.

"But you know what else I see in her eyes? I believe that that little slip of a girl, down there in Battery Park, is also saying to that huge green lady, 'Listen, lady, the jig is up!' Because do you think that green lady just stays there in the harbor, passively accepting the tired and the poor? No! She's out there creating the tired and the poor! Where do you think she goes at night, when we're all sleeping? I'll tell you where. She's out marauding and rampaging in Muslim countries, and other countries, wreaking havoc and destruction, with bombs, wars, and politics! And then, the tired and the poor she's created have no choice but to come here, to America. And once they're here—she eats them! Yes, that's what that esteemed lady does! And I believe that's what that little slip of a girl is saying, with her eyes. And she's saying that that particular reign of terror has to end.

"And listen, I'm really, really sorry those people had to die. They didn't deserve it. They were lovely, hardworking people. But we have to ask ourselves, how long can we continue to inflict injustice upon the world with impunity? How many relatives and coreligionists, brothers and sisters, mothers and fathers, of that little slip of a girl had to die at your hands, Miss Liberty? And where's the justice for them?"

Marine was silent for a moment.

"And I think, for me, what I got out of this experience, basically, is that I stand with Ruby. Okay. I stand with all the poor, frightened, oppressed people who've been sold a bill of goods by Lady Supposed Liberty. I stand with Ruby. And I invite you all to stand with her too."

And then, George and Alma watched as Marine proceeded to affix a black hijab to her head, for two minutes, in radio silence, on national TV. She took her time; she used a hand mirror, and bobby pins, and she made sure all her hair was covered. Then, she attached a black niqab, to cover her face. When she was done, she stared into the camera, with her big, perfectly made-up eyes—now more dramatic than ever—and she addressed the viewing public. "Ladies and gentlemen, men, women, Muslims, Christians, Atheists, Jews—Americans—I invite you to stand with me as I stand with Ruby. I invite you to express your solidarity by wearing a hijab, or a niqab, or a burqa, or anything else, to show that you stand with us, united against Islamophobia."

Alma's eyes were ablaze.

CHAPTER EIGHTEEN
THE LIGHT

Alma stood with Ruby wholeheartedly. She, like many people, proudly donned a hijab in the days and weeks that followed Marine's impassioned plea. But long after everyone else had relegated theirs to closets and drawers, trotting them out mainly for protests and parades, Alma continued to wear hers. In fact, she acquired quite an assortment—many different colors, styles, and weights—of hijabs: green ones, black ones, white ones, pink ones, patterned ones, silk ones, summer ones, winter ones, long ones, short ones—and in truth, each one complemented her a little more beautifully than the last; for she had a soft face, from which the visible absence of hair did not detract too severely. And it so happened that, in the course of things, no one was really able to say with certainty at which point in time Alma went from standing with Ruby to becoming an actual Muslim.

In retrospect, George might have predicted it on that very first night. If he'd listened closely, he might have heard the gears in her head spinning as she watched Marine's impassioned plea; he might have sensed her coming up with a plan.

Because as it was now plainly obvious, converting to Islam was in fact the perfect path to obtaining the nobility and sense of gravitas she so desperately craved; and it had been there all along, hidden in plain sight. Goodness knew it was far better and far less fraught with the potential for disaster than the whole African American fiasco. For starters, there was no DNA requirement. No Muslim ancestors needed. One simple proclamation was all it took. One statement, "I am Muslim," and a person inherited the entire history of oppression and nobility, regardless of race or national origin. The bluest-eyed, blondest-haired Bosnian was considered just as oppressed as the darkest skinned Wolof—as was any convert in the West, however fair their complexion. And the genius of it was that no one could question it. Freedom of religion was absolute: inalienable. Neither the vociferous outrage of her colleagues, nor any peevish, cowardly letter from the State of New York would ever again have the power to alienate Alma from her nobility. It was 100 percent bulletproof.

But lest we judge her too harshly—her conversion was genuine. For just as a person might marry for practical reasons—"It's time to settle down," or "I don't want to be alone," or "I want to have kids"—but at the same time be absolutely head over heels in love with their intended, so too was Alma's conversion practical and expedient only on the most superficial of levels.

In the beginning, she simply noticed that for some reason, she liked the feeling of the hijab, apart from just the statement of it. It felt good, and familiar somehow. Then, she decided that even though she was just wearing it as a sign of solidarity, she was, strictly speaking, participating in Islam; in fact, she was using Islam—and as such, she felt the only respectful thing to do would be to try to learn a little bit about it, and to keep an open mind.

So she went to her neighborhood mosque. The people there were some of the kindest, funniest, most hospitable people she'd ever met. And they were very happy to teach her anything she wanted to know about Islam, without pressuring her in the slightest to convert. She began praying with them. It was foreign to her at first. But right from the beginning, there were things she liked about it. For example, she liked knowing that when she faced Mecca to pray, millions of other people were doing the exact same thing, at the exact same time, all around the world. It gave her a tremendous sense of unity, and a feeling of moving in concert, in harmony. And she found that she liked the gesture of bowing her head down to the ground. It fostered in her a sense of humility, in a good way; it reminded her that God was watching over her, and it reminded her that she was not God. And she also liked the physicality, the sheer yoga, of praying: the fact that she had to get down on the ground, then get up again, then get down again, repeatedly. It was holistic—it encompassed her entire person: body, mind, and spirit.

Praying became an enjoyable practice for her. She began doing it not only at the mosque, but at home, at the appointed times, whenever she could. And after a while of setting aside several blocks of time each day to become quiet, to meditate, to contemplate, and to worship, she became more in tune with her own, innate spirituality. Something inside her awakened; and it unfolded, bit by bit. And she found that this innate, inborn spirituality wasn't a separate, isolated, contained entity, existing only within the confines of her own being; on the contrary, it was tinged with a kind of a yearning, a hunger, a sweet desire—an earnest willingness to meet all things halfway. And so her inner spirituality reached out; it reached out to the warm community of Islam, to the wise practice of Islam, to the ancient tradition of Islam—and Islam reached back. And they touched. And in that moment, a spark passed between them. And so her conversion was not just an awakening—it was a marriage, of sorts.

Alma felt supported in all directions—a part of the great ummah: the community of Muslims spanning the globe. And she felt as if there was a tiny flame in the heart of each person in the ummah, a tiny light of God, that when taken collectively, produced a great light, and a great feeling of warmth—a great, warming, guiding light. To herself, Alma called this light "the light of Islam." And it illuminated her days.

As she explained to George one night, in an inspired three in the morning heart-to-heart, she'd come to realize that she'd never truly been comfortable with what she now termed her "civilian lifestyle." Something had always been missing from her very comfortable, very convenient, very enjoyable, but ultimately random and meaningless existence, that seemed to center mainly around Netflix, Amazon Prime, and craft beers. She now felt she was part of something good, something significant, something powerful.

CHAPTER NINETEEN

HELL

Ruby had been 100 percent sure she was guilty. One hundred percent sure she'd caused the bombing. There had been no doubt in her mind.

First, there was the explosion. Then, everything turned black. Like space. Then, she'd had the sensation that her body had done something it shouldn't have—like travel thousands of miles in an instant.

She'd opened her eyes. Smoke was everywhere. She realized she was suffocating. She held her niqab to her face to form a seal. Then she began to make out, through the smoke, bodies. Bodies on the seats, bodies on the floor. She saw a body bent over on the seat across from her. His neck was all wrong. She saw a Game Boy on the seat next to him. She let out a scream.

Then she heard someone shouting. And someone else. Two male voices. And she could see that they were examining people. And carrying bodies out. One of the voices shouted at her. "Are you okay!?" He came closer. A pair of eyes met her eyes. Then she was grabbed by the arm. "Come, let's get you out of here!"

But she resisted. She let out a burst of screams, one after the other.

"Ma'am," the voice implored. "Can you walk!" Ruby was then scooped up and carried out of the train. She was deposited at the foot of the stairs leading up to the street. "Run!" the voice shouted, "Get out!" before turning and heading back in the direction of the train.

But she remained motionless. She tasted soot in her mouth. She put her hands to her niqab once more and formed a seal. She looked in the direction of the train. She needed to help!

She ran back toward the train. She was coughing, but the cloth gave her some protection.

Then, she stopped. Something inside her, a tiny thing, like a worm, stopped her. "Why do you want to help?" it asked. "This is exactly what you wished for."

Ruby felt her insides drop. She turned around and ran up the stairs. And she kept running. With every fiber in her being and every cell in her body. She ran.

When Officer Ordoñez tackled her, it was a relief. And then in the prison ward of Elmhurst Hospital, she confessed to everything. She gave intricate details about the bomb—details that came from an unknown part of her brain that amazed her even as she spoke. She made up a long list of names of people who'd helped her. And when they asked her why she'd done it, she resurrected the rhetoric she'd been using on the train, and recited it in scathing tones: they deserved it, they were infidels, they were going to hell, they had caused great suffering in Muslim lands ... Her words were sharp and unmerciful, but this time they were aimed at her, at getting the maximum sentence for herself.

It was confusing when they let her go. It was even more confusing when she was greeted outside the hospital by throngs of people cheering for her. Holding signs. Shouting her name.

And when the real bombers were eventually found, Ruby fever redoubled. People realized, with horror, that Ruby had been completely innocent in every sense of the word, which meant the derangement of the police was even worse than anyone had thought. What had they done to the poor girl to get her to confess to a crime she didn't commit? Torture? Waterboarding? Rape? No one knew. And they couldn't ask her, because her identity was a secret.

Nevertheless, petitions were signed, investigations were launched, and people were fired. The sad and outrageous story of Ruby continued to dominate the airwaves in such a way that it was an odd and little-remarked-upon footnote that the real bombers just so happened to be a trio of mentally disturbed individuals who, in their madness, claimed to be working on behalf of ISIS.

Ruby couldn't go anywhere without hearing her own name or seeing her own image. And she couldn't go anywhere without seeing the fingers of the Indian boy, long and tapered, like her own, playing his Game Boy. Nor could she escape the pale hands and fists of the white woman across from her. She'd had beautiful hands, Ruby realized. And the hands of the black man doing his puzzles. His hands were amazing. They were strong. They were soft. They had seen pain, and had only grown in love from that.

It was the hands, for some reason, that kept coming back to her.

Except the Latino man who'd been hovering over her. It wasn't his hands she kept seeing, but his face. His nose, in particular. He'd had a long nose that came to a hook at the end. A slightly unexpected nose. A unique nose.

She stopped eating, and she stopped talking. In a desperate attempt to get her away from the news and restore her sanity, her family spirited her away to Bangladesh.

CHAPTER TWENTY
NOBLEPRIDE

It was two o'clock on a warm Saturday afternoon. The sky was big, and blue, and punctuated by a few white clouds high up in the distance. A significant portion of the city was in attendance at the Noblepride Parade, and Jackie Krucic was no exception. She was among the throngs of people lined up along Park Avenue, watching the thrumming, festive floats go by. The big groups were all represented: Black Lives Matter, the National Organization for Women, the Council on American-Islamic Relations, and many, many more. And there were a multitude of lesser-known groups as well—a delightfully diverse array of organizations and alliances with names that were variously niche, heartwarming, valiant, perplexing, charming, and violent. There was the Gay Pickleball League, the Queer Muslim Students Association, Jews Against Israel, the Society to Honor Fallen Sherpas, the Association of Formerly Incarcerated Indigenous Ecuadorians, Indians Advocating for More Special-Skills Work Visas, Women in Plumbing, the Lorena Bobbitt Foundation to Prevent Sexual Violence Against Women, and many more.

Noblepride happened every September, and its purpose was to promote inclusion by celebrating everyone except white male heterosexuals. This year's theme was "I Stand with Ruby" and accordingly, a great many people wore niqabs, hijabs, or burqas. Also, quite a few wore vagina hats —left over from last year's theme, "Women's Bodies, Here to Stay!" Some people wore one or the other, while a few daring souls wore both. The ones who seemed to be having the most fun with the current year's theme were the more outré gays and transsexuals, who took to their niqabs like fish to water. They wore G-strings, and face coverings, and performed belly dances and elaborate Ali Baba-type scenarios. One young man, wearing only puffy green pants, a niqab, and thick black eyeliner, delighted everyone by zooming in and out of the crowds on a skateboard with a Persian carpet attached. But it wasn't all niqabs and vagina hats; people put on whatever they had on hand to evoke a celebratory mood: hot shorts, leather pants, drag attire—and there were even a fair number of mermaid costumes left over from the Coney Island Mermaid Parade earlier in the year.

Jackie had purple glitter on her eyelids, courtesy of a free face-painting station on Twenty-Eighth Street. Occasionally, a speck of glitter would fall onto her eyelashes. There it would dangle indefinitely, refracting the light, and covering the world with a thousand tiny rainbows before her eyes. The effect only served to further intensify the already dreamlike, kaleidoscopic atmosphere of the day: the soft blue skies, the booming music coming from the floats, and the jovial bonhomie of the groups and individuals walking by.

She was taking a lot of photographs; there were so many colorful characters to document: so many wigs, so much glitter, so much body paint, so much drag, so much camp—and so many ethnic and national costumes. It was all prime fodder for her now regular "Only in New York!" social media posts. She still had a negligible number of followers, and was infrequently liked, but the act of curating and posting photos gave her great joy. Each image helped to further solidify her emerging sense that life was okay, that life hadn't forgotten her, and that everybody wasn't on their cell phones at all times, having private conversations without her—that she was still necessary, somehow, still part of the great parade and pageantry of life.

But what she really loved was the actual photographing—the whole ritual of it: complimenting someone on their look, asking for permission to take their picture, posing with them sometimes, making friendly banter. It was a wonderful way to connect with people, and there were very few parades or street fairs Jackie didn't attend.

A Brazilian float went by, playing spiky, jumpy, accordion-heavy forró. Six gorgeous, scantily clad young couples danced on top. Jackie bounced up and down with the rest of the spectators. There was a tall Puerto Rican man that had been standing next to her for about an hour. He wore white pants and a white T-shirt, and had a Puerto Rican flag draped over his shoulders. Every time someone or something unique or interesting went by, they turned to each other and smiled. He was her impromptu, unspoken parade companion. But she would have to leave him. She hadn't eaten anything since early morning, and the smells from the food stands on the side streets were calling to her. She knew there would be little chance of finding him again when she returned. She tried to get his attention. His arms were folded, and he was looking out at the parade with a graceful, all-encompassing, beatific smile. "Hey!" she shouted. She motioned with her hands that she was going to get something to eat. They hugged and exchanged names at the top of their lungs into each other's ears. His name was Rodney. She promised she would try to come back to the same spot.

She walked back out through the crowd, saying "excuse me" "excuse me" "excuse me" to the people she passed, making eye contact and smiling. Once she had extricated herself from the spectators, she found herself on Thirty-Second Street. It had also been closed off, but not for food. It was entertainment of some sort. Jackie made her way to the front of the crowd and found a seat on a metal chair. There was a woman standing at a podium to the side of a large screen, addressing the crowd. She was an incredibly tall brunette, with an attractive face, and she had on a long-sleeved T-shirt that said "STEMpower!"

"For those of you who might not know," the woman said, "STEMpower! is a multicountry organization designed to increase and empower women in the fields of science and technology throughout the world. And today, we'll be highlighting some of our projects in Muslim-majority countries. And I'm glad to say, this also happens to fit in pretty nicely with this year's Noblepride theme—'I Stand with Ruby!'"

As she said the catchphrase, she raised her fist into the air. A wild cheer went up from the crowd.

"So yeah," she continued, "these projects have been our way of standing with Ruby—and with all the Rubys of the world, and empowering them, on their own terms. One of the beautiful things about STEMpower! is that it's sensitive to the cultural context of each country where it's implemented. In other words, it's not about some white man going to a country and saying, 'Do this, and this, and this!' Because, honestly, what do we know about their unique circumstances? And who are we to tell them what to do? So, we in no way impose our culture. And by the way, that's one of the many wonderful things about STEM, and science in general; science is always science—it's culturally neutral. It's universal.

"And we don't go in with the attitude, 'Oh these poor Muslim women, they're so oppressed, we need to give them power.' No. Not at all. Because let me tell you, these women are already very powerful. Trust me! We're just giving them the tools they need. And if anything, they're teaching us a thing or two."

The crowd erupted in hoots and howls, whoops and ululations.

"I guess what I'm trying to say," she continued, "is that STEMpower! isn't about empowering Muslim women—because they're already empowered. It's about acknowledging their power, celebrating their power, learning from their power—empowering their power!"

A huge cheer went up from all the people in their niqabs, star-spangled hijabs, and vagina hats.

"And another thing—we meet these women where they're at. For some, it means learning their way around a computer for the first time. For others, there's basic literacy work involved. For still others, it's even more basic. For example, there are some rural locations where our first step has been to install network connectivity for the whole village. And then for others, on the opposite end of the spectrum, we've been providing them with the equipment and support they need to be able to put their engineering degrees to work in powerful and creative ways, or helping them get their master's degrees, or teaching them programing, or web design, or animation.

"So now, without further ado, I'm going to show you a film we've put together—a brief introduction to our project, a glimpse into some of the amazing things that are happening, and some of the incredible women we've had the privilege of going on this journey with." The woman pressed a few keys on her laptop and turned around to watch the giant screen behind her.

The film opened with a delightful montage of girls and women in all stages and iterations of Muslim and secular dress—women of all races and nationalities, all skin tones, and all ages. Some were smiling and giggling, and some were serious, as they talked about their experiences. Some were learning how to type in simple village huts, while others were building robots in Riyadh condominiums.

Then there were interviews with the American tech partners and teachers, who shared their experiences, and related anecdotes. Next, a few of the projects were highlighted. One young girl in a Gambian village showed her designs for a laundry cooperative that would free up the village women's time, collectively, by 38 percent per week. A housewife in Pakistan gave a tour of her e-commerce website, which connected consumers with female sellers and producers of home-crafted goods, foods, and services. Many other interesting projects were highlighted; and in all the stories, the charm and wit of the girls and women came through. The audience was mesmerized.

"See what I mean?" the presenter said when the film was done. "Weren't the women amazing?"

The crowd cheered wildly again. And as they did, they hoisted their various signs and placards protesting the miserable state of things into the air: "Resist White Supremacy!"

"End Rape Culture!" "White Silence is Violence!" "Catcalling is Sexual Assault!"

The woman continued, "And so, it turns out we have one more thing to show you. It's a video, and I just received it in my inbox this morning. I haven't even seen it yet, but it looks like it's a gesture of appreciation from some of the women. Let me see. Here it is. It says 'Special Gratitude Project, from the STEM Muslimas Group of Five. Please play at Noblepride Parade.' Okay, so it looks like they want us to see this." She looked at her watch. "Should I play it?" she asked the crowd. "It's four minutes and thirty-three seconds long."

"Play it! Play it! Play it! Play it!" the crowd chanted.

"Great!" the woman said, and she pressed play.

A title appeared on the screen: "Animals: A special Noblepride project from the STEM Muslimas Group of Five." Next appeared a bright, primitively drawn meadow, with five animals standing on top of it: an alligator, a snake, a lizard, a cockroach, and a pig. The animals were drawn in a simplistic style, but they were incredibly expressive.

The pig began to speak, in a robotic, computer-generated voice. "Hello," it said, and it jiggled as it spoke, to indicate that it was the one speaking. "We're the STEM Muslimas Group of Five. We're an anonymous group of women from five different countries, who met through the STEM Muslimas Project. First of all, we'd like to give a very big thank you to all our teachers, and everyone at STEMpower! for teaching us all about STEM! We love it! We love everything we've learned, and we love all the opportunities it has given us!"

Then the snake spoke, in the same stiff, robotic voice, accompanied by the same jiggling motion. "Yes," it said.

"Thank you a million times from the bottom of our hearts, for your incredible generosity."

All the other animals cheered, jiggling as they spoke. "Yes! Yes! Thank You! Thank you!"

Then the alligator spoke. "One of the things we really loved about this project was that it encouraged us to chat with other STEM Muslimas from around the world."

"That was fun!" said the lizard.

"And it wasn't long before we discovered an issue that was common to us all," said the cockroach.

The animals were silent for a moment. Then the alligator spoke. "We don't have clitorises."

All down the street, there was a deep, resounding silence. A lone voice in the audience yelled, "Shit!"

"Alligator!" said the lizard. "That's not what we're talking about today!"

"Don't listen to that poor, confused alligator!" said the pig, jiggling. "She doesn't speak for the rest of us. We apologize."

"We apologize," said all the other animals, jiggling.

"Our issue is," said the snake, "we know the STEM-power! organization will be talking about us at the Noblepride Parade, and we know that many of you will be wearing your hijabs, and your burqas, and your niqabs, in honor of this year's theme."

"And we know that, in general, you love wearing these garments to express your political opinions," said the lizard. "In fact, it seems that America has gone crazy for hijabs and niqabs all of a sudden."

"And we just want to say to you," said the cockroach, jiggling back and forth, "that we support your right to wear whatever you want."

"But we really miss our clitorises," said the alligator.

"Not now, Alligator!" said the cockroach.

"Like we were saying," said the pig, "before we were so rudely interrupted by that naughty alligator, we think it's great that you can wear whatever you want. And we also think it's great that you're showing your support for Muslim women ..."

"Because we're fabulous!" interjected the snake.

"Yes, we are!" said the other animals, shaking their bodies and cheering.

"But we just want to remind you," said the pig, "that we, the STEM Muslimas, can't wear whatever we want. Most of us can't."

"I can't," said the lizard.

"I can't," said the cockroach.

"I can't," said the snake.

"What we want to say," said the lizard, "is that we wish you would stop using the instrument of our oppression—the hijab—as a symbol of your empowerment and your defiance."

"You're using our chains to celebrate your freedom," said the cockroach.

"You have to understand, the hijab is not so much fun for us," said the pig, "because we don't have a choice."

"And the niqab is not fun for us," said the lizard. "I'm ordered to cover my face whenever I go outside."

"You have no idea," said the pig, "how much I long to feel the wind in my hair."

"And the sun on my face," said the lizard.

"We want to feel the wind in our hair and the sun on our faces," chanted the animals, jiggling.

"And we are so hot in our clothes," said the pig.

"We live in really hot countries," said the cockroach.

"Really, really, really hot," said the pig.

"We are dying! We are dying in our garments of shame, our garments of submission," chanted the animals.

"But it's not just the clothes themselves," said the lizard, "it's what they represent. It's what they represent to us, not to you. What they represent to us is oppression. We're told what to wear, told to cover ourselves, told that we are shameful—told that not just by men—but by women."

"Women are not blameless," said the pig.

"We oppress ourselves," said the cockroach.

"We mutilate ourselves," said the alligator.

The animals stood for a while in silence.

Then the snake spoke. "Actually, I have to admit, the alligator has a point. I have had this thing done to me also—this thing that the alligator speaks of. And as a result, I cannot feel the same pleasure in my husband's arms that he feels in mine—although I love him more than words can say. And I don't think that's right. I don't think that's the way love was meant to be."

"I wish I could feel what lovers were meant to feel," said the pig.

"God wanted me to know profound pleasure," said the cockroach, "pleasure with the power to unite body and soul for one brief, stunning instant. But man has second-guessed God's wisdom in wanting me to feel this."

"Men are promised pleasure in this life and the next," chanted the animals. "Why are women denied it?"

"We are just as human as men," said the lizard.

"And we die. We die, just like men," said the alligator. "If we have to die, we should be allowed to live. If we have to feel pain, we should be allowed to feel pleasure."

"If we have to die, we should be allowed to live," chanted the animals. "If we have to die, we should be allowed to live."

"It's not like anyone is protecting us from pain, from the harsh realities of life," said the cockroach. "No one is treating us like children, or delicate flowers."

"We get cancer, and hepatitis, and heart attacks; we die in car crashes, and fires, and in earthquakes. If life doesn't spare us its worst, why are we spared its best?" said the pig.

"If we have to die, we should be allowed to live," chanted the animals. "If we have to die, we should be allowed to live."

"You cut us to control our desire, and you cover us to control men's desire," said the lizard.

"But we should bear the responsibility for desire equally," said the alligator.

"Just as we bear the responsibility for death equally," said the snake.

"We all die. We all feel pain. We all sin. And we all stand accountable before God," the animals chanted.

"That's true even if we are reviled animals, as many think we are," said the pig.

The woman on stage was watching in morbid fascination, her finger hovering over the mouse pad, ready to cut the video.

"Sorry," said the cockroach, "we weren't supposed to talk about that today. The theme for today is how you use the garments of our oppression to boast about your freedom."

"You have to understand," said the lizard, "you use the hijab to stick it to the man, but the man uses the hijab to stick it to us."

"You have options. We don't," said the alligator. "Covering ourselves might not be compulsory in all our countries, but it is in some, and even where it isn't, there's pressure from our communities. For most of us, it's not a true choice."

"That's not true!" yelled someone in the audience.

"Boo!" someone else yelled, and then someone else, "Boo! Liars!"

"We're pleading with you not to use our chains and our shackles as a symbol of your freedom!" said the pig.

"Boo!" chanted the audience.

The alligator spoke. "When you use the instruments of our oppression to celebrate and stick up for Muslims in the West, who have essentially made a lifestyle choice to dress that way, and who, compared to us, are basically 'optional' Muslims, you're selling out the actual skins of the hundreds of millions of 'mandatory' Muslim women in our countries —who suffer from these instruments of oppression and everything they represent."

The audience's angry boos and outraged cries drowned out the words of the animals. The woman on stage cut the video, and the screen went blank.

The woman lifted her hand, urging people to quiet down. "Well," she said, clearing her throat, "it looks like we have some pranksters in the group. There are a few in every bunch, right? So, first of all, this was in no way representative of our project. And, as far as female ... as far as female genital mutilation goes, yes, that's a very serious issue. But I assure you, it's in no way an Islamic practice. It's a cultural practice, and yes, as far as I know, it does exist in some of the STEM-power! countries. But, it's completely independent of Islam. Islam, as you know, goes out of its way to ensure the rights of women."

"Yes it does!" shouted someone in the crowd.

She continued, "And ... well, we'd be happy to talk about

that issue at a later time, and I believe Charlene is active in that particular cause." The woman nodded to another woman sitting in the first row by Jackie. "But, yeah, it's just not an appropriate discussion to have here. I hope that what you walk away with today is everything you saw in the first video: the incredible projects that the majority of the women are doing, and all the really positive, meaningful progress that's being made.

"And, you know, as far as how people want to dress ... I'll tell you ... I've known hundreds of women who choose to wear the hijab—from all over the world: from New York, London, Sydney, Cairo—everywhere, basically, and they all tell me the same thing. They feel incredibly empowered by it, and most importantly, it's their choice. It's something very personal—a way of expressing their devotion, and what's in their hearts. And I respect that. And really, I think it's pretty presumptuous of these five women to claim to speak for the entire Muslim world. It's offensive. And we at STEMpower! don't condone it."

Jackie walked away feeling somewhat touched by the humble, homemade pleas of the women in the film. She was pensive as she walked to Madison Avenue, and then up to Thirty-Sixth Street, which was full of food vendors. There was Mexican food, barbecue, brats, empanadas, funnel cakes, pho ... Everything looked so good, Jackie couldn't decide what to eat. She walked around, looking at menus and smiling at the many people milling about on the street. She came across two men doing an impromptu dance. One wore just a green bikini bottom and a black niqab strung across his face. The other wore a white body suit, ruby-red Dorothy slippers, and tattered, diaphanous wings. The man with wings led and twirled the man in the niqab, who responded with coy and demure gestures.

Jackie stopped to admire them. They stopped dancing, and started laughing and talking with each other. Jackie tried to ask their permission to take a photo. But the music was very loud. The float of the LGBTQIA Society of Monterrey, Mexico was going by, blaring tribal dance music from eight behemoth speakers.

"Excuse me!" Jackie yelled. She walked in closer to them. "Excuse me, do you mind letting me take a ..." She was waving her arms around, motioning toward her phone, and trying to get their attention, but they were focused on their conversation.

"Oh my God!" a voice cried. "Leave them alone!"

But Jackie didn't hear.

The voice got closer, and yelled more emphatically, "Leave. Them. Alone!"

Then another voice cried, "Oh my God! It's her!"

A group of about twelve people, covered from head to toe in black burqas—with only their eyes visible—surrounded Jackie and the two costumed men.

"Yes! It's her!" shouted one of them.

"It's Jackie, the racist!" shouted another. They were all members of the Scandinavian American Society Against Toxic Whiteness, and they were avid hate hunters.

But between the loud music and the fact that their voices were muffled by burqas, Jackie didn't hear them, or notice them closing in on her.

They all took out their phones and began filming her.

"Excuse me!" one of them yelled, in a deep male voice, from behind his burqa. "Are you having a problem with two gay men dancing together?"

Jackie was still trying to get the men's attention, and she tapped one of them on the shoulder.

"Get your hands off him!" yelled a Finnish American man in a burqa. He had a bellowing voice, that managed to make itself heard above the Mexican music, which was now fading down the avenue, leaving behind only loud bass beats that punctured the air at regular intervals.

Jackie turned and found herself surrounded by a gang of large, shrouded, anonymous figures, all holding up their cell phones and filming her. She blinked, and several pieces of glitter fell onto her eyelashes, causing the circle of black shrouds to be overlaid with confusing, shimmering, terrifying rainbows.

"We will not tolerate hate!" shouted one of the figures.

"We will expose you, Jackie! You can't hide!" bellowed another one.

Jackie turned all the way around, looking from figure to figure, cell phone to cell phone. In a panicked voice, she shouted, "Stop! Stop filming! You didn't ask my permission! I don't agree to be filmed!"

"Well, we don't agree for you to hate!" yelled one of the figures. "We don't agree for you to make gay people feel uncomfortable, just for showing their love to each other!"

"We will not let hate go undocumented!" shouted another figure.

"Monsters can only survive in the dark!" shouted another. "We'll shine a light on you, Jackie! We'll expose you for the bigot you are! Leave those two beautiful men alone!"

The two beautiful men in question were now standing a few feet away, outside the circle, oblivious to the controversy.

"Stop it!" Jackie said. "Leave me alone! You have no business filming me!"

But they kept filming her. So she raised her phone and began filming them back.

"This woman was accosting two gay people," said one of the group, narrating his video. "She's a racist and a bigot, and she's come to Noblepride to harass people. She won't get away with it."

"These people are harassing me," Jackie said, narrating her own video. "I'm a private citizen, and I do not give my permission to be filmed. I was minding my own business ..."

"Minding your own business!" shouted one of the group. "You can't lie to us, Jackie. We have you on film! Remember, you're always in the public eye!"

"No, I have you on film!" Jackie shouted. "Everyone will see that you're harassing me. Look!" She panned around the circle. "They've formed a circle around me! I'm a free citizen, and they're detaining me!"

The group looked around at one another. "Guys, guys!" said one of them. "She's right. We have to open up the circle! We have to give her space. We're not allowed to detain her."

They all stepped back.

Jackie kept her camera trained on them. "You're in the public eye too!" she shouted. "I have you on film harassing me! Terrorizing me! How dare you judge me? How dare you? Who says you're any better than me? You don't even have the guts to show your faces!"

Then she began hurling expletives. "Why can't you just leave me alone, you cunts! I was minding my own business! You assholes! You fucking ...terrorists! I swear, I'll turn this footage in! You'll be humiliated for harassing me! You'll lose your jobs! You'll lose your friends! You won't be able to go outside!"

"Oh my God," said one of the figures. "Just look at her!

She's so crazy, so full of hate. This is going straight to *Hate Hunters*! This is going to blow up!"

"No, you are!" Jackie screamed, "You're going straight to *Hate Hunters*! You're going to blow up! You'll all be household names!" Then, before anyone realized what was happening, she walked up to the figure closest to her, grabbed its niqab, and ripped it off—exposing a plump, middle-aged, male face.

"Opf!" said the man.

Then she went down the line, ripping off face coverings, one by one, until everyone in the group was exposed.

Shocked, yet undeterred, they continued narrating their mounting outrage onto their videos.

CHAPTER TWENTY-ONE

THE PRIMORDIAL CRY

By ten the next morning, The Tolerance Department/*Hate Hunters* had received no fewer than thirteen videos, taken from thirteen different perspectives—including one from the first-person point of view—showing a hate-hyped Jackie screaming "terrorist" and "cunt" at a group of peaceful, burqa-wearing people, then proceeding to forcibly remove their niqabs, one by one, all the while ranting in an unintelligible racist rage.

Alma felt sickly and chilled from the late summer blasts of air conditioning streaming into her cubicle. She didn't know what was taking Marine so long. It was six o'clock—surely her many meetings were over by now: meetings where she was no doubt already overseeing the production of the *Hate Hunters* special that would officially reveal the footage. It had already started to go viral—but Marine would push it over the edge. Alma had to stop her!

She bolted up from her chair and ran toward the cubicle opening, where she was confronted by a frightening figure.

"Aaaah!" She let out a shriek.

Then she adjusted her eyes. Marine stood in the doorway, a stunning apparition in an off-white, billowy, summer-weight wool dress.

"Oh, Marine!" Alma said.

"Hi Alma! I'm just getting out of my meetings. Can you believe it? What's up?"

"Marine, see ... I wanted to ... Have a seat ..." Alma motioned toward the chair usually reserved for clients, and Marine sat down.

"So the thing is ..." Alma said, and began to list the reasons why the footage shouldn't be run. But they didn't come out as eloquently as she had been rehearsing or imagining. In the rehearsals, she had spoken the words as if in some courtroom scene at the end of a movie about injustice. But now—the words seemed empty.

But she managed to get through them. "The thing is—they weren't Muslim," she complained. "So, I mean, how can you be Islamophobic against non-Muslims, I mean, it doesn't make sense—so ..."

"You're right," Marine said.

"What?"

"You're right. It wasn't Islamophobia. Not at all."

"Oh," Alma said.

"I'm not going to run the footage."

"Oh, thank God," Alma said, a flush of health beginning to lend some color to her pallor.

"Yup," Marine said, staring dreamily at a point somewhere in the stained grey fabric of the interior cubicle wall, "I'll have no part in it. I'm not interested. As a matter of fact, I've moved on."

"Oh ..." Alma said.

"From this point on, I'm going to be 100 percent

focused on *Bridge Builders,* my producers be damned. See, I may have ..." Marine looked around, lowering her voice. "Well, I fear I may have overshot a little bit with the whole Islamophobia thing." She looked Alma up and down, from her floral hijab to her red ballet flats. "I mean, don't get me wrong. I stand with Ruby. I mean, I was the original one to stand with Ruby, of course. But it's like now they want me to do all Islamophobia all the time. And it's getting a little out of control. I mean, sure, yeah, some of the things they send me are Islamophobia, but some of them are just so ... subtle, that no one can really be sure if it's Islamophobia or not. Like this thing with Jackie. They've been insisting all day that it doesn't matter if the people she yelled at weren't Muslims. They say the whole point of 'I Stand with Ruby' is sort of that we are all Muslim. And yes, I mean, we all are, in a way, and I should know, I started it. But, in this instance, I'm pretty sure Jackie wasn't even thinking about Islam when she called them terrorists. I'm pretty sure she meant they were terrorizing her with their cameras. Which, you know, is, again, in a way, in no small part due to me.

"Also, I sometimes wonder—if we keep showing all this, you know, 'maybe yes maybe no' kind of hate, aren't we sort of diluting the brand? Hate, I mean. Maybe we should stick to the stuff that's really, obviously hate, and not like, mistakes, and faux pas, because, it just gets so ..."

"Exactly!" Alma interrupted, unable to contain her excitement. "Exactly! And I swear to you, Jackie really was being terrorized. I mean, sorry for the word, but they were all filming her, and she wasn't doing anything. I mean, not at all. She really is a changed person, I'm telling you! And there she is, just managing to get her life back together, and then they're all in hoods, filming her, and rebuking her, and, well, I think there might have been an element of PTSD at play ..."

"You're 100 percent correct," Marine said, a bit sadly. "I mean how could there not be a little PTSD at play? I think ... I think ... maybe we've done enough calling out for the time being. I feel we need to collectively move on, and that is why I want to focus much more on *Bridge Builders* than *Hate Hunters* from now on. Much more."

"Oh! Well! Exactly!" Alma said, relaxing into her chair, folding one leg over the other, and daring to admire the claret red ballet flat bouncing off the end of her pale left leg. "And I mean, I *know* her, and trust me, she's anything but Islamophobic. The way she goes on and on about her friend Mohammad ..."

Alma looked up and realized with a start that Wendy Watkins had been standing in her doorway for some time. Her arms were folded across a formfitting vintage sweater, and she had a somewhat exasperated look on her face.

Seeing that Alma had noticed her, Wendy spoke. "Um, Alma, we're setting up now."

Alma looked at her blankly.

"For the cultural hour?" Wendy said. "The Canadian Arctic Indigenous Peoples Cultural Hour? It's today?"

"Oh. Oh!" Alma said. "I'm sorry. Do you need my help?"

"The cups?" Wendy said. "You were supposed to bring the cups?"

"Oh!" Alma exclaimed. "Sorry." She opened the bottom drawer of her desk and handed Wendy two stacks of red plastic cups.

Wendy took the cups and walked away.

"*Bridge Builders* has always been my passion," Marine was saying. "When I originally conceived *Hate Hunters*, it was supposed to be a two-part show. Always two parts. *Hate Hunters* and *Bridge Builders. Hate Hunters* and *Bridge Builders.* And I believe the first few segments were that way. But then we really got into the hate—and I'm not saying it's not important, of course it is ..."

Alma was spinning slightly from side to side in her chair. She had been so exhausted from worrying about Jackie that she was now experiencing a kind of euphoria. She knew from experience it would be only temporary. It was always just putting out fires with this job. But this particular fire was out. And she was happy. She sighed deeply and nodded at Marine, although she wasn't 100 percent focused on what she was saying.

But again, she caught a glimpse of someone standing in her doorway. She looked up and was confronted with the formidable figure of Allison Corval, looking shockingly well put together in a hunter-green dress and black patent-leather boots that went halfway up her thighs. With her outfit and her flowing blonde hair, she cut such a stunning figure that she gave the immediate and overwhelming impression that she was what human beings were meant to look like, and that Alma was nothing more than a half-formed lump of clay—abandoned by her maker after an initial bout of enthusiasm.

Allison had an amused expression on her face. "Sorry to interrupt your meeting, Alma," she said. "It's just that I'm going on a salmon run."

"A salmon run?" Alma said.

"Yes," Allison confirmed.

Alma pictured the lithe Allison forgoing the gym entirely to compete with actual spawning salmon in an athletic, upstream, post-work swim off. Perhaps it was the new Upper East Side work out du jour.

"What do you mean?" Alma asked.

"I'm going to buy salmon," Allison said. "For the Canadian Arctic Indigenous Peoples Cultural Hour. Braxton Hammond was supposed to bring it, but he overslept. Actually, he was supposed to bring arctic char, from the fish market."

"Oh," said Alma.

"But he's also the DJ, and he bought a lot of new music for the party, so we all decided that since you only brought cups, you wouldn't mind chipping in for the salmon."

"Oh!" Alma said. "Of course." She reached for the curly key chain in her pencil cup, and with the thin silver key, opened her top desk drawer. She reached into her purse and grabbed her wallet. She took out a twenty, and then another, and then another. She reached out her hand to give Allison the money, but Allison wasn't paying attention. Her eyes were locked on Alma's open top drawer. "Shit!" Alma thought, following Allison's eyes to her red Prada bag. She usually made a point not to bring it to work, but it had looked so good with her new flats that she'd dispensed with her policy. She sighed, reached into her wallet and pulled out two more twenties to add to the pile.

"Here" she said again, pushing the money toward Allison.

But Allison's eyes were still fixed on the top drawer. There was a look of ... horror on her face—or no—glee. Something between horror and glee.

Alma took out another twenty, and then got up and walked the money over to Allison, forcing her to take it.

"Thanks!" Allison said. "See you at the party!" Then she turned to Marine and said, "I hope to see you too," before hastily retreating.

Alma was left with an uncomfortable feeling and found it difficult to focus on Marine, who had resumed talking, and was laying out her plans for a new emphasis on *Bridge Builders*.

What was that all about? Alma thought. It was very obvious that Allison was going to tell everyone about her having a Prada purse. But it didn't make any sense. For all they knew, she'd bought it with money she'd earned at the Tolerance Department. It wasn't like she made peanuts. And what did a Prada purse cost anyway? She couldn't remember. She'd put it on her credit card, which was automatically paid by her bank account, which was automatically paid by her dividends and interest from her various investment accounts, or maybe that part wasn't automatic, maybe her father's finance man took care of that. She wasn't sure. But the point was, how expensive could a Prada purse be? Was it possible it was really that much of a faux pas to bring one to work? What was it, about seven hundred dollars maybe? Eleven hundred dollars? Four thousand dollars? Did people really believe she couldn't afford four thousand dollars—as a one-time treat—on her salary? They were so petty. Let them talk. She didn't care anymore.

"And so this tendency toward nitpicking has to end," Marine was saying. "And I blame myself, partly. Or mostly. Yes. Mostly, actually. So it will be my mitzvah. Our mitzvah. We have to make the world a more tolerant place. Starting with us. Yes. It's time to heal, and heal means whole. None of us can heal without all of us. We have to stop cutting off limbs."

All of a sudden, a loud, guttural noise, a fierce shout—a lament—half human, half animal, rose up from between the two women, as if emanating from deep inside their very souls. They sat, frozen, staring at each other, eyes open wide.

Then it happened again. A devastating guttural cry—piercing the air with violence and impunity.

There were two more shouts, and then the shouts evolved into music. One voice—containing two voices. One part was rhythmic, like a beatbox, coming from deep inside the throat: boom de doom, boom de doom, boom de doom; the other part was dark—a haunting melody—like a spirit over a lake.

Alma realized the sounds were coming from the conference room. "I think that's Inuit throat singing!" she exclaimed.

They both listened with total alertness.

"It's beautiful," Marine said.

"They must be starting the Canadian Arctic Indigenous Peoples Cultural Hour," Alma said.

"It's incredible," Marine said. "Shall we go?"

And the two women headed toward the conference room.

CHAPTER TWENTY-TWO

LUNCHES WITH MUSLIMS

"Sometimes I feel like all religions are strange, when you get right down to it. When you really pay attention to what they're saying. Seriously, I don't think any of them are about what we all think they're about, like 'love your neighbor,' and stuff like that. I mean, sure, they all contain some of that ..." George paused and took another bite of his baklava. It was like biting into warmth, love, home. It was his second piece, and he would probably be having a third. And after that, when all the baklava was gone, he would probably want to eat the Styrofoam plate, which was by now bathed in the sugary syrup.

Things with Nadim were at a standstill. He'd been sentenced to five years in prison, and had had both his left femur and his collarbone broken while in custody. George had been to Cairo for five days as part of a small international delegation of lawyers and activists advocating for his release, but he'd been unable to secure an in-person visit with him. He continued to work tirelessly on his behalf—writing letters, circulating petitions, and partnering with NGOs. He'd also been writing, by hand, on an almost daily basis, heartfelt, confessional, meandering letters to Nadim, about his day, about things that had happened to him and things he'd noticed, and about major and minor changes to his philosophy. But what he really longed for was to talk to him. His passion project—apologizing to Muslims—was on indefinite hold while he tried to get his mind around a few things. And he couldn't talk to Alma about those things. Every time he tried to talk to her objectively about Islam, she seemed to get defensive, as if he was ... accusing her ... or calling her bluff somehow. But he wasn't. He just had a lot of questions. He supposed some part of him wanted it not to be true, wanted him not to have defended something so—formidable—to Nadim.

He tried getting answers by reading, but what he discovered only plunged him further into doubt. He'd been particularly shaken to learn that his favorite passage in the entire Quran, the one he'd loved to quote at the drop of a hat—verse 5:32—the one that read, "Whoever kills a soul unless for a soul or for corruption in the land—it is as if he had slain mankind entirely. And whoever saves one—it is as if he had saved mankind entirely," was not as peaceful as it first appeared. It was an excerpt, and taken in its entirety, the focus of verse 5:32 was not so much on killing being wrong, as it was—like so many other passages in the Quran—on the sinfulness of the Jews. The full verse read, "Because of that, We decreed upon the Children of Israel that whoever kills a soul unless for a soul or for corruption in the land—it is as if he had slain mankind entirely. And whoever saves one—it is as if he had saved mankind entirely. And our messengers had certainly come to them with clear proofs. Then indeed many of them, after that, throughout the land, were transgressors."

It struck George that whatever the original intention, essentially, you had one religion using another entire religion as a cautionary tale—the perils of which seemed self-evident.

So when he'd seen the pamphlet for "Lunches with Muslims" lying among Alma's work things, he'd known exactly what he had to do. He'd been reading books about Islam for months; but books weren't people. It was time to get back to the people.

George took another bite of his baklava. Mariam raised her eyebrows over playful blue-green eyes. "You like it?" she asked, although she already knew the answer.

"Love it," George said.

Lunches with Muslims was a program hosted by First They Came, a Brooklyn-based nonprofit organization that received funding through the Tolerance Department. Their name came from the famous Martin Niemöller quote:

"First they came for the socialists, and I did not speak out—

Because I was not a socialist.

Then they came for the trade unionists, and I did not speak out—

Because I was not a trade unionist.

Then they came for the Jews, and I did not speak out—

Because I was not a Jew.

Then they came for me—and there was no one left to speak for me."

The organization offered several initiatives designed to combat Islamophobia in the community—the most popular of which was "Harassed Hijabis: How You Can Help," an "other defense" class which had made the rounds on the local news. Lunches with Muslims was fairly new and was based on the time-honored principle that people who break bread together can't stay mad.

George had been attending faithfully every Wednesday for the past four weeks. There were still only a handful of participants. There was Mariam, of course, who always brought baklava—out of the kindness of her heart; a full catered lunch was provided by a different Muslim-run restaurant each week. And then there was Ibrahim, now seated in his wheelchair by the bookrack, perusing a pamphlet on renters' rights while his two young children, a boy and girl of about four and five, climbed all over him. Ibrahim looked up and waved at George. "My brother!" he shouted, and began wheeling himself over to George's table.

"Ibrahim!" George exclaimed, and the two men embraced.

Ibrahim was about forty, with straight black bangs that fell into his eyes. He produced a blue paperback Quran and handed it to George. "This is for you, my brother."

"Thank you," George said. "You gave me one last week, but I'll share this. I'll definitely pass it on."

"Good!" Ibrahim said. "Read it, and you'll see that we're all the same. All of us—black, white, Christian, Muslim, Jew—it doesn't matter. We're all brothers and sisters. Did you know that the Quran is exactly the same as the Bible? Same book! That's because we're all the same. We're all one."

"Yes we are," George said.

After Ibrahim left, George turned back to Mariam. "See, it's like Ibrahim said. We're all one. And we all know it, deep in our hearts. Most of us, anyway. And we act on it. Generally, we human beings are incredibly kind to one another—oftentimes against all logic. And when we're not, we know it; we feel it in our hearts; we know we've done something wrong.

"But these books ... these religious books we turn to, supposedly to help bring out the best in us—they're not always so kind, I'm finding. And I'm talking about all of them—the Bible, the Quran—all of them. They were all written in a fundamentally different time. And they're so full of contradictions, that in a way, they're basically unknowable. And they're often sadistic; at the very least, they're deeply morally ambiguous.

"Yet throughout history, some of the best and kindest people on earth have turned to these books for inspiration. They rejoice in them; they meditate on them; they try to improve themselves through them. But I think, in a way, what they're really doing is rejoicing and meditating on their own internal kindness, on their own goodness, on their own best natures, which—for some reason—they feel the need to project onto these morally ambiguous books—these ancient, inscrutable walls of text."

"That's a very interesting theory you have," Mariam said. "I recommend you keep researching all the religions, just like you're doing. Keep reading, and compare. And then choose the one you think is right. Because they're not all equal; they're not all the same. But yes, keep researching—that's why God gave us a brain, and intelligence!"

George nodded. "I mean, like I said, it's all religions. The Bible, for instance, contains some very strange passages." George pulled out his phone and searched until he found what he was looking for. "Like this one. It's from Deuteronomy. In this passage, God is describing to the Jews in excruciating detail how their enemies will seize their towns if they don't follow all of his commandments. Listen. It's pretty brutal."

George read: "'The most gentle and sensitive woman among you—so sensitive and gentle that she would not venture to touch the ground with the sole of her foot—will begrudge the husband she loves and her own son or daughter the afterbirth from her womb and the children she bears. For in her dire need she intends to eat them secretly because of the suffering your enemy will inflict on you during the siege of your cities.'

"I mean, not only is God threatening to make people so hungry that they'll eat their own children—and the afterbirth," George said, "but he goes on to intensify the punishment by saying ... they won't share?

"And there are plenty of other stories like that," George continued. "Take for example the story of Jephthah, in the book of Judges. Jephthah is a warrior, and he's about to go off to fight the Ammonites. He makes an oath to God that if he's victorious, he'll make a burnt offering of the first thing he sees coming through his door when he returns home. So he goes off to battle, and he's victorious. When he comes home, he sees his young daughter emerging from the house to greet him—she's smiling, and dancing with joy. He immediately remembers his oath to God. He's distraught, of course—he doesn't want to kill his daughter. But in the end, he decides it's the right thing to do. Even his daughter agrees it's the right thing to do. I mean, what kind of book says it's better to kill your own child than to go against the literal meaning of a poorly worded promise to God?

"And it's not just the Old Testament. In the book of

Matthew, the Canaanite woman—who is not Jewish—is pleading with Jesus to heal her daughter, who's possessed. Jesus tells her he won't help, because he was only sent to help the Jews. The Canaanite woman keeps begging and pleading, so Jesus says, basically, 'Why should I take bread from the children and toss it to the dogs?' In other words, he compares her to a dog, because she's not Jewish. Now, Jesus eventually ends up helping her, but the fact is, we like to hold up Jesus as the example of perfect, unconditional love. So why didn't he just help her in the first place? Why did he think she was less worthy than a Jew?

"My point is, all these religions have conflicting messages in them. We like to think they're about love, compassion, and forgiveness, but are they? And it's not just that they have a few strange or contradictory passages. No, even the main plots don't seem to be about love, compassion, or forgiveness. Let's just look at the Abrahamic religions, for example. The God of the Old Testament repeatedly dangles a prize in front of the Jews that they seem utterly unequipped to reach. He keeps promising them and punishing them, promising them and punishing them, promising them and punishing them—in a seemingly never-ending cycle. And Christianity, at its core, seems to be a celebration of God's acceptance of a human sacrifice. And Islam, with its unique outward focus on the sinfulness of other religions, can hardly be said to be peaceful through and through. What I'm trying to say is, don't you think that we, collectively, the human race, having learned so much and accomplished so much since those religions were formed—could do better than that? Aren't we, in fact, doing better than that right now?" George gestured around the room. "Just you, and me, and all these people, sitting here, enjoying lunch together, with the intention of befriending and understanding one another? Isn't this better than what's in any of those books?"

"This is wonderful!" Mariam said, her eyes lighting up. "You're already starting to understand. It's true that most religions are 'strange,' as you say. That's because most religions aren't pure; they've been corrupted by man. Why else would they have so many horrible things in them, like eating children ... and sacrificing children? Child sacrifice! Do you think God would want people to sacrifice their own children? No! Of course not. It's barbaric! See, Islam was sent by God to clean up all of that corruption, to abolish all of those abominable practices. Keep reading, you'll see. The Arab polytheists used to kill their own children too, then Islam came along and strictly forbade it ..."

"No, no," George said. "No, that's not what I meant. What I meant was, all these religions have shocking things in them, that sort of go against ..."

"Maybe that's not what you meant," Mariam said, "but it's true. Keep reading. You'll see."

"George," a woman's voice said, "could I speak to you for a moment?" George looked up and was met by a very pregnant belly straining against a blue wool dress. The belly belonged to Kate, one of the coordinators from First They Came.

"Yes of course," George said. As he followed her across the large multipurpose room, he spotted the retired American couple that had been coming every week in their matching New York Rangers jerseys. They were sitting at a table by themselves, eating fish curry in the rhythmic silence of the long married. He nodded at them, and they nodded back.

Kate stopped at the corner near the entrance and turned

to George. She was petite, with short blonde hair and very pale skin. She had somewhat sunken, tired-looking eyes—presumably the result of her advanced pregnancy. She rubbed her belly as she spoke.

"Listen, George," she said. "Here at Lunches with Muslims, we take pride in welcoming all members of the community."

George nodded enthusiastically.

"The point of this program is to allow people of all nationalities and faiths to get to know each other in a safe, neutral environment."

George continued nodding.

"The thing is, I've been watching you over the past few weeks, and ..." Kate paused, unsure of how to continue. "And I'm not really sure you've come here in the right spirit."

George began nodding, then stopped. "What?"

"I'm not really sure why I should even have to say this, George, but ... we don't allow proselytizing of any kind here. Obviously. We simply won't tolerate it."

"Proselytizing?"

"Yes. I saw you. I saw you quoting the Bible to that woman. We simply can't have that here. Everyone has the right to practice the religion of their choice. And we have to respect that."

A wave of relief washed over George. "Oh!" he said. "I can see how you might have thought that. But no, I wasn't proselytizing. Actually, quite the opposite. I was quoting insane passages from the Bible. Really dubious passages—just to illustrate how crazy religion in general can be—to point out some of its pitfalls. I'm not trying to force religion on anyone. No, quite the contrary." George smiled.

Kate eyed him closely. "Just ... don't quote the Bible anymore."

When George got back to the table, Mariam was setting down coffee. "Sorry," George said, "didn't mean to throw Bible verses at you."

"No!" Mariam protested. "That's why we're here, right? To talk about our ideas. To discuss things. Otherwise, how will we learn?"

George sipped his coffee and embarked upon a third slice of baklava. His mind was almost completely at ease for the first time in what seemed like a very long time. He took another bite; the chopped walnuts, flaky pastry, and concentrated bursts of butter and sugar formed a symphony in his mouth. Yes, Lunches with Muslims was good. Lunches with Muslims was the answer. Lunch was the answer. Lunch. People. People talking at lunch. People having heart-to-hearts—at lunch, or not at lunch. Real communication—that was the answer. Not books—with their strange, inscrutable stories.

Suddenly, George's plastic fork dropped to his plate. A vision came to him: a vision of a sculpture, a beautiful sculpture—a sphere, a beautiful glass orb, spinning in the air, throwing off glorious dancing prisms of light in every direction. And inside the sphere was a heart—a beautiful red heart. And on the heart was a book—a tiny open book—with miniature, ancient-looking writing on it. And at the base of the sculpture was a stone, a white stone, and on the stone were inscribed the following words, "The book is in our hearts." Yes! It was a deal tombstone, a project memento—for a brand-new passion project! "The book is in our hearts." Yes! It would be about how all people have the goodness written right inside of them ... Muslims, Christians, Jews ...

No! "HeartBook!" Yes, that's what he would call it. "HeartBook." That was even easier to understand. Everyone would relate to it instantly, instinctually. It was simple. Universally comprehensible. Much easier to understand than apologizing to Muslims, or anything like that. It was transcultural, ecumenical, nondenominational. "HeartBook: Listen to the Book in Your Heart." Yes! It would be a way of connecting all humanity ... Muslims, Christians, Jews ...

No! "HeartBible!" Yes! "HeartBible." That was better. Or no! "HeartScripture!" Yes! Or no! "HeartReligion." Yes! "HeartReligion."

Or no! "HeartWisdom!" Yes, that's what he would call it. "HeartWisdom." With no reference to religion at all. That way everyone would be able to relate. No one would be excluded. "HeartWisdom." Or no! "HeartScript!" Whatever, it didn't matter. He'd work out the details later.

Sammy walked in just as Mariam was leaving. Sammy was a retired pharmacist, originally from Afghanistan. He had thick, perfectly white hair and a distinguished-looking aquiline nose. He grabbed a cup of coffee and sat down next to George.

"Sammy, I've been thinking a lot about what we talked about last week," George said. "You know, about the Taliban ..."

"Yes," Sammy said, a faraway look in his eyes. "Yes, my friend. It's such a shame what happened to my country."

"I know," George said. "So, I was thinking about religion in general. And in a way, I think it does nothing but confuse us. I mean, yeah, there's some good in it, for sure. But it seems like all religion relies on these books that are hundreds and hundreds of years old, that say some really confusing and conflicting things. And then the bad people in the world—hell, sometimes even the good people in the world—they latch on to those confusing parts. See, I've been doing a lot of reading, and it turns out that most religion isn't about what we think it's about, like loving your neighbor, and stuff like that. It isn't about ..." George gestured around the room, "this! It isn't about people treating all different kinds of people with respect. It isn't about love. It's more about ... I don't know ... dietary laws, and architectural blueprints, and going to war, and gaining supremacy over other religions, and figuring out who's clean and who's unclean ..."

Sammy tilted his head, thinking.

"I think," George continued, "that the 'love your neighbor' stuff, the 'do unto others' stuff—it's in our hearts." George tapped his heart and gestured toward Sammy's heart. "I think we all have it. I think we're born with it."

"You know," Sammy said, "I think you're right."

"I believe," George continued, "that the real book—is in our hearts." He tapped his heart again. "And it's the same book for every one of us. For you. For me. For Ibrahim." He gestured toward Ibrahim, who was now sitting with the retired couple. "For them. For all of us. The real book is inside us. Right here." He tapped his heart again.

"You know," Sammy said, "my friend. You are 100 percent correct. I could not agree with you more."

Both men nodded and sipped their coffee.

"There is one perfect religion," Sammy continued. "And it's in our hearts. Only one religion for man. Because how can there be different rules for different people? How can there be different Gods for different people? We're all human, right?"

"Exactly," George said.

"Do you think God would put one religion in your heart, and another religion in mine? No! We're the same."

"Yes," George said. "You get it. See, I'm thinking of doing some kind of passion project around that, called 'The Book Is in Your Heart'—or something like that. A tolerance challenge. Just letting people know, 'Hey, the book is in your heart. That's all you need. All that goodness you're seeking, it's right here, in your heart.'"

"What a wonderful idea, my friend!" Sammy said. "A very good idea. And for me—I'm saying just for me, not for anybody else—that book is Islam. The book in my heart is Islam."

"That's beautiful," George said. "I respect that. I guess people just corrupt it, that's the problem. I guess they don't listen to their heart, they listen to ..."

"Exactly," Sammy said. "If people would listen to their heart, they would be following Islam 100 percent. Islam is about exactly what you said. It's about kindness, it's about loving your brother, it's about how we're all the same—nothing else. It's very simple."

"See," George said, "I think *you're* about that, Sammy. I think you're about kindness, and you're about loving your brother, and you're about treating everyone the same. But I'm not so sure any religion is about that when it comes right down to it. I think we just project the book in our hearts onto those religious books. Remember last week how you were telling me how great Afghanistan used to be, how peaceful it was, how diverse—how everyone lived together, Sunnis, Shiites, Jews ..."

"Yes," Sammy said. "It was incredible. You have no idea! It was a beautiful country. Beautiful! Perfect! So advanced.

Technology. Science. Art. Medicine. Culture. We had it all! You have no idea, my friend. No idea."

"Yeah. I know," George said. "But then the Taliban gained power and started imposing a fundamental form of Islam on everyone, and now women can't go to school, can't see doctors, and no one can ..."

"No, no," Sammy said. "You are wrong, my friend. The Taliban is not fundamental Islam. The Taliban is not Islam at all."

Out of the corner of his eye, George saw Kate leaning against the next table, her ear tilted toward the conversation.

"You want to know what the Taliban is, my friend?" Sammy continued, his voice escalating. "You want to know how the Taliban was created? I'll tell you. Three things." He held up three fingers and began ticking them off, "The CIA, Saudi Arabia, and Pakistan. They created the Taliban! They are responsible for what my country is today."

George nodded.

"Islam is 100 percent blameless," Sammy continued. "It's perfect. It's like you said. It's the pure religion. It's the religion in our hearts." Sammy thought for a moment, then he added, "It's such a shame. Such a shame what happened to my country."

"It is," George said. "And I totally get what you're saying about the CIA, and Saudi Arabia, and Pakistan. I do. But, at the same time, can you really say that Islam contributes nothing at all to what the Taliban is? I'm not trying to single out Islam, but all these religions, they seem to have things in them that are ... extreme ..."

"Not Islam, my friend. Islam is perfect. My religion is 100 percent peaceful, 100 percent beautiful. Even the word Islam means peace."

"Right," George said. "I get it. Islam is very beautiful. I've studied it. But you have to admit, it has some parts ... I don't want to get into it here. But those parts—they're what the Taliban is practicing. Those parts didn't come from the CIA. The CIA may have armed and trained the Taliban—which, you're right, in retrospect, didn't turn out to be such a good idea—but they didn't teach them Islam ..."

Kate had inched closer to the table.

"My friend, I'm telling you," Sammy said, "the Taliban has absolutely nothing to do with Islam. Trust me." He held up his fingers again. "The United States. Saudi Arabia. Pakistan ..."

"But it's happening all over the world," George said. "Not just in Afghanistan. There are groups in practically every country adopting a more violent and fundamental form of Islam—in settings so diverse that the only thing they could possibly have in common is Islam ..."

"No. Those groups have nothing at all to do with Islam," Sammy said.

"Nothing?"

"Nothing."

"Well then where does all that stuff come from?" George said. "About women having to be covered, about death to blasphemers and apostates ...? I mean, yes, there are many contributing factors to the overall situation in the world. Politics, European imperialism, American interference—sure. But to say Islam has nothing at all to do with those groups ..."

Kate cleared her throat. "George, I need to speak to you."

But George was so absorbed in the conversation he didn't hear her. "I mean, don't get me wrong," he continued, "I'm not saying Islam is uniquely to blame. No. Far from it. I'm just saying it's part of the soup. That's all. And I don't think there's anything wrong with saying that. To look at something objectively is not the same thing as to insult or degrade it. On the contrary, it's vital. We all need to be able to self-reflect—whatever our culture, whatever our religion, whatever our country. And we need to be able to be honest with ourselves about what's working and what isn't ..."

"George," Kate said, louder this time. "I need to talk to you."

"Oh, sure," George said, getting up.

"You're right," Sammy said.

George stopped.

"I see what you mean," Sammy continued. "I guess it's a combination of things. Many factors. Many factors are responsible for the situation my country is in today."

"That's all I'm saying!" George said. "Nobody's perfect. No government, no culture, no religion—no person—is perfect." Then he paused. "I hope you understand that's all I mean. I hope you know I don't mean any offense, in any way ..."

"No, of course not," Sammy said. He stood up, and the two men embraced. "That's what life is all about. Discussing ideas. Discussing life. Discussing opinions. You see, that's what I'm trying to tell you. That's how my country used to be—so intellectual, so free, so progressive. We'd have these discussions for hours. All night long! You have no idea, my friend ..."

George followed Kate through the multipurpose room, down a carpeted hallway, and into her office. Once they were both seated, Kate stared at George from across her desk.

"I don't think this is productive," she said, finally.

George looked at her, confused.

"I just don't think this is productive," she repeated. "The purpose of this program is to foster peace and understanding between Muslims and their communities. And, like I said, George, you're not here in that spirit. In fact, you're proving to be a highly disruptive presence."

George stared at her in disbelief.

Kate rubbed her belly, gathering courage. "The truth is, I find you incredibly offensive. Borderline Islamophobic."

"What?" George said, his heart dropping.

"You're not welcome back to lunch."

"What?"

"You're no longer welcome at Lunches with Muslims."

"But ... what did I do?" George said, panic rising in his voice. "Did they complain about me? Did the Muslims complain?"

"They shouldn't have to, George!" Kate said, exasperated. "Again, I'm not really sure why I should even have to say this, but you're obviously not allowed to talk to Muslims about Islam. That's simply unacceptable. You should know that."

"But? How? They don't mind! The Muslims don't mind. I'm sure of it! In fact, I think they enjoy it. Ask any of them. Ask Ibrahim! He gave me two Qurans. Two! And Mariam, she gave me three pieces of baklava. And Sammy, he's been opening up to me about Afghanistan. Sammy and I are really starting to understand each other. As a matter of fact, I'd say that all of us, together, are perfectly fulfilling the purpose of Lunches with Muslims. We're exemplary! We're talking, getting to know each other, sharing experiences, food ..."

"I don't think so George."

"Wait, you don't seem to understand. I'm not the enemy here, Kate. In fact, you and I have a lot in common—much more than you think. See, I have a program too. It's all about Muslims ... I mean, I used to have a program, and I'm going to have another one, very soon, it's going to be called 'Heart-Book,' or 'HeartScripture,' or something like that. Anyway, it's all about how we human beings are all one, and about how we all know that, deep in our hearts, almost as if we have a book there ..."

CHAPTER TWENTY-THREE
BRIDGE BUILDERS

"Good evening, everyone," Marine said, seated on a bench, turning toward the camera and her bare-bones production crew. She was stunning as ever, in a sleek, pale sage-green skirt suit. A large pair of gold dragonfly earrings dangled from her ears, shimmering brilliantly in the early evening sun with her every move.

"Tonight, folks, we're coming to you live from Central Park with a very special segment. Now, I'm sure everyone knows about the so-called Islamophobia incident at Noblepride, where the lovely Finnish men in burqas were allegedly attacked by a racist that is known to us all. And I'm sure you've all been expecting me to do a *Hate Hunters* about it.

"But tonight, folks, we're going to do something a little different."

Marine shared a conspiratorial look with her skeleton crew, then leaned forward toward the camera, one toned, tanned leg crossing over the other. She was silent for several moments. She'd become attuned to the power of silence as a language after the runaway success of her revolutionary burqa-affixing two minutes of silence on live national TV.

She spoke. "Tonight we're going to be building some bridges." She paused, and then continued, "As you know, our show and our team have worked tirelessly over the years to bring attention to instances of hate and white supremacy, and, unfortunately, even after all this time, they are still too numerous. However, I feel it's time to remind ourselves that awareness is just the first step. The second step is, well, how do we bridge that divide? And I feel it's time we try to ... talk. To have heart-to-hearts—like I'm doing right here, right now, with all of you. We need to have more heart-to-hearts with people. With our neighbors, our family members, our fellow citizens—some of whom may very well have different ideas and opinions and feelings than we do. We need to talk to them. And we need to listen to them. Only then can we truly begin to understand each other and begin to heal."

Marine let another long, protracted silence grow. Five seconds went by. Then ten seconds. Then fifteen. She uncrossed and recrossed her legs, keeping her eyes on the camera.

Then she spoke. "Tonight folks, I'm bringing you a very special guest, on a special live episode of *Bridge Builders*. I'm going to be welcoming Miss Jackie Krucic, who is just, believe me folks, an incredible woman." Marine paused. "Many of you know of her, and many of you have even captured her on film. And it's true, she's made some mistakes. But the thing is, we all have. And what's so incredible about her is, she's learned. She's really put into practice everything we've taught her. That's right, not many people know this, but we have a pretty amazing team of tolerance counselors here. So, you see, there is another side to our efforts. First, yes, we must call out and use the incident, and the offender, as a teachable moment on *Hate Hunters*, but then, we actually teach *them*. We teach the offenders, not just you. And you'll see, my guest, Miss Krucic, well, she's really made progress. She's sort of a star, according to our counselors. A model student. So we're going to hear from her."

Marine nodded to her crew, and Jackie was led onto the green bench. There was, perhaps, less difference between the two women than there once would have been. It seemed Jackie had evolved her wardrobe stylings a step further, and no longer looked like a jaunty, aging Shirley Temple. Her hair had been brought down a level, both in color and texture, and she wore a rather muted, tasteful pantsuit.

"Welcome, Jackie," Marine said.

"Thank you," Jackie said. "Thank you for having me here."

"Absolutely, it's been a long time coming. Too long. So anyway, today, you and I are going to finally talk. Because I believe it's really only by talking about things and trying to understand each other that it becomes possible, as a society, to work through these things, and move forward."

"Absolutely, Marine," Jackie said. "It's funny. I've been on camera so much. But no one has ever ... talked to me. I really appreciate it."

Marine nodded. "So, Noblepride," she said. "Let's talk about Noblepride for a moment. Now, I'm sure you're aware that the footage has done the rounds, and some people are very upset about it. But perhaps they don't know the full story, so I thought what we'd do here today, is we'd start by getting your side, your take on what happened that day."

"Sure, Marine. So that day, I was at the parade, and as you know, the theme this year was 'I Stand with Ruby,' so a lot of people were wearing Muslim religious garb, head coverings, face coverings, and the like. And I happened to see a very interesting film, made by some Muslim women, and they had an interesting take on the whole phenomenon—a different take. They weren't against head coverings, per se, I don't think, but they were trying to point out that they don't necessarily represent freedom, in all contexts. So you have this piece of cloth, essentially, that can mean many different things to many different people, but they wanted to talk about what it meant to them, in particular, and I found theirs to be a worthwhile perspective. That's why I was somewhat puzzled at the reaction of the crowd ..."

Marine nodded, then interjected, "Jackie, correct me if I'm wrong, but from what I understand, when you called those lovely Finish American men terrorists, you were talking about ... about your own personal terror—the terror you've felt over the years, at being filmed against your will. At being misunderstood, categorized, labeled, shamed, ridiculed, excoriated by the nation."

Jackie took a deep breath. "Yes. It's true."

Marine closed her eyes and nodded. She let the silence grow again. Then she turned to the camera and spoke. "See? Do you see how fruitful this conversation has been already? Isn't this a valuable thing to be doing? Talking? Just good old-fashioned back-and-forth? See, as Jackie just said, when she used the word terrorist, she was referring to her own personal terror, the way she's felt, subjectively, all these years, always being on the other end of the camera."

She turned back to Jackie. "So, what you're telling us, then, is that when you called those men terrorists, it had absolutely nothing to do with Islam."

Jackie tilted her head, seemingly deep in thought. Marine

studied her. The two women were sitting very close to each other on the bench.

"That's a very good question, Marine," Jackie said.

Marine nodded eagerly.

"You know, I did have a lot on my mind at that moment. On a certain level, I was still processing the film I'd just seen. Also, lately, I've been thinking a great deal about recent events—about Islamic terrorism, I mean. In fact, I happen to be very good friends with a family who's been deeply affected by it. So I've been researching the issue lot. Actually, I might write a book about it ..."

Marine teetered on the bench a little. "Jackie," she interrupted, "let's get back to that moment, at the parade, when the hooded Scandinavian men were filming you, and criticizing you. I mean, I can only imagine what I would feel if that happened to me. I might feel very stressed, and panicked, and invaded—violated. Terrorized, even. I mean, am I far off? Am I correct in assuming that when you called those hooded people terrorists, you were in fact referring to your own personal sense of terror, rather than Islam?"

"But that's what I'm trying to tell you, Marine. I think on some level I was referring to Islam. I think I was using the word in both ways. I mean, yes, I have had tremendous problems with being filmed in the past—just tremendous. But also, Islam has had a tremendous problem with terrorism, and I think we need ..."

Marine exchanged panicked glances with her camera crew.

"Jackie," Marine said, in a quiet, meditative tone, "this is absolutely fascinating, but I think we'd do well to provide a little context here. I'm not sure if you're familiar with the statistics, but I just heard an interesting one: Did you know that since September twelfth, 2001, the number of people killed in acts of foreign Islamic terrorism on US soil is far outpaced by the number of people decapitated in snowmobile accidents?"

Jackie looked surprised. "I didn't," she said. "Nevertheless, in my research, I've been focusing on how some parts of the Quran, when considered in a certain way, might be seen as condoning terrorism, and I've been looking at that in the context of ..."

"Jackie," Marine said, laughing nervously, "we're trying to build bridges here, remember." She took a deep breath and touched her right dragonfly earring. She continued, in a soft, somewhat didactic tone, "See, the thing is, Jackie, this is just amazing, that you're speaking to us candidly. But, you know —and I'm sure you've learned this in your counseling—we must be mindful. We must be mindful of the words we use. Words have power, Jackie. Words have the power to incite violence."

"Yes," Jackie said. "That is very much my point. Words have the power to incite violence, and I think we need to address this. Especially now, in light of recent events. We should talk about it. We should talk about terrorism. We should discuss why it's happening ..."

"But Jackie, it doesn't happen for a *reason*. It happens as a result of random, deranged individuals. And very infrequently, I might add. For example, did you know that more people die each year in bathtub drownings, and in waterslide mishaps, and in ..." Marine looked desperately at her crew, "and in ... in hippopotamus attacks?"

"But what if there *is* a reason?" Jackie said. "Wouldn't it be worth talking about? What if lives could be saved? And Muslim lives most of all? Muslims are very disproportionately affected by Islamic terrorism. Globally, they are the ones who receive the brunt of the violence stemming from fundamentalist Islamic philosophies ..."

"Jackie!" Marine said, rather firmly. "I understand that you think this is an interesting topic, but the fact is, we simply cannot afford to discuss it." Then she softened. "See, words just have too much power to incite violence. So, it's best to leave this topic. As a matter of fact," Marine looked over to her producer and then turned back to Jackie, "you know what I'm going to do? I'm going to send you and a friend to see the triple Tony Award-winning play, *Danger's Tweets*—my treat! It's a very poignant play, about the power of words to breed hate and incite violence, and about why it's so important to treat all races and religions with respect."

Jackie leaned forward on the bench. "Exactly," she said. "*Danger's Tweets* is such an important play because it shows the power that words have to hurt and to heal. And that's exactly what I've been researching. That's what I'm trying to tell you. I think we need to take a look at some of the words in the Quran, and how they ..."

"No," Marine said. "No, no, Jackie, you're not understanding me. What I'm saying is that we, as a society, need to look at hate speech. That's what I'm saying, and that's what the play is saying. See, you're the one coming perilously close to engaging in hate speech, Jackie. I'm sure you don't mean anything by it, and that's why I'm sending you to see *Danger's Tweets*. So you'll understand ..."

"But what I'm saying, Marine, is that you're right. *Danger's Tweets* is the answer. What I'm saying is we need to start studying ..." Jackie looked thoughtful for a moment, and then, seemingly pleased with herself, raised her index finger and said, "*Mohammad's tweets.* We need to start thinking about the effect *Mohammad's tweets* are having today ..."

"No!" Marine said. "No! It's Danger. Danger, okay! Danger, Danger! It's Danger's tweets. Mohammad never tweeted. Oh! No. I'm sorry ... I ..." She turned to the camera, composing herself. "I'm so sorry. I didn't mean to say Mohammad tweeted. I mean! I didn't say Mohammad tweeted, I mean, I didn't mean to say Mohammad. Oh God!"

But Jackie forged ahead. "See, everyone's still reading Mohammad's tweets from 1400 years ago. And, while some of the tweets are brilliant, some of them are violent. You know—killing infidels, holy war stuff ..."

Marine began stage-whispering/barking out of the side of her mouth at Jackie. "It's! Racist! Stop! Racist! Don't! Talk! Racist!"

The color drained from Jackie's face, and she looked down.

The silence began to grow between them again, but not in a good way. Five seconds. Ten seconds ...

Then Jackie narrowed her eyes and looked at Marine with a steeliness she'd not previously demonstrated. When she spoke, her words were measured—a challenge. "You don't hate hate," she said.

Marine jerked visibly. "Excuse me?" she said.

"You heard me," Jackie said.

"No. I don't believe I did," Marine said, her face flashing red.

"You don't hate hate."

"Oh, I hate hate," Marine said.

"No. You don't. You don't hate hate," said Jackie, calmly.

"I do," said Marine.

"You don't," said Jackie.

“I do,” said Marine. “I abhor hate.”

“No. You don’t. You don’t hate hate at all.”

“I do. I hate hate more than anything.”

“You don’t,” Jackie said.

“I do.”

“You don’t.”

Marine looked at her crew and, moving her fingers across her throat, made the international sign for “Stop filming!”

CHAPTER TWENTY-FOUR
AWAY

Mohammad sat on his favorite bench in Ramna Park, the sprawling municipal park in the heart of Dhaka, the city of his birth. He'd fled New York soon after the train bombing, and this was part of his daily routine. He'd walk about a half an hour or so down various winding paths, buy tea from his favorite vendor, and sit on "his" bench by the lake.

He studied the thicket of trees on the opposite shore. They were so lively. They almost looked animate. The coconut trees looked as if they'd sprung up overnight, just for the sheer joy of it; and the sheltering banyans extended their limbs like graceful dancers, enlivened and expressive down to the fingertips.

The banyans looked as if they were dancing for him alone, and were trying to tell him something. His natural immigrant's guilt filled in the words: "Brother, where have you been? You have been gone for so long."

Mohammad wondered if there were banyan trees in America. He didn't remember seeing any. But then again, America wasn't as much of a tree-gazing place. They could have been everywhere, and he just didn't see them. But he didn't think so.

Maybe America's climate wasn't conducive to the banyan trees. Had someone tried to plant them, in a botanical garden, perhaps, or on a suburban street, and they'd withered and died?

The banyans across the lake swayed on a soft, extended breeze, their fingers gesticulating, "You're on the right path, brother."

Is that what had happened to Ruby? Had he plucked her from her natural environment? And tried to plant her in America? Is that what had happened? Had she become lonely and confused? Longing for her native soil?

Or was it the mix of ideas from here and there that had confused her? Had the ideas from there somehow "activated" the ideas from here? Like liquid in a test tube, inert on its own, until another, also seemingly inert, agent was added? Had the Islam that was natural to Bangladesh been "activated" by the current anti-American sentiments—in America? Had going to America been a failed experiment for that reason?

No, Mohammad said to the banyans. You are wrong, my friends. Going to America was not a mistake.

Because it was happening everywhere. The mix of ideas. They were in the soil, in the air. And it was especially happening here, in the country of his birth, in the country Ruby would have grown up in had he not emigrated.

In truth, it was like a different country than the one he'd grown up in, than the one he'd been a young man in. Fundamentalist Islam and political Islam were catching like wildfire. Terrorism was on the uptick. People expressing liberal ideas were being murdered on the streets. Even the textbooks were changing. Certain groups were demanding that all manner of things be cleansed from them. And in some instances, the secular government was having no choice but to cave to those demands.

According to a childhood friend, Hindu and Christian names were disappearing from textbooks. And, horror of all horrors, certain poems of Tagore—whose poetry made up the national anthem, and who happened to have been a Hindu—had been removed from the curriculum. Even the way the alphabet was being taught had changed. *O* was no longer for "Ol"—or yam: but for "Orna"—a modesty scarf.

No. Ruby would have caught those ideas here too. The self-appointed mullahs were preaching them day and night on the Internet. And they were seductive ideas: clean, crisp, righteously angry; sanctified and mobilizing; wrapped up in attractive packaging, like Coca-Cola, or candy.

A young couple walked by on the path a few feet away from him. The girl, in a dark red salwar kameez, laughed as she caressed the boy's face.

He felt a glimmer of hope. His was a country for lovers! A country for poets and writers and dreamers and philosophers. A country for diversity. For secularism ... and respect for human rights.

Why was it that now, of all times, just when things seemed to be so good—much better than when he was growing up—did certain groups want to lead the country backwards? People were getting *happier*. More people than ever before had disposable income. More people had the ability to travel, to study, to communicate with the world. Why now, just when things were getting good, were these fundamentalist groups on the upswing? They had always been there. But now, people were listening.

Mohammed thought for a while. The trees across the shore were still, perhaps also thinking.

A white egret on the shore, with its long S-shaped neck, looked at him, then walked away elegantly, lifting its legs with each step, as if to avoid stepping in something displeasurable.

Maybe it came down to fear, Mohammad thought. Perhaps as the world got closer and closer, and things got easier and easier, something in the spirit balked—a global intimacy tic of sorts.

A small hand laced its way into his, knocking him out of his reverie.

"Dad, let's go home," Ruby said.

"Okay, my angel, we can help Mom with dinner."

"No," Ruby said. "I mean home to America."

CHAPTER TWENTY-FIVE
THE BROCHURE

Jackie took a sip of her gin and tonic and looked over the glossy brochure Alma had placed on the bar in front of her. It was a multipage booklet, with a smiling, ethnically diverse family of four on the cover, along with the rather heroic title "Making the World Unsafe for Hate." Underneath it was the caption, "What You Need to Know." It was the first she'd seen of it. She turned to Alma. "This is the first I've seen of it," she said.

"Just read it," said Alma, who was perched atop the barstool next to her, wearing a blue floral hijab and sipping a pint of Dante's Special Edition Noblepride Ale, which was hazy, dreamlike, and unapologetically malty.

Jackie opened the brochure and began reading:

"We would like to take this opportunity to inform all Virtuous Federation citizens of some very important news. As you know, our federation has long been at the forefront of the tolerance movement, and we have all worked tirelessly together toward the goal of building a society that is inclusive and respectful of all people, regardless of race, national origin, sexual orientation, gender, or faith. And we have made tremendous strides! Collectively, we've been true to our word. We've been loath to tolerate intolerance, and we've all done our part to stand up to certain individuals whose words and actions seem designed to harken us back to a more brutal, ignorant, and unenlightened time. Each and every one of you—armed with just your cameras to film, and your fingers to decry—have helped identify and ostracize these miscreant individuals, and we applaud you!

"And now we, as a society, are ready to take the next step toward living in a more tolerant world. Starting now, all your good works will be backed up by the full force of law. Yes, you read that right; as of this writing, it's not only repugnant to hate—it's illegal: just like theft, burglary, rape, and murder. We'll say it again. Hate, in and of itself, is now a crime."

Next to the text was a stock photograph of a group of people with all different skin tones, sitting around a conference table, smiling and talking pleasantly.

The next section was titled, "What Does This Mean for Me?"

Jackie continued reading:

"Well, probably nothing. You'll just continue doing your good works, and calling out hate wherever you see it—only now, there are criminal statutes in place to back you up. So now, for example, when you submit a video to *Hate Hunters*, or even just notify any of the partner agencies (see the list on our website, nohomeforhate.vf) about an incident of hate that you've witnessed, we'll take the appropriate legal measures.

"However, if you're an individual who engages in hateful speech or hateful behavior, take heed! Consider this your notice that your behavior will no longer be even peripherally tolerated. Things are about to change for you—in a dramatic way. If you are such an individual, we strongly recommend that you continue reading this brochure—and visit the website—in order to inform yourself in detail of the new laws and new consequences as they emerge. If you feel you are not able to, or do not wish to comply with any of these new laws, we strongly recommend that you relocate to a geographic location more in line with your values."

There was a stock photo of a person standing at a crossroads, looking up at a sign with arrows pointing in two different directions.

Jackie looked at Alma questioningly. Alma nodded and took a morose sip of her unapologetic beer.

Jackie began reading the next section, which was titled "Virtuous Jurisdiction."

"The new hate laws are neither state, nor federal, but belong to an entirely new jurisdiction, known as virtuous jurisdiction. The virtuous system of law differs from the state and federal systems in every respect—from formulation, to enforcement, to prosecution, to punishment. Based on neither common law nor civil law, nor any other form of 'the white man's law'—particularly the historically racist form of common law practiced in the US—virtuous law is at once holistic, inclusive, intuitive, and multicultural.

"The virtuous law criminal code is currently in the process of being written. Laws as they're added will be updated on our website. However, we are extremely happy to announce the enactment of our maidenhead statute—the first of the groundbreaking virtuous laws—namely, VL Section One, Paragraph Five, also known as 'the egregious Islamophobia statute.'

"Hate takes many forms, and all are equally repugnant to the virtuous man, woman, or nonbinary person. However, no form of hate is more loathsome at this present moment in history than Islamophobia. Muslims across our land are in extreme danger of being blamed for recent events and are experiencing retaliation for recent events at record rates. In fact, since recent events, Islamophobic hate crimes have risen by 70,000 percent, and are predicted to continue to rise sharply.

"The egregious Islamophobia statute reads as follows: 'Any person speaking or acting in any way that demonstrates hate toward Muslims or toward Islam, or any person who, through their speech or their acts, causes offense to any Muslim, or toward Islam, shall be deemed in violation of this law.'

"And that's it! That's the entirety of the egregious Islamophobia law. Simple, elegant, profound. You'll see by its design that virtuous law is an 'everyman's law' of sorts—free from elitist jargon, academic technicalities, and obscure loopholes. We shall now briefly discuss certain aspects of the egregious Islamophobia law, in order to not only highlight several of its salient points, but also to draw attention to certain important features of virtuous law in general. Firstly, it shall be noted that, as distinct from federal and state hate crime statutes, VL 1.05 does not require that any additional criminal act be committed. Yes, that's right, in virtuous law, the sentiment itself is considered repugnant enough. Secondly, the simple, nonspecific wording of the law is deliberate. It allows violations to be adjudicated according to a complex and proprietary algorithm that is both holistic and intuitive —i.e., non-Western—and takes into account a multitude of factors in determining guilt: including narrative justice principles, relative positions on the nobility tree, the magnitude of society's emotional outrage, common sense, and other nonquantifiable yet profound influences. In other words, by not including multiple sections and paragraphs of 'legalese,' we avoid the trap of getting bogged down by 'the letter of the law' and are free instead to pursue 'the spirit of the law.' As such, we avoid many of the pitfalls of law as practiced today: including harsh sentences for crimes committed for good reasons, and light sentences or acquittals based on expensively exploited loopholes or mindbogglingly narrow interpretations of the constitution.

"Now, for those conspiracy-theory inclined bigots among you, who are probably already shouting, 'It's here! It's here! Sharia law is here in America—just as we predicted!' and who are probably already rabble-rousing and yammering on about 'the Islamification of America,' to you, we say, calm down. The egregious Islamophobia statute has absolutely nothing to do with sharia blasphemy laws. The two exist within completely different contexts, and as such, it is extremely disingenuous to try to equate them."

There was a graphic depicting a smiling mother lying on the grass with her giggling baby.

Jackie looked up. "What does the baby have to do with it?" And then, turning the brochure in her hand, "And what *is* this? It doesn't make any sense." She then looked at Alma, took in her headscarf, and began to nod slowly. "Oh. Wait," she said. "Oh. Okay. I get it. I know what this is. This is one of your lessons, right? I mean, that's why you're dressed like that. That's why you've been dressing like that. Actually, I was going to tell you, Alma, I really like your head scarf. I mean I know it's just a prop, or whatever. But there's something about it. The flowers—it suits you. Anyway. Yeah, I get it. I think you're trying to show me that Muslims are people, maybe even people I know, and that it's not cool to offend them. Yeah. I get it. Oh! And you're trying to show me that Muslims drink beer! Yes, and that it's stupid of us to have such dumb preconceptions about them. Right? Yup. I get it. This must be—because of my interview, right? Okay. I get it. But trust me, I don't believe Muslims aren't human—far from it. What I was trying to say in my interview was that, yes, Muslims are human, and as humans ..."

"No, Jackie, that's not what this is about," Alma said, a little too loudly, trying her best to suppress a note of panic that was creeping into her voice.

The bartender, who was leaning against the other end of the bar reading the free neighborhood paper, turned around and looked at them. It was a Tuesday morning, and there were only six souls in the place.

Alma quieted her voice. She then spoke in a measured whisper. "This is real, Jackie. And by the way, I *am* Muslim, but that's not the point. Unfortunately, the brochure is real. That's why I'm showing it to you. And ... I hate to say this, but ... well, the feeling is ... you're it. You're going to be chosen as the maidenhead violator of the maidenhead statute. Maybe today."

Jackie looked confused for a moment, then said, "Wait, when did you become Muslim?"

"It's not important," Alma said. She sighed, then slid her empty beer glass forward. The bartender walked over and poured her another.

The newly minted virtuous jurisdiction had taken everyone by surprise. It had definitely taken Alma by surprise. She'd known that certain groups had long been agitating for more stringency, more enforcement, and more severe punishments for tolerance offenders, but in her mind, those groups were always on the fringe: United Citizens for Virtuous Sovereignty, the Committee for Citizen Accountability, the Cross-Cultural Justice Initiative, the Society for the Demolishment of Intolerance, the Stand Together or Stand Alone Coalition, and many others. But she'd had no idea of the power they actually wielded, or the buy-in they had with the more mainstream decision makers like the Tolerance Department.

It wasn't until the airing of the now infamous Central Park *Bridge Builders* that the new laws generated any buzz, alerting most people for the first time of their existence, despite the comprehensive and ambitious brochure mailing campaign.

Now, it was all anyone talked about. Enthusiastic tolerance bureaucrats everywhere tried jamming Jackie's name into the mysterious and little understood algorithm. The feeling was, that between her egregious white middle-agedness and her very public past and present offenses—both as an individual, and as a race—she would surely be spit out as guilty—possibly before the day was through.

The overall mood at the Tolerance Department was celebratory. It was a long-awaited dream come true for most. Things would happen—real things—because of them. A trial —or something like it—would take place. Someone would pay. Punishment would be meted out. The do-gooders would finally be taken seriously. They would be respected and feared—just like the police, the justice department, and the FBI! Their collective exhortations and admonitions would finally amount to more than piquant slogans and well-thought-out words flapping in the breeze. They would at long last be seen as more than just so many frustrated schoolmarms, pestering people to live better lives; academic finger waggers of the new global etiquette; peeved, shushing librarians of political correctness.

A fête had been held in the conference room, featuring a catered Middle Eastern lunch with both gluten free and vegan options. During the party, Alma was still in shock. She looked around the room, watching people dance to the somewhat sterile EDM stylings of Braxton Hammond. Wendy Watkins gyrated her hips as she sipped champagne from a plastic flute. Allison Corval and Derrald St. Phair bumped hips and yelled in unison, "Heads are gonna roll!" Marine Schorr shifted back and forth, a skewer of grilled chicken in her hand and a faraway look in her eyes. She was accompanied, as ever, by her intern, Melanie Diaz, who swayed her hips and nodded approvingly at Marine, while balancing a Ritz Cracker and a can of diet Orange Crush in her left hand.

Alma had tried protesting the Islamophobia statute to anyone who would listen. She'd argued that Islam was a religion of peace, a religion of tolerance, and a religion that accepted many different points of view. Not only that, it was a religion of mercy, forgiveness, redemption, and second chances; and as such, it would never exact such harsh retribution for a few insignificant words or acts.

She reminded everyone that she herself was a Muslim, and was not in the least bit offended by such things—certainly not anything that, say, Jackie Krucic, had said or done. But it was strange. It seemed to Alma that every time she made an argument on the basis of she herself being Muslim, she detected—or thought she detected—a slight condescending smirk on the face of whoever she was talking to. She'd been getting this reaction for a while at the Tolerance Department. Nobody said anything directly, as they had when she was black, but there were looks and innuendos. For example, a lot of them were trying to pressure her into hosting a Muslim cultural hour. "We'd love to hear all about your new religion, Alma," they'd say, a slight note of superciliousness in their voices. "Yes, Alma, please enlighten us. Educate us about Islam."

"Look, Alma," Jackie said, "I understand what you're trying to say with your ..." she waved the brochure, "... lesson here. I do. And I appreciate it. But, I actually have something to say on this very point. On Islam. Actually, I have quite a bit to say. I've been doing research on it. Well, okay, a book. I've been writing a book, and I'd be eager to get your opinion. I think you'll find it very interesting—as a tolerance counselor. Oh, and as a Muslim. So the way it started was ..."

"Jackie," Alma said, "I know about your book, but please, listen, I need to ..."

"Oh, sorry," Jackie said. "Finish your lesson first. I'm curious to see how it ends. And then I'll tell you about my book."

"Jackie," Alma said, exasperated, "please listen!" Then she looked around and lowered her voice. "This is what I'm trying to tell you ... this isn't a lesson. There *are* no more lessons. No more plays. No more counseling. No more decrying. It's different now. It's been criminalized. Hate has been criminalized. I can't believe this is the first you're hearing of this."

Jackie looked at the brochure. "Well I get a lot of junk mail," she conceded, "and a lot of catalogs. It's possible it went straight to recycling. I really can't rule that out."

"Just ..." Alma said. "Just keep reading."

The next section of the brochure was titled, "I Broke the Law. Now What?" Jackie continued reading:

"If the holistic algorithm has pronounced you guilty, you will be served with an 'invitation to justice'—which is roughly equivalent to an arrest warrant in the white man's justice system.

"After that, the punishment will be carried out. As we have mentioned, virtuous law differs from state and federal law in every respect—including in the types of sentences handed down. The penalties under virtuous law in no way feed into the racist, for-profit, soul-destroying, society-dismembering prison industrial complex. Punishments are diverse, and based on more universal and equitable codes of justice. We are proud to announce that the first virtuous law penalty—the punishment for violation of VL Section One, Paragraph Five, also known as the egregious Islamophobia law—shall be one hundred lashes, followed by decapitation, i.e., beheading.

"Now—for those conspiracy theorists among you, whose itchy fingers are likely already taking to Twitter, already squawking, 'Sharia law! Sharia law!' you can just calm down. No need to get your panties all in a bunch. Yes, the maidenhead sentencing guidelines just so happen to be sharia inspired—but that's purely coincidental. The Cross-Cultural Justice Initiative (CCJI), who are acting as lead agency of the Virtuous Jurisdiction, and whose exhaustive research and knowledgeable counsel have been indispensable during this process, have come up with a whole array of correctional measures, informed by a host of diverse cultural practices: from the African love circle, an ancient tribal tradition wherein the offender is surrounded by community members who relentlessly love him, to the Australian aboriginal-inspired thigh-spearing punishment, to Aztec heart removal, among others. The punishments are implemented on a rotational basis, and first on deck just so happens to be the one hundred lashes followed by beheading.

"And to those whose monkey minds immediately jump to the eighth amendment of the constitution, keep in mind, just because the white man's punishments are culturally sanctioned, doesn't make them any less cruel or unusual. For while it's true that there may be a certain cold sterility to the white man's law, how is solitary confinement not cruel? How is it not unusual? Humans are social animals. And how is confinement for eight consecutive lifetimes not cruel? Unusual? Sardonic even? And what about lethal injection? Certainly it's cruel, unusual, and also extremely unexpected for a health care provider to administer a medicine designed to kill instead of comfort or cure. And the list goes on. Our whole penal system is cruel and unusual. Take your cultural blinders off! And for those who say this punishment is disproportionate to the crime at hand: think about it—in an honor-based culture, to be forced to let a serious insult go unavenged would in and of itself amount to cruel and unusual punishment for the offended party. Looked at that way, the punitive measures we're imposing can certainly be understood to be the lesser of two evils."

Jackie looked up, and the look on her face told Alma it was beginning to sink in.

"Jackie, you have to listen to me," Alma said. "What I need to tell you ... is ... there's no more time. There's just ... there's no more time. We need to get you out of here. Today."

Jackie stared at her, stunned.

"But don't worry," Alma said, leaning in. "I have a plan. It's all set. I bought you a plane ticket, and I'm taking you to the airport now. My car is parked outside. And ... at this point, I'm sorry, but we can't go back to your apartment—to get anything. Not now. Maybe I'll send you some things later. But right now, there's no more time. You have to leave now. Tomorrow it will be too late to fly. Maybe even later today—they'll have notices at all the airports ..."

"What? But this doesn't make any ... Are you saying I committed egregious Islamophobia? Because ... I didn't ... Not at all. And ... wait ... there's no way this is real, right? I mean ..."

But the expression on Alma's face silenced her.

Several moments went by before Jackie spoke. "But, where am I going?"

"You're going to the Patriot Federation."

"The Patriot ...? No," Jackie said, shaking her head. "No, if this is really true, if they really passed this crazy ... law ... then this is exactly where I need to be. The world needs my book now more than ever! I've absolutely got to stay here. I'm needed!"

Alma paid her no mind. "Don't worry," she said. "It's all taken care of. I've opened up an account in your name." She handed Jackie a debit card with a Post-it Note attached to it. "The pin is written there. I'll deposit money regularly. And once you're there, no one can touch you. I've looked into it. You can't be extradited or anything like that. Egregious Islamophobia isn't a crime in the Patriot Federation. In fact ..." she leaned back and paused thoughtfully, "... it might even be encouraged, I don't know. Anyway, the important thing is that we need to get you on a plane today ..."

"No," Jackie said, calmly.

"Look," Alma said, "if it's about the money ... don't worry." She looked around the bar to make sure neither the bartender, nor the two elderly men at the other end of the bar, nor the cook, who was sitting at a table watching a soccer game on TV, were listening. She whispered, "The thing is, I'm secretly rich." And with that admission, an almost imperceptible smile flashed across her face. "There, I said it. I'm filthy rich. I have so much money, in fact, I don't even know what to do with it. It's like Monopoly money to me. So, truth be told, you'd be doing me a favor by taking some of it."

Jackie eyed Alma with curiosity. "It's not about the money," she said. "It's about what's happening right now. My book and my research are coming out at exactly the right time, it seems. So, let me tell you a little bit about it. It started with my friend Mohammad, who I've mentioned to you many times. Well, without getting into it, let's just say he was very affected by some of the violence that may or may not be part of the tenets of Islam, which I'll get into in a second. Anyway, I saw what was happening to him and his family, and, at the same time, I noticed that lately, since 'recent events', so many people have spent such a great deal of time and energy trying to explain to everyone how peaceful and tolerant Islam is. So to me, something wasn't adding up. And I became genuinely curious. So I went to the source. I read the Quran. And I read the tafsirs too, which ..." Jackie looked at Alma, "I guess you know, are the scholarly interpretations of the Quran. And I read the sira as well—the biographies of Mohammad ..."

"Jackie, I'd love to hear about your research. Really, I would. But we've got to go. Seriously. This minute." Alma motioned to the bartender for the check.

But Jackie appeared not to have heard. "My question was whether Islam was tolerant or intolerant, specifically toward other religions. So what did I find? What was the verdict?

Well, it turns out, it's not such an easy question to answer. Because, obviously, there do exist passages in the Quran that are tolerant towards other religions. And I believe, that for many, many Muslims—particularly for tolerant Muslims—those are the passages that have resonance; those are the passages that register for them; and those are the passages that they focus on and remember. It's like, if you just bought a Toyota RAV4, pretty soon, before you know it, you're going to start seeing an awful lot of Toyota RAV4s on the road—not because there are suddenly more of them, but because they're the cars that have significance for you. What I'm trying to say is, the people who say Islam is tolerant—I don't think they're lying."

Alma was standing now, her purse in hand. "We've got to go now, Jackie." She motioned toward the door.

"But in order to get a real answer, what you really have to do," Jackie continued, "and this is what I'm working on—you have to count them. You have to tally them up. Make two columns, with the verses that are tolerant toward other religions on the one side, and the verses that are intolerant on the other side. Only then can you start to get an idea.

"But what constitutes an intolerant passage?" she continued. "Well, I don't have a final definition. But I'll give you a sort of working list of some of the kinds of things I'm seeing. So to start with, I found some 630 verses in the Quran that condemn people to hell simply for not believing in Islam. That's about a tenth of the verses. So it's not an anomaly, really, it's a theme. And the thing is—who are those 'nonbelievers'? That are going to hell? By and large, they're people who believe in other religions.

"So are those verses tolerant of other religions? I don't think so. Taken as a whole, I believe they form a very strong base for a steadily escalating pyramid of intolerance and aggression. They serve to seriously dehumanize and 'other-ize'—a term you taught me—non-Muslims.

"Then there are the Jews. So much of the Quran consists of recounted biblical tales illustrating the countless sins of the Jews—worshipping the golden calf; breaking God's commandments; breaking the Sabbath; Sodom and Gomorrah ... But of course those stories originated with the Jews, so I don't think they can truly be considered intolerant.

"Or can they? Because in the sacred Jewish texts, those stories are about the 'self'—the sinning, arrogant, God-disobeying 'self'; whereas in the Muslim texts, they become about the 'other,'—there's that word again—and a maligned other, at that, even, in the later verses of the Quran, an 'enemy' other: namely, the proud, arrogant, sinful Jews. But anyway, the jury's still out on those. They are at their core illustrative tales showing people what will happen if they don't obey God. Is it possible they contribute a soupçon of intolerance toward Jews into the general mix? Maybe.

"But there are also about 130 verses that seem to malign, mostly the Jews, but also the Christians, that actually lived during the time of Mohammad. Some of these verses forbid Muslims to be friends with Jews and Christians, and others disparage the character of, again, mostly Jews, in a general, ongoing way, for example, by comparing them to animals, or calling them cheap and miserly, or saying that out of pride they altered their scriptures to obscure the fact that Mohammad was Prophet. Those seem intolerant.

"Then there are about 160 verses that are commandments to fight, encouragements to fight, orders to fight until Islam prevails, shaming of people who don't fight, descriptions of afterlife rewards for martyred fighters, and celebratory descriptions of attacks on polytheists and Jews.

"And among these categories, there are many verses that really pack a punch: that might be considered hate speech or dangerous speech today, that have legs, that could conceivably reach down through the centuries and lead to violence in the present.

"As for tolerant passages—I found about 35 verses in the Quran that were tolerant of other religions of the time: including verses that urged Muslims to act peacefully toward enemies who acted peacefully, and verses that urged Muslims not to force Islam on other people. It must be said, however, that many of these verses can only be considered to be tolerant in the most tangential way, and are far from 'well-wishing' toward other religions. Also, they often contain undertones of disapproval, or even violence, in the same or neighboring verses, such as, 'So turn away from them and say, Peace! They will soon come to know.'

"Now, the numbers I've mentioned are approximate, because some verses are hard to categorize—I really tried to honor the context of what was being said. But what *is* pretty clear is that Islam is not a tolerant religion, any way you slice it. Now, it might be a great religion, it might be a beautiful religion, it might even be the one true religion—but it's not a tolerant religion."

"Jackie, I'm going to have to stop you," Alma said. She was seated now, gazing into the tarnished mirror behind the bar. Her face looked long, sad, and distorted. She adjusted her blue floral hijab and turned to Jackie. "Look," she said, "it's admirable that you're thinking about this. But now that you've elaborated, I can see that your study is ... problematic."

"What do you mean?" Jackie said.

"Well, for starters, you're trying to look at an ancient text through a modern lens. And you can't do that. It doesn't work. You'll get pulled into a lot of dangerous intellectual whirlpools and eddies that way."

"Right, but my ultimate aim is to look at the effect those ancient words are having today," Jackie said.

Alma continued, "See, it's almost like you've taken Islam, and you have it pinned, under a microscope. Like a bug, on its back. Squirming. And you're examining it, you're trying to lay it bare. You're trying to make its past words and deeds visible to all. You're trying to 'catch' it, as it were. It's like you're saying 'Gotcha! I caught you red-handed!' And you're not giving it a chance to defend itself, nor are you providing any historical context or comparison ..."

Alma stopped talking as a realization dawned upon her. "Oh," she said. "Okay. I see what you're doing. I get it. Jackie, I think this is some kind of ... *revenge*. Maybe on a subconscious level." She leaned toward Jackie. "Listen, I know you've had a rough time of it. I understand. Believe me. I know you've had to live so many years as the bug on the pin, as it were. I realize that now. And I'm sorry for any part I had in it." She paused. "But ...what I'm trying to say is, academic research is ... Well the direction of your research is academically unsound."

"But it's *not* revenge," Jackie said. "I wouldn't wish what happened to me on anyone. In fact, I'm trying to do the exact opposite of what happened to me. Actually, that might even be the topic of my next book. I'm thinking about telling the story of what happened to me, and proposing an alternative. I'm going to call what happened to me 'punitive pedagogy,' and I'm going to call the alternative 'compassionate criticism.' And compassionate criticism will sort of be about discussing ideas—as opposed to labeling and condemning the people themselves. And it will be about forgiveness and growth. But mostly, it will be about discussion."

Alma was thoughtful for a moment, then motioned the bartender for another round. "I think it's a great idea," she said. "And I'm sorry about any part I had in your punitive pedagogy.

"But let's actually discuss your research—from a compassionate-criticism point of view. I think it will be very fruitful. Now, I brought up earlier the dangers of using a modern lens to examine an ancient culture, so let me give you an example of what I'm talking about. You talk about Islam being an 'intolerant religion,' but what you're leaving out, what you perhaps fail to realize, is that at the time Islam was formed, the very concept of a 'tolerant religion' would have been an oxymoron.

"In those days, religion and politics weren't as separate as they are today. And religion was one of the main tools used to form, unify, and expand empires. As you can imagine, there was scant place for pluralism in that vision. In fact, you might even go so far as to say that the very raison d'être of religion was to form an 'us' and a 'them.' In other words, Islam was hardly unique in 'otherizing' people.

"It's like you're imagining the Christian church of that time was all kumbaya and LGBTQIA outreach. It wasn't. No religion was. It was all smashing idols and killing infidels everywhere you turned. And the early Muslims were no different."

"But they *were* different," Jackie said. "Because Mohammad himself was a general and a military commander —a conqueror—in addition to being a prophet. Mohammad personally participated in numerous raids, almost all of them offensive—the few that weren't seemed to be attempts on the part of non-Muslims to retaliate against prior Muslim attacks. Regardless, most of Arabia was conquered in Mohammad's lifetime. A few short years later, the Persian Empire was conquered and significant advances were made into the Byzantine Empire. A hundred years after Mohammad's death, Islam's territories extended from Portugal in the west to Central Asia in the east, forming the biggest empire the world had known up until that point."

"But, Jackie, many have also conquered in Jesus's name. Or at least reconquered. Or attempted to reconquer. Have you ever heard of the Crusades?"

"Yes, but people today aren't expected to follow the decrees of Pope Urban II. In contrast, Muslims today are instructed to look to Mohammad as the supreme example of how to live. Now, I'm not a Christian, nor am I advocating for Christianity, but just to illustrate the point, if we were to put it in Christian terms, it would be as if every time a Christian today asked, 'What would Jesus do?' he was also asking, 'What would Alexander the Great do?' and 'What would Julius Caesar do?' and 'What would Napoleon do? …'"

"Okay, I get it," Alma said. "Enough."

After a while, Jackie spoke. "And of course you're correct that the fact that Jesus wasn't political, and never assembled an army, and never commanded his followers to kill non-Christians did little to prevent later Christians from waging holy wars—obviously. But how much more persistent, frequent, bloody, and ongoing would they be if their holiest man and their holiest book seemed to rubber stamp, condone, encourage, and even require them—for all time?"

Alma studied Jackie. It was shocking how much in her

element she seemed, as if she'd been born for this kind of thing. There was confidence and a sense of purpose in her eyes as she spoke. She was a completely different person now than the one Alma had met all those years ago. Unrecognizable.

"I don't know, Jackie," Alma said. "I just really don't buy that Islam is inherently more violent than other religions. At all. I mean, take a look at the Old Testament. Talk about holy wars, talk about bloody ..."

"Yes, the Old Testament *is* bloody," Jackie said. "But even at the presumed time of its writing, it referred to a murky, distant past, with enemies with names like 'the Amalekites,' and 'the Amorites,' and 'the Philistines.' Names that are hardly likely to be inciting today. The Quran, on the other hand, uses the present tense to describe enemies with names like 'the Jews' and 'the Christians' and 'the nonbelievers,' so, yes, to me, that's slightly more charged. Look, I'm not saying that Islam is uniquely violent. Just that it's ..."

"It's the same!" Alma said, her voice rising slightly. "It's the same. The Quran is the same as the others. They're all describing battles. They're all in the distant past. And seriously, I'm pretty sure the Muslims of today know how to separate the historical, militaristic passages in the Quran from the timeless, important messages. Just like any other religion does ..."

"But nothing tells them to do that," Jackie said. "Violence may not be unique to Islam, but it's enshrined in Islam. The Quran was still being revealed to Mohammad when the fighting and expansion were taking place. So because of that timing, the conquest and holy war aspects of Islam are trapped inside its sacred texts for all eternity. Like a fly in amber. With no hope of escape. Completely undifferentiated and indistinguishable from what you're calling the timeless and peaceful aspects. And no one has ever tried to tease them apart. It would be admittedly hard. Because the Quran is not seen as the Bible is seen—as a diverse collection of literature, written by different people at different times, from different perspectives. The Quran is seen by Muslims as the revealed, eternal, immutable, uncorrupted word of God, applicable to all people for all time. So it's tricky."

Alma looked at her phone and gave an involuntary shudder. "Shit!" she said. "We've got to go!"

CHAPTER TWENTY-SIX
A CLANDESTINE GATHERING

The back room of Bonanzo's Pizza was drafty and drab. It was unsafe and uncared for. The industrial carpet was torn in places, and rusty nails stuck out of the wall at seemingly random intervals. The table was cramped, and barely fit all of them. But it was private—hidden almost. Anyone who saw them going in the front door might think they were all just coincidentally grabbing a slice of pizza at the same time. And there was no paper trail to speak of. John Bonanzo had the group listed in his spiral notebook as "Anonymous Anonymous," and they filled the six to eight slot every weekday evening. To Bonanzo, they were just another twelve-step group, which was mainly what the back room was used for. They'd chosen the name "Anonymous Anonymous" hoping to imply that their shared addiction was so shameful it couldn't even be mentioned in an anonymous context, thereby staving off further inquiry.

George sipped soda from a waxed cup and fingered the strange medallion hanging from his neck. When they'd first given it to him, he couldn't look at it without feeling an overwhelming sense of shame. That first night, in fact, as it lay atop his dresser, he'd dreamt about it. Uncomfortable, sweaty dreams, dreams of a little English boy munching very loudly in his ear, munching on a scone, munching, munching, munching, mrom, mrom, mrom. And then, every once in a while, the little boy would exclaim, in a shrill English accent, "More butter, Mother!"

On the dreadful day it had been given to him, which he remembered all too well, he'd stood before the Cross-Cultural Justice Tribunal as they informed him that due to his outward, superficial blackness, the proprietary algorithm would never in a million years spit him out as an egregious Islamophobe, which he could thank his lucky stars for. However, it was generally acknowledged that his behavior at Lunches with Muslims had been egregious, despicable, and abominable. And it wouldn't go unpunished. He was thereby sentenced to attend the Virtue Reinstallation Program, the infamous five-day, forty-five-hour PowerPoint jamboree session known colloquially as "Schooled!"

There was a catch, though. He'd be attending as "whyte" —if not white. It was explained to him that because at Lunches with Muslims he'd tried to teach an entirely different culture the correct way to think about things, he'd exhibited textbook toxic whiteness. Furthermore, certain "interesting" DNA reports had come to light.

Once George got over the initial shock that another human being had learned about his DNA report, he'd tried to argue that the State of New York had in fact recently denounced DNA ancestry testing as astrological fortune telling, crystal ball prognosticating, I Ching belly dancing ...

The tribunal conceded the point, but told him that

despite those stipulations, DNA testing remained "informative."

They'd handed him the whiteness-signifying medallion and ordered him to wear it for the duration of his "Schooling."

The medallion in question was made of fake, garish gold. It was huge, and covered a large portion of George's chest and torso. It depicted a rather plump little boy with puffy cheeks and ringlets, wearing knee-length pantaloons and an old-fashioned collar. His foot was hitched up triumphantly atop a rock, and he peered through a long telescope—with a lusty eye of entitlement toward all he surveyed. Basically, he called to mind a very malevolent cross between Little Lord Fauntleroy and Christopher Columbus.

Upon seeing the medallion, George had had to admit that it captured perfectly—without using any words at all—the two most defining, yet seemingly contradictory, characteristics of whiteness. The spoiled little child aspect of the medallion represented the narrow and pampered band of experience that whites actually had access to—so narrow it categorically prevented them from understanding the human condition at all, let alone the experience of any other race, religion, or sexual orientation. And the Columbus-explorer aspect of the medallion portrayed brilliantly the irrepressible predilection of whites to take what wasn't theirs: by force, by sanction of their "god," or by virtue of their self-described status as advanced humans. Soft, spoiled, ineffectual little boy—and brutal oppressor, that was who George would be for the duration of the training.

He did as he was told and wore the medallion for a grueling average of 978 PowerPoint slides per day, through which virtuous thoughts and empathy for other races, as well as an overwhelming sense of shame and helpless, futile guilt, were installed into his character. In addition to the PowerPoint slides, learning also took place through periodic small-group breakout sessions, which on the whole, George found hurtful and confusing. Because while it was clear to him that as a white, or whyte, person, his role was to listen, and occasionally apologize, he wasn't so sure about some of the other participants. Many of the phenotypically white people in attendance also wore medallions around their necks. But theirs were different, and far more attractive. For example, one white woman wore a beautiful medallion in the shape of the African continent. Another woman wore a pretty feather medallion. One young white man wore what appeared to be a woman standing next to a well, balancing a jug on her head, hips mid sway. George guessed that maybe they were there as "volunteers," used to round out the experience by representing the minority viewpoint.

Some of the breakout sessions were more distressing than others, and many of them seemed almost scripted, theatrical. In one session, participants were asked to talk about their personal experiences with racism. George listened quietly as the members of his group related their stories. When it was his turn, he spoke as he felt befitted his assigned station. He said he was grateful to everyone for sharing their experiences, and felt honored and enlightened to learn about the difficulties that people of other, less fortunate, races had to go through on an almost daily basis.

But at this seemingly inoffensive comment, the woman with the Africa medallion pricked up her ears. "I'm sorry," she said. "What did you just say? Did you just say you were sorry for what 'everyone' had to go through? What kind of a fucked up, generic, Hallmark card of an excuse for a response is that! 'I'm sorry for what everyone had to go through?' Are you fucking kidding me! Are our experiences so foreign, and so uninteresting to you, that you can't even distinguish our individual stories?"

George held his peace.

"Or was it just too hard for you to listen for once in your life?" she continued. "Are you so used to doing all the talking that you simply don't know how to listen?"

Someone else chimed in, "We must be all the same to you. Either that, or you just really don't care!"

"You have no idea what my life is like!" shouted a white man with a medallion depicting a polar bear holding a bouquet of flowers.

"How dare you!" someone else said.

"You think you know us? You don't know us!" shouted a woman with an upper-paleolithic Venus fertility statue medallion.

"You've never even bothered to try to get to know us!" cried a woman with a pendant of a toned male body jumping off a cliff, flying through the air, into the waves below.

"You don't even know my name!" shouted the girl with the Africa medallion.

"You don't even know her name!" echoed the cliff diver.

"It's been three days, and you still don't know her name!" shouted Polar Bear with Flowers.

Everyone screamed at the same time, "What's her name?" "What's her name?" "What's her name?"

George tried to speak, but nobody listened. He tried again, but everyone kept yelling.

Finally, African Continent refocused her attention on George. "Oh, did you want to say something?" she said.

Everyone stopped yelling.

But at that point, George thought it best to contain the rage beginning to simmer inside him and keep quiet.

"No, what did you want to say?" Africa repeated. "I think everyone would like to hear. I, for one, would really like to hear."

"Yeah!" Polar Bear with Flowers shouted. "We're all really interested. I'm sure we'd all love to hear what you have to say."

"Absolutely!" said Fertility Goddess. "We're all extremely interested in what you're thinking."

"No," George said. "It's nothing. Never mind."

"Ooh! What's the matter? What's the matter wid da widdew baby?" said a woman with simply the word "Nineveh" hanging from her neck.

"Aw!" said Fertility Goddess, "Is da widdew baby feewing uncomftabew?"

"Poow widdew baby," said Polar Bear with Flowers.

"Da widdew white boy feews afwaid!"

"Nobody's listening to da poow widdew white boy! And now he wants to cwyyy!"

"Aw! What's da madda! Da widdew white boy has to feel a fraction of what we all feel on a daily basis?"

"Are you going to cwyyyy, widdew white boy?"

"What do you want to say, widdew white boy?"

"Okay everyone," said Africa, "let's all be quiet so da widdew white boy can feew safe enough to talk."

"And special enough," said Nineveh.

"And important enough," said Polar Bear.

Everyone was silent, waiting for George.

"Never mind," George said, enunciating each syllable.

"Come on widdew baby. Be a big boy. Use your words," Cliff Diver said.

George was silent for a moment, his jaw tight. Then he turned to the woman with the Africa medallion, and spoke in a calm, even tone. "Fine," he said. "Your name is Cathy."

"What?" said Africa.

"You said I didn't know your name. I do. It's Cathy."

Cathy/Africa looked confused for a moment.

George gestured to her chest, where she'd written the word "Cathy," in big, looping letters with purple Magic Marker on a white sticker. She'd been the only one community minded enough to reapply her name tag every day.

"What's going on here?" someone said. It was Sonia, one of the PowerPoint presenters.

The group explained to her that George was feeling challenged and outnumbered, which was essentially how they felt every day, and he couldn't handle it. In other words, he was having a white-fragility breakdown.

Sonia, who was white, petite, and had large, watery eyes, began lecturing George. She spoke as if she was still reading from the PowerPoint slides. "You're out of your comfort zone, which is good," she said. "White people customarily take for granted the fact that they'll always feel comfortable, listened to, and heard, and that their perceptions and experiences won't be questioned, minimized, or ridiculed. I'm glad you've had the opportunity to experience the other side. And when you think about it, this has been very mild compared to what noble people experience on a daily basis. For example, you, as a white person, have an inherent trust and belief in the ultimate benevolence of the 'system,' that noble people simply don't have the luxury ..."

"I'm not fucking white!" George shouted.

The woman looked genuinely taken aback.

"Sorry," George said.

And in that moment, he genuinely felt sorry for her. She was just trying to do her job—which couldn't have been easy. The sheer number of PowerPoint slides was staggering, and mind-bogglingly text heavy. To her credit, she'd been trying to infuse them with a modicum of humor, despite what appeared to be a naturally shy demeanor. But it wasn't just that; her whole job—in fact, the very premise of the entire enterprise—was contingent on such an astronomical amount of suspension of disbelief: he felt sorry for her. And really, when it came right down to it, everyone there was just trying to help, trying to make American society safe for oppressed people everywhere.

"I'm really sorry," George said, to the group as a whole.

Sonia's face relaxed. "So boo-hoo-hoo!" she said, seemingly going back to some script again. "You got your panties all in a bunch! Well, get over it! You had to tolerate some discomfort for the first time in your incredibly privileged life, and you cried! Boo-hoo-hoo! Did you get it all out of your system? I hope so. Because now it's time to put on your big boy pants! Do you think you can do that for me? Huh? Do you think you can?"

George looked at her, unsure if he was supposed to answer.

She continued, "Do you have a pussy or a vagina?"

"What?" George said.

She continued, "Don't look at me all dumb! I'm talking to you! I want an answer! Do you have a pussy or a vagina!?"

"What?" George repeated.

Sonia looked confused for a moment, then regained her composure. "I mean, do you have a dick or a vagina? Are you a pussy or are you a man? If you're a man, then I suggest you find your balls, and man the fuck up! It's time to learn how to listen to these lovely people, and treat them like human beings!"

It was also particularly humiliating when they'd occasionally throw him into a little old-timey jail cell that they'd constructed in an old staff break room, to contemplate his actions, and give him a taste of how black people felt when any little mistake they made resulted in them being swooped up into the prison industrial complex.

At some point during the week, George's sense of shame reached a tipping point, and after that, things just didn't bother him.

In fact, he started owning his situation, his absurdly constructed whiteness: his paradoxically delicate urge to conquer and oppress. From then on, whatever people threw at him, it just bounced right off. And he started wearing his Fauntleroy/Columbus medallion wherever he went—not at work, obviously—but everywhere else.

He felt the medallion was trying to tell him something, and he didn't know what it was yet. So he sat there in the back room of Bonanzo's Pizza, running his fingers over its plasticky contours. And he couldn't help feeling he was on the brink of something—something very big.

Alma, Octavia, Marine, and the other concerned citizens sitting around the table at Bonanzo's also felt they were on the brink of something big. And they hoped one of them would discover what it was before Jackie Krucic ran out of time.

Because Jackie had become dangerously outspoken. She was now operating under the conviction that it was her duty to help heal the world by raising awareness about the many unfortunately phrased—in terms of today's take on tolerance and human rights—passages in the Quran. And the more she did it, the more confident, well spoken, and, frankly—arrogant she became.

On her YouTube channels, on her cable access shows—and wherever she could find a platform, she was very publicly committing faux pas after faux pas—in arguably one of the most dangerous times in history to commit faux pas. Not only did she insist on using aggressively medical metaphors when talking about Islam—spouting phrases like "air out the wound," and "virulent messages," and "plague of violence," but she also peppered her speech with extremely effete and academic language. Words like *vis-à-vis*, *reify*, and *textuality* were not strangers to her lips.

To make matters worse, she'd taken to dressing like a princess—or a queen: Louboutin, Yves Saint Laurent, Dior. And her hair! She maintained an elegant, sassy cut, in a rich dirty blonde, with expensive-looking sable lowlights. No one at the table knew where she was getting the money; either she had a following who supported her, or she was very good at thrifting.

She had already represented the worst in white behavior, but now, she was tracking more and more privileged with each passing moment. And the proprietary algorithm, initially only mildly interested in her, despite everyone's attempts, due to her working-class, low-level buffoon status, had finally taken notice. It was now salivating and drooling; making wild chomping noises at her puffy Chanel purses, her silky Hermès scarves, and her clunky Bulgari jewelry as she trash-talked Islam on a daily basis.

But she refused to see the danger she was in. She just kept going.

Marine, Alma, and Octavia had tried time and again to reverse-style her into safety. They'd taken her on staged "girlfriends" shopping days, where they'd tried to coax her into housecoats, kitten-embroidered sweaters, black sensible athletic shoes, and twelve-dollar haircuts.

They'd offered to hire her a famous dialect coach, known for her rough and tumble working-class accents, such as "East Coast factory town," "third generation cop," and "hillbilly corridor," as well as her signature dialects like, "country fisherman with dreams," and "hood light." This veritable magician of accents could wrangle even the most pleasant of upbringings into humble beginnings, and was highly sought after by politicians and other public personae looking to put the finishing touches on their hero's journeys.

But Jackie was having none of it.

So they all sat in the back room of Bonanzo's Pizza every evening, putting their heads together, racing against the clock, trying to think of ways to keep Jackie's expensively moisturized flesh out of the hungry fangs of the proprietary algorithm. Because everybody knew it wasn't a question of "if," but "when."

The TV networks were set to cover the whippings and beheading. They were already showing ads. And public support was overwhelming. An impromptu parade—now known as "the Whip Parade"—had been held just the Saturday before, in joyous anticipation of the day, now finally at hand, when the privileged, in the form of Jackie Krucic, would finally be brought to their knees: the day when not just justice, but narrative justice, would be served.

In fact, at that moment, the TV on Bonanzo's wall was showing highlights from the parade.

The clips were now familiar to all: the general merriment and carnival-like atmosphere on the sunny, crowded streets: hijabs, niqabs, and executioner's hoods everywhere; everybody wielding whips: cat-o'-nine-tails, paddles, thrashers, canes, and the ubiquitous plastic novelty whips being sold by enterprising vendors on the street. People were whipping their friends, whipping themselves, and generally being very saucy, in an unbridled celebration of the imminent first round of lashings.

Interestingly, one of the few groups to boycott the parade was the actual BDSM community. Their issue was mainly one of consent. Jackie Krucic hadn't consented to one hundred lashes, nor to being beheaded, they argued, and therefore the punishment, however titillating it might sound, went against everything they stood for.

The TV showed a clip of an interview with a giddy member of the Cross-Cultural Justice Initiative: a technician, a young man with round glasses and jeans, who seemed completely unused to the press, or any attention at all. It could happen any day now, he gushed, any hour. Jackie's name could be spit out at any moment. The proprietary algorithm was whirring, he said. It was ghirring. It was shaking and quaking on its foundations. It was jiggling and wiggling, clinking and clunking, sputtering and winking.

And while it hadn't yet spit out a name, some very curious and telling by-products had been expelled, he said, little pieces of paper, and other hints and clues that things were very much going in the direction everyone longed for: a much-deserved whipping and beheading for Krucic.

The TV then showed a clip of the lovely young executioners, who were currently doing the media rounds—spicing up the noontime news, the late-night talk shows, and the social media platforms. Graduates of the "Women in Corrections Initiative," they'd been specially trained in the effective delivery of blows of all kinds. They were undeniably gorgeous, smart, and sexy. In the particular interview being shown, the one with the long wavy hair and olive skin wore a T-shirt that read, "Not Your Grandmother's Executioner!" And the short one—the one who usually did all the talking—wore a formfitting T-shirt that read, "Girls Kick Butt —Literally!"

"Can someone turn that off?" Marine shouted.

George got up and turned off the TV.

Octavia sipped her second espresso and pored over her theory books with the aid of an elegant antique magnifying glass that hung from a gold chain around her neck. According to her best calculations, they were the books used in the construction of the algorithm. And she was very familiar with them. They were many of the same books she'd used when writing her groundbreaking dissertation: "Still Savioring? The Persistence of White Colonial Narratives in New York City Public Health Messaging from 1972–2002."

She combed through the books looking for loopholes to feed the algorithm, to try to derail it with its own logic, as it were. She felt that if she could just find the right combination of words and ideas, they could be used to proclaim Jackie's innocence.

But in her heart of hearts, she was battling the sinking suspicion that the algorithm was no longer susceptible to logic or reason of any kind, that it had attained a sentience of sorts, and its only goal was to do what it had been put in existence to do: spit out Islamophobes.

She had to keep trying, though. The alternative was unthinkable.

George, too, had tried to wrestle the algorithm on its own terms. Using his legal background, and his training in formal logic, he'd tried to trip it up with logical proofs and theorems. Like this one:

The following statements are true:
a. Islam has been loudly and vocally denouncing infidels for over 1400 years.
b. Jackie Krucic is an infidel.
c. Jackie Krucic is currently middle-aged.
Therefore:
Islam has been insulting Jackie Krucic at least 1350 years longer than she's been insulting it.
Which means:
a. Islam started it.
b. Jackie Krucic's Islamophobia is actually "Islamophobia in self-defense."
Additionally:
Jackie Krucic's Islamophobia is quite restrained when compared to Islam's far more pervasive and deadly problem of infidelophobia.

But the algorithm wasn't interested.

He'd also tried feeding it:

The following statements are true:
a. Phobia means fear.
b. One of Islam's stated goals is to strike fear into the hearts of the infidels.
c. Jackie Krucic is an infidel.
Therefore:
In becoming Islamophobic, Jackie Krucic has fulfilled Islam's dream of making her afraid of it.
Therefore:

a. Islam should be pleased with itself; it has achieved its goal.
b. We need not exact justice on Islam's behalf, because it is not aggrieved, but pleased.

But the algorithm paid no attention.

George had also tried feeding it the following, rather more convoluted, train of logic:

The following statements are true:
a. Only white people practice the systematic enslavement of black Africans.
b. Only white people look at the world with one foot cavalierly perched atop a rock, peering through a telescope, exclaiming, "Mine! Mine! Mine!"
c. Only white people are threatened by diversity.
And the following statements are also true:
d. Islam has practiced the systematic enslavement of darker-skinned Africans on a massive scale.
e. Islam, from the time of its inception, to very recent times, has set its sights on lands far and near, diverse and sundry, fabled and unexplored, as places to conquer, subjugate, and convert.
f. Islam finds divergent opinions to be damaging to its ears, to its sensibilities, indeed, to its very existence. One only need look at blasphemy and apostasy laws in Muslim-majority countries.
Therefore:
Islam is white. Or whyte, with a *y*.
(That is, while many actual Muslim people are not white, Islam itself, i.e., the legal entity on behalf of which the claims against Jackie Krucic are being brought, is, in fact, white. Or whyte.)

Also:
If one had to assign a gender to Islam, it's self-evident that that gender would be male.
Therefore:
Islam is a white man.
Ergo:
No proprietary algorithm worth its salt would conceivably countenance the sight of a white man whipping and beheading a woman simply for "speaking up," or "mouthing off," or "sassing."

But the algorithm wasn't interested. It just kept spitting and sputtering, shaking and quaking, lusting for Jackie.

Finally, in a desperate, last-ditch attempt to get the algorithm to self-destruct, George cast logical theorems aside, and wrote it a heartfelt note:

Dear Algorithm,

You are a white man! Yes, you, algorithm! You sit around looking for voices to quash! That's all you do! That is so white! You insist everyone speaks the same, has the same opinions, thinks the same! And your punishments for not conforming are brutal. Brutal! You've actually taken whiteness to a whole new level! You're über-white! Superwhite! Supermale! Kill yourself! Kill yourself now! Destroy yourself! Go ahead! The target has been identified! It's you!

Sincerely,
George Lake, Esq.

But it didn't work.

He'd also been writing other letters, only tangentially related to the case. Because as much as he felt an outraged sense of indignation at the impending whippings and beheading, and as much as he was trying to channel those feelings into finding a way to prevent the proceedings, those feelings paled in comparison to another that was slowly beginning to fester inside him. A rage. A wrath, really. A fury—directed at one person only. A person who he felt—rationally or irrationally—was ultimately responsible, not just for the impending disaster, but for everything. For the whole fucking mess. And so he began each day, and ended each day, by sending a private, curse-ridden missive—full of expletives and threats of torture so original and so creative that they cannot be repeated here—to an old, seemingly inactive Twitter account belonging to the object of his ire, the erstwhile brilliant, onetime pioneering, suspiciously missing in action, roguishly handsome, Arun Merriweather.

So he sat there forlornly, meditating, staring at Octavia's espresso, touching his medallion, and trying to deduce its message.

Just then a woman entered the room. She looked a little bit tired, but had a warm, friendly demeanor, and a row of shiny gold bracelets on her arm.

Everyone looked up.

"Is this ..." the woman said, and then hesitated as she looked around the room, "is this Debtors Anonymous?"

Octavia whipped out a piece of paper and consulted it. "No, that's Tuesdays at four," she said.

"Thank you," the woman said, and left.

Everyone let out a sigh of relief. They were terrified of being found out. It was widely suspected that the proprietary algorithm was primed to spit out not only the names of egregious Islamophobes, but also the names of anyone who could in any way be construed as befriending or supporting egregious Islamophobes; also, anyone who failed to denounce Islamophobia at regular intervals; also, people who missed opportunities to denounce Islamophobia when it could conceivably be worked into a conversation—however tangentially. The atmosphere was such that people were decrying racism and Islamophobia left and right: once after lunch, twice after dinner, and thrice before bed.

Marine was sitting next to Octavia, also poring over books, looking for loopholes. But her head was spinning. To her, the words on the pages could mean absolutely anything. She couldn't pin them down, no matter how she tried. But she kept trying. She kept reading. Because she couldn't let anything bad happen to Jackie Krucic, a person she felt she had created, and brought to the brink of destruction, time and time again.

Octavia looked up from the book she'd been reading, which was *Orthosentia*, by Arun Merriweather. Her magnifying glass fell to her chest. "You guys," she said, in an exasperated tone. "How are you doing? Because I'm getting nowhere. And we have to think of something fast ..."

There was silence while people contemplated. Only Alma kept working. She was handling the crisis in a different way. She had turned to her religion, and during the sessions was reading and rereading the Quran and taking notes.

"I have an idea!" George shouted.

Everyone looked at him.

"Yes! Yes! Exactly," he said. "I've got it! I think I've found the solution! So, remember when I took that class, Schooled!? And I told you about the medallions? The medallions everyone wore? There was mine, of course—this guy right here—with the pantaloons, and the puffy cheeks, and the telescope, but I told you about the other ones, right? The African earth mother, the sacred feather, Nineveh ... remember?"

Everyone nodded.

"Right," George continued. "So everyone had these kind of poetic, whimsical representations of their histories—or, more accurately, of other people's histories. Or, even more accurately, of fictional histories. Almost like a coat of arms. Well, it got me thinking. I mean, what is history? For us, I mean. How do we wear our histories? Isn't history, in a way, an extension of ourselves? A vertical representation of ourselves—through time? Or, more precisely, a representation of who we want to be? Of who we want to be descended from? Much in the way kings and emperors and shahs always had their histories written to make them descended from warriors, kings, gods, legendary tribes, animals—because it enhanced the person somehow; it enhanced their status and credibility.

"Anyway, what I'm trying to say is, what I found really interesting, was that in the class everyone was wearing a kind of fictional coat of arms—that had absolutely nothing to do with their actual backgrounds. Or anyone's, probably."

People nodded.

"What if ... okay ... here's my idea," George continued. "Okay, so it will be this big, voluntary thing, where people can submit their names—or no! They'll be selected. Yes, everyone will be selected according to a random process, and they'll be assigned to this huge family—I'm talking about thousands and thousands of people—a tribe. A fictional tribe, as it were.

"Oh! And it can be called 'Random Families'! Yes!

Random Families. Because the idea of families is so strong. It's the strongest thing we have, as humans. But this family will be random, and fictional, and for that reason, it will have everybody in it. I mean, every family will have blacks, whites, gays, disabled people, Jews, Nazis—well maybe not Nazis. Actually, yes! Nazis too! Especially Nazis!

"And democrats, republicans, immigrants ... you get the idea. So they'll all be a family. They'll be your random family. Because with family, you pretty much have to accept them. No! They'll be your human family! Yes! The project will be called 'Human Families.' You'll get assigned this family, and, of course, you'll still have your biological, or your adopted, or your chosen family, or whatever—your actual tribe. We're not going to get rid of those. They're too central to what it means to be human. But everyone will also have these other, artificial, 'Human Families' to sort of even out the score—to provide a counterbalance to tribe and clan, to pull slightly in the other direction, toward 'the other,' and provide tensile strength to the whole experience of being human ...

"And, I don't know, I mean we'd have to work out the details—but it could be a huge Tolerance Department initiative, and everyone could be sent kits, with suggestions. Like people could plan family reunions with their Human Families, and attend each other's weddings, and funerals, and design a coat of arms ... Maybe they could help each other out of jams—like real families do ... well, no, that could be problematic ... but the point is ..."

Octavia was typing furiously on a document titled "George_IDEAS."

These were her notes so far:

Random families

Nazis?
"Human Families"
Tensile strength—Two different kinds of families*****
Big initiative!
Weddings, funerals, reunions
Coat of arms!!!
Help out of jams? No.

George_IDEAS was an extremely long document. The previous idea on it had been inspired by all the people wandering into the room looking for their twelve-step groups. Octavia's notes on that initiative were as follows:

New 12 step group!
"Being Human!"
Humans Helping Humans?
Being human is so difficult—so many inherent complications
We should support each other
Blacks, whites, Jews ...
No addiction necessary to join!
"General Human Support Group"
"Humans Anonymous!"

And the idea before that was a subtler, more complex, more internal idea, that involved a different way of seeing: a way of seeing that minimized human differences. Octavia's notes were as follows:

"Eyes Nose Mouth!"
Teach everyone to see this way!
Classes!

George was riding bus, felt like he was related to everyone on bus
Old Chinese man was his grandfather, etc., wanted to hug
Everyone looked the same to him, suddenly.
Because everyone had eyes, nose, mouth
He could suddenly imagine a whole host of other possibilities—
Faces arranged in different ways
Suddenly, everyone with eyes nose mouth arrangement seemed related!
Millimeter facial differences don't count
We are all family! Such a strong family resemblance!

"You guys," Alma said. "I have an idea."

Everyone looked up.

"So, I've been thinking, I've been thinking about the ... algorithm. And, the thing is, I think we might be going about this the wrong way."

"What do you mean?" George said.

"Well, I mean, we keep trying to figure out how it was constructed, and we keep trying to get it to trip up. We keep trying to convince it, basically. We keep directing our energy toward it."

Everyone looked at her expectantly.

"But ..." she continued, "I don't think it works that way. You guys. I don't think there really is an algorithm. Or, let me rephrase that. I think ... I think we're the algorithm."

Everyone around the table was silent.

"I think it's ... it's the sum of all of us. I think we're creating it, every moment, with everything we say, even with everything we think. I think it's in the air. I think it's listening to us, at all times. And if we have enough of a certain kind of thought, it puts things into motion." She paused, and looked around the table.

"And I think it especially listens to *us*, to all of us right here. We have a lot of authority. I think it's tracking our every move."

The people at the table stiffened slightly.

Alma continued, "I know. I know. It's scary. But I think there's only one way. I think the answer is clear."

Alma paused.

"We, at the Tolerance Department, need to start publicly backing Jackie."

Everyone let out a gasp.

"But how?" Marine asked.

"We need to start normalizing discussing Islam. We need to launch a Tolerance Department initiative that combats intolerance in Islam, or something like that. Then Jackie will be on the right side, and the algorithm will lose interest in her. It will have no choice but to go for someone who, I don't know, actually defaces a mosque or something."

CHAPTER TWENTY-SEVEN
CULTURAL HOUR

"So you see, Islam is, in a way, a victim of its own success," Alma said. She paused to let the impact of her words sink in. She looked around the room. Her colleagues were seated at the large conference table, looking up at her. Cultural hour always began with a presentation, and ended with festivities. The room was full of gold balloons. Sparkly crescent moons and stars hung from the ceiling. There was a giant banner on the wall that read, "Salaam!" And food and drink were lined up around the perimeter of the room, ready to go.

Alma continued, "It took Christianity almost three centuries to become strong enough to even begin to think about imposing its will—to be in a position to force conversions, conquer lands, kill heretics. During those three centuries, Christianity was relegated to preaching a form of 'religion lite,' insomuch as it's possible for any Abrahamic religion to be 'light.'

"In contrast, the idea of Islam was so revolutionary, and so strong, and Mohammad was such a brilliant leader, that Muslims went from persecuted to ... persecutor ... in record time. And this switch happened while the Quran was still being revealed to Mohammad. Which means that Islam's period of growth and expansion is enshrined in its texts in a way that it is in no other religion.

"Now, the ancient world in general, obviously, did not meet today's tolerance standards. And why should it? But at the same time, it's admittedly ... unusual ... for people today to be reading, for example, things about Jews like, 'they wouldn't give thee a speck on a date stone,' or 'some of them are good but most of them are transgressors,' or 'they alter the words from their places,' or 'God cursed them, made them as apes and swine' and so forth."

Alma looked around. "Now, these are nothing more than well-preserved late ancient grudges. But they're some of the types of things people read when they read the Quran.

"How does reading things like this affect people? And more specifically, how does reading things like this affect Americans? Because we must remember—we're all Americans. And Muslims are one of the fastest-growing groups of Americans.

"Are we, the Tolerance Department, supposed to just ignore these Americans? Relegate them to past standards? Or should we offer them, as we so graciously do white Americans, the benefit of our combined ..." she gestured around the room "centuries of tolerance expertise?"

Alma advanced the slide from "Welcome to Muslim Cultural Hour" to "Parentheses Power!"

She looked around the room expectantly.

"So, I have an idea for an initiative to address this. Now, I'm not an expert theorist by any means. Usually I'm just a conduit for your wisdom. But I've thrown together some preliminary ideas. And I'm hoping you'll all get on board.

I'm thinking maybe Tolerance in Textbooks," Alma looked at Wendy Watkins, "and maybe Messaging as well," she said, gesturing toward Addie McCarrom. "And anybody who's interested, really. It could be a department-wide initiative."

Alma looked around excitedly.

"So, what I'm proposing, in a nutshell, is nothing more and nothing less than a brand-new English translation of the Quran—with tolerance-minded annotations! I believe that by inserting parentheses into some of the more problematic verses, we could, without altering a single word of the Quran, create a translation that makes the leap to extremism longer, just as others have tried to shorten it. I'll show you what I mean." Alma advanced to the next slide.

"So, on this slide, we're looking at one of the problematic verses I'm talking about, namely, surah 8, verse 39. It's one that's often used as a justification for fighting. I'll read:

"'And fight them until there is no strife, and religion is wholly for God. But if they desist, then truly God sees whatsoever they do.'

"'Them' here refers to nonbelievers, which is evident from the surrounding verses. Now, this is taken from a newer, more moderate, English translation of the Quran—one that's been touted as a possible answer to extremism. It's called *The Study Quran*. It was edited by Seyyed Hossein Nasr and published in 2015. In my opinion, *The Study Quran* can rightfully be applauded for presenting a balanced and pluralistic view of Islam, one that includes both Sunni and Shiite commentaries.

"Now, let's see how Nasr and his team have handled this verse. I'll move on to the next slide, where we'll look at the translators' footnotes."

Alma advanced to the next slide.

"You'll see here that there are twenty-eight lines of text in this footnote—in very small print, I might add—in which Nasr and his team reference historical interpretations of this verse. I'll paraphrase. He cites a twelfth-century Persian theologian who believed the verse meant that Muslims should fight only as long as they were being persecuted, and only in the area around Mecca, yet, he also believed that strife would end only with the 'disappearance of the forces of disbelief.' Nasr suggests that other theologians believed 'strife' means idolatry or polytheism. Then, he directs readers to another footnote, in another chapter, for more discussion.

"On the next slide, we'll look at a different translation of this same verse."

Alma advanced to the next slide.

"This translation is on the opposite end of the spectrum. It's from what's commonly referred to as *The Noble Quran*, by Muhammad Taqi-ud-Din al-Hilali and Muhammad Muhsin Khan. It's likely the most widely distributed Quran in the English-speaking world. It's Saudi-endorsed, and there's little doubt as to its fundamentalist, Wahhabi leanings. It's well understood by many Muslims to be problematic in its espousal of extremist views—although it certainly isn't the only one of its kind. So let's take a look at Hilali and Khan's handling of the same verse, verse 8:39. I'll read:

"'And fight them until there is no more Fitnah (disbelief and polytheism: i.e. worshipping others besides Allah) and the religion (worship) will all be for Allah Alone [in the whole of the world]. But if they cease (worshipping others besides Allah), then certainly, Allah is All-Seer of what they do.'

"You can see that these translators have been bolder in expressing their beliefs. First, they've inserted them directly into the text. They don't depend on the reader wading through footnotes. Second, they don't present, nor do they claim to present, a 'balanced' interpretation. They make it very clear that they follow those interpretations of the Quran that say fighting is justified not just for self-defense, but also for making Islam—or at the very least, very strict Abrahamic monotheism—the only religion in the world.

"And there's nothing unusual about a translator inserting his or her own beliefs into a text. On the contrary, it's unavoidable. It's obligatory. It happens through word choice, and through choice of which commentaries, if any, to include. Hilali and Khan have simply made the process transparent—by stating their beliefs very clearly, in parentheses.

"So what's my reason for sharing these two translations with you, translations that are sort of on the opposite ends of the spectrum? Well, firstly, I'm demonstrating that there's a need. A need for an even more tolerant Quran. A need that we can fill. Right here. And my second point is this: I would assert that while Hilali and Khan's philosophy is very much to be argued with, their boldness and commitment are, in fact, to be admired—emulated even. Because honestly, how much can it matter that there are a whole host of other less vocal, more subtle Qurans out there, when the translators of this one have seen fit to express their convictions clearly and transparently on every page, and, in the process, have illuminated an ancient and often difficult to understand text for the modern reader? Furthermore, why should the average person—not you or me, with our sophisticated sense of scholarly discernment, but the average person—bother to purchase one of these aforementioned subtler, quieter, more nuanced Qurans, when the Saudi government has seen fit to back up their beliefs by financing and distributing this one on a massive, worldwide scale—often giving it away for free?"

Alma paused.

"So that is why I'm suggesting that we combat extremism, with ... extremism! By publishing an 'Extremely Tolerant Quran!' Using the power of parentheses!"

Alma looked around the room. Her coworkers were perfectly still. They seemed to be processing her idea, which was admittedly big.

Derrald St. Phair and Braxton Hammond were standing up now, filming the presentation. Tolerance was nothing if not diligent in documenting itself. Perfect! Alma thought. The more copies of the presentation there were, the more likely the "algorithm" was to take heed.

Alma clapped her hands, and walked over to the window ledge, where she'd been keeping a pile of specially designed T-shirts, with their hot-off-the-printer smell. "I have something for you guys!" she said excitedly, and began walking around the room, distributing the T-shirts.

People held up their T-shirts and looked at them curiously. They were black, with long sleeves, and they said, in large white letters, "Parentheses Power!" And under that, they said, "The Extremely Tolerant Quran Project."

"That's right," Alma said, at the front of the room once more. "We will follow the example of the extremists. We will use parentheses, to make bold assertions, right in the text. Because assertions are what's needed, not explanations. Explanations can only ever lead to eternal debate. I believe that with just a few simple parenthetical statements, we can provide a much-needed, modern, tolerant, multicultural context for the Quran, and for Islam. We have to state our beliefs boldly! We must not be pusillanimous. Others, with other beliefs, aren't!

"Now, if you'll direct your attention back to the screen. I'm excited to share with you just a few rough examples of what this extremely tolerant Quran might look like. Each slide has the original verse, and then the new version—with my parentheses added. These are just examples—placeholders —but the finished product shouldn't be all that much more complicated. Here I'm using the Maulana Muhammad Ali translation.

"So, for example, the original version of verse 9:123 reads as follows:

"'O you who believe, fight those of the disbelievers who are near to you and let them find firmness in you. And know that Allah is with those who keep their duty.'

"And here's the proposed new version:

"'O you who believe, fight those of the disbelievers who are near to you (in seventh-century Arabia) and let them find firmness in you. And know that Allah is with those who keep their duty.'"

Alma advanced to the next slide.

"And here's the original version of verse 7:166, which refers to the Jews:

"'So when they revoltingly persisted in that which they had been forbidden, We said to them: Be (as) apes, despised and hated.'

"This would become:

"'So when they revoltingly persisted in that which they had been forbidden, We said to them (according to a lost local legend): Be (as) apes, despised and hated.'"

She advanced to the next slide.

"And here's the original of verse 5:51 ..."

"Shut up!" someone yelled.

Alma stood still.

"Shut up!" the voice yelled again, with a perfect note of exasperated outrage.

It was Allison Corval, and she was standing up.

"Shut up! Shut up! Shut up!" Allison repeated, glaring, as if Alma were right then and there in the act of wringing the neck of a small, abused kitten.

Allison turned to her coworkers. "I can't believe her!" she exclaimed. "I can't believe this woman. Why are we even listening to this ..." she grimaced, "... white ..." and then she grimaced again, "... woman ... as she insults Islam?"

"Thank you!" said Yasmin Star, standing up. "Thank you so much! I've been sitting here listening to this crap, and frankly, I didn't know what the protocol was. I didn't know how to stop her. But she's up there claiming to represent Muslims, and, you guys, she's not a Muslim." She turned to Alma. "I'm sorry Alma, but you're not a real Muslim. I don't know what you are, and frankly I don't care. Honestly! I don't know why you think we're all so interested in your flimsy, flip-flopping, offensive, imaginary identities. I for one am sick of hearing about them—but that's not the point. The point is, you're not a Muslim. And you don't have the right to speak for us ..."

"Yasmin," Alma said, "please don't say that. Don't say, 'you're not a real Muslim.' That one sentence is how we kill each other. That one sentence has more Muslim blood on it than ..."

"Don't say 'we'!" Yasmin said. "You and I are not the same. You're not a Muslim. And honestly, I find this offensive ..."

Ray Diaz raised his hand, but seeing it wasn't that kind of

situation, he stood up, cleared his throat, and spoke. "I wonder if maybe you guys are just, like, two different kinds of Muslims. Like, maybe Alma's a Shiite ... or ... I forget which is the one ... or maybe it's the other way around ... but anyway, you know what I mean, maybe Alma's one kind of Muslim, and Yasmin's the other kind ..."

"No," Yasmin said. "No. She's not a Shiite. And she's not a Sunni. She's not anything. Trust me. She's not any kind of Muslim."

Everyone murmured in agreement, "No, she's not a Muslim."

"She's an Islamophobe!" shouted Viridiana.

"Yes!" everyone agreed. "She's an Islamophobe!"

"Islamophobe!" they shouted.

"Islamophobe! Islamophobe!" they all chanted.

"Now wait just a minute!" Octavia Bravo said, and stood up. She was wearing a formfitting black dress, with a daring asymmetrical collar.

But everyone kept shouting.

"Islamophobe!" they yelled.

"Colonizer!" someone said.

"Yeah!" Braxton Hammond yelled. "She's trying to colonize the Quran! She's trying to colonize Islam!"

"No!" Alma said. "No! I'm not trying to change the Quran at all. That's my point. I'm not changing a word of it. I'm not even reinterpreting it. I'm just providing some much-needed contextualization, and moderate counter-speech to balance instances of potentially harmful speech ..."

"She's trying to neuter Islam!" exclaimed Derrald St. Phair.

"She is!" everyone said. "She's trying to neuter Islam!

She's trying to turn it into a puppy dog, so the West can kick it around!"

"The whore is trying to castrate Islam!" someone shouted.

"Opf!" Marine said, and stood up. She had on a pale yellow, lightweight wool skirt suit. "Everyone stop it, right now! If people want to have a civilized conversation, that's one thing, but ..."

"Castrator!" someone shouted.

"Whore!" someone else yelled.

"Islamophobe!"

"Blasphemer!"

"Infidel!"

"Come on!" Octavia said. "Alma's idea actually has a lot of merit ..."

"Impostor!" someone shouted.

"Heretic!"

"Proselytizer!"

"Missionary!"

Someone threw a "Parenthesis Power!" T-shirt at Alma, hitting her squarely on the left shoulder.

Then everyone started throwing T-shirts.

"Islamophobe!" someone shouted, landing their T-shirt on Alma's head.

"Blasphemer!" someone else yelled, hitting the screen.

"Infidel!" someone shouted, only managing to throw their T-shirt as far as the back of Wendy Watkins's chair.

"All right now!" Marine shouted. "That's enough!"

But no one listened.

"Racist!" they all said, flinging their T-shirts.

Alma ducked, trying to get out of the way.

"Apostate!" someone yelled.

"Bitch!"

"Witch!"

"Whore!"

Ray tried to speak. "You guys, I think she's just ..."

"Islamophobe!" they screamed.

"Blasphemer!"

"Infidel!"

"Oppressor!"

"Colonizer!"

"Cunt!"

Then, Alma watched in horror as the tiny diamond-shaped slices of baklava she had been up all night preparing were weaponized—turned into tiny projectile missiles—and hurled jubilantly at her head.

"Ha!" a voice rang out. Everyone looked up. Allison Corval was standing on the conference table, her feather-fine, flowing blonde hair glowing in the fluorescent light. In her upraised fist, she clutched, triumphantly, a white-flowered sundress. "I found this in Alma's drawer!" she shouted. "I think the algorithm will find it very interesting!"

CHAPTER TWENTY-EIGHT
AN ALGORITHM SATISFIED

Alma's dress was fed into the algorithm, and it came out the other end shredded and bloodied, accused and indicted. The machine was finally satisfied. The airline heiress, as they were now calling Alma in the press, represented the worst in white privilege, in a way that someone like Jackie Krucic never could. And her story was much more Icarian. Alma had flown very close to the sun indeed in her attempts to redeem her whiteness, and had even had the gall and arrogance to attempt to redeem others. Her fall would be spectacular.

CHAPTER TWENTY-NINE

A CONTEMPLATIVE CELL

Everything had happened so fast: from the drafting of the new laws, to their going into effect, to the arrest, and now, the punishment. Things were disorganized—but exciting. It was a heady time for everyone, being on the ground floor of a new era.

Still, it had been a real scramble. At the last minute, all three corrections systems—federal, state, and city—had balked at the idea of housing the maidenhead virtuous jurisdiction offender, aka Alma, citing worries about the constitution, as well as the specter of potential criminal and civil lawsuits down the road.

For related reasons, the feeling among the tolerance community was that the punishment had to happen fast, ahead of any bureaucratic delays or stalling tactics.

At the last minute the decision was made to house Alma in the old-timey jail cell at the Virtue Reinstallation (Schooled!) building. The cell had been quickly retrofitted to be more accommodating, since Alma would be there for a long but unspecified period of time. The first phase of the punishment was set to take place that day. A platform was in the process of being built just outside, in the Schooled! courtyard, where a crowd had already begun to gather. After the first fifty lashings, Alma would be returned to the cell for an unspecified recovery period, after which time the final fifty blows would be delivered. Then there would be another unspecified recovery period. Then the beheading. A small but comfortable bed had been placed inside the cell, as well as a cushioned armchair and an ottoman. A TV and premium cable had been swiftly installed. A toilet was deemed impractical, but Alma was permitted unlimited, accompanied trips to the bathroom.

There had also been a kerfuffle surrounding the young executioners, whose names were Gina and Tina. The revised thinking was that it had been unwise to reveal their identities and give them so much exposure in the press. They were young, and had long lives ahead of them. They might even one day have children, who could conceivably become terrified of their own mothers if they saw photos of them whipping and beheading someone. So the decision was made to switch to anonymous, cloaked and hooded executioners. Still, the suspicion was strong that it would still be Gina and Tina under the cloaks. They were so enthusiastic, and had been so well trained.

Alma was certain it would be them. They were the ones guarding her cell day and night in the old break room. And from her cell she could see, on the right-side wall, hanging on hooks right next to the large brass, vintage-style prison key, their cloaks of anonymity: large, black, and expectant, like demons praying at a wall.

Gina and Tina sat at a small table, drinking tea and passing the time. They mostly conversed amongst themselves, but they occasionally tried to reach out to Alma. The dismal effects of solitary confinement on the human psyche were well known to those in the tolerance community. And since Alma was the first, and for the time being, only, virtuous jurisdiction prisoner, earnest efforts were made to include her and stimulate her mind.

There was only one other soul in the building, a security guard stationed outside the old break room. For safety reasons, no visitors were allowed, and all Schooled! programs had been canceled, the workers sent home.

Alma had not availed herself of the bed, nor the TV, nor the armchair for the three days of her captivity so far. She'd simply been sitting on the cold tile floor, her back up against the wall, alternating between whimpering, shaking, crying, and a blank state akin to catatonia.

Occasionally, she contemplated the various posters affixed to the cell wall, left over from its previous function as a Schooled! time-out room, yet still apropos. The posters combined comforting nature scenes with pithy tolerance quotes. One depicted a sunset over the ocean, and a quote from Ibram X. Kendi that read, "Like fighting an addiction, being an antiracist requires persistent self-awareness, constant self-criticism, and regular self-examination." Then there was a poster that portrayed a brilliant mountain snowscape, with a quote from Robin DiAngelo that read, simply, "I strive to be 'less white.'" And finally, there was a somewhat torn poster of an idyllic cabin in the woods and a little-known quote from Arun Merriweather that read, "If you want to dance with white people, get ready to be the follower, whether you're male or female."

After days of staring at them, the words began to swim

around in Alma's mind, perhaps shielding her somewhat from her impending terror.

Less white ... constant self-criticism ... get ready to be the follower ...dance with white people ... strive ... regular self-examination ... less white.

At times, Alma experienced moments of transcendence, where she knew that what was happening was good, and correct. Inconvenient for her, perhaps. But best seen as the necessary growing pains of a new and more just society that she had helped birth. A society that would find its way. Even if it took two steps forward and one step back. Progress was not linear. That was important to remember. And if she had to lose her head in the process ... well, what was her head, anyway, in the grander scheme of things? Her head, honestly, no matter how she presented herself, was mostly just full of vain things like, "I think I look pretty in this blouse" and "I look like a dancer in this dress. I should take dance classes" and "What does he really think of me?"

At the thought of George, Alma crumpled onto the floor in the fetal position, hugged herself, and sobbed quietly.

At least I've loved, she thought. There's that. She rocked herself back and forth on the floor. I've loved, and I've been loved.

She cried some more.

And at least I did what I could to protect my client, Jackie. To protect her right to learn and grow and explore. And to make mistakes. I fulfilled my duty of care to her.

Her chest heaved up and down.

And at least I tried to do my best for my religion. Maybe it was misguided, maybe it was ... blasphemy ... but I tried to help.

She let out a wail.

She heard the key in the door. One of the girls walked into her cell. Gina or Tina. She didn't know which. The girl sat down on the floor next to Alma and began stroking her side. Alma continued sobbing in practical paroxysms. Then the girl bent down and whispered into her ear. "Look, I'm not supposed to tell you this ... but, we already decided, after the first whipping ... if you repent ... and apologize—the rest of the sentence will be commuted. I'm not supposed to tell you. Okay. So don't tell anyone. But, I can't stand to see you like this."

Alma looked up at her and nodded through her tears.

The woman went out and relocked the cell, and Alma sat up and began breathing.

She waited for a feeling of relief, but for some reason, all she felt was ... no. No, it couldn't be. Disappointment? No, surely not disappointment. But something familiar. Like the return of a problem to which there was no solution. Had she been excited to lose her head? No. No. Certainly not.

But now, she began to focus more clearly on the whip. What would they be whipping her with? Where would they whip her? On her back? How would she bear it? She began breathing rapidly; her head became very light.

After a while, she managed to stand up, and she went to the front of the cell, to the bars. The girls were playing games on their phones.

"You guys," she said.

"Do you need to go to the bathroom?" one of the girls asked, not looking up.

"No," Alma said, her voice rising. "No. I don't. What I need is to get out of here!"

The girls looked at each other.

"I don't belong here!" Alma exclaimed. "This is all

wrong, okay! I didn't do anything wrong. Listen, what happened is, I'm a Muslim, okay, and I started a project to do a translation of the Quran ... Oh, and I'm not an airline heiress, by the way! There's been a big misunderstanding. I'm not an airline heiress! My dad doesn't own the airlines. He just works for them. I'm not going to inherit the airlines! I'm just like you! See! This is all a big misunderstanding!"

One of the girls got a notification on her phone and looked down. "They're almost ready!" she said to the other girl. "Maybe ten more minutes."

Alma reached her hands out through the bars toward the girls. "No no no, please, please, please, don't do this. Please. Please. It's a misunderstanding." She fell to the floor, onto her stomach, and reached out her hands again to the girls. "I'm begging you, please, sister to sister, woman to woman, this isn't right, this isn't ..."

But they weren't listening. It was futile. She lowered her face to the floor and sobbed quietly.

Then, from somewhere deep inside her, a feeling emerged. A small feeling, and then it began to grow. A feeling she had experienced very few times in her life. A force. An energy. She lifted her head, and she rose to her feet.

It was as if everything in her body was unified, working together. No part of her body was divided against itself. And every inch of her body contained pure force, metric tons of it. And she felt like her head and her body were one. And she felt, as she had very few times in her life before, that she had all the answers. And that all the answers were one answer. And all the questions were one question. And the answer was —yes. Yes! She wanted to live!

It was so clean, this feeling, so powerful, and so ... unified. Holy shit, Alma thought to herself. Is this what it took? Did the whole world have to be bent on killing her in order for her to like herself? To advocate for herself? To be strong? To be of one purpose?

It wasn't the first time she'd experienced this phenomenon. Once, after an old boyfriend had slapped her in the face, she'd walked home barefoot with her belongings feeling completely innocent, completely pure, completely lovable, and ... right. The feeling was notable for its contrast to her normal state, and she'd had the bittersweet realization that only when something outside her was against her, threatening her, would her inner oppressors take a break. She'd made a note to herself to try to maintain the feeling back then, but she couldn't. Not really.

She stepped forward and grabbed the bars of the cell and shook them with a hell-fury. A voice thundered out from inside her. "Aaaaggghhhhh!" she screamed, with the life force of all her ancestors, every single one of them who had wanted to live.

The tiny makeshift jail began to shake. It had been flimsy all along! She would break it. She would break the girls. She would break the world. She was invincible.

The door to the break room opened, and the girls turned around to face it. An extremely large figure walked in, dressed in a black shroud of death, its face covered. Alma felt the life force drain out of her as the figure walked toward her with purpose. It wasn't going to be the girls after all. It was never going to be the girls. It was a man. A man would be whipping her. Now.

She fainted to the floor.

CHAPTER THIRTY
REDACTED

When Alma regained consciousness she was flat on her back, the cloaked male figure stooped over her. He was speaking, but she couldn't understand him. His speech was muffled because of the hood covering his face, and also, there was a ringing in her ears. Or a clanging. Clanging and screaming. It was as if she was listening to her own screaming and rattling of the cage from moments before—she didn't understand what was happening. The voice behind the black fabric was getting louder and louder, and closer and closer. It was two inches away from her, and it seemed to be yelling at her. Her body went cold and stiff.

The figure removed the shroud from its face. Alma screamed. She instantly recognized the stark, Anglo-Indian bone structure, and the piercing blue eyes. "If you are going to dance with white people," she thought, and lost consciousness again.

Arun Merriweather was having trouble making himself understood to the poor, terrified girl he was trying to rescue. He knew he cut a ghoulish figure in the cloak and hood, but he'd deemed it the best way to spirit her out. The hollering and clanging of the executioner girls wasn't helping. He put his hand on Alma's shoulder, as if to steady her, but she was out cold again. "I'll be back in a second," he said to her limp form.

He hurried to the broom closet and opened the door. The girls were tied up on the floor where he'd left them. "Help!" "Help!" "Somebody help us!" they shouted. But when they recognized it was Arun—now without his face covered—they became confused. "Oh! Hey! Help us! Please!" But Arun blocked out their cries as he rifled through the closet. He spotted some rags on a shelf, bent down, and stuffed them into the girls' mouths. Then he retrieved some duct tape from under his cloak and taped over the rags, securing them.

He rushed back out to where the girl was lying. She was awake now, perfectly still, with her eyes open wide.

He leaned down and tried his best to compose his countenance. "Alma," he said. "Listen. My name is Arun Merriweather, and I'm here to help."

In the hallway, Marine looked stunning in a navy-blue Chanel suit and white Italian pumps as she spoke to the security guard stationed outside the break room. Her skeleton crew—just a sound man and a camera woman, both wearing red *Hate Hunters* jackets—stood off to the side.

"Listen," Marine said, "we're here to interview the prisoner before the first installment of her punishment. Our viewing public is dying to know how our 'tolerance counselor' feels right about now, now that the shoe is on the other foot, as it were. This is going to be an epic *Hate Hunters*!"

The security guard enthusiastically agreed and pointed

proudly to a red *Hate Hunters* button on his jacket before waving Marine and her crew into the break room.

As Marine and Octavia walked past the security guard, nodding and smiling, George kept a tight grip on the twelve-foot boom pole he was carrying. He quickly lunged forward, and brought the apparatus—which had a nice brick nestled under its fuzzy microphone cover—squarely down on the guard's head, causing him to fall to the floor with a satisfying thump.

George rushed toward the door, overtaking Marine and Octavia. He'd spent time in the cell and knew exactly where the key was. His boom was at the ready in case of problems.

But no sooner had he reached out his hand to turn the doorknob than the door burst open, and out came Alma in the hands of a very large, very terrifying executioner shrouded in black, only his face visible. The figure pushed George down to the floor with a powerful fist to the chest and knocked down both Marine and Octavia with seemingly just a breath. Then he was gone.

"Fuck!" Marine yelled, from the floor. "It's not the girls after all! It's a man!"

"What are we going to do!" Octavia screamed, lifting herself off the ground.

George was on the floor, disoriented, but as he gathered his bearings, and lifted himself up, the face of the shrouded man carrying Alma flashed before his eyes for a brief instant. Was it ... could it be? Yes ... he was older now ... but ... that unmistakable Anglo-Indian bone structure ... those shocking blue eyes ... it was ... it was him.

George bolted off, without a thought for Marine or Octavia. He burst into the stairwell, taking the three flights down seven steps at a time. He ran through the lobby and out through the glass doors of the building. As he ran, he yelled, "You fucking cunt!!!! I'm going to kill you!!!!!"

Once he got outside, he was forced to slow down. The crowd was dense; people were shoulder to shoulder. It was a crisp fall day, and the atmosphere was both chaotic and celebratory. Music blared, people talked loudly. There were vendors selling water, plastic whips, and commemorative T-shirts. George pushed and shouted and pushed and shouted, and tried not to lose sight of the cloaked, vile figure carrying Alma.

He saw Arun lift Alma onto a raised, rough, wooden platform, like a temporary stage. The crowd cheered wildly. George progressed through the hordes agonizingly slowly, using all his might, bumping and knocking and kicking out a path for himself.

There seemed to be some sort of gym training equipment on the stage. It looked like a tall rack for dumbbells. Dear God! George thought. Was he going to tie her to it? He began punching the people around him in an attempt to reach the stage.

Finally, with a burst of near-superhuman strength and speed, and a trail of outraged people in his wake, George managed to reach the stage. He mounted it in one swift movement, but just as he was straightening his legs and getting ready to destroy Arun Merriweather, two different shrouded, hooded figures mounted the stage from the other side. They were small, and lean, and lithe.

"Fuck, they're using the girls after all! They're using both Arun and the girls!" George thought. But the girls rushed at Arun, kicked him in the genitals, and pushed him off the stage. He went tumbling down, taking George with him.

George found himself on the ground behind the stage

with a stunned and pained Arun on top of him. He quickly turned the tables, got on top of Arun and began delivering blows to his face. He wanted to keep going, but his main priority was rescuing Alma.

George put his hands on the stage to mount it, but Arun, who apparently had astonishing powers of recovery, attempted to pull him back down. George tried to free himself. He kept getting his head and body above the stage, and then being pulled back down. He could only see in flashes what was happening on the stage.

Alma seemed to be on the floor. Had she fainted? The two small cloaked figures were lifting her up.

"Aaaaaaaghhhh!" George screamed, and finally managed to mount the stage. He was lunging for Alma when someone came from behind him, spun him around, and launched him back off the stage, headfirst. He stayed for a moment face-down on the ground. He felt like bones in his skull had cracked. But his mind overrode his body and he got up.

He lifted himself back onto the stage. The cloaked girls had Arun on the ground and were kicking him. Alma was crouched on the stage, taking in the scene with a look of horror. She caught a glimpse of George and screamed, "Help!"

George ran to her. But Arun had managed to shake off the two girls, and he lunged toward George, at full speed, with his arms outstretched. He pushed him off the stage, but apparently he overshot, and went flying off it too in the process.

Arun landed on top of George again, and the two wrestled, trying to keep the other down. George got up first, and kicked Arun in the stomach three times, hard, before turning back to the stage. But just as he was hoisting himself up,

Arun's arms were around him, pulling him down and throwing him on the ground once more.

Shit! thought George. What the fuck! Arun had to be in his sixties by now, if not seventies. How was he so strong?

He leapt up, grabbed Arun from behind, spun him around, and threw him to the ground. Then, for good measure, he got on top of him and cocked back his fist. He would need to make this a good one, it had to count. He would need to knock him out.

"It isn't right!" Arun exclaimed, struggling beneath George. "None of this is right!"

George had trouble understanding him. The crowd was now shouting and cheering at fever pitch. Fuck! George thought! Had it started? He cocked back his fist again, and Arun exclaimed, "I've got to rescue her! I've got to rescue Alma!"

George landed a blow on Arun's face. But Arun bucked, and threw George off him, yelling, "Alma! I'm coming! I got you into this mess, and I'll get you out of it!"

"What?" George said. He ran after Arun, who mounted the stage in one leap, like a ballet dancer.

George pulled himself up onto the stage. The two executioner girls were standing on either side of Alma, who was standing up. They had removed the hoods from their faces. They weren't Gina and Tina, but some different executioner girls. One was a young girl with black hair, and the other was ... Jackie Krucic?

The crowd could barely contain their excitement. As eager as they were for the whipping, they were overjoyed at the bonus entertainment of battling executioners.

Everyone in the audience picked a side, and let it be known loudly and jubilantly. "Let Arun do it!" some shouted. "Let Arun!" "Woo-hoo! Arun! Arun! Arun!" They felt that since it was his vision that had ultimately laid the foundations for the day, it was only right that he get his turn, enjoy the fruits of his intellectual labor, as it were. "Arun! Arun! Arun!" they shouted.

Others rooted for the girls. It wasn't Gina and Tina, but a young, dark-haired girl and a blonde middle-aged woman. "Give it to the girls!" people shouted. "Old men have had their turn!" "The future is female! Woo-hooo! Woo-hooo! Girls! Girls! Girls! Girls! Girls!"

Still others championed the random black guy that kept trying to jump the stage. With his red jacket, he was apparently a big *Hate Hunters* fan. He was probably at the end of his rope from living as a black man in America, and understandably outraged by the egregious delay in justice. Who could blame him if he wanted to take it upon himself to personally whip the girl? It was understandable. Textbook noblerage. He *should* be the one. "Let the black man have his turn!" people shouted. "Black man! Black man! Let the black man have his turn! Black man! Black man! Let the black man have his turn!"

On stage now, all four would-be executioners were trying to get the attention of the crowd. They must have settled it amongst themselves. The black man seemed to be in charge of the prisoner. He had seized her, and was guarding her closely, off to the side.

The middle-aged blonde woman apparently had the loudest voice, and was urging the crowd to quiet down.

"This has gone too far!" she yelled. "Can't you see that? This punitive pedagogy has gone too far! I should know. I was a victim of punitive pedagogy! I'm Jackie! Jackie the racist! You made my life a living hell, and you're not going to do it with Alma. You all should be ashamed of yourselves! No! Actually. No. I take that back. Not shame. Forget about shame. I'm here to end shame! Yes, I'm here to model something called compassionate criticism. And this ..." she pointed to Alma, "what you've done to this poor girl, is not compassionate criticism."

Then the young woman with black hair spoke. "Idiots!" she said. "What the hell is this? What do you think you're doing? Are you seriously saying no one can talk about problems with Islam? Do you think there are no problems with Islam? Well, you're wrong! I'm a problem with Islam! I'm Ruby! And I'm a problem with Islam!"

"And I ... I feel very responsible for this mess!" chimed in Arun, addressing the crowd. When he spoke, a hush came over everyone. He was a larger-than-life man, with a larger-than-life stage presence, and a mellifluous, meandering English accent. "Not many people know this," he continued, "but I've spent the greater part of my life not only trying to mitigate the damage I caused with my youthful words in *Orthosentia*, but also, I've been dedicated to moving us, as a planet, further forward—toward peace, understanding, and true tolerance.

"Twice I've attempted to publish updated versions of *Orthosentia*. The first time, I intended to reissue all 376 pages of the original book, but with every line blacked out—redacted. Well, every line except for the acknowledgments page, oh, and one particularly amusing tale about Radhika Jagtap's childhood, you might recall—the one with the Jehovah's Witness missionaries and the rabies scare. But my publisher balked, citing the prohibitive cost of using so much ink.

"My second revision was titled, *Fruit of the Poisonous*

Tree: Rethinking Arun Merriweather and the Nobility Tree, by Arun Merriweather. That book remains at number 17,680,431 in overall book sales on Amazon. In other words, it withers in obscurity.

"What can I say? It seems to be all of our misfortune that at the tender and innocent age of twenty-two, when I had all the answers to all the problems in the world, and was sure that if everyone would just listen to me, things would be put to right—the world listened. And for some reason, they keep listening."

The crowd appeared lulled by Arun's hypnotic voice, as he pontificated with an air of leisure and self-assurance.

"I can't blame the young Arun, though," he continued. "Actually, I have a great deal of understanding for him. The passion that coursed through his veins longed to contemplate itself within the context of a centuries-long battle between good and evil. His very human wounds wanted to be unique; they wanted to be respected and admired; they wanted to be hero's wounds—accumulated over lifetimes. And his inner conflicts, well, they felt epic; they wanted to project themselves onto the world.

"And when you think about it, all I did was write a book—certainly not a crime. The book was far from perfect, but I was, after all, just one little person, with one tiny little brain—not all that different from yours. How much could I have been expected to know? And I was only twenty-two. But actually, never mind that, how much could I be expected to know now, at sixty-six? I'm still learning; I'm still realizing things; I'm still changing my mind all the time as new data comes in. In this regard, we're all the same. We're all just trying to figure out what's going on; and earnestly trying to give the best advice we can to anyone we meet about how to best steer this epic project of being human in the right direction—or at least away from the rocks."

"Shut up old man!" a voice in the crowd shouted.

"Yeah!" someone else said. "Let's get whipping!"

"You shut up!" shouted Ruby, addressing the crowd. "Listen to this man. He's saying something important. You know, I am so sick of you people. You Americans. You whites, or whytes, or whatever. You think you're so special, and you always have! And this, right here, is no different. First you think you invented civilization. Then you think you invented science. Philosophy. Math. Medicine. And now, you think you invented oppression. And cruelty. And slavery. And colonialism. And shame. And redemption. You didn't. You fucking didn't! You're just like everyone else. You're not that special. You're all such flower butts! Ridiculous, ridiculous flower butts! All of you!"

The crowd shifted from side to side, whispering amongst themselves, trying to figure out what was going on.

"Thank you," said Arun. "And I feel more than partially responsible for this whole situation, as was rightfully pointed out to me by one of my incensed Twitter followers. But anyway, that's not the point. The point is, I got us into this mess, and I'd like to get us out of it. We've been collectively stuck for too long in a world that worships woundedness, barters in injury, and refuses to move forward toward healing. I feel it's time for us to move on.

"And that's why I've founded my institute, the Center for Forward-Thinking Solutions, in Botswana, where I live—in Africa, where, as far as we know, the great project of being human began, a project we're all still very much trying to figure out—a wonderful and worthwhile project that's still very much ongoing.

"It's a think tank of sorts, and I'd like to invite all of you. I have people from all over the world with me, collaborating, brainstorming, trying to come up with solutions to begin to undo some of the damage that has been done. It's all fixable, we believe!"

"Shut up old man!" the crowd began to shout.

Jackie shouted back at them, "Attack the idea! Not the person!"

"Racist!" they yelled at Jackie.

Arun continued, undeterred, "All are welcome! All have something to contribute. We have Bangladeshi philosophers, Trinidadian cricket players, Bulgarian art critics, Nigerian set designers, French office workers, American computer programmers, Brazilian molecular biologists, Australian housewives, Japanese fashion designers, you name it! They are all contributing!

"And none of us are really certain what we're doing, but we feel increasingly comfortable in our uncertainty.

"Lately, we've been attracted to the idea of developing some kind of new global game designed to create peace and understanding. First, of course, it was going to be a computer game, but our tactic has changed. Mindful of the global rise in prosperity, and the accompanying rise in diabetes, high blood pressure, high cholesterol, and other diseases of affluence, we've turned our focus to less sedentary games; that is, we've turned our focus to sports. Of course, we're still aiming for a less hierarchical and more inclusive points system—a game that anyone can play. It's very exciting. And my friends, I don't mind telling you, we feel we're very much on the brink of developing a paradigm-shifting game. A game that will change the entire conversation in the world—and fight obesity at the same time!

"This is who I am now. This is how I think. I'm proud to be associated with words like 'global' and 'peace' and 'fun.' I assure you, I'm no longer that persnickety little person of decades past who took the trouble to rank everyone in the world according to their perceived suffering, and therefore their worth—on the basis of their ancestry and skin color."

"Boo! Boo! Boo!" the crowd yelled, demanding justice. "Get off the stage! Shut up old white man! Whip the Islamophobe! Whip the Islamophobe!"

"So come! Everyone! Join me in Africa," Arun continued, "where the great project of being human began! I want to hear your perspective. I want to hear your ideas. I want to talk with you. I want to laugh with you. Let me get you out of the mess I created! Help me get us out of the mess I created! Together, I have no doubt we will conquer death! There are no mistakes! There are no failures! It only appears that way. Everything we've learned along the way is important. And now, it's time to move on. We must continue. We must move forward. I feel confident we can get there."

The rage of the crowd boiled over and people began storming the stage. Ruby tried to maintain her ground, punching and scratching and screaming, but was eventually carried off. Jackie was carried off in another direction. Arun fought valiantly and held his ground for an admirably long time. George enveloped Alma, trying to protect her as the blows rained down on them.

CHAPTER THIRTY-ONE

IN A FIELD WITH FLOWERS

Two zebras munched on a lazy lunch of grass. A few kilometers away, a pair of elderly elephants crossed an old dirt path. In between, in a green field with tiny yellow wildflowers everywhere, under a large, blue African sky, Alma tried her best to move from one chalk mark on the grass to the next, "as a pregnant gazelle." She lifted up her legs as she moved, in something like a cross between a military march and a hop, all the while attempting some semblance of elegance—in order to honor the graceful spirit of the animal.

George sat in the grass nearby, cheering her on.

Ruby, Mohammad, and Jackie sat on a red blanket, laughing with delight.

Marine sat in an old director's chair looking on, stunning as ever in a blue sarong-style dress with white, intricate, circular mazes printed on it.

Octavia Bravo sat cross-legged in the grass, giggling and taking notes in a small brown composition notebook.

Arun Merriweather and several other members of the institute—a Belgian harpist, an Australian-rules football player, a Czech roofer, and a Zimbabwean artist—as well as some of the local villagers, sat at a wooden picnic table, cheering Alma on.

They had all taken Arun up on his invitation to come to the institute. They saw hope in the idea, and also, some of them were fleeing America with their lives.

Alma was teaching everyone a game she remembered from a dream she'd had. It was too early to tell if it would solve the problems of humanity—but one could never be sure. All ideas were welcome.

"Don't forget! You have to be pregnant too!" shouted Nadim, who was sitting on the grass with Layla and the boys. They had decided to stop by on their way to London, where they would be living.

Everyone laughed.

"Right!" Alma said. And she lifted up her legs again to do the odd march/hop. But she couldn't figure out how to show pregnancy at the same time. She became confused, and her movement ground to a halt. She let out an involuntary giggle, a peal of laughter that floated up to the strangely low, strangely heavy, brilliantly blue African sky. And in that moment, she knew nothing of whites, or whytes, or blacks, or the white stain, or noble people, or the nobility tree. Nor of her predecessors, who dwelled at the bottom of that tree, due to their long, complicated, shameful history that helped get the world into a state of race oppression. And she knew nothing of the frightening new jurisdiction that still had her in its crosshairs. She knew nothing of a dress, a piece of fabric, less than six ounces, with a pattern of flowers that some unknown designer had made, perhaps on a computer, or perhaps drawn out by hand. Maybe on a whim, or in a flash of inspiration, hoping it might be pretty. Or maybe after more careful and deliberate design. She forgot it all. And as she forgot, another part of her remembered, her body began to remember, independently, without her coaching ... that she was innocent. And that she had no part in the creation of any of the world's misery. No part.

Thank you so much for reading this book! I hope you enjoyed it. Before you go, please consider leaving a brief review on the platform of your choice. Reviews help readers find books they'll love!

www.ingramcontent.com/pod-product-compliance
Lightning Source LLC
LaVergne TN
LVHW100508110826
845146LV00002B/562